G000153949

GOING DOWN

GOING
DOWN

Kate Thompson

BANTAM BOOKS

LONDON · NEW YORK · TORONTO · SYDNEY · AUCKLAND

GOING DOWN
A Bantam Book: 0553 812998

First publication in Great Britain

PRINTING HISTORY

Bantam Books edition published 2001

3 5 7 9 10 8 6 4 2

Set in 11/13pt Baskerville by
Phoenix Typesetting, Ilkley, West Yorkshire

Bantam Books are published by Transworld Publishers,
61–63 Uxbridge Road, London W5 5SA,
a division of The Random House Group Ltd,
in Australia by Random House Australia (Pty) Ltd,
20 Alfred Street, Milsons Point, Sydney, NSW 2061, Australia,
in New Zealand by Random House New Zealand Ltd,
18 Poland Road, Glenfield, Auckland 10, New Zealand
and in South Africa by Random House (Pty) Ltd,
Endulini, 5a Jubilee Road, Parktown 2193, South Africa.

The Random House Group Limited supports The Forest Stewardship
Council (FSC®), the leading international forest certification organisation.
Our books carrying the FSC label are printed on FSC® certified paper.
FSC is the only forest certification scheme endorsed by the leading
environmental organisations, including Greenpeace. Our
paper procurement policy can be found at
www.randomhouse.co.uk/environment

Printed and bound in Great Britain by Clays Ltd, St Ives PLC

Acknowledgements

Thanks are due to the following: the staff in Oceantec Adventures in Dun Laoghaire, whose patience was monumental. I will leave it to the dive gods there to speculate about the resemblance to persons living or dead – but because gods are omniscient, they should *know* that the scars, shaven heads, dreadlocks, charisma, breathtaking physiques, sex appeal etc that I make reference to are the stuff of pure fiction. Aren't they? Dan, Declan, Enda, Mick, Tommy, Willy (and Tiernan of Scubadive West) – you were all inspirational! Kathy Brickell – thank you for holding my hand on my night dive. Jan Lee in Lady G'Diver, Jamaica, for the training dives. Moynihan-Russell Recording Studios for allowing me to annoy them for research purposes, and especially Orla O'Kelly in said studio for the brilliant excuses for having lunch. Sandra O'Sullivan for her invaluable musical savvy. Robert Dogget and the bar staff of the Trocadero for the cocktail recipe. The lovely, obliging staff at Leopardstown racecourse. Hugh Morton, expert in trivia. Michael Opperman, my tipster. Laura Philips of the Clarence Hotel. Susannah Godman and Sadie Mayne for always saying the right things, and Lucy Bennett for finding the right face – again! Eileen Cleary for keeping me sane. Marian and Cathy for the support system. Francesca Liversidge and Sarah Lutyens for being so wise. My husband, Malcolm, for instigating the diving, for encouraging me to do the advanced course and for just being so completely amazing. My daughter, Clara, for being such a fearless waterbaby, and to whom this book is dedicated.

For Clara

Chapter One

Endorphins! Those were exactly what she needed!
Ella Nesbit was sitting on the white Formica counter of the small coffee room, swinging her legs and waiting for the coffee to perk. She had filched a magazine from the selection she had fanned out on the glass-topped table in reception earlier, and was idly leafing through the pages. There was a feature in the health section about these things called endorphins that supposedly triggered a chemical reaction in your brain to produce a natural high. Apparently these endorphins kicked in when you were feeling good about yourself and enjoying life – like when you were eating chocolate, or when you'd finished a workout in the gym. The chocolate thing she could understand, the gym thing she couldn't. *'Endorphins are also generated by great sex,'* she read. *'And every time you laugh spontaneously, you experience an endorphin rush.'* No wonder she was feeling so bloody sorry for herself lately. Not only had she not had great sex – she hadn't had *any* sex for months. And she couldn't remember the last time she'd laughed spontaneously.

The coffee was done. She poured herself a mug, wandered back out into the reception area of the recording studio where she worked, and tossed the magazine onto the table. The calendar needed changing. She hadn't done it for ages. Now here was an ideal opportunity to experiment with en-dorphins! There were at least five Gary Larson cartoons waiting to be torn off. She studied the first one. *Nul points* for endorphins. It was the same with the second. And the third, and the fourth, and the fifth. Either the *meister* cartoonist had lost his touch, or she had become terminally challenged in the humour department. What scared her most was that she was starting to feel an increasing empathy with Larson's losers. One of her recent favourites showed a bunch of sad individuals mooching around in a hell so hellish the demons even served up cold coffee. It was strange. On last year's calendar she'd identified herself more readily with his smiley, doolally cartoon characters.

She dumped the cartoons in the wastepaper basket, and was just about to pick up the phone to confirm the availability of a voice-over artist for later that afternoon, when it rang.

'Nesbit & Noonan, good morning!' she said in her best receptionist's voice. She actually wasn't a receptionist, she was a sound engineer, but since Hattie the real receptionist had run off with a Scottish radio producer, she'd been roped in to man the desk. She hated it, but she hadn't much choice. Her Uncle Patrick – who was the Nesbit part of

Nesbit & Noonan – had taken a trainee sound engineer on board a couple of months ago, and he was running a tight ship. Until Patrick could afford to fork out a salary for a new receptionist, Ella was doing him a favour by standing in. And she owed him more than just one favour. Her uncle was her mentor, her friend, her port in a storm. For most of her life he had acted *in loco parentis* when one or both of Ella's parents were in globe-trotting mode – which was more often than not. The walls of the spare bedroom in the house he shared with his two teenage sons and his wife Claudia were still covered in her embarrassing Bros posters, and she sometimes found herself automatically scribbling in her uncle's address instead of her own on any forms she had to fill in. She loved him fiercely, and Patrick in turn doted on her, treating her like the daughter he'd never had. Patrick had booked conjurers for her birthday parties when she was little, he had bawled out Ms Ní Bhriain, her Irish language teacher, for undermining Ella's confidence at school, and he had organized orthodontia when her teeth started to grow skew-whiff. He had picked her up from teenage discos, assessed her boyfriends with a hypercritical eye, steered her ever so subtly away from the jail-bait look that some of her schoolfriends adopted, and nursed her through her first head-exploding, gut-heaving, I-will-never-drink-again-as-long-as-I-live-hangover. Ella suspected that he had done the Daddy stuff miles better than Declan, her own father, ever could have. Declan

11

would have let her kick up her heels and run wild – in fact, the more sand she sent flying in the face of convention, the more he would have sat back and looked on admiringly.

It was Patrick's voice now on the other end of the phone.

'Hi, toots. How's the day shaping up?'

'Busy. The Complete Works have cancelled, but Reflex and PBCF&C have booked sessions.'

'Can we fit them both in?'

'Just about. It's going to be a tight squeeze.'

'I'll pick up extra Danish on the way. I'd have been there earlier, but the traffic on the canal is—'

'Bumper to bumper.'

'Got it in one. Is Julian there yet?' Julian Bollard was the new trainee.

'No. He's late. Again.' She couldn't resist the dig, but her uncle didn't seem to notice.

'Put him on the PBCF&C gig, will you? I want to see how he copes under pressure. That gobshite of a client's going to be there today. This will be Julian's litmus test in the diplomacy department.'

Hah! Ella wanted to laugh. If she was currently challenged in the humour department, then Julian bloody Bollard was most definitely challenged in the diplomacy department – at least when it came to her. From the moment they first met they just hadn't hit it off – and when Ella tried to analyse the reasons *why* they hadn't hit it off, she didn't much like what she learned about herself. Because deep down she suspected that her mistrust of the new

trainee was motivated by nothing more complicated than professional jealousy. Julian was gaining
a bit of a reputation as an engineering wizard, and
she was fed up with people finishing off their phone
calls to the studio with the words: 'By the way – will
you make sure Julian's on the session?' Ella was
feeling very scared that she might find herself
behind the reception desk for longer than she liked.

'OK. Will do. By the way, Patrick, both studios
are booked over lunchtime. I'll be running out for
sandwiches again.'

'Can't you send out for them?'

'No. That delivery service is crap. They keep
getting the orders wrong.'

'Hell. I'm sorry about all this gofering lark, toots.
I know you're fed up with it.'

Ella picked up a pen and started doodling on the
desk diary. 'When am I going to be allowed back
on the technical side of things, Patrick? People treat
me with more respect when I'm wearing my engineer's cap. I'm just not receptionist material.'

'I've had no complaints. And you know what a
huge favour you're doing by saving me a salary.
When the new studio's up and running and we've
all that new hi-tech equipment installed you'll
have a ball, but until then I just have to keep costs
to a minimum. And think what's down the line in
just a few more months. Three studios, four sound
engineers, and a *brand new receptionist.* I promise.'

Ella sighed. *A few more months . . .* If she didn't love
her uncle so much she'd be hurling abuse at him.

But he was right. Although the studio he was having built in the disused garage at the rear of the building was costing him a fortune, it promised to be a technological dream, and she was dying to play with all the latest state-of-the-art toys.

'Patience is a virtue,' Patrick reminded her.

'"*And virtue has its own reward but no sale at the box office,*"' she trotted out automatically.

'Where did I hear that before?'

'Francesca used to say it all the time. It's a quote from Mae West.'

'God, yes! How could I forget?' She could hear the smile in Patrick's voice. 'What was that other Mae West gem she used to chant like a mantra?'

'Um. Let me think . . . Oh yes – "Living well is the best revenge." Except I think that's Scott Fitzgerald.' One of Ella's earliest childhood memories had been of Francesca, her mother, confiding in her girlfriends at some bohemian soirée shortly after her less than amicable split from Ella's father. She'd had a spliff in her elegant right hand, a champagne flute in her elegant left, her Pre-Raphaelite hair had been floating around her like a cloud, and her smoky, kohl-rimmed eyes had flashed fire as she spat the word 'revenge' over and over again. 'I got a postcard from her the other day, by the way. From Gstaad.'

'I didn't know Francesca was into skiing?'

'She's not. But Giorgio is. She's just gone along for the off-piste stuff.'

'There's a bad joke there somewhere,' remarked

14

Patrick. 'But it's too early in the day for my grey cells to figure it out.' An electronic bleep sounded. 'Ah. Incoming call, sweetheart. I'd better take it. See you later.'

'Later.' Ella put down the phone and picked up her coffee. It was cold.

A thud on the floor of the lobby off the reception area announced the arrival of the mail. She wandered through, scooped up the pile of envelopes and sat down at the desk to sort through it. Bills, mostly, and invoices. There was a boring-looking manila envelope marked for the attention of her uncle: a Jiffy bag for Jack, his partner. A trade magazine. A postcard from Hattie in Scotland with one sentence on the back: 'Sorry to leave you in the lurch.' Hah! thought Ella. A circular. A letter for – hey! A letter for her! She hardly ever got letters at work.

'NOTIFICATION: TO CERTIFIED BEN-EFICIARY!' yelled the highlighted copy on the vibrant orange envelope. 'You have in your hands the chance of winning £250,000! Open immediately to find out how!' There was more. Through the cellophane window on the envelope she could make out the words: '. . . procedures are in place to declare Miss Ellen Nesbitt of 14 Lower Winston Street, Dublin 2, Rep of Ireland, the winner of £250,000. Please reply promptly for full prize chances.'

They couldn't even get her name right! She curled her lip at the envelope and dropped it into the wastepaper basket alongside the Larson cartoons. *You have in your hands the chance of winning £250,000!* What kind of a sucker did they take her for?

'Morning.' Jack Noonan came through the door, swinging his motorbike helmet.

'Oh – hi, Jack.'

'Coffee made?' he asked.

'Mm-hm. Help yourself.' She smiled at him as he hung his helmet on the hat stand. You couldn't not smile at Jack. He was a ringer for Pierce Brosnan, and had an identical glint in his eye. He'd been her uncle's right-hand man for the past ten years, and he'd been responsible for her technical training. She'd always secretly fancied him, but she knew it wasn't reciprocated. She just wasn't his type – he was into high-achieving, ball-breaking, post-feminist-type dames (you should have seen them when he was finished with them – you couldn't help but feel sorry for them), and she also knew that Jack would never, ever dream of laying a hand on his partner's niece. He poured himself a cup of coffee and looked over her shoulder at the desk diary. She felt the hair on the back of her neck stand to attention. 'What time's the first session?'

'Nine-thirty. There are two gigs booked.'

'Who's in the main studio?'

'Reflex.'

'Oh, good. I'll do that one. That Angie's a foxy bitch.' Jack smiled at her raised eyebrow. 'Gotta

16

allow us boys a little political incorrectness from time to time.'

Ella shrugged. 'I wouldn't have thought she was your type.'

'Oh? What *is* my type, Ella?'

Not me, anyway, she thought, but: 'I dunno,' she said. 'It's just that Angie's a bit ditzy, if you know what I mean?' Oh, God – was she sounding petulant here? 'Don't get me wrong, I don't mean that in a bitchy way – it's just that she's more . . . well . . .' she realized just in time that she was just about to say 'fun', and stopped herself. 'More – *frivolous* than the kind of woman you usually have strung on your arm, anyway.'

'I'm maturing, Ella. I've got to that enlightened stage in life where a man suddenly realizes he'd much rather talk dirty than talk sense.'

'Oh! Maybe there's hope for me after all!' Ella sent him a ravishing smile.

'You talk dirty, little El? I don't think so. I've known you since the rudest word you knew was "bum", remember.'

'I've learned a lot ruder words since then, Jack.'

'No! What bounder was responsible for your miseducation, Ms Nesbit?'

'You.'

'*Touché*. Don't let on to your uncle. He'd have my guts for garters.'

Jack tipped her nose with his forefinger. Kiss me, you big eejit! thought Ella. But of course she didn't

17

say it. Instead she yawned and started doodling again. 'It's going to be a long day,' she said. 'There's a load of clients due in. I really hate the way those bastards have been treating me like a girly since I've been stuck behind this desk. I keep feeling that I should be filing my nails and saying things like "Mr Nesbit will see you now" into intercoms. And wearing fluffy jumpers.'

Ella wasn't a fluffy jumper type, but she made a bit more of an effort with her appearance when she was doing the desk. Today she was wearing a boat-necked sweater in olive-green cotton, a cream cotton stretch skirt, and heels to make her look taller. She was only five feet two, and she hated having to look up at people all the time. She'd tied back her long, red-setter-coloured hair in a scrunchy and put on tiny silver earrings and a little discreet makeup. At least her hair was long enough to tie back now. She'd tried a Sinead O'Connor crop once, and had spent years regretting it. An enemy in school had told her she looked like a tennis ball with lips. Because her mouth was big and lop-sided she always outlined it with lip pencil now to try and redress the balance, and because she considered her eyebrows to be her best feature she always smoothed them with a smidgen of Vaseline.

'*When* am I going to be allowed to do my proper job again, Jack?' she said. She suddenly realized that the doodle she'd been scribbling on the desk diary was a skull and crossbones.

'When the new studio's finished, that's when.' Jack sat on the edge of the desk and narrowed his eyes at her. 'Anyway, I quite like treating you like a girly for a change, and your ass looks great in that skirt. You might come up to the office and take dictation later, Miss Nesbit.'

The phone rang. Ella stuck her tongue out at him and picked up the receiver. 'Nesbit & Noonan, good morning!' she said into the phone. 'Yes. Yes? *Yes!* No. Not today, thank you!' She put the phone down. 'A telesales rep,' she said.

'You handled that call beautifully, Ella. You might want to start making a few cock-ups, otherwise Patrick will keep you behind the desk indefinitely.'

'Oh, Jack – I just want my proper job back. It's not fair. Patrick's taking advantage of my dynastic loyalty. If he's not careful I just might run off to Scotland with a married radio producer. I can understand now why Hattie did it.' The phone rang again. 'Oh piss off,' she said, picking it up. Then: 'Nesbit & Noonan, good morning!'

She could hear Jack's low laugh as he loped up the stairs that led to the main studio, and left her to it.

*   *   *

Patrick and Julian arrived together. She could see them talking and laughing as Julian padlocked his bicycle to the railings outside the studio. When he'd finished Julian unzipped his jacket and stretched so

19

that his horrible six-pack was displayed to its full advantage, and then he 'casually' flexed his biceps a couple of times. Julian was big into fitness and he rode a state-of-the-art cycle, even when it was raining. But all the hours he devoted to circuit training and weights and Nautilus couldn't disguise the fact that he was quintessentially a nerd.

'Hi, toots,' said Patrick as he came through the door. 'Julian was just telling me about his father's new car. He's invested in a Lotus Elan that will make my little coupé look pedestrian.'

This was yet another reason to hate him – Julian Bollard was *rich*. Or rather, his daddy was, and his rich daddy had contacts. Unfortunately, one of these contacts had turned out to be Jack Noonan, and that's how Julian had ended up working here. Ella had hoped that maybe Julian would get bored with being a sound engineer, the way he'd got bored with all the other groovy professions he'd dabbled in – photography, film production, journalism, acting (someone had told her he'd actually only ever been an extra). But so far he showed no sign of flagging.

'Hi, Ella.' Julian smiled at her with his thin lips, and then he raised one of his black Noel Gallagher eyebrows. 'Great skirt.'

Ella pretended not to have heard. She opened the desk diary and started punching in numbers on the phone. 'Good morning! May I speak to Monica, please? Ella Nesbit here. Thank you.'

Jingly music kicked in as she was put on hold.

'What's the best way of producing a premix and a final mix, Patrick?' she heard Julian ask.

'Mix your premix first,' Ella said authoritatively, pressing the 'on' switch on her computer. 'Load it back into the Audiofile and then play out your mix.'

'Oh?' said Julian, looking at her in a vaguely patronizing way. 'Can't you mix your premix into the Audiofile, and then play out your mix and your premix simultaneously? That would save all that loading time.'

'You're right, Julian,' said Patrick. 'That would do it in half the time.'

Fuck, fuck, fuck, thought Ella. He was outstripping her already. She'd been doing things according to established principle for ages now, while Julian had obviously been accessing all the new software. She'd need to do some hard work if she wanted to keep up. Ella was fed up with watching the new trainee scooting up and down the studio floor on his wheely chair, tweaking and mixing and humming along to the playout. She sat colouring in her skull and crossbones as she waited for her call to be put through, trying not to listen to the conversation the two men were having. Julian sounded so know-it-all she felt sick. 'Blah, blah, blah,' she heard. 'Blah, blah and blah.'

Ella had been working for Nesbit & Noonan for nearly three years now. She'd kind of drifted into the recording business. She'd had problems finding work the year after she'd graduated from music college, and Patrick had taken her on as a part-time receptionist. In those days she'd spent five mornings a week behind the desk, five afternoons a week practising her violin, and occasional evenings as a deputy player with various orchestras. But there were no permanent positions available – apart from one in a Baroque chamber orchestra which would have required her to dress up in a wig and period costume, and she just couldn't hack that idea. So in the end she'd returned her violin to its case, put the case in the back of her wardrobe, and asked her uncle for a proper job. After a year's apprenticeship, she'd qualified.

She no longer entertained ambitions of becoming a professional musician, although that didn't stop her fantasizing about it. It was in her blood, after all. Her paternal grandfather had been the Stradivarius of Irish fiddle makers, producing the most sought-after instruments in the country until the day his liver had packed in; and her father, Declan, was a star on the trad scene, travelling the world with a highly respected and successful band. Her mother, Francesca, had been a violinist with the National Symphony Orchestra before she'd given it up and run away to Tuscany with an Italian tenor. Francesca had sounded only mildly regretful when Ella had made the long-distance phone call telling her she was giving up the violin. 'Oh, well. I'm sure it's the right decision for you, darling,' she'd said reassuringly. And then Ella had heard the sound of the receiver being covered, and her mother's muffled voice saying: 'Open another bottle, *mio caro*. This one's corked.'

She'd waited until her father had come back from tour before telling him. For some reason she'd wanted to tell him to his face. After opening the glossy Fifth Avenue department store bags he'd brought back for her (he did this every time he went away, and Ella knew it was his way of assuaging his guilt at being such a crap father) and admiring the Gucci watch and the Ralph Lauren sunglasses and the Prada handbag, she'd poured him a large Jameson, and calmly informed him of her career choice. Declan had gone ballistic. He'd shouted, gone bright red in the face, and practically frothed at the mouth. 'Look what happened to Patrick!' he'd fulminated. '*He* could have been a contender, but he hadn't the guts! He opted for the safe option. Running a fucking *recording* studio, for Christ's sake!' He'd made the words 'recording studio' sound tackier than 'cat house'. 'Your uncle wouldn't recognize a fiddle now if it came flying at him and took a chunk out of his arse!' Patrick had played once upon a time – played brilliantly, according to Declan – but he had given it up when the recording business proved more lucrative.

When Declan had finally run out of steam on that unforgettably explosive occasion, he had looked at Ella for a long time in silence, and then, registering her stony face and determinedly set chin, he had turned on his heel and walked out the door. She hadn't heard from him again until a week later, when a massive bouquet from Interflora had arrived on her step with SORRY FOR SHOUTING AT YOU printed in block capitals on the card. And that had been the last time her father had ever referred to Ella's non-starter of a career as a violinist. Or to her new-found career as a sound engineer.

All in all, Ella had enjoyed working in her uncle's studio until she'd been shunted behind the reception desk full time. The recording business was buzzy and sociable, and although sound engineering was a mostly male preserve, she liked being one of the boys. She'd always preferred boys to girls. Most of the pupils at her all-girls boarding school had been consummate practitioners in the art of bitchcraft – and she knew that the rarefied world of the orchestra was inhabited by divas with agendas – so she felt more comfortable behind an Audiofile. But occasionally she thought about all those years she'd devoted to the study of music, and couldn't help feeling a little gutted.

Now she looked over at Julian again. He was standing nursing a mug of coffee, sucking up to her uncle. He may have gained a reputation for being a bit of a wunderkind, but Ella knew he was a dilettante at heart, with no real appreciation for – or understanding of – music. This wasn't a major disadvantage, since Nesbit & Noonan specialized mainly in commercial work, and very little music was recorded there. But as far as she was concerned, the only thing Julian Bollard had going for him was his technical savvy. This madly impressed the clients who sat in on recording sessions, but it cut no ice with her. Ella might not be as fluent in technospeak as he was, but intuition was her trump card. She could run her eye over a script, gauge to the nearest nanosecond what the running time would be, and establish immediately whether it needed a pacy or a leisurely read. She knew which voices could safely launch a thousand products, and which ones would have listeners lunging for the 'off' switch on their radios. She established instant rapport with agency creatives and with voice-over artistes because she spoke the same language they did, and because she laughed a lot. Or had done until recently.

The jingly 'on hold' music coming through the receiver was giving her a headache. Ella put the phone down, pressed redial, and scribbled black hair and a big nose on the skull to make it look more like a living person. It just ended up looking like Julian.

*   *   *

Later that day there was an unexpected lull between sessions. Ella unclingfilmed her salad sandwich and sat down on the big leather couch in the reception area to eat it. She was browsing through the *Evening Herald* when foxy Angie, the copywriter from Reflex, came downstairs.

'Finished?' asked Ella, looking up from the paper.

'No. I just want to take a breather. There's some problem with the DAT. It's going to take a while to get it sorted.' Angie flung herself down on the couch beside Ella, yawned and stretched. 'Anything in the paper?'

'A feature on how to be an "it" girl.'

'Ow. Sad. Anything else earth-shattering?'

'A competition to win a holiday for two in Jamaica.'

'Jamaica? Wow! Give us a look.'

Angie leaned forward, tucking a stray strand of glossy silver-blond hair behind her ear, and Ella slid the newspaper sideways to give her a better view. The competition was being run by a food consortium that was promoting a new line of fruit juice called Pirate's Punch. The punch was a blend of tropical juices like mango and pineapple and guava, and the advertising campaign featured a bunch of parrots dressed up as pirates with cutlasses hanging off their belts, bandannas on their heads and eye-patches over their eyes. They were brandishing musical instruments. One had maracas, one a squeezebox and one a trumpet. The one with its beak open was obviously the singer.

'Jesus,' said Angie, looking horrified. 'I wonder what agency was responsible for this piece of shit. Why on earth are they all playing instruments?'

'They do in the telly ad. The parrots play the jingle.'

'How does the melody go?'

'I don't know. I always zap it off when it comes on.'

'I'm not surprised. What a *mélange*! I pity the poor schmuck who got stuck with this account.' She ran her eyes along the copy. 'Let's see – what do you have to do to win the holiday? "Simply answer the following questions blah, blah, blah"' she read. '"And then dream up a name for our band of piratical parrots! It can be as zany as you like – in fact, the zanier the better! And if you're our lucky winner, you could be winging your way to your warmest winter wonderland ever. In the luxurious Salamander Cove resort, Port Antonio, Jamaica!"'

'As zany as you like?' repeated Ella. 'How about Schopenhauer and the Thundering Intellects?'

Angie laughed. 'Excellent. Or Jean-Paul Sartre and the Existentialists?'

'The Exceptionally Sad Dickheads?'

'Yes! Or zanier still – The Plumed Prats!'

'The Feathered Farts?' Ella was laughing too.

'Yes – yes! That's it!' Angie reached for a pen and entered the words 'The Feathered Farts' in the space left blank for suggestions. Then she said: 'Whose name shall we put?'

Ella didn't hesitate. She took the pen from Angie and wrote in block capitals: 'Julian Bollard, c/o Nesbit & Noonan, 14 Lower Winston Street, Dublin 2.'

*   *   *

She was closing down the computer when Jack came through reception, yawning and looking at

27

his watch. 'Holy schomoly – it's half-past six already. That was a day and a half. Patrick gone home?'

'Yep.'

'You closing up now?'

'No. Julian wants to stay on and mess about with sound effects. I'll let him lock up.'

'Dedication, enthusiasm, eagerness to learn – that boy will go far.'

Ella shot him a basilisk look.

'C'mon, sweetie, lighten up. You'll be back at the control panel before the end of the year.'

'But it's only October now!'

'Well, let's look at it in terms of positive thinking. How about this? Next month's one of the shorter ones. Only thirty days.' Jack shouldered on his jacket and reached for his helmet. 'Come on. Let me buy you a drink. A pint of Guinness will put the roses back in those pallid cheeks of yours.'

'All right. I'd love a pint. But let's not go to Daly's – it'll be crowded with media types, and I've a headache looming. Can't we go somewhere a bit quieter for a change?' She got up and fetched her coat from the hat stand.

Jack made an apologetic face. 'Sorry. Daly's it has to be.'

'Why?'

'Angie's going to be there. I kind of made an arrangement to meet her. Nothing definite, but it would be bad form not to show.'

She turned to him, trying to keep disappointment

out of her eyes. 'Cor blimey, O'Reilly. Could this be the start of something beautiful?'

He shrugged as he held the door open for her. There was a blaring car alarm going off on the other side of the street. 'I don't really know. She dropped what might have been a kind of hint during the session earlier.'

'Oh?'

'Of course there may be nothing meaningful about it, but she said she'd just split up with her significant other.' He raised his eyebrows at Ella as they hit the footpath and took a left turn in the direction of the pub.

Ella stuffed her hands in her coat pockets and considered the situation. For some reason the notion of Jack and Angie hooking up together didn't afford her the same stabbingly jealous pain as some of his past liaisons had. Most of her boss's previous women had been worldly and sophisticated – real Bond girl types – and they'd taken pains to keep Ella at arm's length. She suspected that they were jealous of her easygoing relationship with Jack, and she often fantasized about wiping the floor with them. *Sorry, Tamara/Saskia/Magda. Jack and I won't be inviting you to the wedding. We've decided on a small affair on a beach somewhere exotic . . .* But she'd always got on well with Angie. It would at least make a nice change not to be condescended to by a girlfriend of Jack Noonan's. 'So. You reckon she's available? Actually, I think she kind of likes you too, Jack. She always gives herself a quick spray with Gaultier before she goes into a session with you.'

'Does she really?'

'Mm.' Hell. Maybe she should have kept shtum about that. 'I can't say I blame her. You're a very attractive bloke, you know.' A drop landed on her cheek, and she wiped it away. 'Uh-oh. It's starting to rain.'

'You're a doll for saying that.'

Jack slung an arm round Ella's shoulders, and she tried not to tense.

'What? For saying that it's starting to rain?'

'No. For reminding me that I'm not unattractive. I'll be hitting forty soon, and I could do with all the female reassurance I can get. And something tells me Angie is no walkover. I'm going to have to work at this one.' He stopped suddenly and gave her a speculative look. 'Hell, Ella. Look at yourself and then answer me this. Why is there no significant other in *your* life right now? There hasn't been anyone in the picture for ages, has there?'

'No.'

'But you used to have bevies of boyfriends baying after you like – like *beagles*.'

She gave him a cynical look. '*Bevies* is something of an exaggeration, Jack. I had a string of botched relationships, that's all. They were all gobshites.'

'All of them?'

'Every last one. I've had egotists, bullies, misers, sadists, manic depressives. I even went out with someone who didn't find *Father Ted* funny. It's made me fussy about men. I'm waiting for Mr Right to come along.'

'Define Mr Right for me. I suppose he has to be tall, dark and handsome?'

Like you, thought Ella. 'Preferably. But there's a more important prerequisite than that.'

'Let me guess. He has to have a sense of humour.'

'Hey! How did you know?'

'That's what all the girls say. They say that the best way to get a woman into bed is to make her laugh. Can't say it's ever worked for me. They all run a mile at my jokes.'

'I've got a good one for you,' said Ella. 'Knock, knock.'

'Who's there?'

'The Interrupting Cow.'

'The Interrupt—'

'*Moo!*'

Jack gave a gratifying laugh before giving her a ruminative look. 'You might have a long wait for this Mr Right, you know, darlin'. Remember what it says in the song.' A flurry of raindrops fell just as the green man on the pedestrian lights opposite turned to red. Ella made to dodge through the traffic, but Jack tightened his grip on her shoulder. 'Hey! Not so fast, sweetie.'

'Sorry.' She hopped back onto the pavement. 'What does it say in the song?'

'A good man is hard to find.'

No he's not! she thought. *Sometimes he's right under your nose, and he just doesn't realize it!* But she didn't

31

say it. Instead she said: 'And vice versa.'

Jack laughed and cuffed her lightly on the head. 'What would you know about that?'

'Jack. I'm not still Patrick's baby niece, you know. You may not have noticed, but I grew up some time ago.'

'I'd noticed,' he said. 'It would have been pretty difficult not to.'

Ella sent him a coquettish look from under her eyelashes, and was surprised not to receive the usual bantering-Jack look back. Instead there was something so new and so disturbing about the way he was looking at her that she berated herself for automatically sliding into their well-worn we're-such-good-mates-we-can-even-play-at-flirting routine.

Oh God. Change tack, Ella! Quick, quick – *change tack*! In nanoseconds the coquettish look was history, and she was casting around in a panic for a more appropriate, grown-up response to the sudden sexual tension that had sprung up between them. Poor Ella couldn't know it, but she had simply succeeded in making herself look incredibly vulnerable. Suddenly, awkwardly, Jack removed his arm from her shoulders, gave a little, unconvincing cough, and focused his gaze on the horizon somewhere to his right.

There was a long silence while mutual confusion reigned.

'Anyway – how will you know him when he eventually shows up?' said Jack, finally turning back to her. 'Your Mr Right.' He had resumed the expression he habitually wore when talking to her – that amused, slightly indulgent expression that had 'avuncular' written all over it. There was no trace left of the stranger who'd locked eyes with her barely one minute earlier.

Ella forced back her disappointment. More than anything she wanted to meet that stranger again. 'Well,' she said, making sure her voice was light and her smile chipper. 'He'll announce himself, of course, in time-honoured *coup de foudre* fashion—'

'*Coup de* what?'

'A *coup de foudre*, dummy, is French for "love at first sight". You know – like a bolt from the blue.'

Jack gave her a sceptical look. 'Life ain't that simple, little El.'

'Isn't it? Oh, look. The green man.' Ella skittered across the road towards Daly's on light feet, but with a heart that weighed a ton. An image of beautiful Angie had come into her head, and she couldn't stop thinking of her sitting in the pub, waiting for Jack. As he opened the door of the pub, a wave of heat, noise, alcohol fumes and cigarette smoke billowed out.

'Oh God, Jack,' said Ella suddenly. 'I'm sorry. I'm not going to be able to hack it after all. I think I'll just head on home. It's a night for staying in and watching something mindless on the telly.'

'Are you sure? It's not like you to be anti-social. Come in for one.'

'No, no, no. You know there's no such thing.'

Over by the counter Angie had caught Jack's eye and was waving at him.

Ella gave Jack's hand a quick squeeze. 'See you tomorrow.' Before he could twist her arm further, she slid back out through the door.

A bus was at the bus stop – the last passenger in the queue just boarding. She ran towards it, waving, but the driver ignored her and pulled away from the kerb. Shit. There wouldn't be another one for ages, and if she was going to organize something to eat and do her laundry before visiting the video shop, she'd need to get going. She set off up the road at a brisk pace just as the first drops of really heavy rain began to fall.

*   *   *

The next day was Friday. Ella was the first to arrive at work, as usual. She thought longingly of the days before she'd been tethered to the reception desk, when she'd had an extra half-hour in bed.

Julian had obviously worked on until quite late last night. There was an empty can of Diet Lilt on the coffee table, and the remains of a pizza in its cardboard box. He might have had the decency to dump it in the bin, she thought crossly, as she started to clear away the detritus. Yesterday's *Evening Herald* was there amongst the mess, still folded open at the page with the Pirate's Punch competition, and she felt a sudden flush of alarm. What if Julian had spotted his name on the competition entry? She picked up the paper and looked at it blankly. Where the entry form had been was a rectangle of nothingness. It had been torn out.

The door opened, and Ella let the newspaper drop as if it had burned her. Thankfully, it wasn't Julian. 'Oh – hi, Jack!' she said, sounding effusive with relief.

'Why are you looking like a little criminal?' he asked, eyeing her curiously.

Ella lowered her tone even though there wasn't anyone there to overhear her. 'I know this sounds bananas, Jack, but I did something a bit juvenile yesterday, and I'm scared that Julian might have found out about it.'

'You're talking about something juvenile pertaining to Julian? Some sort of practical joke, I take it?'

She nodded. 'Yes. And you know he has no sense of humour. He won't see the funny side of it.'

'OK. What have you done to exacerbate the already precarious nature of your professional relationship?'

She filled him in, and when she'd finished, Jack smiled. 'You don't have to worry that Julian saw it, sweetheart. He couldn't have. Angie sent it off.'

'What?'

'She thought it was an excellent jape. She loved the idea of all these unfortunate competition judges sitting around reading banal suggestions for names for those miserable parrots. She said the idea of someone opening an envelope and seeing "The Feathered Farts" instead of the usual predictable stuff like "The Piratical Parrots" or "The Merry Midshipmen" made her want to crease up, so she couldn't resist sending it. She's going to put something even ruder on today's entry form.'

'Oh, hell, Jack – I didn't just put Julian's name on the form. I put the Nesbit & Noonan address as well! What if word gets back to the copywriter responsible? It could be one of our clients!'

'So?'

'They'll think we're sending them up.'

'They deserve it for coming up with such an appalling campaign.' Jack gave her an amused look. 'Hell. Look at it this way. Maybe Julian'll win. After all, they wanted zany and the Feathered Farts is as zany as it gets. And if he does win, he'll just be extremely grateful to you for a free holiday in Jamaica. Oh, hi – Julian.'

'Hi, Julian!' Ella flashed him a guilty smile as he came through the door. He was looking nerdier than ever in a waterproof suit with bicycle clips round his ankles. She moved to the bin and dropped his pizza box into it.

'Here's the post,' he said, dumping a sheaf of envelopes on the desk and reaching for the diary. 'How many sessions have we lined up for today?'

'We're busy again,' said Ella. 'I don't mind covering for you if you want to take a lunch break,' she added hopefully.

'That's not possible, Ella,' said Jack. 'I'll answer the phone any time I have free so that you can do a sandwich run, but I can't lose Julian today. He has his own set-up on the Audiofile. It would take you too long to change it to your settings in the time booked.'

Ella thought she could detect smugness in the expression on Julian's face, and she hated him more than ever. Git! When she finally got off that desk she would show him a thing or two about sound engineering! She turned her attention to the post that he'd dumped in front of her. A grey envelope with urgent yellow and black type on the front caught her eye. 'Six Sweepstakes numbers allocated exclusively to Mrs Alan Nesbit' she read. With a sinking heart she tore open the envelope and took out a glossy A4 document. 'As an eligible Irish finalist you could be holding a number that is already worth over 1.6 MILLION DOLLARS! Plus this beautiful condiment set could be yours FREE with our very best wishes if you send away for our mouth-watering recipe book . . .'

How on earth had she got on a mailing list for prize draws? She looked at the picture of the condiment set. Who in their right mind could describe it as beautiful? What kind of people were they aiming at? The irresistible offer went into the bin alongside the envelope that had arrived for her in the afternoon post yesterday, exhorting her to *act immediately* because it was her *last chance* to win a *million yes a million lovely smackers* . . .

*   *   *

Over the course of the next few days junk mail streamed through the letterbox of Nesbit & Noonan. All the petitioners offered mind-boggling incentives to potential subscribers. As well as draws and competitions with millions of pounds of prize money on offer, there were other inducements. Ella was offered a free Photo Frame cum Alarm Clock, a home breadmaker, a solar watch, a wall clock that marked the hours with birdsong, a beautiful rose bush SPECIALLY for HER, and a Majestic Garden Arch.

One morning she received a letter that was – amazingly – correctly addressed to her in her grandmother's perfect italic script. She slit open the envelope and took out a card with a photograph on the front of a fluffy blue-eyed kitten poking out of a satin slipper. It had a miniature top hat on, and it was wearing a pink bow. Hang about, thought Ella. This was emphatically *not* Leonie's style. Leonie usually sent the most beautiful cards – reproductions of Matisse or Picasso or Miró. This card was more like a Jeff Koons aberration.

'Darling Ella', she read. 'A card to say thank you for my birthday flowers. Tacky, isn't it! What sad geezer dreamed up the idea of sticking a kitten in a shoe! I was thinking of writing to the ISPCA about it until I remembered that I used to stick Ronan in my slipper when he was a kitten, but at least I never made him wear a ribbon or a top hat. By the way have you won anything yet? With very much love from your doting ~*!# Leonie. XXX'

Leonie hated the word 'grandmother', and always refrained from using it when she could. Hence the ~*!#.

Ella skimmed through the note again. *Have you won anything yet...* Now the competition entries and draws for smart cars and lump sums of money and dream holidays made sense. Her grandmother must have put her on some junk mailing list. Oh God. Leonie had lost it. She was obviously doting in more ways than one. But then, Ella supposed, Leonie had always behaved erratically. She had married Ella's paternal grandfather – a fervent Irish republican – to spite her father, who'd been a colonel in the British army. The marriage had lasted just long enough for her to produce Patrick and Declan in rapid succession, and then Leonie had scarpered, abandoning her husband for a career on the stage. She had been a great beauty, and had done a mean line in celebrity consorts until she decided to give up men and espouse environmental causes instead. She'd dumped her last lover two years ago, and claimed to have been celibate since.

Ella stuck the blue-eyed kitten up on the pinboard behind her desk, and then picked up the phone and punched in her grandmother's number. The answering machine picked up. *This is a recorded message,* heard Ella. *Do not under any circumstances vote for Jim Moran at the next by-election. He is a complete shyster. He has done bugger all about the noise pollution in the Liberties, he connived on the planning permission for that hideous high rise office block, and he also completely ignored my letters concerning recycling. I repeat. Do not vote for Smiling Jim Moran.* Then: *Beeeep* went the answering machine.

'Leonie?' said Ella. 'If you're there will you pick up the phone? Pick up the phone, Leonie.'

There was a beat, and then she heard her grandmother's voice. 'Oh, hello, darling. I'm glad it's only you. I thought it might be that awful Mrs Hardiman from down the road reminding me about her coffee morning. How are things?'

Ella got straight to the point. 'Leonie – have you put me on some kind of mailing list?'

'Oh, yes! Didn't I tell you? Brilliant prizes, aren't they?'

'Leonie – you would not believe the kind of stuff I've been offered. You thought that kitten in a shoe was tacky? How's this for tacky? Personalized writing paper with your photograph on it? A stuffed lamb that plays "Jesus Loves Me"? A garden lamp in the shape of a gnome?'

'Oh – ignore all that crap, Ella. Just go for the big stuff. You know – the cars, the holidays, the cash, the—'

'Leonie – I'm not going to win *anything*. If you think Jim Moran is a shyster, those people who manipulate you into forking out pounds and pounds for their cruddy products are shysters twenty times over. It's a mug's game.'

'All right, darling,' said Leonie with equanimity. 'Just fling them in the bin if you're not interested.'

'Leonie – you're the one who's concerned about recycling.'

'You're right.' A pause while her grandmother digested this. 'I shall demand that your name is taken off every single mailing list.' Leonie was starting to sound animated. 'In fact – this could be my new pet project. Putting an end to mindless junk mail. Maybe I should give Jim Moran another chance. Yes. I'll do that. I'll write to him and see if he rises to the challenge.'

'What made you put me on a mailing list anyway?'

'Because you seemed so out-of-sorts the last time I talked to you. I thought the idea of winning something might cheer you up.'

Ella smiled at her grandmother down the phone. 'You are sweet,' she said. 'Why did you give them my work address?'

'Because you told me some of your mail had gone missing. I suspect it's that man who lives next door to you. He's intercepting it somehow. His moustache is too thin and his eyes are too close together.'

'He's running for the by-election,' said Ella.

'Well, that explains everything,' said Leonie.

*　　*　　*

'Nesbit & Noonan, good morning!' said Ella into the phone later that morning, trying hard

41

to remember to use receptionist's exclamation marks.

'Hello,' came the unfamiliar voice at the other end of the line. 'Could I speak to Miss Ellen Nisbit, please?' He pronounced the name with a precision she found offensive.

'This is Ella Nesbit speaking,' she replied flatly.

'Ah – hello, Miss Nisbit.' The voice was irritatingly cheerful. 'I have some news for you that I think you'll find extremely exciting.'

Oh God, thought Ella. Leonie had obviously given her phone number to some telesales rep. 'I'm sorry, I'm not interested,' she said, hoping the geezer wasn't going to be persistent.

'Oh ho – I think you will be,' said the caller. 'When I tell you the news I have for you, I think you'll be more than interested.'

Hell. He *was* going to be persistent. And the fact that he had actually said 'Oh ho' made it a matter of urgency to get rid of him. She was just about to come out with her firm but polite 'Not today, thank you' when one word made her stop in her tracks.

'Jamaica!' said the voice. 'How does Jamaica sound to you? Two weeks with a lucky girlfriend – or boyfriend, ha ha – in the Salamander Cove resort?'

Salamander Cove? That was the name of the resort in that competition in the *Evening Herald*. 'Sorry,' she said. 'Who is this? Is this some kind of practical joke?'

42

'Ha ha ha! You think you're dreaming, don't you, Ellen? Well, it's a dream come true – or maybe I should say a dream holiday come true!!!' She knew that he'd invested the end of the sentence with at least three exclamation marks. 'My name is Manus McNulty, of Toptree Foods Ltd. You entered our competition recently to win a holiday in Jamaica, and you won – with your wonderful suggestion for a name for our trademark parrots.'

Oh God. How could 'The Feathered Farts' have won? Could it be that they really really *did* want zany, as they'd said in the ad? Not possible. 'The Feathered Farts' wasn't even zany, it was just infantile. Anyway, if it had won, they'd be phoning Julian, not her. 'You – er – you don't mean "The Feathered Farts", do you?' she enquired tentatively.

'Come again?'

'"The Feathered Farts"? Was that the name that won?'

The voice down the other end of the phone sounded confused. 'I'm sorry. I don't know what you're talking about. You're sure you're Ellen Nisbit, aren't you? Of Nisbit & Noonane, 14 Lower Winston Street, Dublin 2?'

She wasn't sure of anything right now. But: 'Yes, yes. That's me,' she said.

'Well, your entry has no – er – feathered farts on it. The name you put down was "The Polly Rogers". That was the name the judges thought bang on for our band of pirate parrots.'

Oh God, she thought. Things were suddenly starting to make sense. 'Of course,' she said. 'How stupid of me. It was "The Polly Rogers", not "The Feathered Farts". I was – er – thinking of something else.'

'Well,' said Manus McNulty. 'When would it suit you to take your holiday?'

*   *   *

As soon as she put the phone down she picked it up again and punched in her grandmother's number.

'Oh, hello, darling,' said Leonie. 'How lovely to hear from you again so soon. Let me just put this stethoscope in the right place.'

Ella didn't ask.

'S-C-O-P-E,' Leonie enunciated carefully. 'There we are. The *Irish Times* crossword isn't getting any easier. Now. What can I do for you?'

'Leonie?' said Ella. 'Do "The Polly Rogers" mean anything to you?'

'The Polly Rogers? No, darling – I can't say they do. Oh – wait a minute. Wasn't Polly MacPherson married to somebody called Roger?'

'No, no, Leonie,' said Ella patiently. 'I'm talking about a competition. Did you put my name on a competition entry form recently?'

'Oh, yes.' Leonie's tone was careless. 'I've been doing that for weeks now, as well as those prize draws. I rather hoped you might win that set of

Hugh Grant videos and invite me round to watch them one night. I keep missing *Four Weddings* every time it's on the television. I've drafted a brilliant letter, by the way, telling all those purveyors of tack to remove your name from their junk mailing lists with immediate effect. I told them Jim Moran would be down on them like a ton of bricks if they didn't. That should make them sit up and take note, eh?'

'Have you taken that defamatory message about him off your answering machine?'

'Yes, yes. Smiling Jim has got a reprieve. Stop that, Ronan. Ronan's eating the geranium. Stop it, you evil cat!' There followed a pause full of muttered expletives before her grandmother spoke again. 'Sorry about that,' she said, breathlessly. 'I think he's addicted to that geranium. Now – tell me. *Did* you win those videos?'

'No, Leonie. I didn't win any videos. I won a holiday.'

'Oh, excellent! Where to?'

'Jamaica.'

'Jamaica! How exotic! Now – which competition was that? You have to be reminded of things like that when you get to my age.'

'The one where you had to make up a name for that band of parrots dressed up as pirates.'

'Oh, God yes. Now I remember. Horrific creatures, aren't they, those parrots? I zap them off the television every time they come on. What name did I call them?'

'You called them the Polly Rogers.'

'The Polly Rogers! An appropriately *ghastly* name, don't you think? I was actually tempted to call them something like The DTs but I restrained myself. "My beautiful Ella needs a holiday", I thought to myself. "And she's not going to get one if I give in to the temptation to write down something smart." So I came up with "The Polly Rogers" instead. That's the sort of thing they're looking for, isn't it? Oh listen – Ronan's purring.'

A noise like a sewing machine came down the phone as her grandmother stuck the receiver next to the cat. After a minute of listening to Ronan purr, Leonie came back on again. 'So, the jolly old Polly Rogers won, did they? Good for them. I wonder did "Grant My Wish" get anywhere?'

'Grant My Wish?' echoed Ella, perplexed.

'Yes. That's what I put down for the Hugh Grant video competition.'

'If it didn't win, it should have.'

'Better than the Polly Rogers anyway. I can't believe they bought that!' Leonie gave a scornful laugh, and then resumed. 'So – Ella, my darling – you'll be jet-setting off to Jamaica soon! You lucky, lucky girl. I've always wanted to do the Caribbean. How sad to think I never will. That's the grimmest thing about getting to my age. You start eliminating things from the list of "Things I've Always Wanted to Do" and "Places I've Always Wanted to Visit". I finally got round to scratching off "Snorkelling on a Coral Reef" last week.'

'I think you should put it on again,' suggested her granddaughter with a smile.

'Really, darling? Why's that?'

'You're coming with me,' said Ella.

Chapter Two

Friday evening in Daly's was always the busiest of the week. When she swung through the door with Jack at around six o'clock the place was heaving with media types, but this evening Ella didn't mind. She was feeling sociable again, and so full of gratitude to Toptree Foods that she very nearly ordered a Pirate's Punch when Jack asked her what she wanted to drink. Word had got round that Ella had won a holiday for two in Jamaica, and as she made her way towards the corner table that her uncle always took pains to commandeer on Friday nights, the regulars were speculating vociferously about what lucky man she might be taking with her. One extremely attractive (married) actor generously volunteered to accompany her if she was stuck. 'Who *are* you taking then, Ella?' he asked when she turned him down. She raised her eyebrows at him and gave him an enigmatic smile. 'C'mon – who is it?' persisted the actor. 'One of your groovy musician friends, I suppose?'

'No,' she said. 'I'm taking my grandmother.'

'El*la*!' groaned the actor. 'You're taking your

grandmother to a romantic tropical paradise! What a waste!'

'I'll call you if she gets cold feet,' said Ella. 'But it ain't likely. Leonie's hot to trot.'

Her uncle was sitting in his usual corner, a pint already in front of him.

'Hi, Patrick!' she said, plonking herself down beside him and giving him a kiss on the cheek. She'd picked up a brochure from a travel agent's after leaving work, and she pulled it out of her back-pack now and started leafing through the glossy pages. 'Look!' Her voice was sing-songy with delight. 'That's where I'm going! Palm trees! White sand! Cocktails on the beach!' She spread the brochure out on the table in front of him.

Patrick shook his head in disbelief. 'I can't believe you're bringing Leonie, Ella.'

'Why can't you believe it?'

He indicated a blue-sky, blue-sea photograph in which two smiling thong-clad babes were promi-nent. 'Can you imagine my mother sitting on that beach? You haven't given this very much thought, have you?'

'I couldn't not take her, Patrick,' she replied reasonably. 'She was the one who won the compe-tition, after all. And she's not a prude, if that's what you're worried about. She told me that she used to go skinny-dipping in the Mediterranean when she was my age.'

'It's not that I'm worried about,' said Patrick. 'It's

just that she's getting dottier by the day. I'm not sure you could handle her on your own – especially on the other side of the Atlantic. What did she say when you invited her along?'

'She told me to get real.'

'Get real? She used those actual words?'

'Yes. She told me to get real and bring a friend my own age. She was absolutely adamant about it until I told her that I wouldn't go at all if she didn't come. Then when she knew there was no way round it, she started getting excited. She rang me back later to tell me she'd been in touch with some scuba diving outfit in Portdelvin.'

'Jesus!' said her uncle. 'Leonie can't go scuba diving. At her age she'd have problems learning how to snorkel.'

'Don't worry, Patrick. She was checking it out for me. Apparently you can start learning here and complete the training anywhere in the world.'

'That sounds like a bloody good idea.' Jack had rolled up. He set two pints down on the table and sat down on Ella's left – close, but not close enough for physical contact. The banquette was narrow. Ella resisted the temptation to shift to her left, congratulating herself on her self-restraint. God! What a sad bitch she was, mooning over this man! 'That time I went to Australia I cursed myself for not having done a course in scuba beforehand,' he continued. 'Leonie's dead right, you know. You *should* investigate having lessons.'

'You really think so?' Until that afternoon Ella

had never even entertained the idea of taking up scuba diving, but now she could see it made sense. Diving in the Caribbean would be like diving in Paradise.

'I absolutely think so. I'll never forget the afternoon I saw a dive boat coming back from the Great Barrier Reef, full of people comparing stories about what they'd seen underwater. They were high on it – euphoric. It's one of my biggest regrets ever that I travelled halfway across the planet, but let a whole new world go unexplored.'

'A new world?'

'The world under the waves.'

The world under the waves . . . It sounded so romantic! She'd seen a diver on a *National Geographic* programme once, feeding fish in the Tropics. She pictured herself swimming through Caribbean water, picking up shells and surrounded by flocks – no, shoals – of multi-coloured fish, looking slinky and svelte and streamlined in her scuba suit, and with her hair drifting around her like the Little Mermaid's. Hell. She'd have to do it.

'OK,' she said. 'I'll book a course first thing on Monday.'

'When are you off?' asked Patrick. 'To Jamaica?'

'Whenever I like,' she said breezily. 'Or rather – whenever suits you. Around the beginning of December might be good. Things will be easing off by then.' Hooray! she thought. He and Jack would have to think seriously about finding a receptionist now.

Her uncle looked pensive. 'We'll have to think seriously about finding a receptionist now,' he said.

* * *

The following Monday, along with an envelope that exhorted her to: 'HURRY! We're giving away a Philips Mini Hi-Fi System to each of the first 50 replies drawn', and another which was obviously meant to set her heart racing with excitement at its 'URGENT' invitation to enter a prize draw which could win her £100,000, there was a third envelope addressed to her. It contained a brochure with the portmanteau word 'ActivMarine' emblazoned on the front across a picture of a diver silhouetted against an underwater background of aquamarine blue. A spotty blue and yellow fish hovered in the foreground, and a whole shower of little stripy ones were surging over a reef below. There was a stream of silver bubbles emerging from the diver's mouth, which was clamped around a rubber tube. Leonie must have given the scuba outfit her address.

Ella opened the brochure and perused the contents. Inside was a list of the diving courses available. There were beginners' open water courses and advanced open water courses. There were wreck diving courses and night diving courses, rescue diving courses and Blue Shark diving courses. There were dive weekends away in the West of Ireland, and dive holidays in more exotic locations. Barbados, the Red Sea, Thailand.

There were photographs of people looking happy and windswept on dive boats, and pictures of people gliding effortlessly through deep blue water. It looked enormously seductive.

A colour-coded calendar showed her when the next beginners' classes were starting. This Wednesday, at 7 p.m. Every week for six weeks! It seemed a ridiculously long time to learn how to float around underwater sucking air in through a tube. She had a friend who'd gone scuba diving in Australia once, and she hadn't had any training at all. The geezer who'd taken her down had done all the necessary fiddling round with tubes and gauges and whatever, and she'd just trailed along behind him, holding onto his hand. Still. It would be nice to be independent instead of being a mere water baby. To have some diving education. Her friend had tried to pick up a shell at one point, and her guide had practically given her a Chinese burn in his efforts to prevent her. Admittedly she'd found out afterwards that that particular species of cone shell had a highly venomous barb. If she trained she'd learn about all that jazz. She might even invest in an underwater camera. It would be a lot more interesting to bring home wonderful photographs of coral reefs and exotic fish and divers rather than the usual run-of-the-mill 'Me on the beach. Me sipping a cocktail. Me diving into the pool' holiday shots.

'Morning,' said Jack, coming through the door. Today he was wearing his motorbike leathers and looking more like Pierce Brosnan than ever. 'What's that you've got?' he asked, glancing at the brochure as he pulled the zip on his jacket all the way down and peeled it off. Ow, thought Ella. 'More offers of millions of pounds?'

'No,' replied Ella. 'It's a scuba diving brochure.'

'Let's have a look,' said Jack, sitting down on the reception desk and leaning in to her, as was his habit every morning when he arrived at work. He whistled through his teeth as he scanned the glossy pages. 'Oh, yes, Ella! You've gotta do it. Wow. I can just picture you emerging from the water with a dagger on your hip like Ursula Andress in *Dr No*.'

'Ursula Andress I ain't,' said Ella.

'Well – I'll concede that you're not as well endowed. Still. It's a seriously glamorous sport. Sure as hell beats golf for sex appeal. Go on. Give them a ring now and book yourself in.'

'It's a six-week course, Jack.'

'It'll be worth it. Go on, Miss Intrepid. Didn't you do a parachute jump once? This has got to be less scary.'

'OK.' Ella took the brochure from him and gave him a challenging look. 'I'll bring you back a shark's tooth necklace,' she said as she punched in the number. 'One that I'll make from teeth plucked from the jaws of death by my own fair hands.'

'Way to go, Ella. You'll make Lara Croft look like Goldilocks.'

The phone rang for ages. Then, finally: 'ActivMarine, good morning,' she heard. Whoever had picked up the phone had forgotten the mandatory exclamation marks. It was a man's voice.

'Oh – good morning!' said Ella in her brightest receptionist's tones. 'I'm ringing to enquire about diving lessons. Can you tell me something about the beginners' course, please?'

'Sure. There's one starting this Wednesday at seven o'clock.'

The accent was Galway. Quite attractive, she thought. She decided it might be worth giving him her full warm receptionist's treatment, and she replied with a smile. 'Yes. I saw that from your brochure. It's an hour-long class, is it?'

'No. We do two hours of academic work between seven and nine, and then two hours of practical pool work. You'll be out of the pool by eleven o'clock.'

'Eleven o'clock!' Ella was horrified. 'But that's four hours!' She made a rapid calculation. 'Four hours a week for six weeks – that's twenty-four hours altogether!' She looked up at Jack and opened her mouth in a silent scream.

'There's not a lot wrong with your mental arithmetic. Can't you spare the time?'

'Well – yes, I can. I just didn't realize there was so much work involved.'

'You're training to be a certified open water diver. It's not like taking night classes in flower arranging.'

Ella narrowed her eyes at his tone. Who did he think she was? Some bored dilettante who'd been flicking casually through the *Guide to Evening Classes*? 'I understand I can complete the course abroad?' she said, adopting a rather more distant tone. There was obviously no point in wasting friendly exclamation marks or warm smiles on this individual.

'That's right. You can do your certifying dives at any affiliated dive outfit in the world.'

'Oh? Does that mean I could do four weeks' training here and two in Jamaica?'

'You're off to Jamaica, lucky lady?'

'Yes.'

'Well, I'm afraid it doesn't work like that. You do your twenty-four hours here, and then you sit a written exam. You then have to demonstrate that you've mastered the skills you've been taught.'

'In a pool?'

'No. In open water, in four separate dives. You can choose to do them here – in which case you'll be already certified when you hit Jamaica – or we'll refer you on and you can perform your qualifying dives once you're there.'

Oh God. It all sounded horribly complicated. She was beginning to wish she'd never hit on this learning to dive idea. 'Where do you do the open water dives?' she asked, suspecting she wasn't going to like the answer very much.

'Sheep's Head Bay, near Portdelvin.'

'But it's nearly winter!'

That irritating smile was in his voice again. 'You'd be amazed how hot you can get in a wetsuit, even in the Irish Sea, even in the month of November.'

'Actually, we're in October.'

'If you manage to get through the six weeks of training, it'll be November when you do your dives.'

If you manage to get through the six weeks of training! He'd obviously got her totally wrong! Ella Nesbit was no wimp. She was one of the lads – able to equalize, compress and mix with the best of them. *And* she drank pints. 'OK,' she said with authority. 'Book me in for the course starting this Wednesday.'

'Sure. What's your name?'

'Ella Nesbit.'

'All right, Ella Nesbit.' Wow. He'd actually got her name right. 'You're down. You might like to come out to us beforehand to pick up your manual.'

'My manual?' Ella made another face at Jack. He was earwigging shamelessly, and was obviously highly amused.

'Your dive manual. It goes over the course step by step, and it'll give you a taste of what's in store. It's a good idea to have read the first chapter before you come to class.'

The first chapter! Phooey. She wasn't going to go all the way out to Portdelvin to pick up a poxy manual. He probably thought she had the IQ of an idiot, and wouldn't be able to understand a word of her lesson without having laboriously read the whole thing through in advance. She'd never been one for swotting – she'd winged every exam she'd ever taken. She could pick up whatever she needed to know in the classroom.

'Um. No. I think I'll pass on that,' she said.

'That's your lookout.' This was obviously not the 'very helpful and charming' individual Leonie had spoken to when she'd made her enquiries. 'We'll see you on Wednesday, then, Ella Nesbit. The class starts at seven o'clock sharp.'

'I'll be there at five minutes to,' she told him, and then – just as she was about to put the phone down she said: 'Oh – by the way! How much does it cost?'

'Three hundred and ninety-five pounds.'

'Oh!' She was so taken aback at the amount that she found herself trying to cover her confusion. 'A snip!' she said in a jokey voice. 'Thanks for your help!'

Ella put the receiver down with a heavy hand, and – she realized to her dismay – a heavy heart as well. What in God's name was she letting herself in for? An opportunity to indulge in a relaxing recreational sport, or the prospect of forking out £395 for boot camp? The person she had spoken to was obviously some despotic Pol Pot type. And it sounded as if he was totally challenged in the humour department, which wouldn't help matters. The word 'fun' had featured a lot in their glossy brochure. She wondered if she should draw it to the attention of the trades description people.

'Having second thoughts?' Jack raised an eyebrow at her pensive expression.

'No,' said Ella. 'It just costs a lot of money.'

'What costs a lot of money?' Patrick had swung through the door with a flurry and shake of his wet umbrella.

'Ella's just enrolled on her scuba diving course.'

'Oh? When do you start?'

'Wednesday. I'd better get in touch with Toptree Foods and find out about booking the dates for the holiday today. I should just about have time to get all my training out of the way before I go.'

'Are you still thinking about disappearing in December?'

'Yeah.' Ella dragged the desk diary towards her and drew a big smiley face on the page marking the first Monday of December. 'That's my optimum date. Is that cool with you, Patrick?'

'That's cool. The Christmas rush will be just about over by then.'

'You'll miss a lot of agency parties, Ella,' cautioned Jack.

She shrugged. 'I won't miss the hangovers.'

Patrick picked up the scuba brochure. 'They mention the word "fun" a lot in here,' he remarked, as he flicked through the pages.

'Well, if they're all going to be like that geezer who answered the phone it's not going to be a barrel of laughs. Twenty-four hours of training, Patrick! Two hours a week desk work, followed by two hours in a pool! And an exam, and you have to get through four dives in the Irish Sea.' She shuddered and then reconsidered. 'No. I'll go for the referral

option. I'm not diving in Sheep's Head bloody Bay.
I'll definitely do those dives in Jamaica.'

'Aw, come on, Scubagirl. Give us a laugh, why
don't you?' said Jack. 'I'll sit on the beach in my
sheepskin jacket with a hip flask and a picnic and
cheer you on.'

'A hip flask sounds like a very good idea,' said
Ella. 'Maybe you should drive me out and then
whisk me off to the Harbour Bar for copious hot
whiskies afterwards.'

'Talking about transport – how are you going to
manage the long haul out to Portdelvin every
Wednesday?' asked Patrick.

'I'll get the DART.'

'What? And DART it home again after spending
two hours shivering your ass off in a pool? C'mon,
Ella – get real. I'll lend you the car.'

Patrick occasionally lent her his car if her need
was greater than his. It was very handy – she had
friends out in Wicklow whom she would probably
never have managed to see at all if it hadn't been
for him. And she loved driving it – it was a seriously
smart little two-seater Merc convertible.

'Every Wednesday, Patrick? I can't expect you to
do that.'

'It's not a problem, Ella. You can drop me off on
your way, and leave the car back when you're
through. And it's a way of saying thank you for
being such a sweetheart and bringing Leonie to
Jamaica with you. She hasn't had a foreign holiday
for years, and I was starting to feel guilty about it. I

was even toying with the idea of inviting her to come to France with us next summer.' Patrick and his wife Claudia owned a small villa in the Midi.

'But that would be disastrous! Claudia would go demented!' Leonie and her daughter-in-law did *not* get on. In fact, they couldn't even bear to be in the same room.

'I know. That's why I really owe you, Ella.'

'Well, thanks, Patrick! I feel awful now for all that moaning I've been doing about being the receptionist. I promise you won't hear another peep out of me between now and December. It'll be like Home, Home on the Range in here.'

'Home, Home on the Range?' repeated Jack.

'Where Seldom is Heard a Discouraging Word,' explained Ella.

'And the Sky is not Cloudy All Day.' Julian came in, and Ella's smile faded. She snuck a look at her watch. It was bang on nine-thirty. He was on time. 'It's cloudy out there, though, I can tell you. Some amateur weatherman said on the radio this morning that we're going to have the worst winter in a decade.' He was wearing his waterproof suit, and there was a drip on the end of his bony nose.

'Well, if that's the case, Ella, you're one lucky baggage.' Jack got to his feet and performed that lovely lazy stretch he did so well. The fact that he was so completely unselfconscious about how well he did it made it even lovelier.

'What's so lucky about the worst winter in a

61

decade?' asked Julian, divesting himself of his bicycle clips.

'Ella's not going to be here,' explained Jack. 'Well, for two weeks of it, anyway. She's heading off to go scuba diving in the Caribbean.'

It was the first Julian had heard of it. 'Oh? When?'

'The beginning of December, with a bit of luck.' Ella tried not to look smug. 'I've won a holiday to Jamaica.'

'Oh. Great.' Julian gave her his thin-lipped excuse for a smile. 'I didn't know you were into scuba.'

'I'm not. Well, not until now, that is. I'm taking a six-week course before I go.'

'Where?'

'ActivMarine, in Portdelvin.'

'Ah. Yeah.' Julian nodded his head in an irritatingly knowledgeable way. 'That's the outfit I trained with.'

'*You* did?' She couldn't prevent her jaw from dropping a little.

'Yeah. I did my advanced open water training with ActivMarine last year.'

Oh shit. She couldn't bear it. Not only was Julian a certified open water diver, he was an *advanced* open water diver! She thought she might get sick. Why was life so unfair? Now she'd have to sit through hours of him droning on about scuba diving as well as showing off in the studio.

'They're a great bunch of lads out there.' Julian did something with his chin that she supposed was meant to look manly. 'Know their stuff. You'll be in good hands, Ella.' He put his bicycle clips in the pocket of his waterproof suit and hung it on the hat stand. It looked like a dripping bat. 'Scuba's tough, but it's fun. I've had some great experiences in tropical water, but there's some excellent diving off the West Coast of Ireland. In fact, I might head west for a dive weekend over the Christmas break,' he added, nodding his head again, this time in a nauseatingly contemplative way.

'Christmas? In the worst winter of the decade?' said Jack. 'Won't the water freeze your bollocks off?'

'Not when you're wearing a dry-suit,' said Julian. 'Mine's a customized state-of-the-art compressed neoprene. Keeps me warm and bone-dry.'

'I wouldn't have thought the visibility would be much good in December, either,' remarked Patrick.

'Well, it depends on conditions. It can be murky, sometimes. But even in poor visibility you can encounter marine life. Wrasse, for instance.' Wrasse? Ella had read somewhere that 'rass' was Jamaican patois for arse. Was Julian trying to put her off? 'And pollock. And I saw a shark down in Killary once. Yeah. You can see some amazing stuff off the West Coast. Tubeworms are totally astonishing.'

Thank you for sharing that with me, Julian, thought Ella. So. Scuba diving was fun, was it? Freezing water, crap visibility, nerds like Julian floundering around in murk, wrasse and pollocks, for Jesus' sake, and *tubeworms* – yeuch – and, and – sharks and Pol bleeding Pot types like the one she'd spoken to on the phone earlier . . .

'You'll have fun, Ella,' said Julian. The f-word again! 'If you get through the training, that is.'

She bloody well would.

Chapter Three

The following Wednesday evening, Ella slid into the driver's seat of her uncle's cherry red Merc feeling quite chuffed with herself. Here she was in a groovy car, heading off to learn all about one of the sexiest hobbies in the world! Recreational diving! She slid the seat forward, adjusted the rear-view mirror and changed the channel on the car radio. Time Saver Traffic told her that there'd been an accident on the coast road, and that traffic was backed up as far as Booterstown. Uh-oh. Maybe she should have got the DART after all.

Progress was slow. She'd allowed herself an hour to get to Portdelvin, but she now realized it wasn't going to be enough. Well. It wouldn't matter if she was a few minutes late, would it? Pol Pot had said seven sharp, but nothing in Ireland ever started on time. The Irish were a laid-back race – that was part of their charm, after all. Visitors to the country were always commenting on how refreshingly easygoing the Celtic nature was.

Forty minutes later, looking round her at the other motorists stuck in commuter belt hell, she saw high-achieving, stressed-out Celtic tiger types snarling with road rage behind the wheels of their Beamers and Mercs. Somewhere along the line the sleepy-village mentality of the average Irish person had been given either a shot in the arm or a kick up the arse. Even she was starting to whimper a little with mild road annoyance, despite the lazy jazz she'd put on the CD player to conjure a mellow vibe. By the time she reached Portdelvin it was seven o'clock on the dot. Shit. She hoped that Pol Pot wouldn't remind her that she said she'd be there at five minutes to. She cruised along the seafront, looking for ActivMarine. When she hit the little harbour, she knew she'd gone too far. She turned the car, drove back the way she'd come, and looked some more. Finally she stopped a passing dog-walker. 'Excuse me?' she said. 'Would you happen to know where ActivMarine is?'

'The scuba-diving place?' said the man. 'Yes. It's right there.' He indicated a shop front two doors down. She wasn't surprised she'd missed it. The joint looked shut.

'Thanks,' she said. 'Enjoy your walk.'

A parking space was what she needed next. Again she drove up and down the seafront, starting to feel a little panicky. It was ten past seven now. At last she saw someone pull out and she swooped down on the vacant space, thanking God for her uncle's power-steering. She grabbed her bag, zapped the locks and ran down the road, cursing her girly heels. Her receptionist's garb of the day was the stretch cotton skirt that Jack had said made her ass look great, teamed with a plain black FCUK top. When she got to the dive shop she rang the bell. After a minute or two spent peering through the window at the dim interior lined with rails of scuba suits and serried ranks of tanks, she rang again and eventually saw a door opening at the back of the shop. A shaven-headed man in his twenties approached and looked at her questioningly, and by pointing to the door and to her watch and spreading her palms apologetically she managed to convey that she was there for the class. A bunch of keys was produced, and the door unlocked. 'Sorry I'm late,' she said as she teetered through. 'The traffic was a bitch. I'm Ella Nesbit – I'm starting your open water course this evening.'

'No problem. You haven't missed much – they've just been filling in forms. You can do yours later.' He smiled at her and held out his hand. She noticed that a long scar zigzagged along the back of his wrist. 'My name's PJ Farrell.' Was this Pol Pot? She thought not. Pol Pot would have given out to her for being late, and this geezer had lovely crinkly eyes and an easygoing manner.

'Are you an instructor?' asked Ella, shaking his hand. She hoped he was.

'Yeah. I'm not doing any of the academic stuff with you, but I'll be helping out in the pool later. Come on through.'

She followed him through the door at the back of the shop, along a corridor whose walls were hung with framed photographs of underwater scenes featuring divers and reefs and exotic fish, and into a fluorescently lit room where a dozen or so individuals were sitting at rows of desks. They were all male, with the exception of one sporty-looking woman in an olive-green tracksuit.

A tall bloke was standing at the top of the classroom writing on a blackboard. Long blond dreadlocks snaked down his back beyond his shoulder blades. He turned when Ella came through the door, and then referred to a clipboard. 'Ella Nesbit,' he said, raising an eyebrow at her. He didn't bother with a question mark, and she was reminded of the way he hadn't bothered with exclamation marks either, that time she'd talked to him on the phone. He looked at his watch in an irritatingly meaningful way. This had to be Pol Pot. Somehow she'd imagined him as looking very different. More of a sergeant-major type. The last thing she'd have predicted would have been dreadlocks. He even had quite good bone structure – apart from a broken nose.

'We've a full quota now,' said PJ Farrell.

Pol Pot nodded, and motioned her to a seat. The only ones free were at the very front of the class, and she felt a bit stupid as she high-heeled her way to the top of the room and slid out of her coat and into a chair. She'd immediately registered that everyone else in the room was dressed in jeans and sweaters and sensible-looking shoes, and she could feel their eyes taking in her girly gear.

'Here's a form to fill in,' he said, handing it to her.

She noticed a diagonal scar running from the edge of his jaw to his cheekbone. It terminated just below the outer corner of his left eye. Ella decided she was going to do an inventory of scars. If scars were a feature on every single instructor's anatomy she might have serious second thoughts about taking up recreational diving as a hobby. 'It's to verify that you're in good physical nick,' he added, as she opened the questionnaire.

'I am,' she said.

'Oh?' His look of amused enquiry invited elaboration, and she felt herself colour. Infuriating git! He was *smirking* at her!

'I had an assessment done at my gym recently,' she explained in brisk tones, taking a pen out of her bag.

'You still need to fill it in. No cheating.'

No cheating! Where was she – at a night class or in kindergarten? She scanned the checklist of questions on the form and mentally crossed them all off. No, she didn't suffer from obesity; no, she didn't suffer from a collapsed lung; no, she didn't have a history of drug or alcohol abuse, blah blah blah. The list went on and on.

Only one of the conditions made her think twice. Claustrophobia. She had suffered from it as a child, but she hadn't had an attack for ages – which was just as well, because one of the recording booths she was required to work in was pretty poky.

Pol Pot leaned back in his seat, splayed out long, combat-clad legs, and addressed the class. 'OK.

Hands up who hasn't read the first chapter of the manual you were issued with?'

Ella looked round. Not one person in the room had raised their hand.

Pol Pot resumed. 'Everyone's done their homework? Good. It's important that you familiarize yourself with the relevant chapter before coming to class because—'

'Excuse me?' said Ella. 'I don't have a manual.'

He narrowed his eyes at her and she found herself going pink again. 'So, Ella,' he said. 'You're at a disadvantage. Please come prepared next week because I don't want to have to waste time doing remedial work.' Remedial work! Ex*cuse* me? 'It's not fair on the rest of the group.'

Oh. The old guilt trip tactic never failed with her. 'Of course,' she said quickly. 'I'll do two lots of homework next week. I don't want to run the risk of ending up in detention.' It was a pathetic joke, and possibly ill-timed, but Pol Pot acknowledged it with what could best be described as a perfunctory smile.

'We don't do detention here. We're more into traditional maritime forms of punishment.'

Ella didn't want to ask, but somebody else in the classroom did. 'Hey! Whips and manacles are considered forms of *punishment*?' came a male voice.

'Only if you're a deeply unimaginative individual,' said Pol Pot, raising an amused eyebrow. 'I might have known you'd suss that one, Richie.'

Ella turned round. Pol Pot had directed the remark at a good-looking geezer who she gauged was somewhere in his early twenties. He had eyes the colour of blue denim, an open, extremely engaging expression, and he was sitting back in his chair with his feet up on the one in front of him. Timberlands, noticed Ella. She also noticed the rather sexy way his brown hair flopped over his forehead and the jacket in a truly appalling shade of green he was wearing. He smiled at her, and she smiled back before returning her attention to Pol Pot.

'Here's your crew pack.' He passed her a blue nylon folder. 'Happy reading, Ella.'

Ella opened the folder. There was a logbook in it, and some Filofaxy pages and a plastic card with DIVE TABLE printed at the top. It was so busy with figures that it looked as if a spider had been tap-dancing across it. She took out her manual. There were the usual seductive pictures on the cover of rainbow-coloured fish and aquamarine scenery and graceful divers. Flicking through the introduction she saw that the 'fun' word featured heavily, along-side similar nouns such as 'excitement' and 'adventure' and 'new friends'.

But the pages further on told a different story. They were dense with text and diagrams and photographs of divers doing complicated stuff with equipment. As she leafed through the book, her heart plummeted. There were sections on contami-nated air and nitrogen narcosis and decompression

sickness. There was advice on problem management such as Running Out of Air, Near Drowning
and Entanglement. Where was the fun and excitement in all that? she wondered. Although nitrogen
narcosis sounded cool. Apparently it induced feel-
ings of euphoria.

'OK,' said Pol Pot. 'Let's get going.' He reached
behind him and turned a dimmer switch, then
aimed a remote control device at a television
monitor. 'We'll start by watching a video. It's pretty
seductive stuff – a lot of it shot off reefs in the
Tropics. Diving in Irish waters is more – challenging.'

'Module One,' Ella read on the screen. 'The
Principles of Buoyancy . . .'

* * *

The video contained a lot of footage of people on
beaches fiddling about with scuba equipment.
They all smiled a lot, to show what fun they were
having as they strapped huge tanks onto each
other and gave each other high-fives and waddled
around sideways on flippers. Except they weren't
called flippers, the soothing mid-Atlantic voice-
over told her. They were called fins. Ella tried hard
to concentrate, but by the end of the video she still
wasn't sure what a BCD was and what SPG stood
for, or what blind bit of difference there was
between a J-valve and a K-valve.

When the credits finally started to roll, Pol Pot
turned the monitor off and then went over every-

thing they'd just watched on the screen. By the time the two hours was up, Ella's mind was reeling. The only thing that really had made sense to her in Module One was the bit about always having a buddy at hand as a support system. She hoped it wasn't considered mandatory to high-five each other, as well.

'Does everyone have transport?' enquired Pol Pot at the end of the class. 'The pool's a couple of miles away. Hands up anyone who needs a lift.'

A couple of hands were raised.

'And hands up who's prepared to give lifts?'

Ella stuck her left hand up. Her right was busy filling in answers about her fitness level on her questionnaire.

'OK – Gerry, you go with Stephen. Have I got the names right? Good. And Richie, you go with Ella.'

Ella turned round to face the bloke with the great smile and the vile green jacket.

'Hi,' she said. 'You're Richie?'

'That's right.'

'I'm Ella Nesbit.'

'Ellen, or Ella as in Ella Fitzgerald?'

'You got it right second time.' She returned her attention to her form. She'd got as far as the question about claustrophobia. Should she answer yes or no? Fuck it, she thought, scribbling in 'no'. It was highly unlikely her childhood condition would recur now she was halfway through her twenties. She quickly filled in 'no' to all the other questions, and then she got to her feet, slid her manual into its blue folder, and zipped it up. Everyone else was doing the same, in that pseudo-absorbed way that people do when they need some business to cover their awkwardness at not knowing anyone. At the top of the class Pol Pot was leafing through the forms that had been filled in earlier. 'Excuse me, P—' said Ella. 'I mean, excuse me. Please. Here's mine.' She handed it to him and he ran his eyes down her filled-in form.

'Well, Ella,' he said. 'You were right. You *are* in good physical nick.' Ella made to move away, but he reached out a hand to stop her. His hand against the white skin of her wrist was as brown, hard and rough as the pad of an animal's paw. 'Hang on,' he said. 'You missed a bit. I need your signature here.'

As Ella rummaged in her bag for her pen, Pol Pot yawned and stretched. The fabric of his T-shirt rode up, and Ella immediately slid her eyes away from the tanned expanse of skin that was exposed. Stop stretching, she thought crossly. Jack Noonan's the only man in the world who's allowed to stretch like that. She quickly signed the form, and made to back off again.

'I like the way you loop your L's,' he remarked.

'What?'

'Your L's,' he said, indicating the form. 'You've a great signature.'

'Oh. Thanks.' She tried a smile out on him, but he wasn't looking at her any more. He was yawning again. Ella turned away before he could ease himself into another stretch.

The class had started to file out of the door and back through the shop. Ella followed them past a group of people who were talking in the arcane language of scuba. Seasoned divers, obviously, to judge by the scars.

Outside, PJ and some helpers were just finishing loading equipment into a white van with ActivMarine emblazoned on it in blue. 'I'd appreciate it if you could all help unload once we get to the pool,' said PJ. 'Does everyone know the way?'

'I don't,' said Ella.

'I do,' said Richie. 'I'll direct you. Where's your car?'

'This way.' Ella indicated where she'd parked, and she and Richie set off down the road. The rest of the class climbed into various vehicles and started their engines, and Ella got her car keys out of her bag and zapped the locks on Patrick's Merc.

'Wow. Class car,' said Richie.

'It's not mine. It's my uncle's,' she explained with alacrity. She didn't want this bloke to think she was some super-cool rich bitch with a Merc for a runabout. As she slid into the driver's seat, the dive van lumbered past with Pol Pot at the wheel. PJ was in the passenger seat. 'What's the name of the geezer who lectured us?' she asked, putting the car into gear and moving away from the kerb.

'That's Ferdia MacDiarmada,' said Richie.

'Bit of a crosspatch, isn't he? Kind of gives the lie

to all that guff in the book about scuba diving being fun.'

'He's just a bit depressed at the moment. His dog died last week.'

Ella looked surprised. 'And he felt he had to share this news with the entire *class*?'

'Jesus, no.'

'So how come you know his dog died, then?'

'He's my cousin.'

'Oh.' She bit her lip. 'Sorry for bad-mouthing him.'

'No problem,' said Richie. He turned to her and smiled. 'I won't tell him what you said if you promise to give me a lift to the pool after class every week.'

'OK,' she said, smiling back as she put the car into fourth. 'It's a deal.' She turned on the CD player. The jazz she'd been listening to on the way out oozed through the speakers, and she quickly switched back to 98FM. Slow jazz was way too sexy to be playing for a mere acquaintance. 'What did you think of the class this evening?' asked Ella. 'Could you make sense of all that stuff?'

'Pretty well,' Richie admitted. 'I took Ferdia's advice and did my homework.'

'I felt like a bit of a dilettante,' confessed Ella. 'He obviously thinks I am, anyway.'

'Ferdia? Why? Just because you hadn't read the first chapter?' Richie shook his head. 'Nah. His bark is worse than his bite, you know. But be warned. He doesn't suffer fools gladly.'

'I'll swot all week, then.' She furrowed her brow.

'Hell – I'll need to. I got completely mixed up with all those technical terms. Why can't they just call a regulator "the breathing thingy" or a BCD "the blowy-up floaty jacket". And what's an SPG when it's at home? I find all that acronym stuff really confusing.'

'It gets worse,' said Richie. 'I've heard Ferdia come out with shit like "OK, then we had to lose the DV and the BCD and get the ABS on to the RIB for CPR ASAP."'

'Jesus!' Ella laughed. 'It's just as well PJ wasn't involved in that particular scenario.'

'He was. And to add to the confusion, another of the divers was called TP.'

'Well. It looks like I'm going to have to learn a foreign language as well as everything else.'

'It'll be worth it.'

'So everyone keeps telling me. I just thought it would be more straightforward.'

'Can't you handle technical stuff?'

'On the contrary,' she said, with a small degree of hauteur. 'I'm a sound engineer by profession. But that's a very different kind of technology.'

'A sound engineer? Wow. Do you work with any famous bands?'

'No,' she admitted. 'Sorry to disappoint you. The studio I work in specializes mainly in ads. We do some film and television stuff too.'

'So you get to work with famous actors?'

She smiled and shrugged. 'Sometimes. What do you do, Richie?'

'I'm a student. With a bit of luck I'll be graduating in marine archaeology in a couple of years.'

'Cool!'

'Not as cool as sound engineering. What made you decide to get into that?'

'I had the most important qualification for the job.'

'Oh? What's that?'

'A good ear,' said Ella.

Richie looked quizzically at her. 'It's funny,' he said. 'To look at you, the last thing I could imagine you doing would be engineering of any kind.'

'Oh? What could you imagine me being?' If he said 'receptionist' she'd stop the car and boot him out.

'I dunno really. Something classier, I suppose.'

'Classy! Me! Get off! I stagger through life making mistakes all over the place.'

'I can relate to that. I made the huge mistake of buying this jacket today. I hate it.'

'Then why did you buy it?'

'It seemed like a good idea at the time – the colour didn't look so acid in the shop. And it had been marked down three times in a sale.'

'I'm not surprised. It's really horrible.' They smiled at each other and an idea struck her. 'Hey! Will you be my buddy, Richie, in the pool sessions?'

'With pleasure, Ella,' he replied urbanely.

The archway they finally drove through was hung with a sign that read *Rosemount Leisure Centre*

78

in wavy aquamarine lettering. Ella pulled up along-side the ActivMarine van and killed her lights. People were already unloading equipment from the back of the van.

'Time to heave-ho,' said Ella to Richie as they joined the queue. She dragged out a tank and stag-gered sideways on her high heels. 'Holy shomoly – this weighs a ton!'

'Take it easy,' warned Ferdia, who was passing down the gear. 'You don't want to strain your back. Take this instead.' He handed her a box full of masks.

'No, no, I'm fine with this,' said Ella, stung by the implication that she was a wimp. She struggled through the door of the leisure centre after the other divers, noticing that the one other girl on the course was handling her tank with comparative ease.

They changed, then assembled by the poolside, and were divided into groups of four. Ella was teamed with Richie and Jan – the sporty-looking girl – and a middle-aged man called Dan. Crinkly-eyed PJ was their instructor. It took ages to assemble the equipment, and Ella felt utterly ridicu-lous when she was finally kitted out. The length of the fins strapped onto her feet meant that she could only shuffle backwards or sideways, and entering the water was an exercise so humiliating it might have been devised by someone with a grudge against recreational divers. Her tank got stuck on the side of the pool, and she dangled for a while, unable to move either up or down. At least it was

smiling PJ who extricated her from her predicament, not grim-faced Ferdia. She'd seen him
barking instructions at some unfortunate assistant
earlier.

The water was cooler than tepid. Her group of
four lurched around in the shallow end for a while,
watching PJ demonstrating the skills they'd be
required to learn. Down at the other end of the
pool, the other members of the class had already
disappeared under the water, learning fast. She was
obviously in the duffers' group.

'Some buddy you are,' she remarked as Richie
went bobbing off in the direction of the deep end.

'I can't help it,' he said, laughing over his
shoulder. 'I've no control over where I'm going. I
feel like an inflatable beach toy.'

She realized what he meant as soon as she
pressed the inflator button on her BCD and found
herself colliding into Dan, feeling very foolish.
'Sorry,' she said, as she bounced off his chest.

'That's all right,' he said to the back of her head
as she took off in the opposite direction. The only
one who didn't seem to have a problem controlling
her manoeuvres was Jan.

'OK,' said PJ, when they'd all somehow managed
to reunite. 'Regulators in your mouths, take a few
breaths, then deflate your BCDs and you'll find out
what it's like to breathe underwater for the first
time.'

They did as they were told, and as Ella felt the
water creep up her face and over her head she felt a

frisson of excitement. Endorphins at last! She found herself smiling as she inhaled once – a long, slow breath – and then again and again. She had gills!

She might have had gills, but the thermoplastic fins she'd strapped to her feet weren't much help to her in her new incarnation as mermaid. When they eventually got round to exploring the deep end of the pool she felt as if she was free-falling in slow motion. Her uncoordinated movements on the surface were positively balletic compared to her underwater manoeuvres.

But at least she wasn't the only one who was finding it impossible to manage. Divers were drifting surreally all around her. It was hard to make out who was who behind the masks, but it was easy to distinguish the masters from the pupils. The instructors, kitted out in neoprene suits, swam around effortlessly, like elegant aquatic shepherds tending their flock. At one stage she noticed Ferdia glide past, his blond dreadlocks rendering him instantly identifiable. The way they drifted around his head reminded her of a film she'd seen as a child, which had starred a palomino pony. In slow-motion sequences of the horse galloping, its tail had looked just the way Ferdia's ponytail did now, streaming out behind in feathery tendrils. He glanced briefly at her as he passed. Mortified by her own clumsiness she looked away, only to see Dan's head sticking out from between her splayed legs. The expression on his face under the mask was one of such profound apology that Ella wanted to laugh.

But when she did, water trickled into her mouth through the gap she'd made between her lips and the regulator. She began to cough.

'Are you OK?' PJ signalled to her, raising his eyebrows into question marks and making a circle with his thumb and forefinger.

'I'm OK,' she signalled back, before realizing that she wasn't. She scrabbled back up to the surface and took her regulator out of her mouth so that she could cough freely. PJ joined her.

'Are you all right?'

'Yeah. I'm all right now,' she insisted after she'd recovered herself. 'I've just realized that it's probably not a very good idea to laugh underwater.'

'Oh, yes it is,' said PJ. 'In fact, I can guarantee you'll be doing a lot of it.' He smiled at the sceptical look she gave him. 'I mean it,' he said. 'Ready to go back down?'

'Yeah,' said Ella, taking a deep breath. 'I'm ready. But I still don't believe you about the laughing bit.'

As they descended, she caught sight of Ferdia and one of the other instructors sharing a private joke in sign language on the other side of the deep end. They were laughing their asses off.

*   *   *

'How did you get on?' asked Julian the following morning after he'd divested himself of his cycling gear.

'Fine,' returned Ella airily. She wasn't going to tell him that she'd floundered around like a drunken mermaid and nearly choked to death.

The aftermath of the training session had been a bit grim. Her duffers' group was the last one out of the pool, and they'd had to dismantle their equipment before they could get dressed. The changing rooms were very end-of-dayish, and she wished she'd remembered to bring flip-flops. She was certain she was going to end up with athlete's foot. Verrucas, too, probably, knowing her luck.

'Who did your academic stuff with you?'

'Ferdia.'

'Sound bloke, Ferdia. We go way back – I was at school with him. Who took you for the pool work?'

'PJ.'

'Hey! PJ!'

Oh shut *up*, Julian, she thought.

'It's fun, isn't it?' he said, sitting on her desk the way Jack did. She thought it a bit over-familiar of him.

'Yeah,' said Ella, wishing she was a better actress.

'Not very glamorous, though. Especially when you end up with a bad case of diver's face.'

'What's diver's face?'

'Well, the deeper you dive, the more pressure there is on your sinuses. When you get back up to the surface and take off your mask you find your face is covered in snot.'

Jesus! She'd looked in the changing-room mirror last night, and while there'd been no sign of snot, the mask had left a vivid red mark across her fore-head and along her cheekbones. Her face had looked like the muzzle of some badly drawn cartoon animal. 'Thank you for sharing that with me, Julian,' she said, crisply, sorting through mail.

He smirked. 'It's only fair to let you know what you're in for. Did you go for a drink with the boys afterwards?'

'No. I was tired.' PJ had mentioned that the dive-masters usually gravitated to the leisure centre club after the training session, and that their neophytes were welcome to join them there, but Ella had been too self-conscious about how idiotic she looked with her cartoon face to take him up on the invitation.

'You should. You get to learn a lot from those boys just by talking to them. Tell them I said hey next time you're out there, will you?'

'Sure.' She bloody wouldn't. The last thing she wanted was to be associated with a nerd like Julian Bollard. *Hi, PJ! Julian Bollard says 'hey'!* Oh, no.

He stood up and stretched, and Ella got the impression that he was trying to look like Jack when he performed his gloriously languid morning stretch. 'Right,' he remarked, looking at his watch. 'It's time to hit the Audiofile.' He helped himself to the latest copy of *Pro Sound News* that was fanned out with all the usual suspects on the coffee table, and set off up the stairs. 'See you later, toots,' he said, as he disappeared from view.

Toots! How fucking dare he! Ella swigged back her coffee, and set the mug down on the table with a bang. She picked up the phone and pressed the button for the upstairs studio. 'Julian?' she said in her frostiest tone. 'I'd just like you to know that my uncle is the only person in the world who gets away with calling me "toots".' She put the phone down before he could reply. Then she reached down and pulled her dive manual out of her bag. There was a half-hour lull before the next session. She flicked through until she found the relevant page, and then she steeled herself. 'Module Two', she read.

*   *   *

Over the course of the following weeks Ella studied hard. By reading each module in advance of the actual class, she got a better grasp of the academic side of things, and she was glad to see that she never scored less than 90 per cent in the written tests they had to take.

The pool work was a different matter, though. She found it gruelling, and every Thursday morning she'd wake up with bruised and aching limbs. It was all right for blokes like PJ and Ferdia and all those divemaster types. They were big and hulking or tough and wiry, and they strode around the poolside swinging heavy tanks of pressurized air as if they were as lightweight as carrier bags from Marks and Sparks' lingerie department.

Out of the water, Ella was about as graceful as a beached walrus. She just couldn't get used to feeling so clumsy. Underwater, things were improving a bit because she was learning more about controlling her buoyancy, but on land she felt ridiculous. She would trudge along the side of the pool with Richie, laden with tank and weight-belt, and muttering imprecations.

'I hate this hobby,' she found herself saying one evening.

'Why don't you give up then?' he asked.

'Because I don't give up easily,' she returned.

'Time for your Giant Stride, Ella,' pronounced PJ, and she tried to ignore Richie's snigger.

She dreaded having to do her Giant Stride. It had to be the single least elegant physical manoeuvre she'd ever performed in her life. It involved shuffling sideways to the very edge of the pool and then stepping out into mid-air in the goose-step style favoured by the Gestapo, clutching your mask to your face. Richie had doubled up with laughter when he'd first seen her do it.

But every week she improved, and every week she learned a new skill. She learned how to flood and clear her mask underwater, she learned how to buddy-breathe and she learned how to communicate in sign language. She also learned how to laugh underwater without running the risk of drowning, and she and Richie spent a lot of time communicating in a rather juvenile makey-uppy sign language when PJ was busy testing Jan and Dan's skills.

They were still the duffer group, she was sad to admit. When she looked at the other groups she could see that they were all miles ahead in the skills they were mastering, and every week she and Richie and Jan and Dan were the last ones out of the pool. It was really Dan's fault, she reckoned, that they were lagging so far behind. He never did his homework, and she'd seen him cheating in the weekly test, riffling through his manual when he thought no-one was looking.

On the fifth Wednesday of the course Richie took her off for a drink with 'the boys' – as Julian had called them. Ella had loosened the strap on her mask at the start of the session, and she was relieved to see that there was no cartoon character's muzzle on her face when she looked in the mirror, and no snot either.

Richie was waiting for her when she emerged from the changing room, her heels echoing on the tiled floor. It was bitterly cold outside, and they legged it fast across the car park to the club.

'What'll you have?' asked Ella.

'I'll get it,' said Richie. 'As a reward for giving me all those lifts.'

'I won't hear of it,' said Ella. 'You're an impoverished student. I'm on an income.'

'A good one?' asked Richie.

'I wish.'

'But one that means you can swan off to Jamaica?'

'I *won* that holiday, Richie, remember?' She'd filled him in on the holiday thing a couple of weeks ago, when she'd given him his lift to the leisure centre. 'Or rather, my grandmother did.

87

Now, go and find somewhere for us to sit.'

She ordered two pints. At the other end of the bar Ferdia was ordering drinks too. Ella avoided his eyes. She paid for the pints and took them over to the table where Richie was sitting. She was happy to see that PJ was there too.

'I hear you're off to Jamaica,' said PJ, when she'd settled herself down between him and Richie. 'When are you going?'

'Beginning of December,' said Ella. 'I'm going to do all my training dives when I get there.'

PJ gave her a look of appraisal with his wonderful crinkly eyes. 'You might think about doing at least one dive while you're here, Ella. That means there won't be such pressure on you while you're on holiday, and you can do more dives in Jamaica for the sheer pleasure of it.'

'But that means I'd have to dive in Sheep's Head Bay! It'll be freezing!'

'You'll be wearing a wetsuit,' he pointed out. 'And it's a good idea to get a dive out of the way here before you go off diving in tropical waters. If you can master a dive in the Irish Sea in the month of November you can master a dive anywhere in the world.'

Ella laughed.

'I mean it,' said PJ.

'I believe you. I'm laughing at the idea of me swanning around the world on dive holidays like something out of Condé Nast's *Traveller*.'

'You don't have to do it the Condé Nast way.

Lots of people work up to instructor or divemaster status and work the dive sites.'

'That would be a brilliant way to see the world,' said Richie. 'Better than sitting on your arse having servants bring you iced Pimm's like those *Traveller* readers.'

'I feel sick every time I open that magazine,' said Ella with a heavy sigh. 'Who can *afford* those kind of holidays?'

'You'd be amazed. The Celtic tiger and his wife bugger off on them all the time.'

PJ gestured to Ferdia, who was standing in the middle of the floor with two pints in his hands, looking around him. 'Over here, Ferdia!' The other instructor clocked him and started to move towards their table. 'Not all dive holidays are unaffordable, you know Ella,' he resumed. 'We organize packages a couple of times a year. And we have brilliant dive weekends away in Lissamore in the west of Ireland every month.'

'Is the diving there really that good?'

'Yeah. Some of the best in the world.'

'How's that?'

'There's spectacular scenery – you would not believe some of the walls and cliffs out there – and there's no pollution.'

'Yet,' said Ferdia, putting a pint in front of PJ and sitting down beside him.

'I'd love to go on one of those dive weekends,' said Richie.

'Then you should think about doing an advanced

course,' said PJ, 'and go for the dry-suit speciality option. Dry-suits take some getting used to, but they're kinda mandatory for Irish diving.'

'Why?' asked Ella.

'Because they do what they say. They keep you bone dry, and you don't get as cold. You can stay down longer in a dry-suit.'

'I'm going to do a wreck diver speciality course some time,' said Richie. 'I'm dying to dive a wreck.'

Ferdia was lounging back in a seat across from Richie, nursing a pint and looking ruminative. He looked up at his cousin's words. 'You won't be specializing in anything if you carry on messing about the way you have been, Rich,' he remarked. 'I've noticed that your group's lagging behind. It'll be your own fault if you don't pass your exam.'

'No it won't. It'll be Duffer Dan's fault,' argued Richie.

'Duffer Dan?' queried PJ. 'Who on earth is Duffer Dan?'

Ella tried not to laugh.

'That's what Ella calls the middle-aged geezer who's holding us up.'

Ella gave Richie a dig in the ribs. 'That's not fair,' she hissed at him. 'I called *myself* a duffer. You were the one who came up with "Duffer Dan."'

'See what I mean?' said Ferdia, leaning back further in his chair and surveying the pair of them as they tried not to giggle. 'You're a pair of messers. I saw you tonight, clowning around and making daft gestures at each other instead of concentrating on what PJ was demonstrating.'

'We only did that when he was working with Jan and d-Dan,' said Richie. He and Ella burst out sniggering again, and kept their heads averted.

'It's a good idea to watch your divemaster all the time, even when he's concentrating on other individuals in the group,' said PJ equably. 'That's the best way to learn.'

'That's right,' concurred Ferdia. 'You want to show your instructor a little more respect. What he teaches you could save your life one day.' He took a swig of his pint and the pair of them sobered instantly.

'OK,' said Richie humbly. He turned to PJ. 'Sorry, PJ. I promise to stop messing in the pool. Maybe Ella and I should swap groups.'

She saw PJ and Ferdia exchange glances, and she knew that they were thinking the same thing. Oh, no! she thought. Her dive buddy's juvenile sense of humour was the only thing about Wednesday evenings that was keeping her sane.

'That's probably not a bad idea,' said PJ. 'You'll catch up faster if you stop distracting each other.'

Ferdia said nothing. He just raised an eyebrow and shot Richie a sceptical look. 'Well? Are you going to wise up a bit?'

'Yeah, yeah.' Another sceptical look from his cousin. 'I'm determined to qualify, you know, Ferdia!' protested Richie. 'I'm going to dive the

Lusitania one day. Maybe I'll even get to dive god status, like you.'

'Then you are going to have to work your ass off, Rich.'

'I damn well will,' said Richie, with feeling. 'I'm going to do as many courses as I can afford. I'll end up getting hooked, I suppose. Like you did.'

Ferdia smiled. It was such a rare a sight that it took Ella a bit by surprise. 'That's right,' he said. 'The first time I went down I never wanted to come up again.' He looked at Ella suddenly. 'You're a lucky woman to be heading off to Jamaica to dive. I spent three months diving the reefs there once.'

Ella was surprised. 'Three months on holiday?'

He gave her a pitying look. 'No,' he said. 'Working for a dive outfit.'

Of course. How stupid of her.

'Whereabouts are you going?' asked PJ.

'Salamander Cove, on the north-east coast. Near Port Antonio.'

'I know it,' said Ferdia. 'It's a classy joint.'

'Is that where you worked?'

'I helped out from time to time. Desirée had a reciprocal arrangement with the resort that employed me. She used to call on us if she was stuck.'

'Desirée?'

'She runs the outfit. She's some lady. If you're very lucky she might take you down herself.'

Ella said nothing. She'd actually prefer to go down with some gorgeous dive god type like PJ. She snuck a look at him from under her lashes, and was pleased to see he was looking back.

'Ella's thinking about doing her first qualifying dive off Sheep's Head,' said PJ, smiling at her. 'So that she can get a taste of what it's like to dive in less than perfect conditions.'

Ferdia cocked his head to one side. 'Thinking about it? People who think about it never do it.'

That decided her. 'I *am* going to do it,' she said.

PJ gave her another smile – of approval this time – and she felt the same small thrill of smugness she used to get when her teacher at prep school told her she'd come top of the class. It hadn't happened that often. A girl called Shetty Deepak had usually come top. She had never forgotten the name.

*　　*　　*

A little later she said good night to Richie and the rest of them and went to get the car. The leisure centre car park was a bit scary. There was nothing parked there now apart from the dive van, and the place wasn't particularly well lit. As she took the key from her bag and went to zap the locks, she froze suddenly. Something had whimpered. She stood motionless for a moment, listening. A low whining noise was coming from beneath the dive van, which was parked in a dark corner under a tree. Ella moved cautiously towards it, and then she got down on her hunkers and peered under the van. A black-and-white collie dog was looking back at her with a fearful expression on its intelligent face.

'Hello, boy,' said Ella gently, stretching out a tentative hand, ready to withdraw it at once if the dog growled. It didn't. It licked its muzzle and then it leaned towards her, sniffing cautiously. Its breath was warm on her cold fingers. 'Come here, boy,' said Ella. 'C'mon. I'm not going to hurt you.' Slowly the dog advanced towards her, keeping its belly low against the ground and moving in that way that dogs do who have been beaten regularly. It was painfully thin. Ella remained crouching on her hunkers. 'Hello, darling,' she said, as her hand made contact with the dog's ear. 'What are you doing here? Why aren't you at home? It's a horrible night to be stuck outside in a car park.' She rubbed the fur of the dog's ear, and as she did so, she saw its tail begin a tentative movement. 'There, now!' said Ella. 'Good boy!'

'It's a bitch.' A voice came from just behind and above her, and she turned, startled. Ferdia was silhouetted against the navy-blue sky, looking down at her. From her crouched viewpoint he looked even taller than usual.

'Jesus – you gave me a fright!' she said, nearly losing her balance on her heels. The hand that had been stroking the dog's ear had flown to her throat in alarm.

'Sorry,' he said, not sounding sorry at all. He lowered himself to his hunkers beside her and looked at the collie. 'Hello, beautiful,' he murmured. The dog responded by moving her tail more vigorously and raising a paw. Ferdia took it

94

and then he sucked in his breath. 'Ow. Who did that to you, darling?' he asked. For the first time Ella was aware of a gaping wound running from just above the dog's right front paw to the very top of its skinny leg. Ferdia ran a hand along the animal's flank, assessing her physical condition. Her eyes took on a dazed look. It was as if she'd never been caressed before. 'You've been starved, too, haven't you, sweetheart?' He examined her some more, and then sucked in his breath again. 'Jesus, hell. Oh, darling, you need to be seen by a vet. This is urgent.'

'Oh, God – is it really? You'll never get a vet to come out at this hour of the night.' Ella had wrapped her arms around herself, and was hopping from foot to foot to try and stay warm.

'I will,' said Ferdia. 'I've a mate who's a vet, and he owes me a favour.'

'Oh?'

'Yeah. He had to put my dog down for me last month.'

Oh, hell. 'I'm sorry,' she said, getting to her feet.

'Don't be. She had a massive tumour. It was a mercy killing.' He stood up, unlocked the back of the dive van and pulled out a worn woollen blanket. 'Here, sweetheart,' he said to the dog. 'You're coming with me.' He kneeled down and wrapped the dog in the blanket, then picked her up very carefully and laid her in the back of the van. Ella was so used to seeing Ferdia barking orders and striding along the poolside like a conquistador marshalling his forces that it came as something of a surprise to see him suddenly behaving like Saint Francis of Assisi. The dog was looking up at him with liquid brown eyes. The expression on her face as he closed the door verged on worship. It reminded Ella of the expression on the dog's face in a painting she'd seen once of *The Adoration of the Magi*.

Ferdia stood back from the van and looked down at Ella. 'That's your car, isn't it?' he asked, nodding his head at Patrick's shiny little Merc.

'Yes,' she said. She didn't bother explaining that it wasn't her car. She didn't think he'd be interested.

'I'd park it outside on the road next week, if I were you. There's a lot of vandalism in this car park after the pool closes. They always go for the posh ones.'

'Thanks for the advice. Good night, and good luck with the vet.' She shimmied across the car park, zapped the locks and slid into the driver's seat, kicking off her heels as she always did when she drove. Across from her, Ferdia was climbing into the van. 'See you next week,' she called, before closing the door.

'Yeah,' he remarked absently. 'Good night, Ella.'

Wow. He'd actually remembered her name.

Chapter Four

The following Wednesday was their final session in the pool. Ella had got a headache from trying to work out dive tables on the dive planner earlier, and she was cross because she and Richie had been split up. 'It's for your own good,' she'd been told, which made her feel more than ever like a badly behaved schoolgirl. Richie stayed with PJ's group, Ella was banished to Ferdia's.

The group descended at the deep end of the pool, and Ferdia began his demonstration of how to take a scuba unit off underwater. Ella couldn't imagine ever wanting to do this in a real-life scenario, but she'd been told it might be necessary if her unit ever became entangled in weed. The instructor went through the manoeuvre effortlessly, step by step, and after the demonstration he turned to Ella. 'You,' he signalled with an authoritative index finger, indicating that she follow his example. She undid her waistband with relative ease, and snapped the release catch on her shoulder straps. She then extracted first her left arm and then her right from her BCD. To her embarrassment, as she slid the BCD away from her right shoulder, the strap of her swimsuit came with it, and when she looked down she saw that her right breast was fully exposed. There was nothing she could do – she needed both hands to keep hold of her unit. Well, the geezers in her new group were pretty damn lucky, she thought resignedly, having a nice flash of tit to keep up their morale.

She couldn't see the hand that made contact with her upper arm because her peripheral vision was restricted by her mask, but she felt someone drawing the strap back up until it was securely in place on her shoulder once more. She turned to find herself looking directly into Ferdia's vigilant eyes. She was glad that he'd had enough cop-on to come to her aid. Another man might not have had the nerve to touch her, and might just have pretended nothing had happened.

Now she had to put the damn unit on again. But the incident with her swimsuit had seriously messed up her concentration. She tried to struggle back into her BCD, without success. Again Ferdia came to her assistance. He held the unit out for her, and she finally managed to twist herself into the jacket and refasten the belt around her waist. The shoulder straps had to be adjusted next. She'd always had trouble with them – even above water. They needed to be given a sharp tug downward in order to tighten them fully. She pulled and pulled, but the bloody things wouldn't budge. Her buoyancy was banjaxed now, as well as everything else. She added a quick blast of air to her BCD, and suddenly she was ascending rapidly.

Ferdia was beside her again. He turned her to face him, and then pulled her down till she was on a level with him. Ella felt absurdly small and absurdly inept as she was dragged back down through the water, but worst of all she felt absurdly passive, like a rag doll. As the instructor vented the air from her BCD she was aware that the upper part of his leg had wedged between her own awkwardly splayed limbs. She almost choked in surprise. She shifted her hips in an effort to put some distance between them, but only succeeded in gliding further along his leg.

Oh! She was totally unprepared for the sensation of the black neoprene-clad thigh as her crotch slid against it. It was quite electrifyingly erotic. She felt charged by a thrill so shockingly intense that she had to resist a sudden overwhelming impulse to pull herself closer. She struggled a little to disentangle their limbs, and then gave up. She was back in limp rag doll mode as he took hold of the rings on her shoulder straps and jerked hard. Again her pelvis was rammed into his thigh, but he was oblivious, concentrating as he was on adjusting her BCD. Once it was snug, Ferdia's hands moved down to her waist. He inserted an expert finger between her belt and her belly to ensure that the clasp on her belt was as secure as the shoulder straps now were.

Ella could feel her breath coming fast, and she made an effort to control it. But the bubbles soaring upwards were a giveaway. Her instructor looked at her curiously, signalling to her to take it easy. *Breathe slowly*, he gestured with an eloquent hand, and as she tried hard to concentrate on her breathing she found herself wanting to laugh out loud at the sheer ludicrousness of the situation. How totally bizarre! Here she was, drifting around underwater, half naked, being manhandled by someone she barely knew . . .

You really wouldn't want to have any hang-ups about intimate physical contact in this sport, she thought, as he finally finished checking her straps to his satisfaction. Then he resumed eye contact and asked if she was OK. Yes, she signalled back, she was OK. But when he turned his focus on the next novice she was aware that she was actually extremely confused.

The next novice was gazing lustfully at Ella, and she wondered how much he could read in her face under the mask. Then she heard a muffled rapping noise, and realized that Ferdia had taken his diving knife from the sheath on his thigh, and was striking it against his tank to attract attention. *You*, he signalled to his pupil, jabbing his finger at him. The guilty-looking novice immediately diverted his gaze and started to take off his unit. She was glad to see that he was almost as inept as she'd been, and that she wasn't the only one in the group who needed the assistance of the divemaster this evening.

Later she adjourned to the leisure centre social

club with Richie. 'How did you get on?' she asked, taking hold of a hank of damp hair and shaking it dry. She was glad she wouldn't have to do any more sessions in the pool. The chlorine wasn't doing anything for the condition of her hair, and she suspected that the blond streaks in Ferdia's dreadlocks were due more to the effects of chemically treated water than to hours spent bumming around on beaches.

'OK,' he said. 'I'd a few problems getting into my unit at the surface.'

Ella could relate to that. She'd spent more minutes than she'd have liked bobbing around with her tank between her legs, while Ferdia had held her steady. 'Hey! That manoeuvre could save your life one day,' she intoned solemnly, mimicking the instructor's Galway accent. Then she made a little grimace of apology. 'Oops. Sorry to take the piss out of your venerable cousin.'

Richie smiled. 'He's in much better form these days, as a matter of fact. He's found a dog to replace the one who died.'

'Oh?' Ella wondered if the dog was the one she'd come across last week.

It was. Minutes later the door swung open and PJ and Ferdia strolled through. The black and white collie was at Ferdia's heels. The instructors ambled up to the bar and the dog sat patiently while the barman pulled their pints. The animal looked a million dollars compared to the waif she'd been a week ago. She had gained some weight – although she was still very thin – and her coat was noticeably glossier. Her right front leg and her tail had been bandaged, and she wore a collar of red leather. She was gazing up at her new master with a totally lovesick expression.

PJ and Ferdia picked up their pints and moved over to sit at a table by the door. Ella felt a bit miffed that they hadn't gravitated towards their table. She loved the way PJ smiled at her from underneath his eyebrows.

'Will you have another?' asked Richie, draining his pint.

'No,' she said, doing likewise. 'I'm driving, remember? I've got to make tracks.' She shrugged into her coat and slung her bag over her shoulder.

'Enjoy swotting up on Module Five during the week,' said Richie as he moved in the direction of the bar.

'I will damn well have to swot. If anything's going to mess up the exam for me next week, it'll be those hellish dive tables. See you, Richie.'

She made her way across the room trying to remember what she'd learned this evening about surface intervals and bottom time.

'Final exam next week, Ella,' PJ remarked with a smile as she passed by his table.

'Thanks for reminding me.' She stopped, and smiled back at him.

'You won't have any problems.' She was mildly surprised that the encouraging words came from Ferdia, and that *he* was actually bestowing a smile on her, too! 'Your academic work's fine.'

'Oh! Thanks!' And then: 'Um. I see you've adopted the dog we found,' she remarked, mainly to disguise her surprise at Ferdia being nice to her.

'Yeah. She's a lady.'

'What have you called her?'

'Perdita.'

'Perfect. That's Latin for "lost one".'

He sent her an amused look. 'Smart girl.'

'Hi, Perdita,' she said, stooping down and caressing the dog's ears. Her tail gave a gratifying thump against the floor. 'Hi, gorgeous! You look a lot better than you did the last time we met.'

'That's because her master's been stuffing her with prime fillet steak,' remarked PJ. 'She's going to get spoilt rotten if you're not careful, Ferdia.'

'Not a chance. It's just to fatten her up a bit. No more gourmet meals for you once the scales hit twenty kilos or thereabouts, you gorgeous girl.'

Ella looked up at him and he smiled again, and she suddenly remembered how her breast had been exposed earlier that evening. She found herself going pink, and then pinker still as she recalled the impulse she'd had to grind herself into him when he'd pulled down on the shoulder straps of her BCD.

To cover her embarrassment she delved into her bag and produced her Filofax. It was a rather smart pigskin one her father had brought back for her after his last American tour. She could feel Ferdia's eyes on her as she leafed through it. 'Is the weekend after next still pencilled in for the open water dives?' she asked PJ. She'd put her name down for two dives that weekend. One wasn't mandatory – it was just a skin dive without scuba – but she'd been advised to do it anyway because it would familiarize her with the suiting-up procedure.

'Yeah. It seems to suit everyone.'

'What time?' she asked, pen poised over the page. There was a big party marked in for that Saturday night. Patrick was throwing a bash for Jack's fortieth birthday.

'Nine o'clock on Saturday morning. Same again Sunday. That's when the tide's at optimum height. You'll need to get out here at eight, though, to allow time for briefing and suiting up.'

Eight o'clock on a freezing cold November morning! And it *would* have to be a morning after the night before! Hell's bells. Why was she *doing* this to herself? And then: Oh God, oh God, she thought in a panic – would Patrick be an angel and let her have the car for that weekend? The idea of trailing hungover through early-morning DART stations filled her with dread.

'OK,' she said, trying to sound keen as she scribbled in the relevant space in her diary. Then she closed the book and snapped the popper. 'Well – see you next Wednesday.'

'Yeah,' said PJ. 'By the way, Ella – if you want to do a pool session after your exam there'll be a master available to take care of you. Some trainees like to hone the skills one last time before performing their open water dives.'

'Oh.' She'd hoped she wouldn't have to do any more pool work, but she could see the sense of this. 'Well. I'll think about it.' Ferdia caught her eye and smiled, and she remembered what he'd said last week. *People who think about it never do it.* 'It's probably a good idea,' she conceded. 'I could do with another go at taking my mask off underwater. I found that a bit spooky.'

'You might want to practise taking your BCD off underwater, too,' said Ferdia. 'That didn't go as smoothly as it might have.'

Ella thought of her exposed breast again, and his thigh between hers, and she couldn't meet his eye. She was saved by the arrival of Richie with a fresh pint. 'Still here?' he asked unnecessarily.

'No, no – I'm off now. *A bientôt.*' *A bientôt?* Where had that come from? Shit. She'd a feeling that that little sally into French would strike 'the boys' as being madly pretentious. Before she could blush again she turned towards the door, painfully aware of the three pairs of male eyes that were scrutinizing her retreating rear.

*   *   *

Ella studied hard that week, and passed her exam with no problems. She fouled up on only three of the fifty questions on the paper, and that was because she hadn't read them properly. She'd even worked out how to use the dive tables.

As the class trailed out of the room, she asked Richie if he was going to the pool to practise. 'Nah,' he said. 'Can't be bothered. I'm going to the club to celebrate never having to read that fucking manual again.'

She asked Sporty Jan and Duffer Dan if they were going. Jan couldn't and Dan wouldn't. He should, if he has any sense, thought Ella. He needs all the practice he can get. She'd spotted him cheating in the exam, frantically flicking through Module Five.

As far as she could ascertain, the only person going to the pool was the bloke who'd sent her lecherous looks underwater last week. She didn't fancy the idea of practising buddy-breathing with him, so she decided to go for the club option with Richie.

Ferdia was already there, ordering a pint at the bar, but there was no sign of PJ.

'He's gone off to the Red Sea,' said Ferdia when she asked. 'For two weeks of dive heaven.'

They took their pints over to the table by the door, where Richie was tethering Perdita to a chair.

'Well, Ferdia?' said Richie, when he'd finished showering the dog with compliments. 'What's your verdict? Are Ella and I divemaster material?'

'Could be,' was Ferdia's measured response. 'You both did OK tonight. Should've taken the opportunity to do some extra pool work, though.'

Ella knew this was directed more at her than at Richie. 'I'm not divemaster material,' she admitted.

'You'd be surprised.' Ferdia gave her an appraising look. 'You might get hooked. You may even decide to do the advanced course after you've qualified.'

'What's involved?'

'There are a number of options. Navigation, night and deep dives are the toughest. We go to a flooded quarry near Blackwater. A place known as the Blackpits.'

The idea of navigating a flooded quarry at night was about as appealing to Ella as getting into a bath of cold sick blindfolded. 'Pass,' she said in a jokey voice. 'I'll stick to the Caribbean.'

'I thought you'd say that,' said Ferdia.

There was something faintly patronizing about his tone. Jesus Christ – would he ever lighten up? She hadn't meant it seriously, for heaven's sake! She wished PJ hadn't taken his infectious smile and crinkly eyes off to the Red Sea. An uneasy thought struck her suddenly. 'Who's supervising the dives this weekend?' she asked. She hoped she wasn't going to be landed with Ferdia.

'Whoever's least hungover. Diving and hangovers don't go together. Throwing up underwater is possible, but it's not something I'd recommend.' He looked at Ella, and she thought there was something of a challenge in his eyes, as if he was assessing how squeamish she might be.

Richie gave his cousin a sceptical look. 'Come on, Ferdia. I've known you to dive on mornings after you've been on complete benders.'

'That's my prerogative. I'm a master instructor, remember? You're only a trainee.'

'Hey! I heard a good one this evening.' Richie gave Ferdia a shrewd look. 'What's the difference between God and a master scuba instructor?'

'Tell me. What *is* the difference between God and a master scuba instructor?'

'God doesn't think he's a master scuba instructor,' returned Richie.

'Very droll.' Ferdia took a swig of Guinness. But his eyes above the rim of his pint were smiling.

Ella wasn't much liking all this stuff she'd just heard about diving and hangovers. She'd have to take it easy at Jack's birthday party on Saturday night. She should be taking things a bit easier, anyway. She'd been spending too many evenings in the pub after work, having her arm twisted by the reprobate Pierce Brosnan lookalike. She looked at her watch. 'Time I was off,' she said.

Richie gave her a pleading look. 'Don't go yet,' he said. 'Have another drink to celebrate passing your exam.'

She gave her watch a second glance, and then relented. 'All right then. But I'd better stick to Ballygowan.'

Richie stood up and headed towards the bar, leaving Ella stuck with Ferdia. She racked her brains for something to say, and then gave up. She knew that he thought they had about as much in common as Barbie and Action Man. She wouldn't waste her breath.

'Are you going to Jamaica with a boyfriend, Ella?' he asked politely after a beat or two of silence.

'No, I'm going with – a girlfriend,' she said. She didn't want to tell him she was going with her granny who'd won a holiday from Toptree Foods. It sounded so naff.

'You'll have a blast. It's a beautiful country.' He gave her that look of assessment again, that slightly superior look he was so good at. 'Of course, you may decide not to bother exploring. When you stay in a resort as luxurious as Salamander Cove the temptation is to stay put, lounge around, eat too much and drink too much.'

'And dive,' put in Ella, stung by the implication that she had no sense of adventure. She tried to think of more adventurous things to do. 'I might hire a car and explore the island. I'd like to visit Montego Bay, and I definitely want to do the Blue Mountains. And go rafting.' With her *granny*?

'I'd think twice about hiring a car if I were you. You'd be unlikely to get something as nifty as that little Merc you're used to running, and it'd actually be a better idea to opt for something a lot heavier. The roads are worse than they are here, and Jamaicans are even lousier drivers than the Irish. The best thing for you to do would be to hire a taxi for the day. Sometimes the driver will act as a minder for you.'

'A minder?'

'Yeah. Two white women on their own can be vulnerable. You'll have cameras, money-belts, credit cards. Most Jamaicans are desperately poor. The temptation can sometimes be too much. I got mugged once.'

She found herself looking at the scar on his cheekbone.

'No,' he said. 'That's not how I got that scar. That one's from an accident I had on a reef. The scars I got from being mugged are lower down. They slashed me here.' He briefly indicated an area low down on his hip, but she didn't allow herself to look.

'There was more than one?'

'There were three.'

'Jesus. You're lucky to be alive.'

He looked down at his pint, and then back at her. There was something lacklustre about the expression around his eyes. '*They're* lucky to be alive,' he said. 'I didn't want to hurt them, Ella. They were desperate, they were poor and they were punks. Something just possessed me.'

'You sent them packing? On your own?' Bruce Willis eat your heart out.

'Yeah. I was so consumed with rage that I scared the shit out of them. I'd had a bad day and I was mean drunk. I'd just found out my girl had been cheating on me, and to make matters worse it was my birthday. They just happened to choose the wrong man on the wrong day.'

Wow. How breathtakingly macho. She looked down at her nails. She wouldn't give him the pleasure of looking impressed. But she knew she had to say *some*thing.

110

'Did you end up in hospital?' she asked.

'Only as far as Outpatients. That was the worst thing about the whole unpleasant incident.'

'Oh? Are Jamaican hospitals that bad?'

'No. I just hate getting injections,' said Ferdia MacDiarmada. 'Needles scare the shit out of me.'

*   *   *

The next morning, Thursday, Julian rang in sick. His adenoids were at him. They were at him again on Friday.

The studios were booked back-to-back and mayhem ruled. Ella spent the last two days of the week running between the reception desk and the sound desk trying to wear her receptionist's cap and her sound engineer's cap simultaneously. Inevitably, one of them kept slipping off, and she was delighted when Claudia was roped in to man reception on Friday afternoon. In spite of the extra pair of hands, they ended up working right through until nine o'clock on Friday, when they'd finally hit the pub. That evening Ella fell into bed absolutely knackered and more than a little pissed.

She woke on Saturday morning with a smile on her face, having just emerged from a gloriously erotic dream about Jack. They'd been indulging in incredibly streamlined sex underwater, and Jack had been swathing her in some kind of black satiny stuff just before she woke. Ella stretched and rolled over onto her tummy, and her smile became even broader as she action-replayed further details of the dream in soft focus in her mind's eye, pausing occasionally to freeze the frame. Then she allowed her mind to wander back to the night they'd walked together through the rain to Daly's, and the way he'd looked at her then with eyes that had positively glowered with sexual attraction. He hadn't looked at her that way since – not once. Maybe it was time to make him look at her that way again? Hell. It was worth a try. There was no woman in his life at the moment, and because Reflex hadn't booked a session for weeks, there'd been no distractions in the form of foxy Angie.

She finally reached out a hand for the alarm clock. It read half-past nine. The dream receded abruptly, and real life came swilling back into her brain. Fuck. She should at this precise moment be performing her skin dive in the Irish Sea. Ella let her head fall back on the pillow and turned her face to the window. It was drizzling with rain outside. That made it even worse. There was no way Ferdia would believe that she hadn't just wimped out on a rainy day. Sleeping in was such a pathetically unimaginative excuse.

Cursing herself, she flung back the duvet and shambled into the kitchen to put the kettle on. Her dive manual was lying open on the table at the page that outlined the skin-dive performance requirements. 'A skin dive isn't required for certification,' she read again. She chewed her lip and thought. She'd be all right. It just meant that she'd be at a

112

slight disadvantage tomorrow when it came to the suiting-up procedure, that's all. And suiting up couldn't be *that* demanding, could it? She looked at the manual. OK. So she'd blown it today, but she was damned if she'd blow it tomorrow. She'd just have to make sure to stay sober tonight at Jack's party.

The thought of Jack reminded her of her dream. Before the black satiny stuff had materialized, she'd been wearing something really weird in the dream. No, she hadn't. She hadn't been wearing anything at all. But there had been something on her body. *What?* It came back to her with blinding clarity. She'd had delicately curved tattoos on either side of her spine in the shape of the arabesques that are carved into the surface of a violin. Oh! How beautiful! Like Man Ray's *Violin d'Ingres* . . . Jack had been playing her like a violin in the dream! She re-ran more footage. His elegant fingers had certainly known how to build through a crescendo to a climax – he'd hit the right notes unerringly. Except his fingers hadn't been that elegant, had they? They'd been kind of calloused . . .

As she tried to remember what melody he'd been playing, she thought of how she'd played every single day up until the decisive date three years ago when she'd consigned the instrument to the back of her wardrobe, and given up on her dreams of playing professionally. Ella was suddenly overcome with an intense, nostalgic yearning. This happened to her occasionally, and when it did she

113

took her violin out of its case and tuned it. It wasn't what you'd call serious practice – more messing around. Sometimes she'd get pissed off by how many mistakes she made, and she'd return the instrument to the wardrobe after only minutes of playing.

She fetched a pile of sheet music from her bookshelf, walked thoughtfully back into her bedroom and retrieved the case from the bottom shelf. She ran the square of silk that she kept in the case over the polished wood of the violin, and then she tuned it, tautened the bow, rubbed the horsehair with a little rosin and tucked the instrument under her chin.

Bruch was on the top of the pile of scores. It was strange to hear the notes fill the room. She bit her lip, frowning in concentration. She was rusty, but not so rusty that she didn't still sound OK. She played tentatively at first, then with increasing confidence, swaying along with the music as it spilled out of the instrument, unable to resist the physical compulsion to move. Beethoven next. The slow movement from the Seventh. Holy shomoly, she thought, as she drew the bow across the strings, ignoring the few bum notes that tumbled out – she'd forgotten how sexy it was! This was music to seduce by! She let the bow drop a little way into the allegretto. It felt silly playing a symphonic piece all by herself.

The third book of sheet music was Irish. The music her father had taught her. She swung into a little virtuoso improvisation of grace notes as a kind of preamble to the main treat. Then, just as she was about to launch into 'Pull the Knife and Stick it Again', the phone rang.

She came to with a start. The electronic jangle struck a harsh, discordant note in the aftermath of the thrillingly rich music that had filled the room moments before.

Setting her violin down carefully on the bed, she picked up the receiver.

'Ella?' she heard. 'Hi – it's Angie from Reflex. Listen – I'm sorry for disturbing you at home, but I'm in a bit of a tizzy. The thing is – I ran into Jack in Fitzer's restaurant late last night, and he invited me to the party Patrick's throwing for him this evening. The quandary for me is that I forgot to ask whether it's formal or casual. What do you think I should wear?'

*   *   *

Tom Jones's cover version of 'Sex Bomb' was blasting over the speakers. Ella was scanning the party to see if Angie had arrived, and sipping at the first of the two glasses of champagne she was going to allow herself that evening. Ferdia's advice about diving with a hangover had sunk in. As she hummed along to 'Sex Bomb' she couldn't prevent her eyes from sliding towards Jack. He was looking like Pierce Brosnan might in a scene from *The Thomas Crown Affair*.

Suddenly Patrick's hand was on her shoulder. 'D'you mind if I give you some avuncular advice, toots?'

'Sure.' She swung round to face her uncle. 'Fire ahead.'

'Stop wasting your time hankering after Jack.'

Ella had just taken a gulp of champagne. She nearly spat it out. 'What? What are you talking about?'

'Come on, Ella. You know what I'm talking about.'

She knew there was no point in pretending otherwise. She'd always been crap at dissembling. 'How – how on earth did you guess, Patrick?'

'I've known you since you were a baby. I can read you like a book.'

'Oh! Oh, hell, Patrick! This is *embarrassing*!' She knew that her face had gone scarlet.

Patrick was twisting his glass round and round in his hand. 'Look. This isn't easy for me either, sweetheart. But I just can't let you carry on blindly trotting down the wrong road. Let it drop, Ella.'

She bit her lip and looked away from him, down at the carpet. When she raised her eyes it was to find Jack in her direct line of vision. Oh, no! He was giving her his wonderful smile! Instantly she diverted her attention to her uncle without returning Jack's smile.

'I know why you *think* you want Jack Noonan,' persisted Patrick, 'but he's not right for you, believe me. Think about it. Jack is practically *family*. It's

116

time you stopped looking for the daddy you never had. Oh, hell.' Patrick had stopped twisting his glass and reached for his cigarettes instead. There was a pause while he lit one and inhaled deeply. Then: 'I'm sorry to be so blunt, sweetheart. Really I am. I've never been good at straight-talking.'

He sounded so miserable that Ella jumped in with alacrity. 'No, no. No. It's OK, Patrick. Honestly. You're right – you're *absolutely* right to tell me what you think. I'm just – I'm just feeling a bit mortified now.' She took another hefty swig of champagne, and another.

There was something else she needed to know. 'I haven't – I haven't made too much of an eejit of myself, have I? Have people been sniggering at me behind my back?'

Now it was Patrick's turn to jump in with re-assurance. 'No, no. No-one else would have a clue. Not even Jack. But if you'd ever – well, you know . . .'

'You mean if I'd ever made overtures?'

'Yes. I'm not saying you would, but if you *had* – well – it would put him in a very awkward situation. You know – what with being your boss and all that. Because I suspect he might find it difficult enough to resist . . . I mean, you're a very – well – attractive young woman, and—'

Patrick was clearly so uncomfortable with the situation now that Ella couldn't let him struggle on any more. 'It's OK, Patrick. I know what you're trying to say. Please don't worry. I promise I won't

117

do anything stupid to compromise you or—'

'Patrick! Ella! Hi!' It was Angie from Reflex, looking foxier than ever.

'Angie!' A little flurry of kisses followed.

'Did you just get here?' asked Patrick.

'About ten minutes ago. And I must say I am im*pressed.* Perrier Jouet is my very favourite champagne.' She drained the remains in her flute.

'Then let me get you another one. Ella? Another glass of champagne?'

Ella considered. 'Actually – d'you know what I'd love, Patrick? I'd love a shot of tequila.'

Patrick sent her a look that was half warning, half apology as he disappeared in the direction of the kitchen.

'Fab dress, Ella,' remarked Angie.

Ella had worn her sexiest little slip dress to the party. There'd been no way she was going to give up without a fight. But with Angie looking sensational in gold lamé, there was simply no contest. 'Thanks. But look who's talking. Is that a Galliano, by any chance?'

'Mm. I decided to push the boat out tonight.' Angie slid her a confidential smile. 'Shall I let you into a secret? I'm crazy about your boss.' She reached for a bowl of cashew nuts and casually fired one into her mouth.

So am I, Ella wanted to say. But she didn't. Instead she found herself saying 'And he's crazy about you'. She didn't even kick herself for saying it. There was no point.

Angie's champagne arrived. Ditto Ella's tequila. She knocked the shot back in one and then stood watching miserably as Angie wove her way through the party to where Jack stood watching Angie. Their body language said it all. They were going to end up in bed together tonight.

Patrick looked at the expression on Ella's face. 'I'm sorry, toots,' he said.

'No problem, Patrick.' Ella executed a little, stoical salute for her uncle's benefit, and then she made her way into the kitchen to locate the bottle.

The last thing she had any recollection of doing that night was booking an alarm call for seven o'clock, just before she hit the futon in Patrick's spare room. She'd managed to kick off her shoes and pull off her stockings, but she was still wearing her best Agent Provocateur underwear and her sexy little slip dress. She didn't dream of anything.

*   *   *

The phone by the bed woke her, and she knocked the receiver to the floor. She lay there with her eyes clamped shut for ages, anticipating with dread the pain that was going to kick in when she opened them. Was it going to be that blinding kind of Sabatier-sharp pain, or the dull thudding kind? She couldn't decide which was the worst.

It was the dull thudding kind. She edged her way out from under the duvet and sat on the edge of the futon for a minute or two with her head in her

119

hands. Then she got up and tiptoed into the bath-room, anxious not to wake Claudia and Patrick and her two sleeping cousins. There was a packet of Solpadeine propped up on the basin, with a Post-It from Patrick stuck on the side. 'Take this before you take the car,' she read. 'If you trash it you're in big trouble. Good luck with your dive, love P. XXX.' She splashed her face with water and scrubbed her teeth with the toothbrush Claudia had given her the night before. Her tongue, too. God, she was thirsty!

In the kitchen she drank two pints of water, made strong coffee, and looked glumly round at the post-party mess. Claudia and Patrick and the boys would have their work cut out for them today. But if she had to choose between clearing up party detritus and diving off Sheep's Head, she knew which one she'd rather do.

She'd left herself very little time to get out to Portdelvin, she realized. Only thirty minutes. But at this hour on a Sunday morning the roads would be clear. Unfortunately there was no time to go home and get changed. She rolled on her stockings and slid her feet into her high mules. She was going to look utterly ridiculous arriving at the dive outfit decked out in satin and tat, but she didn't care. She was hungover and she had a broken heart and she was going to have to get into the Irish Sea. As she shrugged into her fake leopardskin coat she found herself thinking that life really couldn't get much worse.

Outside the sunlight was blinding – that cold,

crisp end-of-November sunlight. She shielded her eyes with her hand as she rummaged in her bag for the Ralph Lauren sunglasses that had been a present from her father, and then she got behind the wheel of Patrick's Merc, kicked off her shoes, took a deep breath, and started the ignition.

The journey out took her twenty-five minutes, and she got to the dive shop at exactly eight o'clock. The dive van was just pulling up alongside the kerb outside. The driver's door opened and Ferdia got out, followed by Perdita. Ella swung her legs out of the Merc and stood on the footpath in her stocking feet, swaying a little in the dazzling sunlight. She was glad of her dark glasses. It meant that Ferdia couldn't see how bloodshot her eyes were.

'Hi,' she managed, sliding on her shoes and trying to sound bright. The 'hi' came out as a croak. She seemed to remember having smoked a cigarette last night.

Ferdia took in the fur coat slung round her shoulders, her tight, silk-embroidered frock with the maribou feather trim, and her Agent Provocateur enhanced cleavage. He let his eyes run down her glossy-stockinged legs to her feet in their baby-blue mules, and then up again to her black lensed, gold framed shades. Then he flung back his head and laughed.

'Jesus! What a girl!' he said.

She could tell it wasn't meant in any complimentary sense. There was too much disparaging emphasis on the word 'girl'.

She didn't need any more grief in her life. 'Oh, fuck off, Ferdia,' she said. Then she turned on her high heel and strode into the dive shop. Except her tight dress meant that she couldn't 'stride'. She actually *minced* into the dive shop, followed by her incredulously smiling instructor and his devoted dog.

The trainees were assembled in the classroom for their briefing. A chorus of wolf whistles and appreciative catcalls greeted her entrance. Ella walked up to the top of the room and executed a perfect curtsy before sitting down in the front row where Richie was sprawled open-mouthed. 'What the *fuck* are you wearing?' he asked.

'I was at a party last night,' she said. 'I didn't have time to go home and get changed.'

'Well, all I can say is, he was a jammy bastard, whoever he was.'

She felt rather than saw the sideways look Ferdia gave her as he moved to the top of the class to start the briefing. Her skirt had ridden up, exposing the lacy trim on her stocking-top. Ella crossed her legs ostentatiously, took off her sunglasses and flashed him a dazzling smile. She'd give him *girly*, but she'd bloody well prove him wrong. She, Ella Nesbit, was one of the lads. Always was, always would be. Hangover notwithstanding, she was damn well going to do that dive today.

After the briefing, Sporty Jan and Ella got themselves kitted out with wetsuits and gloves and bootees and suited up in the ladies' changing room.

Because she had no swimsuit to get into, Ella was obliged to put the wetsuit on over her sexy underwear. Sporty Jan pretended not to be looking, but Ella could tell that she was slightly nonplussed. The other woman was at an advantage, having already done the skin dive the day before. She did expert things like spray the cuffs and ankles of her suit with silicone before putting it on, and when she'd finished she gave Ella a hand. It took forever to get the gear on. The neoprene felt clammy against her naked flesh, and when she slid her bare feet into the bootees she thought she might get sick. It reminded her of the time she'd got out of the car and stepped on a slug.

'Are you sure you're OK?' asked Jan, looking at her curiously.

'Sure,' croaked Ella, dead enthusiastically.

They fetched their fins and masks from the rental area and then waddled back along the corridors. The divers were all congregated in the shop, looking like Michelin Men in their thick neoprene suits. Only the masters looked good, in professional, stylish black and neon suits. The poor trainees had to make do with more proletarian designs.

'How do we get down to the shore?' asked Ella. 'It's too far to walk.' She'd presumed there'd be some kind of bus to take them to where they were to perform their dives.

'You take your cars,' said Ferdia.

'I've got to drive in *this*?' said Ella, astonished.

'You got it, Ella. Unless you want to put your leopardskin coat on over your suit to disguise it. You might try wearing your sunglasses as well in case anyone recognizes you.'

Richie sniggered.

'Ha ha, Ferdia,' said Ella.

*   *   *

The drive took them five minutes, and by the end of it Ella and Richie were creased up with laughter. They'd folded down the soft-top, and passers-by stopped and gaped in open amazement at seeing two people in wetsuits bowling along in a Mercedes. Ella had put her film-star sunglasses on for a lark, and was waving her neoprene-gloved hand in the manner of Her Majesty Queen Elizabeth of England. She had got to that stage of hungoverness that makes the sufferer behave in a very giddy, juvenile fashion, and when she and Richie got out of the car, they were laughing so hard they were hanging on to each other.

'OK,' said Ferdia when he caught a load of them. 'You two are definitely not diving together. You and Dan can be buddies, Ella. Richie, you team up with Jan.'

Richie and Ella stole guilty looks at each other and nearly giggled, but when Ferdia said: 'Do you really want to dive the *Lusitania*, Richie? Do you really want to dive that reef, Ella?' they wised up a bit.

Ferdia appointed himself dive leader to her and Dan, and Ella wished harder than ever that smiley PJ wasn't away in Dive Heaven on the Red Sea. When the water trickled its way into Ella's suit and snaked down her spine she squealed – but Ferdia had been right when he'd told her it was easy to get hot in the Irish Sea, even in the month of November, because the sea-water soon reached body temperature. In fact, when they had donned their tanks and weight-belts back on shore, Ella had been perspiring with exertion.

They performed the entry into the water walking backwards, over rough terrain strewn with treacherous boulders. She and Dan clung to each other for support, and Ella was relieved beyond words when they eventually hit water deep enough to float in. Her hangover was really starting to kick in now.

When they'd finned out far enough, Ferdia dropped a line with a weight attached, and they went through the pre-dive signalling ritual. Ella copied her instructor's fluent sign language with clumsy fingers, not really sure of what she was doing. Then she groped for the deflator button on her BCD, pressed it hard, took her last surface breath – and she was going down. She took a few shallow, nervous breaths, and then she did something stupid. She looked down. She couldn't see the bottom. She looked at Ferdia. Though he couldn't have been more than a metre away, the water was so murky that she could barely make out his features under the mask. Beside her, Dan was descending with relentless determination. She looked up. She couldn't see the surface. This was her idea of hell.

In a panic, she bit down hard on the rubber of her breathing apparatus. Water began to trickle through into her mouth. It tasted of salt. She was used to chlorine. This fazed her even more. She waved wildly to attract Ferdia's attention, and then, forgetting everything she'd been taught in her twenty-four hours of training, she scrambled madly to the surface. Her instructor was beside her in an instant, and then Dan's head appeared. He looked mildly quizzical under his mask.

Ferdia took his regulator out of his mouth. 'Calm down,' he said. 'Calm yourself.' He waited, studying her with concern until her rapid, shallow breathing gradually became more measured. 'OK. What's the problem?'

'I couldn't see,' said Ella. 'You said it was shallow, but I couldn't see the bottom and I couldn't see up to the surface, and I just got completely disorientated.'

'A kind of claustrophobia?'

'I guess.' She'd been hit with a touch of nausea, too, but she didn't want to tell him that. She knew the nausea was hangover-induced, and although he'd plainly guessed she was hungover, she didn't want to admit it.

'Do you want to go down again, or do you want to abort the dive?'

She was calmer now. She thought hard. She

couldn't abort the dive! She couldn't wimp out. She remembered the expression on Ferdia's face when he'd called her a *girl*, and she took a deep breath.

'Let's go again,' she said.

'OK. And if you want to come back up, Ella, remember what you learned. Slowly Ascend From Every Dive.' She registered the capital letters and nodded. Ferdia reinserted his regulator, and they repeated the procedure.

Again, Ella panicked. Slowly Ascend From Every Dive, she thought uselessly as she frantically kicked her way back up, Ferdia and Dan following at a less frenetic pace.

She wanted to cry. Beside her Dan was looking vaguely puzzled by all the fuss. 'Come on, Ella,' he said encouragingly. 'It's great down there. Remember what the manual says? When we finish demonstrating our skills we can tour underwater for "pleasure and experience". You don't want to miss out on that, do you?'

'No,' she said in a small voice. The idea of touring underwater for pleasure and experience was actually anathema to her at this stage, but she was determined to do it. 'I'll try one more time.'

'Are you sure?' asked Ferdia carefully. 'Don't feel under pressure, Ella. Not if you're not feeling happy about it.'

'I'm sure. If I can't hack it this time I'll abort,' she said.

'I was watching you,' he said. 'You're tensing up your jaw muscles. Relax your lips. Keep them firmly wrapped round your regulator, but don't bite down, OK? The most important thing is to stay relaxed.'

Third time not so lucky. Ella was so disorientated when she bolted for the surface this time that she wasn't sure whether she was heading upwards or downwards.

'I'm sorry,' she said when she got her breath back. 'I can't do it. I'm going to have to abort the dive. I'm really sorry, Ferdia. Dan.'

'That's all right,' said Dan mildly.

'D'you mind waiting here for me while I take Ella back to the shore?' asked Ferdia.

'Not at all,' said Dan. He gave her a big smile. 'Take care, Ella. Have a good holiday.'

Ella thought she hated herself more at that moment than at any other time in her life. How dare she make fun of him and call him Duffer Dan when she was the one who was the Duffer and the Wimp and the Big Girl's Blouse all rolled into one? Under the mask she could feel tears of humiliation start to come. 'Thanks, Dan,' she said. 'Good luck.'

She and Ferdia finned back to shore leaving Dan bobbing imperturbably alongside the float. They swam in silence for a while. Then Ferdia spoke. 'Hangover?'

'Yes,' she admitted. 'You can say "told you so" if you like.'

'I never say "told you so". It's a really pointless thing to say to anyone.'

Ella bit her lip. 'God! I'm so crap!'

'Hey. Stop beating yourself up. Once you get to Jamaica things will pan out. The visibility there is phenomenal. You won't have a problem with orientation.'

They'd reached the shallows, and Ferdia helped her out of her BCD. As she was relieved of the weight of the tank she gave an audible sigh.

He looked down at her and smiled. 'You really are tiny, aren't you? No wonder you find it difficult.'

'What do you mean?'

'I know it's not a terribly politically correct thing to say, but there's a very obvious design fault in women. You compensate for it by being cleverer and by living longer and by being more dextrous than men, but you just don't have the same physical strength. Next time you dive, Ella, celebrate the fact that you're different, and do the clever thing. Take advantage of some sucker's superior strength and ask for help if you can't manage your equipment. I know we encourage you to handle your gear yourself, but in Jamaica you can tip the boatman to do it for you. I used to feel so sorry for you when I saw you staggering down the poolside, determined at all costs to be one of the lads.'

Ella was staring at him in astonishment. This was the last thing she expected someone like Ferdia to come out with.

'But I hate being perceived as a girly sort of girl!' she blurted.

Ferdia laughed. 'I'm surprised you can say that after the way you showed up here this morning.

You cut some girly swank then. Even I had to compliment you on it.'

'That was supposed to be a *compliment*?'

'When I called you a girl? Absolutely.'

'Oh,' said Ella, feeling really silly now. 'I thought you were making fun of me.'

He shook his head, still smiling down at her. Then: 'I'd better get back to Dan,' he said, looking over his shoulder.

'Oh, God,' she said. 'What's poor Dan going to write in his logbook about his first ever dive? "Abandoned by buddy?" ' She sighed again. 'I don't think I'll hang about for the debriefing, Ferdia, if you don't mind. I feel too embarrassed at being the only one not to have done the dive, and Richie will take the piss bigtime.' She also didn't much like the idea of sitting in the classroom in her party frock sans underwear – subjected to the ultimate debriefing. She'd have to leave the tiny sodden items off or she'd freeze to death. 'Say goodbye to Rich for me, will you?'

'Sure I will.'

She paused and looked thoughtful for a moment. 'It's funny – I'll probably never see him again. Or you, for that matter. Bye, Ferdia. Thanks for everything.' She actually meant it.

'Don't say bye. Say *sayonara*. This time next year you might be doing your Underwater Hunter course.'

'Hah!'

130

'Be sure to send Desirée my love. And enjoy Jamaica.'

'Desirée?'

'Remember I told you about her? She runs the dive outfit at Salamander Cove.' He allowed himself a small, nostalgic smile. 'My favourite dive goddess in the world.'

'I'll do that.' She smiled at him, then turned and headed for the car, feeling water uncomfortably slooshing round in her wetsuit. She'd have to put newspaper down on Patrick's leather upholstery to prevent it from getting watermarked. She could hear Ferdia whistling something as he made his way back into the sea. For a moment she couldn't place the melody, although it was incredibly familiar. Then the whistling stopped mid bar.

'Ella?' he called after her. 'Can I say something else politically incorrect?'

She looked back. He was hip deep in water. 'Sure,' she said. 'I never was a stickler for political correctness.'

'I loved the stockings,' he said. Then he turned, laughing, and struck out for the float bobbing around in the Irish Sea where Duffer Dan was still waiting patiently for him.

She watched him go, and then she realized what it was he'd been whistling. It had been from Beethoven's Seventh. The slow movement.

Chapter Five

Ella spent the next week organizing clothes to take with her on holiday. It felt weird to be looking out little bikinis and sunhats and sandals and sarongs when the skies outside her window were leaden. It felt weird to walk into Boots and fill her wire basket with suntan lotion and calamine lotion and aftersun lotion when everyone else was filling theirs with cold remedies and vitamin C. And it felt weirder still to emerge from the taxi at Dublin airport in nothing warmer than a cardigan when the wind-chill factor was sharp as a spiv's suit.

In Heathrow she and Leonie stood in a queue of other summer-clad individuals at the Air Jamaica desk. There were a lot of stressed-out, bewildered-looking travellers milling about, but Ella wasn't one of them. She loved the buzz of airports. She'd negotiated them since she was tiny: a young flyer in the charge of jolly air stewardesses, flying out to visit her father wherever he might be on tour, or heading off to the sun to spend holidays with her mother. Now she and Leonie were playing a favourite airport game – looking around and speculating about the people travelling with them. Ella loved doing this, watching complete strangers and making up stories about them. The couple who couldn't keep their hands off each other were obviously honeymooners, the smiling black couple were emigrants returning home after years of soulless London living, the man with the Rolex and the designer shades was a drug dealer. Leonie decided that the leather-clad youth checking into first class was a member of a boy band.

'I'm seriously pissed off that they had nothing left in first class.' A peevish female had just joined the queue behind them. Ella resisted the impulse to turn round and have a good look.

'You were lucky to get anything at all at such short notice.' A man's voice. 'Now. Have you taken your Becalm tablets?'

'Yes. I took two already today.'

'Maybe you're immune to them now. They don't seem to be helping much these days, do they?'

'Nothing could help me with the amount of stress I've had to put up with recently. I sincerely hope this holiday works. I'll probably only just have begun to unwind by the time I have to come home again.'

'It's ideal for you, darling. A holiday where you can just chill and lie on the beach and read.'

'I won't get much reading done for pleasure. I've all those scripts to get through, remember?'

A sigh. 'I wish you'd taken my advice and left them behind. You need a complete escape. Try to read only the ones that need immediate attention.

Put the others on the back boiler until you get home. You'll end up having a total breakdown if you don't ease up.'

'I'll have to read the one that Juliet Rathbone-Lyon sent. She wants an answer ASAP or the deal's off.'

Ella was fascinated. She was earwigging so hard that the muscles in her ears had actually gone taut.

Beside her Leonie kicked her hand luggage. 'Oh dammit,' she said. 'I forgot to pack my St John's Wort. Did you know, Ella, that it's meant to be an excellent preventative cure for – what's that disease called? Anyway, I've been taking it religiously since – what on earth's the matter with you?'

Ella was making frantic facial signals to Leonie to shut up. She beetled her brows at her, and rolled her eyes backward to indicate that Leonie should join her in eavesdropping on the couple behind. She'd obviously got quite good at sign language since she'd taken up scuba diving because her grandmother quickly registered what Ella was trying to convey.

'I'm just so sorry I can't come with you,' the male voice was saying. Ella was convinced that his tone had an insincere tinge to it.

'Yes. What a shame you decided to do that bloody panto. It's not as if we need the money.'

'I've always wanted to do pantomime. You know that, Soph.'

Ella couldn't stand it any more. She turned to her left on the pretext of studying the flight monitor,

and swivelled her eyes as unobtrusively as possible.
A very beautiful blonde woman was standing next to
a trolley piled high with expensive-looking luggage.
She was wearing a pale pink linen suit and a pair of
sunglasses so dark she had to be somebody famous.
In fact, Ella was pretty certain she'd seen her somewhere before. Her peripheral vision took in the
male half of the duo. Tall, dark and impossibly
handsome. A perfect pantomime prince. Ella tore
her eyes away from him and returned her attention
to the pink linen woman, who had removed her
sunglasses and laid her head on his shoulder in a
cuddly, proprietorial fashion when she'd seen Ella
eyeballing her man.

'Oh, Ben! Oh, God – I'm going to miss you so
much! Do you realize that we've never been apart
for as much as a week since we first met?' The tetchy
tone had been replaced by one of heart-searing
anguish. Was she imagining it, or was the woman
putting on a performance for Ella's benefit? 'And
now we're going to be separated for a whole *fortnight* – with an entire *ocean* between us! Thank *God*
for mobile phones – you will remember to carry
yours with you at all times, darling, won't you?'

'I can hardly carry my phone on stage with me,
Sophie,' he pointed out reasonably.

'Don't be facile, darling. You know what I mean.
I just need to know that I can contact you any time
the agony of separation gets too unbearable.' Ella
predicted that it would end in tears. She was right.
Out of the corner of her eye she could see the

woman called Sophie starting to dig about in her handbag. 'Oh! Oh! Why does life have to be so *stress*ful? I can't even find my *hanky*!'

'Here you are darling,' said Ben. 'I have one here.'

'Oh! Oh, no! I don't think I can bear it!'

'There, there. What is it, Soph?'

'It smells of you! The handkerchief! Oh *God*. Why am I going off on this hateful odyssey all by myself?' She blew her nose. 'I expect the resort will be full of odious Germans.'

'Well, at least you won't have to talk to anyone. When they ask for your autograph you can just smile sweetly and sign and say "Ich spreche kein Deutsch."'

'What does that mean?'

'It means "I don't speak German."'

'A very useful phrase to know. "Ich spreche kein Deutsch." Write it down for me, sweetheart, will you?'

There was a hiatus, and then the Sophie person spoke again. 'Guess what I'm going to do, Benny?'

'What, sweetheart?'

'I'm going to take this hanky with me and sleep with it on my pillow every night.'

'Oh, darling. That's so typical of you. What a totally sweet Sophie thing to do.'

'Will you do the same?'

He sounded uncertain. 'Sleep with one of your handkerchiefs?'

'No, no, darling. Maybe something a little more

intimate?' There came a sound of whispering, followed by a girlish giggle.

Ella and Leonie exchanged glances and smirked. This was brilliant! Ella hoped that this Sophie woman would sit near her on the plane. She'd be better entertainment than the inflight movie.

*   *   *

In fact, she *was* the inflight entertainment. She was Sophie Burke, best supporting actress Oscar nominee and winner of a BAFTA. Also the star of the inflight movie, a weepy romantic drama that Ella had had absolutely no interest in seeing when it had been released a month or two previously.

To her delight, Sophie was seated just across the aisle and a little forward from her, so Ella and Leonie could observe her while remaining unobserved. When the opening titles of the movie began unfurling on the screen in swirly purple lettering, Sophie had given a little theatrical gasp and immediately lunged for her handbag. She'd extracted her black glasses and fitted them to her face, and then she'd bent her head forward so that her profile was obscured by a curtain of silver-blond hair. The disguise immediately attracted attention, and a little murmur of interest started up among those passengers who hadn't already recognized her. When the movie ended, a respectful round of applause pittered around the plane, and Sophie got to her feet, removed her sunglasses so that her fans could gaze upon her beautiful but emotional face, and made a little bow. 'Thank you. Thank you so much,' she murmured, before resuming her seat and putting her glasses back on.

*　　*　　*

They stepped off the plane to be shrouded in air as warm and soft as a pashmina. The airport was buzzing. Hers and Leonie's and Sophie Burke's and the honeymooners' and the drug dealer's were the only white faces going through immigration. Sophie Burke, with her straight platinum hair and porcelain skin, looked especially out of place, and attracted a lot of looks, especially from the men, who were quite openly appreciative.

The Jamaican people were stunning. The women didn't walk – they swayed. They sashayed. The men were loose-limbed, graceful as gazelles. It was obvious that they'd descended from a breeding stock of princes and warriors, with their proud bearing and their exceptional bone structure. This must be what angels look like, thought Ella, gazing around at the most beautiful race on earth.

Outside on the tarmac Jamaicans milled around Ella and Leonie as they hovered helplessly, looking out for the coach that was to take them to Salamander Cove. They saw the honeymooners get into a minibus that had HUMMINGBIRD HOTEL printed on a cardboard sign in the windscreen. The drug dealer was swooped upon by a stretch limo.

Across the concourse Sophie Burke stood beside her mountain of luggage, looking lost. Leonie and Ella exchanged glances.

'D'you think she's going to Salamander Cove?' asked Leonie.

'She could be,' said Ella looking across the tarmac to where the film star shimmered with film star-ishness. 'Should we ask?'

'Do,' said Leonie. 'Lucky for you if she is. It'll be nice for you to have someone of around your own age to play with.' She responded to Ella's sideways look with a disingenuous smile.

Ella approached Sophie with a tentative 'Excuse me?'

The actress gave a little sigh, and produced a Mont Blanc pen from her handbag.

'You wouldn't happen to be going to Salamander Cove Villas, would you?' asked Ella.

The look of resigned condescension in Sophie Burke's green eyes turned to relief. 'Oh, yes! Are you?'

'Yes, I am. Or rather, *we* are. I'm travelling with my grandmother.' Ella indicated Leonie who was smiling at a small Jamaican child.

'Oh, I'm so glad there's someone else in the same predicament! What are we to *do*? They told me there'd be a coach waiting at the airport.'

'That's what they told us, too. I expect the Jamaicans are as laid back about things as the Irish.'

A spark of interest ignited in Sophie's eyes. 'You're Irish?' she said. 'Of course, I should have known from the accent. I'm Irish, too, although I've been living in London for the past few years.' Ella had read somewhere that Sophie Burke was Dublin born and bred, but there was absolutely nothing about her accent to indicate that this was so. It was polished mid-Atlantic. 'Nice to meet you.' Sophie extended a perfectly manicured hand. 'My name's Sophie Burke.'

'Yes. I know. Congratulations on your performance on the plane this evening.' Sophie couldn't know that it wasn't her screen performance Ella was referring to.

'Oh, thank you!' The actress gave a coy little shrug. 'And you are . . . ?'

'Ella Nesbit.' A pause ensued – the kind of pause that happens when people are thrown together and don't know what to do next. 'Well,' said Ella. 'I wonder what's the best thing to do. Maybe I should—'

'Yo! White ladies!' Ella turned to see a gangling black man bearing down on them. He was wearing loose pyjama-type trousers, a baggy Hawaiian shirt and a crocheted tam-o-shanter. He flashed an enormous smile at them, showing off great gaps in his mouth where teeth had once been. 'You going to Salamander Cove Villas?'

Ella nodded. 'That's right.' She looked at Sophie. Sophie was staring at the black man, incredulity scrawled all over her face.

'I yo' chauffeur. You wait here. My bus done

been impounded. I come back, I pick you up when they give me my bus back.'

'Oh. OK. How long is that likely to be?' asked Ella politely.

'I come back soon.' He gave them another wide smile, and then he turned and started to walk away.

'Excuse me,' said Sophie peremptorily to his retreating back. He paused, looked over his shoulder, and walked slowly back to them. 'How long is the journey to Salamander Cove?'

'Oh – 'bout two hours.'

'Two hours!' Sophie was plainly horrified.

'But it's only about sixty miles on the map,' observed Ella.

The black man nodded sagely. 'We go slow. We go Jamaican time.' Then he threw back his head and laughed. 'You in Jamaica now, lady. You take things easy. No white man time here. No problems in Jamaica.' Then he shambled off and was swallowed up in the maw of the heaving throng.

'Oh, my God!' exclaimed the actress. 'That's our chau*ffeur*?' Sophie Burke set herself down on her pile of luggage as delicately as if she was a piece of Sèvres porcelain. And started to cry.

*   *   *

The journey actually took three hours. Four, by the time the driver's bus had been liberated from the pound.

When Sophie had got a load of the transport she was expected to travel in she started to whimper. No luxury air-conditioned coach pulled up on the airport concourse. This was a vehicle that might best be described as 'basic'. The suspension wasn't that hot, either. Not surprising, thought Ella, given the condition of the roads. They were worse than the worst Irish boreen she'd ever driven down. At times the driver had to slow to a crawl to negotiate potholes. At other times he careered around hairpin bends at a speed so reckless that Sophie started to hyperventilate. He pumped his horn frequently at other drivers, sometimes belligerently, sometimes as a greeting, shouting 'Yo, man!' and 'Yo, brudder!' at fellow taxi drivers out of his open window. On one occasion he stopped and had a conversation in almost unintelligible patois with another man. 'He my friend,' he threw over his shoulders to his passengers. 'He taxi driver too.'

The friend squinted in through the open window and grinned when he saw the women. 'Nice girl passengers,' he said, grabbing hold of his crotch and gesturing graphically.

Sophie looked away immediately. 'They're all obviously out of their brains on pot,' she hissed at Ella.

They passed through townships brilliant with early Christmas decorations. The coloured fairy-lights which festooned the little houses looked like sequinned spider's webs. Thumping reggae blasted out at them through massive speakers set up at intervals along the streets, and Leonie, who was wide awake, nodded her head in time to the music as they passed from one street party to the next, smiling out of the window at the locals and provoking periodic shouts of 'Yo! Whitey!' She found this so amusing that she was disappointed when they didn't shout it.

'Dear God,' moaned Sophie, clutching her head. 'Do they never sleep?'

By the time they reached Salamander Cove Villas the film star was slumped against her leather luggage, and her linen suit, once crisp, looked almost as limp with exhaustion as she did. Her complexion had lost its delicate pallor, and her face now looked as if someone had powdered it with grey chalk dust for a joke.

They pulled up under the *porte-cochère* in front of a pair of cerulean-blue louvred doors. Bougainvillaea trailed over the pale pink stucco that fronted the building. The airy reception area was tiled in terracotta, with arched windows over-looking a plaza.

Ella went to the desk where a big, rotund Jamaican man smilingly invited her to check in. A smiling bell-hop took their luggage, and a smiling housekeeper told them that, although the restaurant and bar were now closed, they would find refreshments waiting for them in their villa. They all *smiled*! And although she was knackered, Ella couldn't help smiling back.

Sophie staggered past them, announcing that

there was no way she was checking in at this hour. 'Just show me directly to my villa,' she demanded, pronouncing it 'veelya'. 'I'll check in tomorrow. I'm so exhausted after that hellish journey that I couldn't even manage to sign my own name.' That was surprising, thought Ella. She'd signed autographs like a polished automaton on the plane earlier.

Ella and Leonie followed the bell-hop down a wide, winding flight of stone steps and across the floodlit plaza. A tinny bell in a miniature clock tower chimed midnight as they walked into Paradise.

Above them Orion hung at a lower angle than usual in a midnight-blue velvet sky. Ella couldn't remember the last time she'd seen it. You'd count yourself lucky to find even one star in the night sky back at home in Dublin. The bell-hop led them along a path flanked by villas with balconies, villas with verandas and villas with roof gardens. Tree frogs and crickets serenaded them as they descended more steps alongside a miniature waterfall. She could hear the sea now. They rounded a bend in the path and found themselves on a grassy esplanade. Beyond a low wall that bordered a turquoise-blue swimming pool, waves danced and beckoned to her.

Their villa was a stone's throw away from the pool and maybe two stones' throw away from a small but perfectly formed white sand beach. There were two bedrooms, a bathroom and a well-equipped little kitchen off a central sitting room.

The furnishings were quietly sumptuous, and Ella couldn't wait to fall into the king-sized bed with its filmy mosquito net. She'd cherished a fantasy about sleeping under a mosquito net since seeing some madly romantic film set in the Tropics when she was ten years old.

The bell-hop told them that breakfast was served in the beach restaurant from seven-thirty onwards. They tipped him in Jamaican dollars and he smiled and wished them an enjoyable stay in his beautiful country. Jah-may-kah. He pronounced the syllables slowly, as if enjoying the feel of them on his tongue. Then he turned and loped slowly away back up the path.

Ella and Leonie looked at each other, smiling incredulously, and then they hugged each other. 'Oh, Leonie!' said Ella. 'You totally clever thing!'

'Aren't I just?' said Leonie, with a feline smile. 'Now – where's the minibar? I'm dying for a drink.'

Ella located the minibar in a carved wooden cupboard. 'There's champagne!' she said. 'Two snipes. Shall we crack them?'

'Absolutely,' replied Leonie.

Ella popped the corks, and filled their glasses.

'I want to propose a toast,' Leonie said, raising hers solemnly.

'To whom?'

'To the Polly Rogers of course, darling,' said her grandmother, laughing.

*　　*　　*

The first thing Ella did when she woke the next morning was make a beeline for the pool. It was early, and there was no-one about apart from a beach attendant raking the sand, and a gardener wandering between ranks of bright flowerbeds. She dived and splashed and performed somersaults, and then she floated on her back and watched buzzards lazily cruising the periwinkle-blue Jamaican skies. By the time she climbed out of the pool some twenty minutes later, a life-guard was ascending his lookout post, a platoon of pink-frocked, white-aproned chambermaids were peeling off into villas, and an army of Germans was marching towards the beach with heaps of towels.

Leonie was sitting on the step of the veranda painting her toenails when Ella returned to their villa.

'We'd better get a move on,' she told her grand-mother, as she towelled her hair. 'The Germans really do do that thing with the towels.'

'Just wait till I finish the top coat,' said Leonie, sticking out the tip of her tongue as she concentrated on painting her pinkie cherry red. 'Guess what was the first thing I saw when I opened my bedroom curtains this morning?'

'What?'

'A hummingbird. It was hovering at eye level right outside my window, sipping nectar from a hibiscus blossom.'

'Wow! We really are in the Garden of Eden, aren't we?' Ella leaned over the wooden rail of the veranda and breathed in the scent of a pink hibiscus flower. It was growing alongside a ginger lily which was growing alongside a bird of paradise flower which was growing alongside something even more exotic, with dangling red blossoms.

'There! Finished,' said Leonie, putting the top back on her nail varnish. 'Let's get ready to strut our stuff. Are you going to breakfast in your swimming costume?'

'I'll put a sarong on over it.'

They walked barefoot to the restaurant on the beach. It was thatched with palm leaves. A coconut palm grew through a ceiling festooned with vines, and glossy black birds hopped cheekily in and out of the open windows, scavenging for leftovers.

There was a dish laden with fruit at the breakfast counter. Until now, Ella had only ever eaten mango that tasted of some vaguely unpleasant oil, and watermelon that tasted of water. This fruit was *fragrant*. As well as mango and watermelon, there were guava and papaya and pineapple. There were freshly baked croissants, there was fried plantain, there was a spinachy-looking dish called callaloo, there was kedgeree. A smiling chef prepared an omelette for Leonie, and a smiling waiter poured Blue Mountain coffee for Ella.

They'd decided to do nothing on their first day. 'Let's just chill,' said Leonie. She had splurged out on an expensive swimming costume, and she looked sensational in her flower-splashed sarong, cartwheel sunhat and shades. When they strolled onto the beach a little later they made an impact, but Ella suspected that the appreciative looks were focused more on her glamorous grandmother than on her.

'When are you going to check out the dive outfit?' asked Leonie as she removed towels from two sun-loungers and made herself comfortable.

'I don't know. I'm not really sure I want to dive ever again after that grim fiasco in Sheep's Head Bay.'

'Oh, you must, Ella! You can't miss out on the opportunity of diving in the Caribbean! It's a once-in-a-lifetime experience!'

'Yes, I know,' said Ella, ruefully. 'But I think I've lost my nerve.'

'Well, just mention that to the instructor! They probably have to reassure nervous divers every single day. You won't be the first one, darling, you can depend upon that.'

'I suppose you're right.'

Ella looked over at the dive outfit. It was housed in a timber-built shack further down the beach. She came to a sudden decision. 'I'll book a dive now,' she said, getting off her sun-lounger. 'If I procrastinate I'll never do it.'

She walked across hot sand and stood by the counter of the dive shop, drumming on it with nervy fingers while she waited for someone to show up. There were stickers plastered over the walls. 'Happiness is Being In over your Head,' she read on one. 'Remember when Sex was Safe and Diving was Dangerous?' on another. And finally: 'Dive Deep, Dive Hard. Fear Nothing.'

She was studying this last sticker, uncertain of what response it produced in her, when a voice came from behind her. 'Dive deep, dive hard. Fear nothing,' she heard. 'The first rule of diving.'

'I thought it was "Never hold your breath"?' Ella turned to confront the person who'd spoken, and her breath was snatched away. She thanked God she was wearing shades, because they hid the expression in her eyes that she was quite unable to disguise. It was one of naked stupefaction.

He was the most beautiful man she had ever seen in her life. He stood more than six feet. He was ebony. His dreadlocks gave him the air of a Pharaoh, and his eyes invited you to dive right in. He was smiling, showing teeth white as pearls set in the most kissable mouth she had ever laid eyes on, and he carried himself like an insouciant prince.

'You know your scuba,' he said. 'You wanna book a dive?'

'Please,' said Ella. 'Are you an instructor?'

'No,' he said.

Ella hoped disappointment didn't register too obviously on her face.

'I don't dive.' Disappointment number two.

'You wanna talk to my woman.' Ow! Disappointment number *three*.

The terrestrial god moved to the door of the dive outfit. 'Desirée!' he called. 'There's a lady here wants to go divin'.'

149

The woman who emerged from the dive shop could have been any age from her late twenties to her early forties. She wasn't much taller than Ella, but she had a neat, lean, almost wiry physique. Her face had the high cheekbones, full mouth and slanting eyes of a Buddha, and she radiated chutzpah. She moved towards the Rasta, who laid a relaxed arm across her shoulders, and they both gave Ella the kind of smile that would be impossible not to return.

'You certified, honey?' The woman had a sweet, low voice.

'Not yet. I'm on referral from Dublin, in Ireland.'

'Ireland!' The woman's eyes gleamed with interest. 'I had an instructor from Dublin, Ireland work here for me once.'

'I think I know who you're talking about,' said Ella. 'You're Desirée, right?'

'That's my name.'

'So you're talking about Ferdia MacDiarmada? I trained with him.'

Desirée's smile became even broader. 'Hey! Ain't *no* instructor I trusted more than that Ferdia. How is my main man?'

'He's doing fine.'

Desirée nodded. 'Yeah. Him a fine t'ing. When you go back to Ireland you tell him that. Anytime he want to come back to Jamaica, he come to Desirée. Desirée find him work anytime.' She strolled across to the counter and picked up a desk diary. 'Now, honey. How many training dives you need to do?'

'All of them.'

'And when you wanna do them?'

'Um.' Oh God. Did she really *want* to do them? 'Whenever *you* want,' she said.

Desirée scanned the pages of the diary, humming a melody under her breath, while Ella chewed her lip. She suddenly realized that she was being observed, and she looked round to find the eyes of the beautiful Rastafarian on her. He was leaning against the jamb of the door, hands resting low on lean hips like a gunslinger. 'What's your problem?' he asked.

Ella was baffled. 'My problem?'

'Yeah, man. You have a problem. I see it in your face.'

Desirée glanced up at him and then turned to Ella. 'What is it, honey?'

'I'm scared,' confessed Ella. 'I wimped out of my first dive in the Irish Sea.'

'Oh? Why did you do that?'

'I felt a bit claustrophobic. I had a kind of panic attack.'

'What was the visibility?'

'Two metres.'

Desirée threw back her head and laughed. 'Two metres! Oh, look, girl – here you can see for twenty, thirty, forty metres no problem! You won't have no problem with claustrophobia!'

'Are you sure? Are we going to be going down very deep?' God! How she *hated* herself for being a wimp!

Desirée looked at her appraisingly. 'What's your name, honey?'

'Ella Nesbit.'

'OK, Ella Nesbit. This is what I am going to suggest to you. I am going to hand-rear you. I am going to finish the job my friend Ferdia started, and this is how I am going to do it. I will take you round to the Blue Lagoon, OK? There the water is very calm, very still – not choppy like the sea out there today. We go in off the dive boat there, OK?' Her laid-back Jamaican accent sounded wonderfully reassuring. 'We stay on the bottom for as long as it takes you to get comfortable. We maintain eye contact at all times. I won't take my eyes off you until I sense you are a happy girl, OK? Then I take you by the hand and we explore a little. Cruise around.'

Ella considered. There was something about this woman that inspired absolute trust. She remembered how Ferdia had told her that she'd be damn lucky if she got to train with Desirée. She nodded her head. 'OK,' she said. 'This sounds good.'

'That's what I like to hear. I think this girl has guts. But if at any time you feel nervous, even a little, you just signal to me and we'll go up. How are you fixed tomorrow morning?'

'I'm free as a bird.'

'OK. Show up around ten-thirty, Ella Nesbit, and

I will take you down. And when you go back to Ireland you tell our friend Ferdia that you were hand-trained by Desirée.'

Ella smiled at her. 'I'll do that. Thanks a lot, Desirée. I'll see you in the morning.' As she turned away, she made eye contact once again with the beautiful Rasta. 'Goodbye – ?' she said.

'Raphael,' he said, bestowing a beatific smile on her. Ella remembered how she had compared the Jamaican people to angels when she'd arrived in Kingston. This man didn't just *look* like an angel! He even had the name of one.

'Goodbye, Raphael.' She walked back across the beach to rejoin Leonie, with a song singing in her heart. It was the song Desirée had been humming, and Ella suddenly knew what it was. It was: 'Don't worry. Be happy.'

As she drew nearer the stretch of beach where she'd left Leonie, she became aware that someone had commandeered her sun-lounger. There was a man sitting next to her grandmother, and they were laughing away together as if they'd known each other for years. Ella gave Leonie a questioning look.

'Hello, darling. Let me introduce you,' she said. 'This is Dieter Bleibtreu. He and his son-in-law were responsible for hogging the sun-loungers. He's apologized for it, so we're friends now. Dieter, this is my granddaughter, Ella Nesbit.'

Dieter Bleibtreu rose to his feet and executed a little bow. '*Enchanté.* It is a pleasure to meet two so charming ladies on my first day here.'

You wouldn't have thought it was his first day. He was tanned to a dark honey colour, which made his blue eyes look bluer and his white hair whiter. He had an urbane manner, he wasn't in bad shape for a man whom Ella guessed to be somewhere in his sixties – and he was rich. Ella could tell by the gold Rolex. Trust her grandmother to find a man like this on the first day of her holiday!

'Let me get you something to drink,' he offered. 'It is a little early in the day for champagne, but perhaps you would care for a fruit punch?'

'It's never too early in the day for champagne,' said Leonie. 'It's the only alcoholic drink one's allowed to drink at any time of the day. Thank you. I'd love a glass.'

Dieter Bleibtreu smiled. 'Ella? Champagne?'

'No thanks, Dieter. I'll stick to punch.' She wasn't going to start knocking back alcohol at this hour of the morning. She didn't want to end up with a hangover tomorrow in the Blue Lagoon with Desirée.

Dieter headed off in the direction of the bar, and Ella sat down beside Leonie. 'Honestly! You are incorrigible! I leave you alone for ten minutes, and when I come back you've picked up a complete stranger. What am I going to do with you?'

Leonie looked smug. 'He's rather gorgeous, isn't he? He's a divorcee, and he's here on holiday with his daughter and her family. They have the poshest villa in the joint, with their own private swimming pool. He's invited me for cocktails later.' She looked over at Dieter, who was leaning on the bar, and sent him her wonderful smile. Then she turned back to Ella. 'How did you get on? Does that woman you were talking to run the dive shop?'

'Yup. Her name's Desirée, and she is the Man. Or rather, the Woman.'

'So who was the man? He was pretty damn sexy. Is he a diver?'

'No. He's also a strictly no-go area. He and Desirée are an item.'

'So when are you diving?'

'Tomorrow. Desirée's taking me down.'

'Good girl!' said Leonie approvingly. 'That's the spirit. Never give up too easily. Oh, look. There's that film star person.'

Sophie Burke was walking across the grassy esplanade. She was wearing a thong, a skimpy sun top, high-heeled gold sandals and a sunhat with the widest brim Ella had ever seen. There was gold at her ankle, her wrist, her throat and her earlobes, and a diamond sparkled in her belly-button. Men gaped, and women looked away. Sophie kicked off her shoes, doffed her hat with a flourish of her left hand and her shades with a flourish of her right, and swept back her shiny platinum hair. Then she removed her sun top and dived into the pool.

'Goodness,' said Leonie. 'She's got amazing bazookas. Do you think they're real?'

Sophie swam one lap, and then rose up like Aphrodite at the other end, lifting both hands to push back her wet hair from her forehead and looking around with a Bambi-ish blink for a sun-lounger.

A blond youth obliged the starlet immediately, jumping to his feet and indicating that she could use his lounger before hurling himself into the pool to cool off. Sophie settled down on the lounger, produced a tube of suncream from a beach bag, and began to unscrew the lid. This time everyone on the beach looked away.

Dieter returned with drinks on a tray.

'Thank you, Dieter,' said Leonie, raising her glass of champagne at him. 'Here's to happy holidays.'

*   *   *

Some time later Ella got bored listening to her grandmother and Dieter flirting, and decided to go to her villa to fetch something to read. As she passed by the pool, she heard her name being called.

'Ella! Hi!' Sophie Burke was waving at her.

Ella veered reluctantly round the pool to where Sophie was reclining. 'Hi,' she said. 'How's your jet lag?'

'Pretty awful, really. I had a massage in the beauty parlour earlier to perk me up. What do you think of the resort?'

'It's heavenly, isn't it?'

'So-so. I've seen better. And there are so many *Germans.* The masseuse told me that 90 per cent of the residents at any given time are German. Shall I give you some advice? Just say: "Ich spreche kein Deutsch". That'll put them off trying to harass you.'

Ella couldn't imagine being harassed by any of

the people she'd seen so far. And Dieter had turned out to be perfectly charming, with a nice line in irony. If only her grandmother would stop monopolizing him. Ella had barely been able to get a word in edgeways.

'It's lucky for us, isn't it, that we met up at the airport? Otherwise we might never have run into a single other English-speaking person. Oh – look. That sun-lounger's free. Grab it, quickly, before anyone else can.'

Sophie flung a towel across the next-door lounger, and Ella found herself sitting down beside her.

'Here,' said Sophie sweetly. 'Would you like to have a look at my *Harper's*? You might do my back for me first though. I need to use a total block because my skin's so fair. And having a tan is so deeply untrendy, don't you think? I mean, look at all these Germans. Their skin's like leather. And did you know that the highest proportion of skin cancer . . .'

Uh-oh, thought Ella. If she wasn't careful, life on this holiday could turn out to be more of a bitch than a beach . . .

Chapter Six

The following morning saw Ella on board a boat
beating its way towards the Blue Lagoon, looking
svelte and sexy in Lycra at last. No horrible slugskin
neoprene necessary in Dive Holiday Heaven! She
sat in the stern with her hair streeling out behind
her like a scarf and her skin all aglow from the sun
and the sea wind. The sad thing was there was no-
one to look svelte and sexy for. There was just her
and Desirée and the boatman on board.

She'd discovered that Salamander Cove Villas
wasn't exactly bursting at the seams with people
her age. It seemed to cater for an affluent, upmarket
clientele, and most of the residents were dripping
with gold and sagging with middle-aged spread.
This was emphatically *not* a swinging singles
holiday resort. How ironic that her sixty-something
grandmother had managed to embark on a whirl-
wind flirtation with a gorgeous German, while her
young and not screamingly unattractive granddaughter hadn't hooked up with anyone! Pah –
she didn't really care. Since Jack and Angie had
become an item she'd lost interest in men.

She disengaged a strand of hair from the zip of her exposure suit, and turned her thoughts to a more immediate consideration. Her dive. Desiree had told her that she wouldn't test Ella on her dive skills today. She just wanted her pupil to get comfortable in the underwater environment. She had radiated reassurance, but Ella was still feeling antsy. Was she going to wimp out again? Had all those lessons been a complete waste of time and money? Would those twenty-four hours of struggling with dive tables and J-valves and ton-weight tanks have been better off spent doing something else? Studying *Pro Sound News* to keep up with Julian? Practising her violin?

The dive boat rounded a headland, and there, suddenly, was the Blue Lagoon, surrounded by high escarpments covered in verdant forest. It was every bit as beautiful as the photographs in her guidebook, but the photographs hadn't done justice to the colour of the water. It was of a blue-green so smooth and dense that when Ella dipped her fingers in the water she half expected them to come out dripping with colour like thick gloss paint.

The boat chugged to a halt, and Desirée leaned forward. 'OK, Ella. How are you feeling?'

Ella's heart started to beat a little tattoo. 'Fine,' she lied.

'We'll do a backward roll into the water. Let me go first – and remember to signal to me that you're OK the minute you surface.'

Ella donned mask and fins, inflated her BCD, and, feeling like a condemned prisoner, stuck her regulator in her mouth.

Desirée performed an elegant backward roll, and surfaced. 'Go, Ella!' she urged.

She leaned back and the weight of the tank pulled her over. The warm water churned round her in an explosion of bubbles and refracted silvery light, and then she was at the surface, floating calmly amidst the wavelets she'd made, signalling to Desirée that she was OK.

'Hey!' Desirée gave her a great, broad grin, and Ella found herself smiling back. 'Not a lot wrong with your backward roll, girl! You ready to go down?'

'I think so, yeah. That was cool!'

'OK. Let's take it real easy, Ella. Remember to breathe slowly.'

Ella pressed her deflator valve. Very slowly, she felt the Blue Lagoon close over her head. She looked down. The bottom was only a few metres away. It was sandy, strewn with pebbles. She looked up. She could see sunlight dancing on the surface. A shoal of tiny, jewel-coloured fish went by, and she laughed. She looked at Desirée and made the OK signal with thumb and forefinger. Then she signalled that she wanted to go back up.

'What's the problem?' asked Desirée when they were buoyant on the surface. 'Ain't you comfortable, honey?'

'Oh, hell – yes! I just wanted to say – can I do the skills today?'

Desirée laughed. 'Hey! She's hooked!'

'Oh, Desirée – it's blissful down there! I saw fish!'

'Blissful? Phooey. There ain't much to see in the Blue Hole. You ain't seen nothing yet, Jacqueline Cousteau. Just wait till you dive a reef.'

Ella laughed again. She had stuck her regulator back in her mouth and was rapidly going through the pre-dive signalling sequence.

'Hey! Not so fast, honey!' Desirée was laughing too. 'You gotta wait for your old lady!'

*   *   *

She spent the next three days performing her training dives in open sea. After each of the tests, she and Desirée would tour the reefs together. They glided over caverns and precipices so vertiginous that Ella kept catching her breath, and had to remind herself of the first rule of scuba diving. *Never* hold your breath. She spiralled slowly downwards, feeling weightless and wonderful and – well – *watery*.

The reef was a revelation. She had never seen such extraordinary beauty. She saw shoals of spotty fish, stripy fish and neon fish. She bought a book on fishes of the Caribbean so that she could identify the creatures. She saw shy hamlets, indigo hamlets, butter hamlets. She saw fairy brasslets, flamefish, cardinalfish and trumpetfish. She saw angelfish and cherubfish and neon blue parrotfish kissing. She saw an aptly named rock beauty poised provocatively in her boudoir like an Amsterdam whore, wearing the prettiest makeup. A yellow base, blue lipstick to accentuate her pout, and blue eyeshadow to emphasize her *beaux yeux.*

The reef itself was like an underwater tapestry. It was as if someone had draped the most luxurious cashmere shawl they could find over the seabed and scattered it with soft cushions of coral. She could picture mer-princesses reclining on them. Some were embroidered in gold thread, some had been spangled with sequins, some gleamed with mother-of-pearl buttons, others with tortoiseshell. The fabrics were chenille and velvet and angora; the hues were purple, amber, red ochre, saffron, rose, moss green. Lainey Keogh would have been in seventh heaven!

The architect that had been employed to design the mer-kingdom had been a visionary. There were castles, turreted and castellated, there were gorgeous palaces, there were magnificent garden urns and mazes and statuary. The beauty of her surroundings made Ella feel like an alien intruding on the habitat of a superior species, but she thanked her lucky stars that she was a privileged alien, able to feast her eyes on all this sub-aquatic sumptuousness.

And it moved! Little shrubs decorated like Christmas trees swayed to the rhythm of the ebb and flow, and intricate lace fans undulated alongside silken fronds and ostrich-feather plumes and tendrils of mermaids' hair. The mer-princesses had plainly abandoned their kingdom at the first sign of human invasion, and they'd abandoned it in a hurry, knocking over jewel boxes and spilling gems onto the rich carpet. They'd been having a party. There were coral cups and exquisitely-wrought goblets strewn around. She'd seen goblets like that once in an expensive craft shop in Temple Bar. Temple Bar! How far away that place seemed now, and how pedestrian!

'Let's look for starfish,' Desirée suggested one day, writing on her underwater slate. They searched under rocks on the seabed for the creatures, and Ella thought how bananas it was that underwater she could heft around weighty-looking rocks with ease, while on the surface she could barely manage her own tank. Desirée found the first starfish, and passed it to Ella, who watched the delicate creature glide across her palm with laugh-out-loud delight. She had found her gills at last, and was so reluctant to return to the real world that she wanted to swim away and hide in the reef every time Desirée made the signal to ascend.

She had a problem once only. As part of her training she was required to take her mask off underwater, and put it back on again. Without a mask it was impossible to see anything with any degree of clarity, and she found herself disorientated again. Her breathing was verging on hyperventilation when she struggled, panicking, to the surface with Desirée following. It was an action replay of the dive she'd performed in Sheep's Head Bay. Desirée calmed her, then they descended and tried again. Again Ella panicked and bolted for the surface. 'I'll try it one more time,' she said. 'But if I can't hack it, I'm aborting the dive.' It would break her heart if she had to abort. She knew that if she did, she would never certify, and she would never be able to dive again. She'd be like an addict denied a drug.

'Do it, honey,' said Desirée, 'and I will ask Otis to invent a cocktail specially for you.'

'What? Who's Otis?'

'Otis is the head barman in Salamander Cove Villas. He dreams up special cocktails for special people. So some evening before you go, you and I are going to celebrate, Ella. With a cocktail named after you. All right?'

'That's a lovely idea, Desirée,' said Ella, giving a self-deprecatory shrug as she strapped her mask back on. 'But you could hardly call me special.'

'Anyone who overcomes a fear is special, Ella. You did it in the Blue Lagoon. You can do it again. Now. Tell me when you're ready to go down again.'

Ella stuck her regulator in her mouth, took a couple of deep breaths and forced herself to relax. She looked at Desirée, registered the reassurance in her eyes, and then made the OK signal. This time when she hit the bottom the mask was off, on again, and cleared of water before she could allow herself to think about what she was doing. Dive deep, dive hard, she thought. Fear nothing. Desirée clapped her hands and then scribbled something on her slate. *I can tell you are a fighter!* read Ella, and she laughed. She laughed with relief and pride and pure euphoria. She remembered what PJ had said all those weeks ago on her very first training session. He'd told her she'd be doing a lot of laughing underwater. He'd been right.

Later, back on dry land, Desirée signed her logbook for her, and stamped it.

'Congratulations,' she said, handing it over to Ella and giving her a big kiss on the cheek. 'You are now a certified open water diver, Ella Nesbit. And you've earned that cocktail.'

'Wow,' said Ella. 'It's hard to believe. I honestly thought I'd never do it.'

'You're persistent. That's how you did it.'

'Yeah,' said Ella, with a rueful laugh. 'That's how I lost my last boyfriend. He told me I was a stubborn bitch.'

Desirée smiled. '"You don't give up easily" is a nicer way of putting it.'

*   *   *

Later that afternoon she took her logbook down to the poolside so she could enter her dive. PJ had told her how important it was to keep a log, but she was getting lazy and her descriptions were becoming less and less detailed. She had just finished scribbling in 'Marine life: the usual stunning suspects' when a shadow fell across the page. She looked up to see Sophie Burke. 'Hi,' said the actress, commencing her daily striptease ritual.

'Oh – hi.'

Sophie discarded her sarong as if it was the seventh veil in the dance, and then stretched out on the sun-lounger beside Ella. You could almost hear the collective male groan. 'Diving again, were you?' she asked, sliding what looked like a film script out of her beach bag.

'Mm.'

'All that salt water won't do your skin any favours, Ella. Look how chapped your hands are compared to mine.'

Ella looked down at her hands. Sophie was right. They were dry and chafed, and she'd broken a couple of nails while assembling her gear. 'I'll worry about that when I get home,' she said. 'Anyway – I think I'll only dive on alternate days from now on. Now my training's out of the way I can take some time out to explore the island.'

'Drop by my villa later. I'll let you have some hand cream.'

'Thanks.' Ella reached for her Lonely Planet guide. 'D'you fancy hiring a cab and heading off somewhere tomorrow, Sophie? I'd hate to stay cooped up in this resort for the entire duration of the holiday, and Leonie wouldn't be able for the more strenuous stuff.'

Sophie looked suspicious. 'What did you have in mind?'

'Well, there's masses to do.' Ella leafed through the pages. 'We could go hiking, or rafting or canoeing. Or bicycling in the Blue Mountains – and I think I saw paragliding mentioned somewhere . . .' She trailed off as she registered the blank expression on Sophie's face. It was obvious she was wasting her breath.

'Paragliding? Eeyoo. I don't *think* so.'

'Well, maybe we could opt for something more cultural, then? There's a walking tour of Port Antonio. We could visit the craft market afterwards.'

'Ella?' Sophie swiped her sunglasses away from her face and looked at Ella with a pitying expression. 'I didn't come here for an *adventure* holiday. I came here to escape from the stresses and strains of my career. Because I am very much in demand as an actress, my life is fraught with responsibilities and decision making. Which script?' She held up a spiral-bound volume and started fanning herself with it. 'Which agent? Which charity? Even here I cannot escape. I sign dozens of autographs every day. I do not resent it, because I have a duty to my public. But sometimes it seems to me that there is nowhere on this planet where I can bask in blissful anonymity. This –' she indicated the pool, the beach, the kaleidoscopic gardens with an expansive gesture '– is as good as it gets. But still I feel eyes staring at me from behind all those dark glasses.'

Ella looked perplexed. What had she done to invite this discourse? Sophie sounded as if she was rehearsing lines from the film script she was wielding. 'I only suggested that we maybe hire a taxi and—'

'Ella.' Sophie placed a perfectly manicured index finger on her glossy lips. 'I am here to *chill.* I am here to relax by the pool, have massages and facials, maybe take a modicum of exercise in the gym or play a little tennis. I am under doctor's orders to take it easy. I cannot be hurtling through mountains on a bicycle, or slashing my way through rain forests. I have no intention of venturing into the ghettos of Port Antonio and running the risk of being mugged or raped. *Capisci?*'

The actress bestowed a patronizing smile on Ella, and Ella shrugged. 'OK. I just think it's an awful waste to travel all the way to another country and not see any of the local colour, that's all.' It had been stupid of her to try and interest Sophie in an excursion. She might have known that the starlet's interest in this tropical island paradise wouldn't extend beyond the parameters of their exclusive resort. She looked down at the picture of a smiling Rasta in her Lonely Planet. Hell's bells. She *couldn't* spend all her time in Jamaica surrounded by European faces! Maybe she could cajole Leonie into visiting some of the sights with her? But she knew now that paragliding and cycling would be out of the question.

Sophie had cast aside her film script with a dismissive 'pah!' and had started to leaf through *OK!* magazine instead. Ella was now beginning to bitterly regret the charitable impulse that had made her take pity on the actress at the airport. She wished she'd had the good sense to pretend that she was German.

'Oh, look!' said Sophie with a pleased smile. 'Hasn't Jodie Kidd got enormous! She's put on at least half a stone since I last saw her. At the BAFTAs, I think it was.' She turned another page. 'Eeyoo. I don't think much of the Spring collections, do you?' – flashing a glossy photograph at Ella and resuming her commentary without waiting for a response. 'That dirndl shape is *sooo* unflattering, isn't it? Even I couldn't carry it off. Oh look – somebody else I know!' She looked at Ella, plainly waiting to be asked Who?

'Who?' obliged Ella dully.

'Rory McDonagh. I knew him before he became a Hollywood big shot, you know.'

'Oh?' Ella perked up a bit. Rory McDonagh was an actor she'd always liked. There was something of the maverick about him. 'What's he like?'

'Well, he's quite a private individual, so there's not a lot to tell.'

'He married that actress who used to be in that soap opera that was axed, didn't he? What was the name of that soap?'

'*Ardmore Grove.* I was in that as well, you know.'
Sophie sounded vexed that Ella hadn't remembered. 'And yes, Rory did marry that actress. Her
name was Deirdre O'Dare.' She looked pensive for
a minute and then she said: 'Poor Deirdre. She
didn't have any success at all as an actress after she
left the "soap", as you call it. I prefer to use the term
"urban drama."' She gave Ella a sweet smile, and
then continued: 'Not like me. My career went into
the ascendant when *I* left. Now Deirdre's having
babies! Ha ha ha! What a joke. She once said she'd
never settle down.'

'I wouldn't mind settling down and making
babies with someone like Rory McDonagh.'

'He's not that good in bed, actually,' said Sophie,
and then her eyes went very wide and her hands
shot to her mouth. 'Oh! How indiscreet of me!
Forget I ever said that, Ella, will you?' She turned
imploring eyes on Ella.

'Sure,' said Ella. She really wasn't interested in
Sophie Burke's sex life.

But Sophie obviously was, because she continued
to fill Ella in, keeping her eyes demurely downcast.
'It was before I met Ben, of course. When I met Ben
he just swept me off my feet, and I had to let Rory
down. It was awful. He begged me to stay, but Ben
and I just had this incredible instant rapport – do
you know what I mean? It was – quite simply – love
at first sight.'

'Mm.'

'Then poor Rory went off and married Deirdre

170

on the rebound,' concluded Sophie happily. Suddenly she gave a little scream. 'Oh my God!' she said, clapping her hands to her mouth.

'What is it?' asked Ella.

'It's Eva Lavery!'

'The film star? In *OK!* magazine?'

'No. In real life – over there! Look!' Sophie had sat bolt upright, and was pointing to a blonde woman and a dark-haired man, who were strolling along the path that bordered the lawn. 'Oh my God! Eva! Eva!' Sophie grabbed her sarong, got up and teetered across the esplanade on her high heels, clutching her enormous sunhat to her head, and practically pratfalling in her desperation to reach Eva Lavery and her companion. The heads of all the men on the poolside turned to follow her progress, eyes glued to her jiggling breasts as she ineffectually attempted to wrap the sarong around her.

The couple stopped and turned towards Sophie, and Ella could see them exchange glances as the actress bore down upon them. They stood stoically while she showered them with air-kisses and then regaled them with a non-stop torrent of words, all the time gesticulating theatrically. Ella resisted the impulse to applaud. She felt as if she was watching a one-woman show.

She studied Eva as Sophie prattled on. Eva Lavery in her late forties was more beautiful than most women are in their prime. Ella had seen the actress in loads of films, but she looked different off screen. On screen she was a chameleon, famous for being able to change her look for each movie she made. Today her golden skin was devoid of makeup, her blond hair was piled messily on her head and her feet were bare. She was wearing tiny silver earrings and a very simply-cut long cotton dress splashed with flowers. The only thing remotely film-starrish about her were her sunglasses.

After about two minutes of chat, Sophie allowed her victims to beat a retreat, and then she tottered back across the grass, and collapsed onto her sun-lounger. 'Isn't that the most amazing coincidence!' she gasped. 'That was Eva Lavery, the film star and David Lawless her husband, the famous director! Gorgeous, isn't he? I've known them for the longest time, ever since I turned professional! The first show I ever did was for David Lawless – it was *A Midsummer Night's Dream* in the Phoenix theatre – Rory MacDonagh was in it as well!'

Ella murmured something polite, but Sophie wasn't listening.

'Goodness! How *wonderful* to have run into them!' Sophie's exclamation marks were even more irritating than usual. 'They're staying around the corner, in a villa near the Blue Lagoon. David's here to discuss some project he's working on with a famous producer – I'm not allowed to say who – that's top secret!' Sophie turned a radiant smile on Ella, as if she was bestowing on her the most magnificent gift on the face of the planet. 'Would you like to meet Eva?' she asked, magnanimously. 'I'm joining her at the bar for a drink.'

Actually, Ella would, quite. She really admired Eva Lavery's work. 'That would be nice,' she said.

They meandered down to the bar on the beach. At least, Ella meandered. Sophie made a beeline towards where Eva was sitting on a stool sipping Planter's Punch. Her husband was at an umbrella-topped table on the terrace, engrossed in conversation with some dripping-with-gold type.

'Ella Nesbit – this is Eva Lavery. Eva, Ella,' pronounced Sophie when she joined them.

'Hello, Ella,' said Eva in honey tones. 'Pleased to meet you.' She actually made the clichéd greeting sound genuine.

'Likewise,' said Ella. 'I'm a fan. I loved your last movie – I went to see it twice.'

'Well, thanks!'

'My friends will be dead jealous when I get back to Dublin and tell them that I stayed in a joint frequented by celebrities!'

'Hey! You're from Dublin? I thought I recognized the accent.'

Ella smiled. 'It's a giveaway, isn't it?'

'Mine isn't,' said Sophie, in polished mid-Atlantic.

Ella noticed the corner of Eva's mouth twitch, and decided she was going to like this woman.

'Let's see,' resumed Eva in a speculative voice. 'Your accent's somewhere south of the Liffey – but not as far south as Dun Laoghaire.'

'Right first time. I'm from Portobello.'

'Hey! I used to live there! In Pleasants Street.'

'Then I lived just around the corner from you. In Grantham Street.'

'Hang about. Grantham Street? Wasn't there another Nesbit there? I seem to remember that Declan Nesbit from Celtic Note had a house in Grantham Street.'

Ella laughed. 'He still does, but he's hardly ever there. He's my dad.'

'No shit!' Eva threw back her head and crowed. She had one of the most full-bodied laughs Ella had ever heard. 'Dear God, but it's a small world!'

'What d'you mean?' asked Sophie.

Eva's expression changed suddenly. She wore the look of a guilty pussycat. 'Oh, it's just I – er – knew him, back in the early eighties some time . . .' Her voice had a rather contrived vagueness about it.

Ella smiled. 'You knew my dad?'

'Um. Yeah.'

Ella's smile grew broader. She suspected from the way Eva was demurring that they'd had an affair. Her father had gone through the eighties and early nineties having a string of affairs with gorgeous women all over the world, before he'd settled down with his current wife, an Alaskan Innuit. 'Did you – um – know him well?'

'Mm. Afraid so.' Eva smiled back, acknowledging that further prevarication was pointless. 'He

174

was pretty bloody irresistible, your dad. I imagine he still is.'

'He is,' conceded Ella. 'But he's on the straight and narrow now. In fact, he's going to present me with a baby brother or sister early next year.'

'Wow. And we were of the generation who thought we would never settle down.' Eva leaned over and shook Ella's hand. 'Well, neighbour,' she said. 'What'll you have to drink?'

'I'll have what you're having, thank you.'

'Sophie?'

'I'll just have a mineral water, thanks.' Sophie sounded virtuous. 'How long are you staying, by the way?' she asked as Eva signalled to the barman.

'We're flying out late tomorrow night.'

'Oh, no! What a shame!' An expression of devastation ravished Sophie's beautiful face. 'We could have hung out together, Eva. Visited a few beaches. *Discovered* Jamaica.'

Ella's jaw dropped.

'I've done loads of jaunts since I've been here,' said Eva. 'I discovered a wonderful guide. He knows everything there is to know about the island.'

'Look – if you're leaving tomorrow, why don't you have dinner with us tonight?' suggested Sophie. 'The Pavilion restaurant here is wonderful.'

Ella's jaw hit the deck. Sophie had done nothing but moan about how mediocre the Salamander Cove cuisine was since they'd arrived.

'No thanks, Sophie,' said Eva. 'We're going out

175

to dinner this evening. We've arranged to meet someone in the Blue Lagoon restaurant at eight o'clock.'

'Oh.' Sophie couldn't hide her disappointment. She let a little hiatus dangle in the conversation, waiting for Eva to suggest that she join her and David for dinner at the Blue Lagoon, but no such invitation materialized.

Then: 'How about meeting up tomorrow?' suggested Eva. 'David's got an appointment to see some backer. He'll be stuck in discussion for hours, and I'll die of boredom if I have to hang around that villa all day. I'd love to visit Navy Island.'

Ella cheered inwardly. At last she had a chance to escape from the luxury compound! 'Yes! I'm on for that!' she said.

'Navy Island?' said Sophie. 'Where's that?'

'Just off the coast at Port Antonio. You take the ferry. There are beaches, and some lovely walks, apparently. A good reef, too, for snorkelling. And you can visit Errol Flynn's mansion.'

'I don't have a snorkel,' said Sophie. 'But I'd love to see the mansion.'

'OK. It's a date.' Over on the terrace Ella could see David Lawless getting to his feet and shaking hands with his colleague. Eva waved at him, and then slid off her barstool. 'Say I pick you up here at around ten o'clock tomorrow morning?'

'Ten's cool. Thanks, Eva,' said Ella.

The actress started to walk across the sand towards her husband, and then she paused. 'Oh – by the way,' she called back to them. 'Remember to wear sensible shoes.'

'Sensible *shoes*?' said Sophie Burke.

Chapter Seven

The next morning Ella and Sophie waited in reception for Eva to arrive. Sophie seemed to have more outfits than Barbie. Today she was wearing a kind of Jemima Khan flowing white embroidered tunic and the most sensible shoes she had: a pair of barely there flat Jimmy Choo sandals with criss-cross leather thongs. Ella had filled a backpack with the usual day tripper's paraphernalia and was wearing gingham shorts and a T-shirt over her bikini.

'Are you going to swim off the island?' asked Sophie.

'Sure. There are three good beaches, according to the Lonely Planet guide.'

'I hate swimming in the sea,' said Sophie. 'I only ever swim in pools.'

Ella was swotting up about Navy Island in the Lonely Planet. 'It says here that one of them's a nudist beach.'

'Really?' said Sophie, brightening. 'Maybe we should go there. It would be nice to go home with an all-over tan.'

'I thought you said you didn't want to get a tan?' said Ella.

Sophie looked vague. 'Oh – I wouldn't mind just a touch of colour, you know. It lets people know you've been away somewhere exotic.'

Ella suspected that Sophie was rather more intent on showing off the amazing physical symmetry that had all the male residents of Salamader Cove agog every time she unknotted her sarong.

'Miz Nesbit? Miz Burke?' A low voice came from behind her.

Ella turned round and gave a little 'oh!' of surprise. There, standing at the reception desk, was Raphael, Desirée's partner. She hadn't seen him since her first day in the resort.

'Raphael! Hi!' she said.

He gave her his wonderful smile. 'Glad to see you again, Ella.'

'Hey! Glad to see you, also!'

'I'm driving you today. I'm Miz Lavery's guide.' He leaned against the desk, pushing back his heavy dreadlocks, and for the first time Ella noticed the sickle moon of a scar etched in silver on his cheekbone. It did nothing to diminish his beauty. 'Desirée tells me you got certified?'

'Yeah. I'm a total convert.'

'I knew she'd see you right. My old lady's the best teacher in the business.' Raphael turned his attention to Sophie. 'Are you Miz Burke?'

'That's right. Is the car out front?'

He gave Sophie a look of narrow-eyed assessment, and then he gave a slow nod. 'Yes, ma'am.'

There was nothing remotely servile about the 'ma'am'. 'Follow me.'

A gleaming Lexus was waiting under the *porte-cochère*. Eva was sitting in the leather-upholstered front seat, looking like the cat that got the cream. 'Isn't he *gorgeous*?' she mouthed at Ella as she slid into the back seat, and Ella gave an appreciative smile back.

'Nice car,' said Sophie. 'It'll make a change from that bloody awful bus that brought us here.'

Today Eva was wearing baggy cotton trousers, flip-flops, a T-shirt and sunglasses. There were diamonds cascading from her earlobes. Sophie's gimlet eyes assessed them at once.

'Eva?' she said. 'I'm not sure it's a good idea to wear real diamonds into Port Antonio.'

'Goodness, Sophie – you're absolutely right. How inconsiderate of me to flaunt my good fortune in the face of poverty.' She unhooked the diamonds and flung them into glove compartment.

'I was thinking more along the lines of being a target for mugging,' said Sophie, fastening her seat-belt as the car took off down the driveway. 'But, er – do you think the glove compartment's a safe place for them?'

'Right again.' Eva retrieved the jewels and handed them to Raphael. 'Will you look after them for me?' she said. The look on Sophie's face when she saw Eva pass her driver a small fortune in diamonds was so appalled it was comical.

'No problem,' said Raphael, sliding the earrings into his pocket.

Ella took the opportunity to study him further as he drove. His eyes slanted upwards at the corner, his cheekbones were razorshell sharp, and when he laughed – which was frequently – he showed the tip of a tongue like red satin. Eva flirted shamelessly with him, and the appalled look on Sophie's face intensified.

When Eva turned to them and said, 'Wonderful country, isn't it?' Ella felt guilty. She'd been so transfixed by the vision that was Raphael that she'd barely clocked the scenery.

Jamaica was dazzling. She found it hard to believe that there were only forty shades of green in the spectrum – this place was greener than Ireland on St Patrick's Day. They drove through countryside dense with trees dripping moss and looped with vines. They passed coconut groves and orderly plantations of broad-leaved banana trees. They passed colonial-style palatial homes like giant wedding cakes, and small villa-style houses so neat and dainty they looked as if they were prinking themselves in proud testament to pernickety housekeeping. They passed garages that looked like relics from the fifties, with pump attendants gyrating to blasting reggae on the forecourts, and stalls selling everything from jerk pork to frocks to raffia baskets.

Some of the townships they drove through were more rundown than others. There were shacks so wretched it was difficult to imagine how people lived in them. These were patchwork houses of haphazard construction, with roofs of corrugated iron. Goats bleated and chickens scratched around in the dusty growth by the side of the road. Most of the shacks were painted in vibrant colours – cerulean blue or hibiscus-blossom pink – and decorated with jewel-like patterns, but much of the paintwork was washed out and peeling, and Ella was appalled to find herself contemplating how picturesque poverty could be.

Port Antonio was crammed with people and bicycles and parping beat-up cars, and when they emerged from the car in the ferry car park Sophie was the instant target for appreciative remarks and graphic gestures. Luckily there was a ferry waiting, because the remarks were becoming more and more voluble, with lots of references to 'rasses' and 'battys', and Sophie was looking more and more tight-lipped.

'They're not abusing you, Sophie,' said Eva mildly as they boarded the ferry. 'They're complimenting you. They think you've got a great ass.'

'Pardon me, Eva, but I don't consider being called a "yum-yum tart" much of a compliment,' said Sophie, bristling.

The ferry ride was short. Ella took out her camera and snapped views. Then she snapped Eva and Sophie and the ferryman, and finally she snapped Raphael. 'Do you mind?' she asked, and he shook his head slowly and gave her that heart-stopping smile again. She actually found herself blushing as she smiled back. There was something about his eyes – something *unfathomable*. It felt as if he was looking into her soul.

On the island, he left them on the jetty and went into the waterfront hotel to check out the refreshment situation. There was no-one else around.

Ella sat down on the grass and watched him go. He had the familiar Jamaican gait she found so attractive, but for the first time she noticed that he walked with a barely perceptible limp. 'What a beautiful man he is!' she observed.

'Mm. Isn't he devastating?' Eva produced a bunch of bananas from her bag and handed them round. Sophie shook her head. She had divested herself of her Jemima Khan robe, and was spreading out a towel so that she could sunbathe. Ella noticed that she kept her top on. She'd obviously received enough compliments for one day. 'I'm genetically predisposed to fancy the pants off attractive men,' resumed Eva. 'David's forever telling me off for flirting with the riggers on location. Flirting is as far as it goes, I hasten to add. I have all the man I need at home.'

'I can't say I'm really into dreadlocks,' said Sophie. 'I always imagine they must be alive with all kinds of unpleasant creatures. And he's spoken for, anyway. I saw him wrapped around a rather strange-looking woman yesterday.'

'That's Desirée, his missus,' said Eva. 'She's a real dynamo. We had both of them round for dinner the other evening.'

'Did you?' said Ella. 'I know her. She's my dive instructor.'

'Hey! You dive?'

'Yeah,' said Ella, feeling inordinately proud to be able to answer in the affirmative at last.

'Oh, wow!' breathed Eva. 'You totally lucky thing! I've always wanted to scuba dive, but I've never done it.'

'Ow, that sun's hot.' Ella peeled off her shorts and T-shirt and took a bottle of water out of her bag. She took a long swig, and then passed the bottle to Eva.

Eva peered at her through her dark glasses. 'Ooh. Look at all your lovely freckles!'

'The sun brings them out. I hate them,' said Ella. 'I was called Freckle Face at school.'

'It's funny the way some people hate having them, isn't it? It's a bit like people with curly hair envying people with straight hair, and vice versa. I used to paint freckles all across my nose and cheekbones when I was a teenager.' She screwed the lid back on the bottle of water and handed it back to Ella. 'How long have you been scuba diving?'

'I only just certified. You should give it a go, Eva. It's amazing.'

'I tried to once, but I failed my medical. Like Raphael, I'm not allowed to dive, on doctor's orders.'

'Oh?' Sophie's eyes gleamed as if she'd just found a gold nugget. 'Why's that?'

'None of your business,' returned Eva amiably.

'Raphael failed his scuba medical?' Ella was

184

surprised. He seemed such a prime specimen of physical rude health.

'No. But he's been precluded from diving ever since he got the bends. It's a pretty tragic story.'

'The bends? Hell. It must have been a really bad case if he can't dive any more?'

'It was. According to Desirée he underwent months of treatment before the doctors put the final kibosh on his career.'

'He was a pro?'

'Yes. Top level.'

'A master instructor?' That explained the scar. 'Wow. And he doesn't dive at all now?'

'Absolutely not. He won't ever dive again.' Eva carefully wrapped her banana skin in a paper bag and then lobbed it into her beach bag. 'Desirée told me he was completely, utterly floored when he heard the news.'

'Oh, God – how awful!' said Ella. 'How did the accident happen?'

'I'm not sure. During some deep dive, I think. He wasn't at fault, though. The outfit responsible forked out a lot in compensation.'

'Still. It's terribly sad that he won't ever dive again.'

'Yes, it *is* sad. He turned his back on diving completely after that, apparently. He even left the running of the shop – which he had originally been responsible for setting up – to Desirée.'

'But he didn't have to do that! Couldn't he have carried on working as an instructor in the classroom? There's loads of academic stuff involved in scuba.'

'Think about it, Ella. If you were as passionate about something as Raphael was about diving, how would you feel if you could only sit back and watch from the sidelines?'

'Oh – I agree absolutely!' said Sophie earnestly. 'If I had to stop acting, I'd never set foot in a theatre again!'

Ella looked pensive. 'So. What made him decide to become a guide?' she asked.

'He'd earned a living through learning all there was to learn about his underwater habitat. So when his career as a diver was scuppered, he decided to earn a living through learning all there was to learn about his terrestrial habitat. He knows Jamaica inside out.'

'He can't earn that good a living as a guide,' sniffed Sophie.

'You saw the car.'

'The Lexus?'

'Yes.'

'It's his?' Sophie looked sceptical.

'Yes. He didn't want to be dependent on anyone else for work. So when his compensation money came through, he sank a load of it in the car.'

'It's funny,' said Ella. 'He's obviously been through the emotional mill, but you wouldn't think so to look at him. There's something incredibly – *serene* about him.'

'The spirit of Jah shines out of his eyes. He's a Rastafarian, after all.'

'Pity about the dreadlocks. But, yes,' Sophie conceded, 'he does have lovely eyes. Kind of soulful.'

'I'd have soulful eyes too if I lived in the most laid-back marijuana-producing country in the world.' Eva took a tube of suncream out of her bag and shimmied out of her trousers and T-shirt. Underneath she wore a plain black bikini. 'Be a doll and do my back, Ella, will you?'

'Sure.' The actress was still in pretty good nick for a woman her age, thought Ella, as she drizzled cream down her spine.

Sophie was sending them sideways looks. 'Have you managed to get in a workout since you've been here, Eva?' she asked.

Eva looked blank. 'A workout? You mean a gym kind of workout?'

'Mm-hm.'

'Good God, no. That's my idea of hell.'

'How do you manage to stay in shape, then?'

'Lots of rampant sex, of course, darling. Do you want me to do you, Ella?'

'Please.'

Eva took the tube from her, and started on Ella's back. 'What's the tattoo?' she asked. Ella had had a bar of music tattooed onto her shoulder blade in her first year in college, and had regretted it ever since.

'It's – um – the first bar of Beethoven's Seventh,' she said. 'The slow movement.'

'One of my favourite pieces.' Eva slapped the last of the cream onto Ella's back. 'D'you need some, Sophie?'

'No thanks. I plastered myself with factor 30 before I left the villa.'

Eva lay back on the jetty and looked up at the sky. There was a vapour trail wisping across it. 'Hell. I wish I could stay here for ever, and not have to take that flight back to real life tonight,' she said.

'What's real life got in store for you?' asked Ella.

'A film première, unfortunately.'

'Oh? Which one?' asked Sophie.

Ella kicked off her espadrilles and sat down on the edge of the jetty, eating the banana Eva had given her and kicking up little spatters of water with her toes. What did real life have in store for *her* when it was time to re-enter? Nothing as exciting as a film première, that was for sure. But at least she'd be off the Nesbit & Noonan reception desk. Beside her, Sophie prattled on in film talk, which was punctuated by the occasional 'mm' or half-hearted 'really' from Eva. It was getting hotter. Gradually a drowsy silence descended.

'*Mesdames.*' Ella blinked and looked up. Raphael was standing on the path that led from the jetty to the hotel. His back was to the sun, giving his dread-locks the appearance of a burnished nimbus. 'I have arranged for beer to be brought to you on the beach in around one hour.' Angel Raphael.

188

'*Beer?*' said Sophie, as if she'd never heard of the stuff. 'Haven't you any white wine? I'd really prefer a chilled Chablis.'

'Oh come on, Sophie,' said Eva. 'This isn't a chilled-Chablis-on-the-beach kind of place. Let's go for the Red Stripe option.'

'Oh, OK,' said Sophie, a touch ungraciously. 'When in Rome and all that jazz rules, I suppose.' She looked around her. 'Whereabouts on the island is Errol Flynn's mansion, by the way?' she asked.

'That's Errol Flynn's house,' said Raphael, nodding his head at the timberbuilt hotel. 'You gonna eat there later.'

'Sorry?' said Sophie. 'Did you say *that* was Errol Flynn's *mansion*?'

'Sure. One of them. That man owned a lot of property on Jamaica.'

'Ee-*yoo*,' said Sophie contemptuously. 'Call that a mansion? You'd think he might have built something a bit more luxurious than *that* kip.'

Raphael just smiled at her. Then he turned his attention to Eva. 'OK. I tell you the best way.' He pointed to a track that led along the tree-dense coast. 'You go there. That path takes you right round the island.'

'Aren't you coming?' Ella remembered what she'd been told about white women on their own being vulnerable.

He looked at her with toasted almond eyes. 'You safe here, Ella. Ain't no-one on this island I don't know. And you are the first visitors here today. You

189

will be taken good care of. There will be someone waiting on the beach for you with beer and coconuts.'

'But *you're* our guide!' protested Sophie.

'Lady. I have a friend here who works in the hotel. I ain't seen him for a long time. I will stay here, talk with my friend, then I will bring you back to the resort when you are ready.'

'It's cool,' said Eva, in response to Sophie's mutinous look. 'Raphael and I talked about this earlier. We're perfectly safe, and there's no point in him wasting his time trailing round the island after us if he's got something better to do.'

'It's a small island,' said Raphael. 'You gonna end up on a beach on the west side, near here. Or maybe you want to go to nudist beach?'

'Good God, no,' said Eva, pulling on her trousers. 'Are you out of your mind – at my age? I'm not into strutting my stark naked saggy stuff in front of a load of nubile young things.'

Raphael looked her up and down and laughed. 'You look in pretty good shape to me, Eva,' he said.

'Thank you, darling.' Eva gave him her wickedest smile and slung her beach bag over her shoulder. 'We'll see you back here later. You'll join us for something to eat?'

'Sure.'

Sophie was still looking doubtful. 'I'm still not convinced we'll be all right on our own,' she said.

'Trust me,' said Raphael. And then he turned and strolled back into the hotel.

Ella shucked into her shorts and Sophie swathed herself in Jemima Khan, and they set off up the path Raphael had indicated, with Sophie bringing up the rear. She looked like something from a fashion shoot in her flowing white garb, which kept getting caught on foliage, and she was soon 'tching' noisily. 'Have you noticed,' she said, 'that this path is getting muckier and muckier? The hem of my garment is bogging with mud, and my Jimmy Choos are going to be ruined.'

'Jimmy Choos? I told you to wear sensible shoes,' Eva reminded her.

'These *are* sensible. They're the only ones I have that don't have heels.'

'Take 'em off,' suggested Ella.

'And have this swamp oozing between my toes? No thanks,' said Sophie.

'Actually, that sounds good,' said Eva. 'I love the idea of mud oozing between my toes.' She kicked off her flip-flops and hooked her finger through the straps. 'Ooh – *wow*!' she said. 'It's heavenly.'

Ella took off her espadrilles and wriggled her toes. 'Hey! So it is! Oh – go on, Sophie – have a go.'

'Are you out of your mind?' said Sophie. 'That mud is probably crawling with poisonous insects.'

The path got narrower and narrower the higher they went – and Sophie had been right about one thing. It was getting muckier, too. They were ankle deep now, and at times it was like negotiating a swamp. Ella and Eva had to keep waiting for Sophie to pick her way round on any dry bits she could find, which were becoming increasingly scarce. At one stage Eva fell on her arse. Ella went to help her up, and felt a flash of panic when the actress bent double, but a peal of laughter reassured her that Eva was doubled up with laughter, not agony.

'Oh, God, look at my bum!'

'Oh – Eva, that's awful,' said Sophie. 'What label are your trousers?'

'I dunno. I think I got them in Hennes,' said Eva indifferently.

They'd reached the top of a hill, and rhythmic seashore sounds drifted up to them. It was a steep descent all the way from now on.

'Oops,' said Eva. 'It's going to be tough doing this without suffering another pratfall.'

They inched their way down the slope, Sophie making occasional whimpering noises that featured the words 'Jimmy Choo' quite a lot. Suddenly she slipped backwards. Immediately she lunged forward to compensate, and without any warning whatsoever the lunge suddenly turned into a run, and Sophie was off, like an albino bat out of hell. Away she sped down the hill at full pelt, sending showers of mud spattering all over her white robe, obviously unable to stop or slow down. Ella and Eva stood and looked on in open-mouthed astonishment as Sophie hurtled downwards, her feet running away with her so fast that they became a blur of movement. Her arms were flailing, and her dress billowed out behind her like a parachute.

'The flight of the snowy egret,' remarked Ella,

and all at once the two women were laughing, clutching each other for balance. They couldn't prevent a loud hoot escaping when Sophie finally slipped and tobogganed onto the clearing below flat on her rear end. Gradually her trajectory slowed to a halt.

Ella and Eva sobered suddenly. Sophie's descent had been punctuated with 'oh-oh-ohs' of alarm, but nothing prepared them for the scream of terror that came reverberating back up the hill.

The pair descended rapidly, squelching as they went. When they emerged from the forest they found her sitting on the ground, frozen in an attitude of abject terror. 'What is it, Sophie?' asked Eva.

Sophie raised a trembling hand and pointed to something behind them. Ella turned to see a tall Rasta standing there. He had a machete in one hand and a stout stick in the other. 'Oh my God!' said Sophie in a croaky voice, clutching her throat. 'Oh my God!'

The Rasta looked perplexed. 'Everyt'ing irie?' he said, mildly. Then he grinned and indicated his machete. 'Hey! You ladies want coconut? I ready for you thirsty white ladies with coconuts.' He rattled the stick among the high branches of a nearby palm tree and a shower of coconuts descended. Then he slashed one open with the machete and handed it to Eva.

'Cool! Thanks!' said Eva, lifting the coconut to her lips and drinking long and thirstily.

'Good for drinking after long walk.' The Rasta

repeated the process for Ella and Sophie.

'No, thank you,' said Sophie, looking as if she'd just been offered a poisoned chalice. Her eyes wandered warily to the machete in his hand.

'Hey, lady! You no trust me?' said the Rasta. He laughed. 'Why you white lady not trust we Rastafarians? We gotta trust in one another, man. Trust and respect, they go hand in hand.'

He turned to Ella and proffered a high-five, which she automatically found herself returning. It was the first time she'd ever performed a high-five without feeling utterly ridiculous. How amazing, she thought as he went through the ritual with Eva, to land on a verdant island and be offered coconut milk to drink!

'How much?' asked Eva.

'Two hundred Jamaican dollar.'

'OK,' said Eva, dipping into her bag.

The Rasta looked shocked. 'Hey, lady – you don' wan higgle wit me?'

'Higgle, hell,' said Eva. 'I am a rich woman. If I get an opportunity to spread some of my money around, I'm glad to do it.'

The Rasta shook his head and laughed. 'You some lady,' he said. 'You damn bad higgler. But you damn pretty.' He took Eva's hand and shook it. 'Respect,' he added, as she handed over a wad of dollars. Then he gave her one last appreciative grin and loped off down the path.

'Ow!' Ella and Eva turned back to Sophie, who was now looking like a bedraggled snowy egret that

194

had been swept off course. 'What is it? Quickly, someone. On the back of my neck! Quick! Get it off! Get it *off*!'

Ella plucked a leaf away from where it had got caught in the hair on the nape of Sophie's neck. 'It's OK, Sophie,' she said. 'It's only a leaf.'

'You should have seen the look on your face when you spotted our friend, Sophie,' said Eva, draining her coconut. 'It was priceless. I should have taken a picture.'

'How was I supposed to know he was only felling coconuts?' replied Sophie indignantly. 'He looked like he'd just walked out of *The Blair* bloody *Witch Project* standing there with his machete and his cudgel. Oh *shit*!' This was said with great feeling.

'What's wrong now?'

'I broke a fingernail trying to grab onto passing branches.'

'Well, thank God there's a beauty parlour in the resort!'

'Too right,' agreed Sophie earnestly. Hell's bells! This woman had the worst case of irony deficiency Ella had ever encountered.

*   *   *

It would have been a perfect day, if it hadn't been for Sophie. She turned her nose up at the beer that was waiting for them when they hit the beach, she refused to swim, and she also refused to talk with the Rastas who were hanging there, convinced that their friendliness concealed sinister ulterior motives. Instead she plugged herself into Andrew Lloyd Webber on her CD player.

Some hours later, as they sat waiting for Raphael to join them in the restaurant of the waterfront hotel, Sophie announced that that was the last time she intended leaving the luxurious confines of Salamander Cove. 'I'm sorry,' she said. 'I just don't enjoy wading through swamps and being attacked by sandflies and mosquitoes. I came on holiday to enjoy being pampered a little, and that's the way it's going to be from now on.'

'What'll I do?' said Ella morosely, when Sophie was in the loo. 'I've no-one to explore Jamaica with. Although, come to think of it, Sophie's so completely uptight she's actually *worse* than no-one.'

'Mm. That coconut-felling Rasta was dead right, you know. There's not enough trust in the world. If Sophie trusted people more she might learn to relax a bit.' Eva stretched. 'Ow. I'm going to have very stiff muscles after that hike.'

'Maybe it wasn't such a good idea: going for a trek through a rain forest on the same day as you're flying.'

'What do you mean?'

'Well – trying to get comfortable in those sardine-can seats isn't going to be easy.'

'Oh – I'll sleep like a log, darling. That's the best thing about being able to afford first-class travel.'

Ella laughed. 'Of course you're going first class!

How daft of me even to imagine you in economy! Oh, Eva – I will miss you, you know. It's been fun today. I wish I'd run into you earlier in the holiday. We could have gone on loads of jaunts.'

'What about your grandmother? Couldn't you get her to go places with you? She sounds like a pretty laid-back individual.'

'Since she discovered Dieter and his villa, she's not too keen on leaving the resort either. I can't say I blame her. They're so into each other that I'm starting to feel like a total gooseberry.'

The waiter arrived with their beers, and they moved to a table on the balcony overlooking the jetty. 'Oh, look,' said Eva. 'There's Raphael.'

She pointed to where Raphael was sitting on the small jetty that protruded into the bay. He sat cross-legged, very straight and very still, gazing out to sea.

'How beautiful he is, and how utterly serene,' remarked Eva in an admiring voice. 'I must get a photograph.' She rummaged in her bag, then upended it. A lot of junk spewed out, including a dog-eared *Rough Guide to Jamaica*, but no camera materialized. 'Shit,' said Eva. 'I must have left it on the beach. Lend me yours, Ella, will you? And be sure to send me a copy.'

As Eva snapped happily away, Sophie returned from the loo. 'Why's Eva using your camera?' she asked.

'She left hers on the beach,' said Ella. 'We'll have to go back for it.'

Sophie gave her an incredulous look. 'There's no point in doing *that*, Ella. One of those Rastas will have claimed it by now.'

On the jetty, Raphael had been joined by one of the youths from the beach. They exchanged a few words, and then Raphael turned and looked up at the hotel, shading his eyes against the sun. He located Eva on the balcony, and pointed at her. The two men high-fived each other, and then the newcomer turned and headed in the direction of the hotel. Eva's camera case was hanging from his shoulder.

'Hey! Thanks!' Eva leaned over the balcony and shouted down at him. 'You've saved me a journey back to the beach!'

'No problem!' returned the youth.

Sophie sat down stiffly and picked up a menu.

'What's everyone having?' asked Eva, doing the same.

'Oh, God,' said Sophie. 'More jerk food. My heart sinks every time I walk into the restaurant in the resort and look at the specials advertised on the blackboard. Jerk pork, jerk chicken, jerk beef. I can't wait to get home to some decent fresh fish.'

'Don't worry, Sophie,' said Ella in a jokey voice. 'Maybe we'll walk into the restaurant tonight to find the words Jerk Off on the blackboard.'

'Very funny, Ella,' said Sophie, shooting an unamused look at Eva, who had burst into paroxysms of laughter.

On the jetty below, Raphael had finished his

contemplation of the sea, and was strolling towards the hotel. He raised a hand at them in salute. There was something beneficent about the gesture.

'Hey, Ella!' exclaimed Eva. 'I know who you can explore Jamaica with! How stupid of me not to have thought of it earlier!'

'Who?' asked Ella.

'Hire Raphael, of course.'

*　　*　　*

And that's exactly what she did. For the rest of the holiday she alternated between one day exploring with Raphael, and the next diving with Desirée. By the end of the holiday she wasn't sure which of the two terrains she preferred – the world under the waves, or the world above. But she *was* sure about one thing. She had fallen head over heels in love with the island.

Chapter Eight

Every single time Raphael took her out, she had a blast. They did all the things she'd hoped to do, and more. He took her to a reggae bar, he took her body surfing on Long Beach, and he even took her to his cousin's birthday party. His aunt and uncle lived in a shantytown shack on a dirt road beyond the ghettos of Port Antonio, and although Raphael's cousin was only ten, it had been one of the most kicking parties she'd ever been to. She'd spent the whole night dancing to pounding reggae. She'd danced with children and with women and with old men who moved like demons. She'd been plied with birthday cake and sweets and ganja, and had flirted bigtime with the birthday girl's teenage brother. Hers had been the only white face there.

On the second-last day of her holiday, Raphael came to pick her up as usual.

'Where are we going today?' she asked, climbing into the front seat beside him.

'Reach Falls,' he said, sliding a cassette into the player. Mellow Marley thrummed out. 'And then I will take you to a beach that no tourist knows about. There is a good reef there.' He put the car into gear, raised a hand in farewell to the doorman, and they took off down the drive, scattering peacocks as they went.

Ella checked her bag. 'Shit. I left my snorkel in the villa,' she said. 'D'you mind going back for it?'

'Have you your mask?'

'Yes.'

'Then it's cool. You can borrow my snorkel. I seldom use it.'

Oh God. Ella remembered what Eva had told her about Raphael contracting the bends. She wondered if it even prevented him from snorkelling.

'I can dive without a snorkel,' he said. 'I got gills.'

Eva laughed. 'What?'

'I can hold my breath a long, long time.'

'Like how long?' asked Ella.

'Like three, four minutes.'

She opened her eyes very wide. 'Wow. You *do* have gills,' she remarked.

'I used to do a lot of free-diving. Still do, sometimes.'

'Free-dive? What's that?'

'Diving without scuba.'

It was the first time he had ever referred to his career as a diver. 'You must miss it tremendously, Raphael, do you?'

He turned his golden eyes on her. 'I have learned to accept what I must accept. When you have a gift you are grateful and full of praise. Jah gave me my gift. Jah gave me my gills. But Jah has the right to

201

take away that gift also. I will not question that right.'

They were passing through one of the more run-down townships now. Advertisements for Craven A cigarettes and Guinness, Red Stripe beer and over-proof rum were plastered on shop fronts with names so uncool they were cool. DR MUFFY'S NATURAL VITAMINS AND HERBS, SHAGGY'S PLACE, KOOL KAT KORNER and SIR PLUGGY'S JERK SHOP. WELCOME TO KATHY'S LITTLE BAR AND GROCERY, she read outside a shack that was festooned with bunches of exotic fruits. A woman wearing a pink taffeta dress straight out of the fifties and clutching a matching purse was waiting by a bus stop with two equally prinked little girls. They were obviously on their way to somewhere special. The woman stood tall and erect, and gazed at Ella with solemn eyes in a proud face as she glided by in the passenger seat of the Lexus, feeling shameful and inadequate. These people existed at subsistence level, struggling to put food on their tables. Raphael, with his business, was one of the luckier ones. But even in the face of crippling poverty these people managed to behave with more dignity than almost any other race on earth.

They swept past a timber church painted in blue and white, and crowned with a red corrugated iron roof. 'The Grace and Truth Temple,' she read out loud. 'Your churches have such beautiful names, Raphael! My local church is called St Sepulchre. No wonder I'm a heathen.'

'Grace and truth. That's what it's all about, man. Grace and truth. Peace. Unity. And love.' She realized he was looking at her again. *One love*, she heard, as a new Marley track slid over the speakers. 'One love,' he echoed. 'Do you know what that means, Ella?'

She smiled and gave a little shrug. 'One love? I suppose it means true love, doesn't it?'

'It can mean that, yeah. But for Jamaicans it also means "Unity". When we part with someone, that is what we tell them. One love.'

*   *   *

The graffiti in the dingy café at Reach Falls read 'Peace, Love, Unity – Strengthens'.

Ella was the only white person there. She hadn't felt self-conscious about this at Raphael's cousin's party, but now she did – especially when she stripped down to her bikini. Jamaican women hanging out on the rocks by the waterfall eyed her with suspicion, while the men's eyes were full of carnality they didn't bother to conceal. As she passed a group of geezers swigging Red Stripe, she heard a chorus of muttered patois. Raphael said something in patois back. His was the kind of tone you don't mess with, and the geezers shuffled a bit, and looked at her more furtively.

'I take you upriver,' said Raphael, obviously sensing her discomfort. 'There will be fewer people up there.' He took her backpack from her and they set off, away from the curious eyes that regarded her without friendliness and made her seethe with discomfort.

They made their way past the rushing waterfall that cascaded down over the rocks like a dense bridal veil, and waded upriver for about half a mile in crystal-clear water that was only ankle deep in some places, and deep enough for swimming in others. In those places where the water ran deep, Raphael carried her backpack on his head, in the way she'd observed Jamaicans walking on the roads carry bundles. There was no-one else around, and Ella started to feel more relaxed. It was utterly silent, apart from the gurgling of water and the occasional burst of unfamiliar birdsong from some exotic species of bird. The forest on either side was full of fauna and exotic flora, like something out of a Rousseau painting. There were fabulous insects, and dragonflies and beetles, and shrubs that were so thick with yellow butterflies they looked as if they were covered in fluttering blossoms. She was wandering through a terrestrial Paradise. But after twenty or more minutes of perfect tranquillity, Ella gradually became aware of men's voices drifting upstream. Soon she spotted three shapes in her peripheral vision. They were distinctly masculine shapes, and they were moving purposefully towards them.

With a flash of fear she realized that they were the men who'd muttered and laughed about her earlier. As they gained on her and Raphael, Ella started to feel very panicky indeed. If these men were after what she suspected they were after, one bloke on his own wasn't going to stop them. She could tell that Raphael was aware of the maleficent vibe, because as soon as the men got too close for comfort, he stopped.

'Go on upriver,' he instructed Ella. 'I gonna talk to these boys. These boys are makin' you nervous, Ella, and if you are feelin' nervous then I am not doin' my job right. You go up to the first deep pool you find, and you have a little swim around. Relax. I will follow you up when I done finish dealin' with these facety boys.'

'Are you sure?' asked Ella uncertainly. She knew the fear on her face was graphic.

'Trust me,' said Raphael. 'I will teach these boys respect.'

Ella turned and continued on shaky legs, trying to resist the temptation to look back. She stumbled occasionally on the pink and gold rocks that were strewn over the river-bed, and at one point found herself wading through a chest-deep fissure where the current ran so strong it was almost impossible to negotiate, but eventually she reached a calm green pool.

Now she allowed herself to look back. Raphael was standing thigh deep in the river. The men he was talking to were all bare-chested, and the water hit them around their midriffs. As Ella watched, one of them moved towards the bank. He turned in her direction and then he pulled his penis out of his swimming trunks and proceeded to urinate into the water, watching her as he did so. She turned away immediately. When she looked back again, very covertly, two of the men were heading off back down the river, and Raphael and the most powerful-looking of the three were exchanging an unsmiling high-five. Then the burly individual turned and followed his cronies back the way they'd come.

Silhouetted against the sparkling water Raphael watched them go, one hand on his hip. She remembered how he'd reminded her of a gunslinger the first time she'd met him. Now his stance had even more of an insouciant arrogance about it. Gunslinger, warrior prince, guardian angel – he was all of these. Finally he turned and made his way up to where Ella was floating in the pellucid water. He stood looking down at her, and she found it difficult to read the expression on his face because his back was to the sun. 'You OK?' he asked.

'Yeah.' She pushed her wet hair back from her face. 'What did you say to them that made them back off?'

'I made them see sweet reason, Ella. Those boys are wolves, but I know how to talk to wolves. I understand their language. How-ev-er,' he drawled the word, extending it into a kind of growl: 'maybe it is a good time to get out of here. I know a short cut that will take us back up to the road. Come with me. I am going to take you to the prettiest beach you ever saw.' He held out his hand and pulled her, dripping, from the water.

*   *   *

On their drive to the beach, they passed the same woman still waiting at the bus stop, still standing tall in her Sunday best. Ella wanted to weep for her, and Raphael told her not to.

'What good are your tears to her?'

She was about to suggest that she could offer money instead, but some wise instinct advised her against it. That would be possibly the ultimate sign of disrespect – the ultimate slur on her dignity: to be offered money she hadn't earned.

It wasn't a long drive. Ella sat up front with Raphael and helped him smoke a spliff. By the time they reached the beach she had a totally blissed-out smile on her face. There was no-one else there. This beach belonged exclusively to them, and it was Bounty Bar perfect. She and Raphael gazed out over talcum powder sand towards the sea. Golden, golden sand, thought Ella. Blue, blue sea. She remembered the blue-sky blue-sea picture in the holiday brochure she'd looked at all those weeks ago, and how she'd fantasized about being in that picture. The reality was even more fantastic.

The water was inviting them in with seductive whispery splashes.

'Let's swim,' said Raphael.

Ella took her last deep drag of pungent smoke, opened the door and floated out of the car. Quite suddenly they were chest deep in water that shimmered in dinky little wavelets to where it met the baby blue blanket of the sky. She had no idea how they'd got there.

'Are you some kind of a pooka?' she asked, laughing.

'A pooka? What do you mean by pooka?'

'A pooka's a kind of Irish genie. It wouldn't surprise me if you *were* one. This place is magic.'

They swam out about thirty metres until they reached the shallow reef. Then Raphael took Ella's hand and they dived. She could not believe how shockingly pale her hand was in his. The tan she had acquired since arriving in Jamaica seemed to have been washed away. She felt like a phantom, feather light and whiter than white. He turned to her underwater and gave her his blissful smile, and she smiled back, incredulity written all over her face.

His claim to have gills wasn't an arrogant one. Ella would let go of his hand any time she needed to surface for air, but he remained underwater for what seemed to her to be an eternity. Occasionally he would disappear from sight, and then she would look down and see him patrolling the reef like some sleek aquatic beast, or she'd look up and see him swimming above her, hands casually clasped together like a guardian angel at prayer, dreadlocks haloed round his head. At one point he took up an anemone from the seabed and split it. Myriad jewel-like fish came to feed on the flesh, and Ella clapped her hands and smiled too broadly. She found herself at the surface again, spitting water out of her snorkel.

Raphael surfaced beside her. 'Time to go,' he said, and the switch behind her smile clicked off. 'It gets dark fast, remember?'

Reluctantly she swam back to shore. She didn't want to go. This was the second-last evening of her holiday!

'Why so sad, Ella?' asked Raphael, when they hit the beach.

'I'm dreading going back.'

'You don't want to leave our country?'

'No. I don't. It's just so beautiful.'

'Yeah, man. That is what all the visitors say. Most of them say that they will return some day, and some of them do. A Dutch girl has come to live on the beach where I live. She is the only white person living there, but she has the soul of a Rastafarian. She gave up a good livelihood in Holland to come and live with us.'

'Where do you live, Raphael?'

'Me and Desirée's got a house on Hummingbird Beach, just round the headland from Salamander Cove.'

'On the Blue Lagoon side?'

He laughed. 'What! You think we live in one of those white palaces? On the other side, Ella. On the Rasta side.'

In the car, Bob Marley accompanied them all the way back to the resort. Raphael pulled up under the *porte-cochère* and killed the engine.

'Where you want to go tomorrow, Ella?' he said. 'Or you gonna dive tomorrow?'

'I can't leave the resort again, Raphael,' said Ella, feeling gutted. 'Dieter – my grandmother's friend – is going back to Germany tomorrow. I can't abandon her.' What had started as a mild flirtation between the two sexagenarians had developed into something a lot more meaningful, and Ella suspected that Leonie was going to be feeling very bereft on the last day of her holiday.

She rooted in her bag for the money she owed Raphael, and in return he handed her a slender spliff. 'Keep it for later,' he said. 'When you are looking at the moon on the bay. That's what I do most nights. I sit on the headland down from my house. Smoke a spliff and watch the moon.'

'Thanks,' she said, pocketing it.

When she looked back at him he was watching her with an infinitely wise expression in his slanting, golden eyes. 'Remember, Ella, what I told you earlier. Be grateful for what you have. Be grateful, and full of praise.'

For some reason the words made the hair rise on the back of her neck. 'I will,' she whispered. Then, impulsively, she leaned forward and kissed his cheek. 'I won't see you again, Raphael. It's a really horrible thought. You and Desirée made this holiday incredibly special for me. Thank you, both. For everything.'

'Why you say you won't see me again? Maybe you come back one day, like my Dutch friend.'

'Maybe.' She tried a smile, but couldn't manage

it. Feeling really choked now, she slid out of the car and turned to wave at him.

Raphael sent her his blissful, blissed-out smile, and saluted her with a relaxed hand. 'One love,' he said. And then he was gone.

Chapter Nine

The following morning they saw Dieter and his family off on the coach that was to take them to Kingston airport. Dieter was the last passenger to board.

Leonie stapled a brave smile onto her face. 'Goodbye, my darling Dieter,' she said. 'It's so amazing that we found each other!'

'Don't say goodbye, Leonie,' said Dieter, looking down at her with tender eyes. 'Say *Auf Wiedersehen*. Till we meet again.'

Ella had never felt more like a gooseberry in her life. She stood slightly to one side of the star-crossed lovers, pretending to be fascinated by a buzzard that was circling overhead. On the coach, Dieter's family were obviously feeling equally embarrassed. They too were studiously ignoring their father, while the rest of the passengers were gawping shamelessly. The love story between the two sixty-somethings had engendered a lot of interest among the guests in Salamander Cove, to the extent that it had become a kind of running soap opera, and now everyone was anxious to see how it was going to end. Ella snuck a surreptitious glance at the pair.

Yikes! Now they were kissing! Oh God – it really was too much. Her uncle had been right – she should never have asked Leonie to come on holiday with her. She was a complete liability.

Eventually the coach driver pumped his horn, and Dieter freed Leonie from his embrace and boarded, lobbing endearments over his shoulder as he went. 'Auf Wiedersehen, mein Schatz, mein schöner Liebling, mein Herz, meine—' Thankfully, the doors cut him off before he could come out with any more.

Ella and Leonie stood and waved as the coach sailed down the driveway, and then Ella turned to her grandmother. 'Honestly, Leonie,' she began, 'don't you think it's a bit—' And then she shut her mouth like a trap. Leonie was crying.

* * *

'There, there, Leonie.' Ella handed her another wad of tissues. They were sitting side by side on the couch in their villa. 'Blow your nose and have another swig of champagne. That'll do you more good than anything.'

'Oh, Ella – I'm sorry.' Her grandmother's tears had dried up but she was still a bit sniffly. 'It's just *awful.* If I'd known I was going to fall in love I would never have come on this holiday.'

'Don't say that, Leonie! I think it's brilliant that you had a holiday romance.'

'But at my age! It's too absurd for words!'

'No, it's not. I'm madly jealous, you know.'

'Oh, darling – it's not fair! You're young and gorgeous. You should be the one being wined and dined and having glorious sex.'

Ella's jaw dropped. 'Glorious *sex*?'

'Yes.' Leonie gave her a look of mild reproach. 'Just because I'm fifty-nine doesn't mean I can't still enjoy it, Ella.'

Leonie had shaved a few more years off her age, but it wasn't that that surprised Ella. She'd just never thought of her grandmother as being sexually active.

'Was it *really* glorious?' she ventured cautiously.

'Yes. I'm not sure whether the fact that I haven't indulged for a while made it glorious, or whether it was all down to Dieter. He was terribly special.' Leonie looked as if she was about to burst into tears again, and then she took a deep breath, blew her nose and shook her head, as if to shake off the glooms that were threatening to overcome her. 'Now,' she said with decision, chucking the damp wodge of tissue into the wastepaper basket. 'I must shut up crowing on about how splendid my sex life is, and concentrate on yours instead. How come you didn't fancy anyone in the resort, Ella? You could have lifted a little finger and any number of men would have come running. I've seen the way they look at you.'

'There was only one man I found attractive, Leonie. And he wasn't available.'

'Let me guess. That Rasta you told me about?'

'Right first time.'

'Was he a dish?'

'You don't really call good-looking men dishes any more, Leonie.'

'Oh? What do you call them? I'd hate to think I was too terminally unhip.'

'Well, you call them "babe". Or "dude".'

'I prefer "dude". Dieter's a dude, isn't he?'

Ella smiled at her. 'Absolutely.'

'So this Rasta was also a dude?'

'Yeah. But it wasn't just that. We had a great rapport. And he had the most trustworthy eyes of any man I've ever met.'

'I imagine the ganja helped.'

Ella shot her grandmother a look. '*Leonie*! What makes you think I smoked ganja?'

'Don't look so injured, Ella. It doesn't suit you to protest too much. Of course you smoked ganja. *My* generation invented sex, drugs and rock 'n' roll, remember? And no self-respecting granddaughter of mine would come all the way to Jamaica and not get potted.'

Ella laughed. 'Oh, all right then. Yes. We indulged.'

'Good weed?' asked Leonie, with a kind of knowledgeable insouciance.

'Yes. Excellent. Hey!' She remembered Raphael's present to her. 'I have a reefer he gave me. We might smoke it later?'

'You keep it all to yourself, darling. It's so long since I had a blast that I'd get completely out of it

215

and wind up embarrassing you bigtime. I'll stick to champagne.' She swigged back the rest of the champagne in her glass and looked at her watch. 'Holy shomoly! Is that the time? I can't believe that I wasted so much of my last day in Paradise boo-hooing. And you have a dive booked, Ella, haven't you? You'd better hurry if you're not going to miss it.'

'Oh – I'd written that off. I'm not going swanning off around coral reefs when you're so miserable. I'm going to stay here and feed you champagne until your broken heart has mended a bit.'

'Don't be daft, darling. Go and enjoy the last day of your holiday.'

'But what will you do?'

'Read.' Leonie reached for a magazine on the coffee table and started to leaf through it. 'There's a competition in here for a holiday in Thailand, and it's a cinch. "Answer the following questions. What colour is your hair?"'

'What?' said Ella.

'I'm kidding. But it's nearly as facile. "How many years are in a millennium? How many nights did Scheherazade regale the Sultan with stories? A regular Hollywood beanfeast is the Night of the – how many – Stars?"'

'What's the tie-breaker?'

'"I use Matt Miller's Thousand Island Dressing because – dot dot dot".'

'How many words?'

'A thousand. Only joking, darling. Hah! I crack

myself up. Twelve, actually. Now. Run along and do your dive.'

'Are you sure you'll be all right, Leonie?'

'Absolutely.' Leonie looked at her with eyes in which only a trace of misery remained. 'And doing this asinine competition will take my mind off Dieter.'

*   *   *

After her dive, as Ella stripped off her exposure suit and rinsed down her gear she realized that this was the last time she'd dive for the foreseeable future – unless she won the lottery, or Leonie won her Thailand competition. She said as much to Desirée.

'No chance, sweetheart,' said the dive mistress. 'You are hooked now. Ain't nothing going to stop you diving again. I know people like you who work their asses off all year just so's they can get the money together to come back here and dive for two weeks. Anyhow, you can always carry on diving in Ireland.'

Ella's mind went back to Sheep's Head Bay, and she shuddered.

Desirée registered the grimace. 'Come on, Jacqueline Cousteau! Where's your fighting spirit? That Ferdia – he told me that your country has some incredible diving. I always did threaten that I would come visit him there, just to check it out. Sloosh out your BCD now, sweetheart,' she said, handing Ella the hose before disappearing back

217

into the dive shop. 'And don't forget I promised you that drink.'

'It's me who should be buying *you* a drink, Desirée, after all you've done for me.'

'No, no, Ella. The cocktail is on the house. I've even thought up the perfect name for it.'

'Oh? What?'

'You'll find out later. But I'll give you a clue. All those special cocktails are named after fish.'

'Oh? Just don't call me a wrasse, OK?'

Desirée laughed. 'You got a sweet rass, honey! Will I see you in the bar on the beach later? How does nine o'clock sound?'

'I'll be there,' said Ella.

*　　*　　*

Later that evening she and Leonie were sitting together on the veranda, sharing a final celebratory bottle of champagne. They were showered and scented, and dressed for dinner in the kind of casual-formal clothes required for dining in the Pagoda restaurant. Leonie was wearing something long and fluid in silk, and Ella had on one of her mother's cast-offs – a loose white dress by Ghost. Tree frogs were serenading them, a blue dusk was descending, and the gentle rhythm of mento was drifting up from the beach, where the resident band was playing. It had rained earlier, and the earthy smell of wet grass mingled with the scent of expensive cigar smoke from the villa next door. The mood was bitter-sweet; redolent of nostalgia and a kind of regret.

'Well,' sighed Leonie, raising her glass. 'Here's to the last evening of our dream holiday.'

'Here's to our next one,' said Ella. 'In Thailand. Did you come up with any ideas for that Thousand Island Dressing competition?'

'Nothing madly inspired, I'm afraid,' said Leonie. 'I was torn between "I use Matt Miller's Thousand Island Dressing because *it's so much classier to dress up than dress down,*" or the rather more pragmatic "I use Matt Miller's Thousand Island Dressing because *it's cheaper than Paul Newman's.*"'

'Mm.' Ella considered. 'In this case I don't think honesty's the best policy. Not if we want to win that holiday.'

'How about this?' A man's voice came from the adjoining veranda. A rich, velvety, German-accented voice. 'I *don't* use Matt Miller's Thousand Island Dressing because it is cheap and nasty, and if I accept my wealthy consort's proposal of marriage I can go to Thailand any time I damn well please.'

'Dieter!' Leonie had gone very white, and her hands had flown to her face. 'Dieter!' she exclaimed again, jumping to her feet and parting the branches of the hibiscus bush that separated the two verandas.

There he was, lounging back on a cane chair with a cigar between his fingers and with his long legs elegantly crossed. 'Do you ladies mind if I join

219

you?' he enquired politely, getting to his feet in a leisurely fashion, and setting the cigar down in an ashtray.

'Dieter!' said Leonie again.

'The very same.' His tone was urbane as he stepped off his veranda and on to theirs.

'Dieter!' It was Ella's turn to address him. 'What on earth are you doing here?'

'I'm here to ask for your grandmother's hand in marriage, *Fräulein*. Do you think she'll have me?'

There was a beat of shocked silence. Ella looked from Dieter to her grandmother, and then back again. Dieter's face was smiling and handsome, Leonie's was ghost-white. She had sunk back down on her chair, and was gazing at Dieter with an expression of such profound shock that Ella felt a sudden rush of concern for her. 'Leonie!' she exclaimed, dropping to her knees and taking her grandmother's hand in hers. 'Are you all right?'

Leonie nodded, mutely. A tear rolled down her cheek. Dieter got down on one knee on the other side of the cane chair, and gently wiped away the tear with his thumb. Then he took a box from his inside jacket pocket and held it out to his inamorata. 'Will you marry me, Leonie?' he said.

Leonie nodded again. 'Yes,' she said in a voice so tiny it was barely audible. 'Yes please, Dieter. I would love to marry you.' She leaned forward and kissed him very gently on the lips.

Ella knew she was *de trop*. 'Um,' she said, casting around for an exit line. Then: 'Champagne!' she pronounced in ringing tones. 'Let me fetch you a glass, Dieter.' She escaped inside and loitered there a while to give the lovers a chance to do whatever lovers did in situations like this. Oh God. Patrick was going to *murder* her when she went back to Dublin. He'd told her to keep Leonie under strict surveillance, and now her granny had gone off and got herself proposed to by someone she'd known for only a fortnight!

Dieter was sitting next to Leonie when Ella re-emerged with the champagne flute. Their hands were joined on the table between them, and they were gazing at one another with supremely foolish expressions on their faces. There was an exquisite diamond on Leonie's ring finger.

'Thank you, Ella,' said Dieter, when she set the glass down on the table. He poured, raised his glass, and then said solemnly: 'To true love.'

'To true love,' chorused Leonie and Ella, smiling at each other. Then Leonie added: 'And to the Polly Rogers.'

'The Polly Rogers?' echoed Dieter.

'Yes. That was the name I dreamed up for the Toptree Foods competition. Without them, Dieter, you and I would never have met.'

'What a truly horrible thought,' said Dieter, with an expressive shudder.

'When did you decide to turn round and come back?' asked Leonie.

'At the airport,' he said. 'I realized in a blinding flash that I simply couldn't live without you.'

They spent the next ten minutes listening to the tale of his *crise de coeur*. He had spent the journey to Kingston agonizing over how he might get to see Leonie again. At the airport he'd abandoned his astonished family on the tarmac, climbed into a cab, and instructed the driver to take him back to Salamander Cove, stopping off in Kingston to buy the ring and some basic items of clothing. All his luggage was on the plane, heading for Berlin.

'You mad, impetuous fool,' said Leonie, taking his head between her hands and covering his face with kisses. 'I am not worthy of you, you utterly amazing man.'

Oh God. Now her granny was talking Mills-and-Boon-speak. It was obvious that the lovebirds needed some time to themselves. Ella rose to her feet and glanced at her watch. The fingers of her right hand curled around the joint Raphael had given her. She'd transferred it earlier from the pocket of her backpack to the pocket of her dress, anticipating that she might like a little blast on her last evening in the greatest ganja-producing country in the world. 'I think I'll have a stroll before dinner,' she said. 'I'll see you two in the Pagoda in half an hour or so?' The radiant couple smiled at her, and then turned and smiled at each other.

Ella wandered off in the direction of the beach, passing halfway there to light up the spliff. The band was playing that sexy, lazy, rhythmic mento, and people were dancing. She veered to her left, towards the sea wall. Swinging her legs over it, she sat there and looked out to sea, listening to the wavelets match their rhythm to the mento, watching darkness fall.

By the time she'd finished the spliff, the stars above her head were more beautiful than the most beautiful diamond necklace ever sold by Tiffany's, the ambient song of the tree frogs was more melodic than Beethoven's Seventh, and the light breeze on her neck was the most erotic sensation she'd ever experienced. The band on the beach had taken a break, but Ella was still clicking her fingers to the rhythm that had crept into her head and lodged itself there. She made a mental note to herself to buy some mento when she got back to Ireland. Then she chucked the roach into the sea below, and stretched luxuriously before turning round to head in the direction of the restaurant.

Suddenly she remembered something. She looked towards the bulky mass of the headland that was silhouetted against the dark sky to her right, and stood quite motionless, waiting. There! For a split second she saw a tiny dot of red light glowing against the blackness of the rocky outcrop . . . But when she looked harder there was nothing. Her eyes were playing tricks on her. She pressed the cool pads of her fingers against her closed lids momentarily, then opened her eyes and looked again. And then she saw the pinpoint of red light shine again, briefly, and she knew immediately what it was. It was the glowing end of Raphael's ganja spliff.

She remembered the way he had sat cross-legged on the jetty on Navy Island, the time Eva had photographed him, gazing out to sea with serene eyes. Now she pictured him sitting loose-limbed and relaxed on his stone headland, contemplating the Caribbean. Her pooka. Her guardian angel, Raphael. She blew a kiss into the air, hoping that the wind would take it to him, and stood with her eyes closed and the warm breeze lifting her hair, waiting for the kiss to be returned. The breath that grazed her cheek moments later was so palpable that she was surprised when she opened her eyes to find nobody there.

Ella drifted across the grass to the path that led past the Pagoda restaurant with a dreamy smile on her face. Dieter and Leonie were sitting at a table on the long veranda, with a bottle of champagne in a cooler between them. She floated up the steps, and Dieter rose to his feet and pulled out a chair for her. 'What's on the menu tonight, Leonie?' asked Ella, sitting down and sending them both seraphic smiles. She picked up the printed sheet and squinted at it. The words formed themselves into the prettiest hieroglyphics she'd ever seen.

'The jerk prawns are excellent,' said Dieter. 'Here. Have a taste.' He peeled a prawn, stabbed it with his fork and passed it to her.

'Mm. Oh, my God, you're right,' agreed Ella. She thought she'd never tasted anything quite so delicious. 'Definitely prawns for me.'

'And champagne.' Dieter took the proffered flute

from the waiter and filled it. Ella took a sip and sneezed as the fizz went up her nose. The sneeze was so brilliant she laughed. Then she looked round the room with soft-focus eyes, taking in the exotic décor, the elaborate trelliswork of the veranda, the backdrop of midnight blue velvet beyond the open windows, the flowers and candles on each table, the low murmur of the other diners, the ceiling fans swishing currents of air, the rich vibrato of the solo violin that was playing . . .

'Oh!' Ella was overcome with nostalgia. 'My favourite Brahms!'

'Did you know, Dieter,' said Leonie, 'that my granddaughter is an exceptionally talented violinist?'

'No, I did not know that,' said Dieter, turning interested eyes on Ella. 'Did you train?'

'For years,' sighed Ella, turning yearning eyes on the elegant dark woman playing the violin on the other side of the room. 'And years. I adored it. But I couldn't get a job. So I renounced the first true love I ever had.' She gave another great sigh and then turned her attention abruptly back to the table as her prawns were set in front of her. 'God – I'm ravenous,' she said, falling upon her plate.

She was glad that she'd chosen finger food. It meant that she didn't have to worry too much about her manners. When she'd finished her prawns, she dabbled around in the finger bowl and then wiped each digit fastidiously to get rid of any traces of oil. It didn't work. Her fingers actually felt oilier every time she dipped them in the scented water, and the smell of prawns was becoming more and more intense. 'Excuse me, please,' she said, getting up from the table. 'I think I need something a bit more heavy-duty to shift this prawny smell off my fingers.'

In the loo she spent at least five minutes with her hands under the tap. What on earth was the scent of the soap she was using? It had the most glorious perfume she'd ever smelt. Musky. Slightly masculine, with top notes of . . . vanilla. She wanted it as a memento. Every time she smelt it, it would remind her of Jamaica, just like Proust's madeleine reminded him of – whatever it was that it reminded him of. She stuffed a cake of soap in her pocket, dried her hands on a soft-as-swansdown towel, and went back to the table.

The dark violinist was standing next to Dieter, talking with him and smiling.

'Ah – here she is!' announced Dieter with satisfaction as Ella joined them. 'Ella – this is Diandra. She has very kindly volunteered to let you take a turn on her violin. Will you oblige us, please, by playing something for us?'

'What?' Ella's eyes were huge with astonishment. 'I can't. I – it's ages since I've played. I'm completely out of practice and – No no no.' She shook her head violently.

'Oh, do play, darling. Please?' cajoled Leonie. 'I'd love to hear you. It must be three years since I last heard you play a note.'

226

Diandra was holding her violin and bow out to Ella with an encouraging expression on her face. Around her the faces of the other diners were all looking at her expectantly. 'Please do,' echoed Diandra. 'The gentleman has offered me a generous fee for the loan of my instrument.'

Oh, God. There was no getting out of it now. What had Eva Lavery said that day on Navy Island? *If I get an opportunity to spread some of my money around, I'm glad to do it* . . . The image of the woman waiting for the bus with her two children came back to her, her dignity in the face of poverty, and Ella's aborted impulse to give her money. She couldn't deny this woman the opportunity to earn a little more . . .

Ella bit her lip. 'Thank you, Diandra,' she said. 'I'd consider it an honour.'

She took the violin and tucked it under her chin, adjusting the angle until she felt comfortable with it. Then she raised the bow and drew it experimentally across the strings. Though inferior to her own, the instrument hadn't a bad tone. A little flurry of scales came next. An adjustment to the tension, with a 'May I?' to Diandra before screwing one of the pegs a fraction tighter.

Then Ella took a deep breath, centred herself, and launched into 'Erin Shore'. The first notes were gentle – almost tentative – as she familiarized herself with the instrument. Then, as her confidence increased and she drew the bow more vigorously across the strings, the plangent strains swelled, filling the room and filling her heart. Ella shut her eyes, smiled, and gave herself up to the music.

When she finished, the applause took her by surprise. It was a long, long time since she'd played in public. She opened her eyes and registered the smiling, appreciative faces around her, and felt colour sweep into her face as she bowed her head in acknowledgement. Diandra was clapping too, and joining in with the calls for an encore. Wow! Ella was blown away. She laughed out loud. She'd played stoned before, but never in front of an audience.

She paused for a beat or two before raising the bow again, casting around for what to play next. Something livelier would be good. She'd show them that Irish music could be sexy – less laid back than mento or reggae, but a serious contender in the world raunchiness stakes. Which piece, though? There were so many to choose from 'The Clare Jig?' 'The Hag's Purse?' 'Pull the Knife and Stick it Again?' No. She hadn't played that for ages – she'd make too many mistakes.

'Toss the Feathers!' That was the one! She tapped her foot – one, two – before launching into the jig with a flourish. Yes! The notes soared out of the violin in a stream of indescribably beautiful colours. Emerald green, hot pink, lapis lazuli . . . They hung quivering in the air like exotic insects. Looking around, she could tell by the way that people were moving in their chairs – swaying, drumming their fingers on tabletops, tapping their feet in time to her playing – that they were aching to dance. It was the greatest compliment she could have got – apart from the cheers that rang out when she finished. The audience whistled and clapped their hands high in the air and stamped their feet. The applause only subsided when she finally returned Diandra's violin to her and sat back down, feeling breathless. 'Thanks a lot,' she said to the other violinist. 'I'm really glad Dieter approached you. I haven't played in public in a long time, and it's kind of reassuring to know I can still just about hack it.'

The dark girl smiled back at her and gave that wonderful slow, Jamaican nod of the head. 'You can hack it for sure,' she said. 'No problem.' Then Diandra moved gracefully back across the room and took up her position on the little podium where the resident musicians played. 'I dunno how I gonna match that!' she remarked, with a laugh. But the sweet strains of Debussy were soon floating through the room, and once again Ella was swamped with nostalgia.

'Oh, Ella,' said her grandmother with a rueful smile. 'You really shouldn't be recording sounds for a living.'

'Oh?' said Ella, perplexed. 'What should I be doing, then?'

'You should be making them, of course, darling.'

*   *   *

After dinner, Ella remembered that she'd arranged to meet Desirée at the bar on the beach. Her instructor was there already, talking to the barman.

'Desirée! Hi!' Ella danced up to the bar and perched on a stool beside her.

'Hey! How's my Siamese Fighter!'

'Siamese Fighter?'

'It's a beautiful little fish. A feisty little fish. And it's the name of the cocktail Otis has made for you. I thought it right for my fighting girl. Tell Ella what's in it, Otis.'

The barman was expertly juggling ingredients. 'I mix Bombay gin with pink grapefruit juice. Then I squeeze in the juice of one blood orange, and rim it to the top with vodka.' He gave her a big smile and handed her the colourful concoction with a flourish. 'Here you go. My congratulations on adding a new cocktail to the list, Miz Siamese Fighter.' The glasses were set ceremoniously on the counter in front of them.

'Wow! I feel so chuffed,' said Ella, 'to have a cocktail named after me. It's like having a star named after you, isn't it? Or a rose.' She lifted her glass. 'Cheers.'

'Here's to you, Siamese Fighter,' said Desirée. 'And here's to a long and happy diving career.'

Ella took a sip. 'Wow,' she said. 'That packs some punch!' She'd better take it easy. She was already woozy from champagne and wine and that excellent weed of Raphael's. She ran her eyes down the expansive cocktail list. 'Will it ever get listed here?'

'Sure. Otis gets a new list printed up every season.' Desirée indicated a name halfway down the list. 'Look. There's your friend Ferdia.'

'Leopard Shark,' said Ella. 'Why did you call him that?'

'Because he's streamlined and sexy.'

'And dangerous?'

'Hell, no. Those leopard sharks are big pussycats. You get close enough to one, you can pet him.'

I think not, thought Ella. 'Um. Who's that beneath him? Rock Beauty?'

'That was his girl at the time. Miss Jamaica.'

'Oh.' Ferdia and Miss *Jamaica*? 'And – er – are you here somewhere too, Desirée?'

'Sure honey. That's me there.' She pointed to Starfish. 'Ferdia chose the name for me.'

Ella smiled. 'He chose well,' she said.

'Excuse me?' An American accent came from behind them. 'I wanna congratulate you on your playing earlier. That was some virtuoso performance.'

'What? Oh – you mean my fiddle playing? Well, thanks very much indeed.' Ella raised her glass at the middle-aged geezer who'd rolled up at the bar.

'Are you a professional?' he asked.

'No. I just play for fun, really.'

'Well. I was seriously impressed. I have a bar? – an Irish bar? – in Manhattan? If you're ever in New York give me a call. We have sessions there every night of the week. You'd be more than welcome, and I'd be glad to let you have work as a resident player.' He slid his wallet out of his pocket and handed her a card.

'Well. Thank you.' Ella glanced down at it, registered the name Bob O'Mahony, and then pocketed it. 'I'm really very flattered, Bob.'

'You're welcome,' said Bob O'Mahony. 'You're a very gifted young lady.' And he shook hands with her before moving off down the beach.

'What was all that about?' asked Desirée.

'Oh. I played a couple of tunes in the restaurant earlier. Diandra lent me her fiddle.'

'Yeah? You must be *good* honey! It's a real Irish thing, isn't it? The fiddle? Doesn't everybody over there play it?'

'Well, not so much nowadays. But once upon a time every household in the country would have had a fiddle – just like every township here has those massive speakers, blasting out reggae. The Jamaicans and the Irish have loads in common when you scratch the surface. Music, green countryside, bad roads . . .'

'Desirée!' A passing woman called to her. 'I'm not going to be able to make that dive tomorrow after all. Can we make it the day after?'

'No problem, honey.'

'Thanks!'

Desirée turned back to Ella. 'Ferdia tried to teach that Miss Jamaica, but she couldn't master it.'

What! Why was Desirée harking back to Miss Jamaica again? For some reason Ella didn't want to hear about Ferdia and Miss Jamaica. She decided to change the subject.

'Is Raphael on the cocktail list, Desirée?' she asked, opening it again.

'He sure is, honey. He's right at the top. Look there.' She indicated the first name on the list with a calloused forefinger. It was Angel Fish.

Ella nodded. 'That's perfect!' she said.

'I know,' said Desirée. 'I'm a very lucky woman.'

Chapter Ten

Ella was mildly surprised to find Dieter shaving in the bathroom of their villa the following morning, and had to remind herself that he was going to be part of her family. The three of them breakfasted together, and packed, and went to wait for the airport coach in the lobby.

Sophie was already there, sitting in a hilly landscape designed by Louis Vuitton, wearing the pink linen suit she'd worn on the flight over. Thankfully the coach that arrived to drive them to Kingston was so state-of-the-art that not even Sophie could find anything to complain about. Hell's bells! Imagine being such a sad individual that moaning was your favourite hobby, thought Ella, as she observed the actress looking around trying to find fault with something. And then she remembered how down in the dumps she herself had been before heading off for her Jamaican idyll, and she wondered if she'd be back down in those dumps by the time she got home to Dublin.

Dieter and Leonie re-enacted the farewell episode from their real-life soap opera at Kingston airport, although this time there were no tears from

Leonie. After Dieter's flight to Berlin was called and the lovebirds had exchanged final kisses, Ella and her grandmother wandered around the duty-free shops to kill time and escape from Sophie. Most incongruously, 'Frosty the Snowman' was playing over the airport speakers as the Jamaican sun blazed down on the tarmac outside. It was just as bonkers, Ella thought, that her grandmother should be going home with such an outrageously romantic tale to tell, while she, Ella didn't have so much as a romantic anecdote.

They said goodbye to Sophie at Heathrow. Practically the first thing the actress did upon arrival was to switch on her mobile phone. 'Thank God I'm in range again,' she said, fingers flying across the keypad faster than a concert pianist's. 'Tch. Engaged.' She made a little face, then turned to Ella. 'Give me your phone number. The next time I'm in Dublin I'll give you a bell and we can meet up somewhere hip for coffee.'

Ella hoped she didn't blanch too visibly, but Sophie was absorbed in locating the electronic organizer she kept in her handbag.

'OK?' she resumed, finger poised over the gadget. Ella was on the verge of obliging when someone in the arrivals hall called out Sophie's name. The actress dropped the organizer back into her bag as if it had given her an electric shock. 'Ben!' she shrieked, propelling herself and her luggage trolley into his arms. 'Oh, thank God! I've had the most appalling time. You would not believe—'

Leonie and Ella slid a look at each other and sidled in the direction of Flight Connections. They needn't have bothered sidling. As far as Sophie Burke was concerned, Ella and her grandmother were no longer part of her universe.

When they arrived in Dublin airport, festive songs were jingling around all over the place. 'Go, Frosty, go!' trilled Leonie as they looked about for Patrick, who was to meet them.

The place was milling with expats returning for Christmas, all hugging and kissing their family and friends and gabbling delightedly. Bah! Humbug! thought Ella, hating herself for being sour. She couldn't remember ever having had a Christmas when all the members of her family had been present. Every Christmas at least one family member cried off, either because they couldn't tolerate the icy vibe between her mother and father, or because they'd had a better offer elsewhere. If she wasn't flying out of the country to visit one or other of her parents, Ella generally Christmased with her uncle and Claudia and her cousins; but the last couple of Christmases had been spent with her musician friends in Wicklow. She hadn't a clue what she was going to do this year. Before she could think Bah! Humbug! again, she stapled a big smile on her face, determined to make an effort. 'There's Patrick now!' she said brightly to her grandmother.

Leonie made a beeline in his direction. 'Oh darling,' she breathed when they drew level with him. 'You'll never guess what's happened!'

Patrick took in Ella's averted eyes. 'I've a feeling I'd hate to even hazard a guess,' he said, giving his niece a dark look as he commandeered the luggage trolley. 'But I'll try. Let's see. You met the man of your dreams and you're getting married?'

'Right first time, clever clogs!' Leonie gave a tinkling little laugh. Then: 'Oh – I love this bit!' she said with a rather alarming enthusiasm. And she continued to sing along to 'Frosty the Snowman' with blithe brio.

Ella stole a look at her uncle's face. 'Merry Christmas, Patrick,' she said.

*　　*　　*

The subject of Leonie's forthcoming nuptials were deftly skirted round on the drive back to Dublin. Ella could tell that Patrick was reluctant to make any comment until he'd grilled her about it. He left her off at her gaff first, telling her in an ominous voice that he'd talk to her later, and then he and Leonie went to pick up Ronan the cat from the posh kennels he'd been staying in for the past fortnight.

At around six o'clock, Ella poured a hefty glass of red wine and braced herself to phone her uncle.

'What in *God's* name made Leonie decide to get married?' was the first thing he said.

'Oh, Patrick – don't be angry. Dieter's gorgeous, really he is. He's an absolute gentleman. You mustn't have no worries about him and Leonie.' The double negative had just slipped out. She prayed she wouldn't start speaking in a Jamaican accent as well.

The bummer about having a musician's ear meant that she always ended up talking in the accent of the region she'd most recently visited. She was sure everyone thought she was madly pretentious the time she'd been to New York, because she kept lapsing into *Friends*-speak when she came home.

'Of course I have worries – she's my mother. You worry about *your* mother, don't you?'

Ella considered. 'Um – no,' she said, matter-of-factly. 'Francesca's really happy. She's got her gorgeous villa and her lover and her collection of paintings. Why would I worry?'

'I can't understand this family's predilection for getting involved with glamorous foreigners,' said Patrick in a voice groaning with incomprehension. 'Your mother bolts with an Italian, your father shacks up with an Alaskan Innuit, and now your grandmother's running off with a German. I suppose you'll tell me next that you've fallen in love with a Jamaican.'

'I *wish*,' said Ella. 'My love life's still emphatically a no man's land. Anyway, Patrick – you married a glamorous Swiss model, so you're hardly one to talk.'

'Well, at least Claudia has Irish connections.' Patrick sounded defensive. 'We know nothing about this man who's knocked Leonie for six.'

'You've *got* to let her do it, Patrick. It's what she wants more than anything. I think it's wonderful that she should find romance at this stage of her life. She didn't even have to do the personal column thing or go on *Blind Date* to do it.'

Patrick sucked in his breath. 'Jesus. I suppose you're right. I wouldn't have put it past her to have volunteered herself as a guinea-pig to Cilla.' Ella could tell he was thawing a bit. Leonie's unexpected *affaire de coeur* was at least preferable to the idea of her conducting a holiday romance on a television show. 'How are they going to keep in touch, by the way?' he resumed, as if trying to pick as many holes as he could in this bizarre scenario. 'Her phone bill's going to be astronomical.'

'They'll do it by e-mail.'

'Don't be daft, Ella! Leonie's a complete techno-phobe! She doesn't even have access to a computer!'

'Dieter's offered to buy her one, and supply her with tuition.'

There was a fractional pause while Patrick digested this information. His voice when he replied sounded resigned. 'So. When are we going to meet this munificent Dieter?'

'Not for a while. He can't take any time off before the summer, so Leonie'll be jetting off to Berlin on a regular basis. Before you know it she'll have acquired Frequent Flyer status. Dieter's coming over in July. It'll be his first trip to Ireland.'

'And that's when the wedding will be? In July?'

'No. They're delaying that until November, when the rainy season's over.'

'What rainy season? It's always bloody raining in Ireland.'

Ella took a swift swig of wine before answering. 'They're not getting married in Ireland, Patrick. They're getting married in the Grace and Truth Temple.'

'The Grace and Truth Temple? Where in hell's name is that?'

'Jamaica. Near Port Antonio. At least, that's what they're hoping to do. They'll be happy enough to have the wedding on the beach if they can't organize a church ceremony.'

'Holy shit,' said Patrick.

*   *   *

By the time Christmas arrived, everyone had grown to accept the fact that Leonie and Dieter were perfectly serious about getting married. Patrick and Claudia decided to 'do' Christmas, and Declan, Ella's father, flew in from the States to be with them for a few days. He'd left his gorgeous Alaskan girlfriend behind because she was too heavily pregnant to fly. Ella's mother had phoned just before Christmas to say she was sorry she couldn't be there, but a long-lost daughter of her lover had arrived on their doorstep quite out of the blue, and she felt it was only fair to stay on as a kind of surro-

gate mother for the child. 'The child' was, it tran-
spired, older than Ella. Ella had received this latest
news with unfazed equanimity. Nothing her family
could do had the power to surprise her any more.

It was a hectic, buzzy week. On Christmas Eve
Declan and Ella snuck away from the drinks party
Claudia and Patrick were hosting to try and grab
some time to themselves. Ella had expected the
local pub to be heaving, but in fact it was surpris-
ingly quiet, and they even managed to get the snug
to themselves.

She'd brought her holiday photographs to show
to her father. There were lots of smiling shots of
Dieter and Desirée among them, but for some
reason hardly any of her shots of Raphael had come
out. There were only two that were halfway decent,
and they'd both been taken by someone else. One
was the picture that Eva had taken of him in the
pose she would always associate with him – sitting
on the jetty at Navy Island, so absolutely at one with
everything around him; the other had been taken
on the evening of his little cousin's birthday party.
She and Raphael were looking into the camera with
beatific, slightly stoned smiles.

'I recognize that smile,' said her father indul-
gently. 'Good weed?'

'*Very* good weed.'

'So. Jamaica rocks?'

'Jamaica rocks.' Ella gave him an oblique look.
'You know I met an old friend of yours there?'

'Who?'

'Da-dah!' She produced a photograph of Eva on board the Navy Island ferry. Her hair was whipping around her face, she was laughing, and although you couldn't read the expression in her eyes behind the black, black lenses of her sunglasses, you knew that it was wicked.

'Eva Lavery?' Declan gave an incredulous smile. 'Wow. There's a real blast from the past. How is she?'

'She was great. If it hadn't been for her, I don't think I'd ever have set foot outside the resort. I'd have been stuck inside with all the other pampered prisoners.'

Her father's smile had gone from incredulous to nostalgic. 'She always had an adventurous spirit, that girl. And a charm that was irresistible.'

'That's what she said about you.' Ella smiled at him. 'She said *you* were irresistible.'

Declan raised a sceptical eyebrow. 'That was a long time ago, sweetheart.'

'I dunno. You're still pretty charming.' She laughed. 'Eva remembers you as having long blond hair like a Viking.'

'Hah! She'd get a shock if she saw me now, wouldn't she? A balding middle-aged git.' He handed back the photograph. 'She's hardly changed at all.'

'You're not a balding middle-aged git, Declan. You're a charming balding middle-aged git.' She drained her pint and set the empty glass down on the table. 'Your round, pater.'

Declan went up to the bar and came back with two more pints of Guinness and two packets of peanuts. They sat in companionable silence for a while, and then came the question Ella had been expecting – the question he always asked her when he came back on his visits. 'How's your form these days?' he said.

She looked a bit guarded. 'D'you mean my musical form or my mental form?'

'Both. Try running the musical bit by me first.'

Ella poured a small pile of peanuts into the palm of her hand and started to eat them one by one. 'Well. It's not brilliant, I'm afraid.' She was realistic enough to know that the euphoria she'd experienced the evening she'd played in Jamaica was down to the excellent ganja in the spliff that Raphael had rolled for her. Her rendition of 'Erin Shore' and 'Toss the Feathers' had been mediocre at best, and the rapturous response of the diners in the Pagoda restaurant had been merely polite. It was amazing how easily you could fool yourself into believing you were a ringer for Sharon Corr when stoned.

'I'd really love to hear you play, Ella,' continued her father. 'It's ages since I last did.'

No you wouldn't, she thought. I sound like shit. But she didn't want to admit that to Declan. He was so *proud* that she'd inherited his talent! So instead she just said: 'I'm a bit rusty, Dad. I don't have much time to practise.'

'You've *got* to practise, Ella.' Her father turned

243

uncharacteristically solemn eyes on her. 'You have a God-given gift. You can't let it go.'

She looked down at the photograph of Raphael that was still lying on the table, and remembered what he'd said to her on the last day she'd spent with him. *When you have a gift you are grateful and full of praise. Jah gave me my gift. But Jah has the right to take away that gift also. Be grateful for what you have, Ella. Be grateful, and full of praise . . .*

Ella slumped in her seat. She didn't want to be having this conversation. 'I'll never be a professional like you. You know that.'

'You still dream about it though, don't you?'

'Of course I do, Dad. But those kind of dreams don't come true.'

'On the contrary, Ella. Dreams can come true if you pursue them hard enough and want them badly enough.' He gave her a penetrating look. 'But that's beside the point. Think of the pleasure you get playing for yourself. Think of the pleasure you can give your friends and family. Sakatook loves it when I play. She says it's the best aphrodisiac there is. You know she thought I was a pretty nondescript kind of a guy when we first met in a bar in Chicago? It wasn't until I invited her along to a gig that she got the hots for me bigtime. Having mastery of an instrument is very sexy, Ella.'

Ella laughed. 'I can just imagine producing my fiddle the next time I fancy someone and sending him big seductive looks as I woo him with Weber.'

Her father gave her a pitying glance. 'Not Weber,

Ella. You know yourself who the sexy guys are.'

'The Irish guys?'

'For sure, yeah. But classical is sexy, too. I used to get really turned on when I watched your mother play. Those boys knew what they were doing, all right. Think of Bach. Think of Bruch. Think of Beethoven.'

She nodded. 'Let me guess. The Seventh?'

'The Seventh, for sure. Bloody critics have been falling over each other since it was first written to read an agenda into that piece. Bollocks to all that theorizing.' Declan threw a handful of peanuts into his mouth and chewed vigorously. Then he gave Ella a look of assessment. 'What do *you* think was in his head while he was writing it?'

'That's easy,' she said. 'It's all about sex.'

'That's right! It's all about sex! It's a musical tribute to the best ride Beethoven ever had.'

Ella smiled at her father. 'Does Sakatook like it?'

'She adores it,' said Declan, returning her smile. He took a hefty swig of his pint and then leaned back in his chair. 'So. Tell me about *your* love life, darlin'.'

'Will not,' said Ella, giving him a supercilious look.

'Why not? You've never been particularly coy about it before.'

'It's not because I'm coy, Dad. It's because there's bugger all to tell.'

Declan winced. 'Oh, baby,' he said. 'I *am* sorry.'

'Don't be sorry, Dad. I'd hate to think that I was

one of those sad singletons whose entire *raison d'être* is whether or not they've got a partner. I'm just not interested in the one-night thing, and I like to think I'm choosy about who I'm going to wind up with. I've had it up to here with gobshites.' She looked contemplative. 'And for some reason all the men I've ever been really interested in have turned out to be involved with someone else. Maybe my subconscious is trying to tell me something.'

'Like what?'

'Like I'm not ready for a relationship yet.'

'That wouldn't surprise me. You come from a long line of broken relationships, Ella. You need to be sure that whoever you end up with really is Mr Right.'

She remembered how she'd said as much to Jack once, before he'd hooked up with Angie. She sometimes wondered if she shouldn't have put up more of a fight where Jack was concerned, but then she thought of what her uncle had said to her on the night of that fateful birthday party, and she knew that he'd been right to discourage her. She sighed, and took another swig from her pint.

'I'm sorry,' said Declan.

'For what?'

'For being such crap parents. Francesca and I really messed up, didn't we?'

Ella laughed. 'Don't beat yourself up, Dad. I got so used to the fireworks after a while that I started to think that conventional families were the weird ones. You know, daddies who worked from nine to five and played golf at the weekends; mummies who looked after the kids and did coffee mornings. I mean – *that's* spooky. And don't think I didn't inherit some good things from you.'

'Well, at least you got your looks from your mother. What did you get from me?'

She raised her eyebrows at him. 'A taste for Guinness, of course.'

*   *   *

Her father disappeared back to the States a couple of days after Christmas. He had some big Irish-American gig in Boston to get ready for – a ceilidh to celebrate the New Year. As well as the presents he'd given her for Christmas – expensive, last-minute designer-label purchases he'd obviously picked up in the duty-free on the way over – he'd left behind a package which contained a rake of CDs. Most of them were recordings of his own band's traditional Irish stuff, but he'd included a handful of classical CDs too. *Have a listen to refresh your memory*, read the accompanying note. *And have fun trying to decide which is the sexiest. Then practise playing them for yourself. With love from your prodigal Dad. XXX.* The penultimate sentence had been underlined. Twice.

*   *   *

Ella spent New Year's Eve at a party given by the creative director of Reflex Advertising. When

247

midnight came she was rather taken aback to be inundated with numerous men – and a couple of women – trying to snog her. Somewhat to her chagrin, she resisted all comers without any difficulty. She'd have quite liked to have found at least one of the snoggees worth making a bit of an effort for.

Across the room Jack and Angie were locked in an embrace that wouldn't have looked out of place in a Bond movie. Bloody hell, thought Ella, grabbing a glass of wine from a passing waiter and turning her back on them, only to find herself face to face with the Christmas tree, which was covered in little papier mâché cupids. Cupid! Pah! He was a complete and utter bastard, and Aphrodite was the biggest bitch who ever walked the planet. She glowered at the cupids for a bit, and then gave a sigh of resignation. She wished she didn't like Angie so much. She hadn't even felt the impulse to indulge in the sabotage fantasies she usually devised about Jack's girlfriends this time round. She wasn't very proud to admit it even to herself, but sometimes the sabotage fantasies had really helped. There had been something enormously satisfying in running footage across her mind's eye of her and Jack shopping for lingerie together while Tamara/Saskia/Magda looked on. *Oh – hi, Tamara/Saskia/Magda! Fancy running into you here in the lingerie department of Brown Thomas! Tell me – what do you think of this teddy? Frankly, I always find the poppers on the crotch a little on the uncomfortable side, but ripping them apart just drives Jack wild . . .*

The volume had been turned up on that awful Slade song about wishing it could be Christmas every day, and a load of drunken people had started jumping up and down and punching the air. Ella had just about made up her mind to get out of there when she heard her name being called. It was Rebecca, a girl she'd been pally with during her time at music college. She was shouldering her way towards her through the pogo-ing revellers.

'Ella! How's it going?' she shouted, when she reached her. 'I haven't seen you in ages!'

'Rebecca! Hi!' Ella shouted back.

Rebecca kissed her on the cheek. 'How've you *mumble?*' she said. 'I meant to *mumble* ages ago, but I've been *mumble mumble mumble . . .*'

Ella squinted at her, trying to lip-read, and then she gave up and laid a hand on the other girl's arm. 'Let's go into another room,' she suggested in stentorian tones.

'What?' said Rebecca, with a blank expression.

Ella pointed towards a door to the right. 'It's – quieter – in – there. We'll – be – able – to – hear – each – other.'

They squeezed through the crowded sitting room into the adjoining study, and sat down on the floor in the corner where no-one could trip over them.

'Well, Beck! How are things?' asked Ella, glad to be able to use her normal voice at last.

'Good, good,' said Rebecca, sliding a spliff out of her breast pocket and lighting up. 'On the social side of things, anyway.' A cloud of smoke escaped her lips in a perfect O. 'If you're talking career-wise, on the other hand, it's more *comme-çi, comme-ça.*' She made a wavy motion with her fingers.

'Oh? What are you up to? Anything interesting?'

Rebecca made an apologetic face. 'I'm working for a computer firm.'

'A *computer* firm? *You?*' Rebecca had been one of the most highly regarded students in college. 'Wow. That's a turn-up for the books!'

'Yeah.' Rebecca shrugged, and drew on the joint again. 'Hell. It's the money thing, Ella. I couldn't afford a career as a violinist. I managed to pick up some work with a chamber orchestra in London for a while, but the money was rubbish. When it got to the stage where I was so poor I was actually contemplating selling my fiddle, I knew it was time to get a real-life job. There's stupid money to be made in computers.'

Ella nodded. She could relate to that. How many other casualties had there been from her year? she wondered. She had an image of a legion of injured musicians, dropping out of their musical careers like flies. 'Do you enjoy it?' she asked, curiously.

'Not much. But I keep myself sane by gigging a couple of evenings a week.'

'Oh? Where?'

'O'Brien's.'

Ella knew O'Brien's. It was a small pub in

Rathmines that held regular sessions. There was a good buzz there, but Ella hadn't been near the place for a couple of years. It was more convenient to hang out in Daly's.

'You should drop by some time,' suggested Rebecca.

'I might do that.'

'And bring your fiddle. Join in the session.'

'I haven't played for ages, Becky. I'm very out of practice.'

Becky passed her the joint. 'So? Start practising.'

*　　*　　*

And she did. She spent the next two months practising and practising and practising – until she was satisfied that her confidence was re-established beyond the shadow of a doubt. And then one evening in early March she dropped into O'Brien's with her fiddle, and had a blast. The band played until well after the official closing time, and she established such good rapport with the other musicians that they paid her the ultimate compliment for a fiddler. They asked her back.

January had gone fast, February faster. But March flew. Ella had never been busier. She ran between her day job and her evening sessions, buoyed up by endorphins.

In April there was an unanticipated lull. Bookings in Nesbit & Noonan took a dive, and O'Brien's changed hands. It was bought by a

London consortium who announced that they were going to turn it into a theme pub. The musicians abandoned the joint like rats fleeing a sinking ship. They made desultory noises about investigating a music option elsewhere, but nothing materialized, and Ella suddenly found herself with her evenings free again. It was the first time for ages that she had no idea what to do with herself.

'Do competitions,' said Leonie when Ella rang her to get the latest update on the Dieter saga.

'Won anything recently?' asked Ella, idly hoping that Leonie might have netted another holiday somewhere exotic.

''Fraid not,' said Leonie. 'I spend all my time e-mailing Dieter these days. It's amazing. On my 56 kps modem I can now send text *and* graphic files in a matter of seconds, *and* get a reply back in as many again.'

Holy shomoly. Leonie sounded like a bad voice-over for an IT commercial. 'Is he still coming over in July?' asked Ella, after listening to five minutes of Leonie's technospeak.

'Oh, yes. We're going to have such fun, Ella! I'll be able to pay him back for all the wonderful places he's taken me to on my visits to Berlin. We're going to dine in the Shelbourne and the Merrion and the Clarence—'

'Leonie, I hate to alarm you, but I think you'll find that the Clarence has changed quite a lot since you were there last.'

'Well, of course it has, darling. It's U2's hotel

now, not the hang-out of some dandruffy priests up from the provinces looking for illicit sex. I'm dying to see how Bono and the boys have done it up. And I'm going to take him to the races. Dieter, that is – not Bono. You'll come too, of course, won't you? I'm going to book a table at Leopardstown so we can drink champagne and eat strawberries all after- noon – and have a flutter too, of course. Oh sorry, darling – gotta go. Call waiting is beeping at me. It might be him.'

'Bye, Leonie.'

'Oh, by the way – have a look at today's *Evening Herald*. There's a big competition you might want to enter. The prize is a romantic trip for two to Paris. Bye, darling.'

Ella put the phone down feeling glum. She had no intention of entering the competition. Even if she did win, who would she take with her on a romantic trip to Paris? Bloody no-one.

She heaved a big sigh and returned her attention to the chore she'd been doing before she'd phoned her grandmother. It was a task she'd been putting off doing for months – sorting out her bureau. Her bureau was a repository for everything and anything – brochures, bills, mail that she should have answered ages ago, instruction manuals on everything from her mobile phone to her coffee machine. As she stuffed an application form for life insurance into a binbag, her eyes fell on yet another brochure sticking out from under an unpaid parking ticket with the reg of Patrick's Merc listed on it. Shit. She'd better pay that, she thought, as she put it on top of her 'to keep' pile.

The brochure she'd spotted had a picture of a diver silhouetted against an underwater background of aquamarine blue. A spotty blue and yellow fish hovered in the foreground, and a whole shower of little stripy ones were surging over a reef below. There was a stream of silver bubbles emerging from the diver's mouth, which was clamped round a – she'd called it a 'rubber tube' when she'd first seen that photograph. Now she knew it was a regulator. She opened the brochure and ran her eyes down the text. *Fun, adventure, excitement . . .* she read. *New friends, weekends away, blah blah blah . . .*

She was just about to bin it when an image swam up before her mind's eye, of the first time she'd performed that backward roll off Desirée's dive boat in the Blue Lagoon. The aquamarine fizz as she tumbled through the water, the rush of adrenalin, the first long breaths of cool, compressed air . . . And then she remembered the endorphins it had produced in her the next time she'd done it, and the next and the next, and suddenly she had an overwhelming urge to do it again.

She reached for the phone and punched in the number printed on the brochure. 'Hello?' she said when the phone was picked up at the other end. 'This is Ella Nesbit. I'd like to book a dive.'

*   *   *

The following Thursday evening she drove out to Portdelvin in the little fourth-hand Renault she'd recently purchased. It wasn't anywhere near as gorgeous to handle as Patrick's sleek Merc, of course, but it was nice to have her own set of wheels at last.

It was such a glorious spring evening that she opened the windows. As she drove along the coast road a flotilla of yachts appeared around the headland like a scattering of paper-white butterflies. A light breeze was up, waves were dancing – sunlight bouncing off them – puffy clouds were scudding in the bright blue overhead, and she had Mozart's Fortieth on the cassette player. All in all, it was one of those special April evenings that reminds you that winter does come to an end, and that life can be pretty damn special.

She congratulated herself on a nifty bit of parking on the seafront, and got her gear out of the boot. As she slammed it shut, she heard a familiar voice call her name. She turned, wind whipping strands of hair across her face.

'Richie! Hi!' She skipped across to where he was lounging outside the dive shop, and, standing on tiptoe, kissed him on the cheek. She noticed that he coloured slightly.

'How's it going, my small dive buddy and cohort?' he said, giving her an awkward little punch on the shoulder. 'It seems ages since I last saw you. How was Jamaica?'

'Brilliant. I got certified!'

'Well done, Ella.' He saluted her. 'I can see you inexorably climbing towards divemaster status.'

She made a face. 'Pah! Some hope. What about you? I suppose you're an advanced diver now, with all kinds of specialities under your weight-belt?'

'Sadly, not.' He sat down on the low wall that fronted the dive shop, stretching out long legs.

'Oh?' Ella perched beside him. 'I thought you were going to go straight into advanced training when you finished the first course?'

'So did I. I had to put it off.'

'But why, Richie? You were dead keen.'

'I broke my foot just after I got certified.'

'Ow. How?'

He looked sheepish. 'I slipped on a copy of *Penthouse* and fell down the stairs.'

'What?' She couldn't not laugh. 'I don't believe you!'

'Strange, but true. This will be my first dive since.'

'And this is my first one since Jamaica. Funny we should have picked the same evening!'

'Not really. Ferdia told me you'd booked yourself in, and I thought it would be cool if we could be buddies again.'

'If Ferdia allows us,' she said.

'He's not going to be here. PJ's the dive leader this evening.'

'Oh? Well then, we'll definitely buddy up.' She wondered where Ferdia was, but didn't want to ask.

'Ferdia's supervising a Rescue Diver course in Lissamore.'

'Oh.'

'Anyway, I thought it would be a good idea to get a dive in before I do my advanced stuff. I'm starting the course next week. Why don't you sign up for it?'

'Me? Hah! What's the point?'

'You learn dry-suit diving. I'm damn sure the next time I dive in Irish waters I'm going to want to wear a dry-suit. And you'd be certified for deeper dives. The deeper you dive, the more you see.'

She remembered the reef in Jamaica with its mysterious chasms, and how she'd yearned to explore them further.

'And of course, there's the fun aspect,' Richie reminded her. 'And the adventure and the excitement and all those new friends. *And* the riveting reading material. Da-dah!' With a theatrical flourish he produced a book from his sports bag. It bore the legend *Advanced Training for Open Water Divers*.

Ella made a cross with her fingers as if warding off a vampire. 'Agh! Do you have to go through the whole manual?'

'No. Only the relevant chapters.'

She took the manual from him and started to flick through it. 'Oh look! There's a chapter on spooky night diving. Yikes! Get a load of the illustration.' She indicated a picture of a couple of divers with big, round, scared-looking eyes.

The dive van was rounding the corner. It drew

up alongside them and PJ got out. He looked sick-makingly fit and sporty, and Ella felt inadequate. 'Hey, you two,' he said. 'Are you both diving tonight?'

Ella noticed that a single magpie had landed on a fence across the road. 'If I can hack it,' she said, blowing the bird a kiss. 'I might wimp out again. How's visibility?'

'Not bad. Four, five metres.'

Another magpie joined the one on the fence, and Ella breathed a little easier. 'Four, five metres,' she repeated. 'I'll give it a lash.' She remembered what Desirée had written on her underwater slate when she'd done her qualifying dive in Jamaica. *I can tell you are a fighter . . .* I will do it, she said to herself. I *will* do it.

PJ looked at his watch. 'We'd better get our act together,' he said. 'We don't want it getting dark while we're out there.'

Richie and Ella got up and followed him through into the shop. There was a selection of T-shirts on display on the wall behind the counter. One of them had a picture of a ferocious-looking eel on the front, and bore the legend: GO WHERE OTHERS FEAR TO TREAD. Thanks for that, thought Ella. How very reassuring.

'So you're all certified?' remarked PJ over his shoulder, as he headed towards the rental area where the gear was stored. He riffled among the wetsuits hanging on a rail and handed one over. 'You're a 36, aren't you, Ella?'

'Yeah. And a size three boot, please.'

PJ laughed. 'It's like kitting out one of my niece's Polly Pockets,' he said, running his hand along the shelf where the hideous neoprene bootees were lined up. 'Here you go.' He handed the boots over, and gave her a challenging look. 'Did you know there's an advanced course starting next week, Ella? Why don't you see how you get on tonight, and then make up your mind as to whether you'd be interested in doing it? You might surprise yourself.'

* * *

She did surprise herself. The visibility was adequate, and she didn't get spooked. Of course, there was no comparison to Caribbean waters, but she went down with a different set of expectations. There was no point in being disappointed that there were no jewel-like fish to feed, or fabulous reefs to visit, or Technicolor vistas to feast her eyes on – this underwater terrain was remarkable in its own way, with a restrained, sepia-tinted, rather grainy beauty. Visuals aside, it was the sensation of absolute tranquillity that enraptured in this silent, slow-mo environment. Real life with its humdrum minutiae couldn't touch her down here. She had found the ultimate escape route from the mundane.

At one point she found herself swimming over another buddy team below. Their air bubbles came gliding up to her through the water like silver spheres, and Ella wondered what it would be like to dive stoned. As she watched the great gleaming globes of air travel up past her towards the surface she found herself gazing in wonder at them, and realized that what she was experiencing really didn't need any drug-induced enhancement. She was on a natural high.

All the other divers that evening were men. Some of them did the usual macho things like haw and spit unapologetically once back on the dive boat; swap stories about the wrecks and the depths they'd dived, and indulge in other ostentatious displays of machismo. But the rather sweet thing, Ella thought, was that while diving was for the most part still a male preserve, the motivation behind it revealed a curiously feminine aspect. Other traditionally male sports were thrill-dominated, like rally driving or motorbike racing, or else they were boring, like cricket or golf. These men were going through a quintessentially macho ritual – suiting up, handling tons of backbreaking equipment with apparent insouciance, sporting fearsome-looking knives and enormous torches and compasses and dive computers and hi-tech cameras – all this so that they could spend an hour underwater teasing crabs, tickling sea anemones and starfish, exploring kelp forests – and in spellbinding slow motion. All that relentless *maleness* was really camouflage for what was actually a rather girly sport.

On the way back to harbour Ella found that she couldn't stop smiling. To the west the sun was setting, turning the water an unreal shade of bubblegum pink. To the east, a full moon was rising like a celestial pumpkin. The sky was hazy now, washed with pale cloud, and she was unable to distinguish any demarcation line between sky and sea. The boat bumped fast over the water, and her hair streeled out behind her. She turned shining eyes on Richie. 'I'm going to do it,' she said.

'Do what?'

'The advanced course.'

Richie grinned at her. 'That's my girl,' he said.

*   *   *

Their first class was in underwater navigation. Oops, thought Ella, whose sense of direction was seriously dodgy. PJ told them that with the aid of a compass and their own natural navigational ability they'd soon be able to navigate for themselves. What if you don't *have* any natural navigational ability? Ella wanted to ask, but didn't. Now that she was doing advanced stuff she supposed she'd better try and put a rein on her juvenile sense of humour.

But it wasn't easy. The class had to practise navigating on the promenade before getting into the water, and they all looked like barking loons as they adopted the required position for compass-reading, with one arm thrust straight ahead and the other hand grasping the opposite elbow. 'I – am – a – dalek,' intoned Richie as he trundled along in a northerly direction. 'Search – and – exterminate.'

'It's meant to be "search and recover", Rich,' Ella reminded him.

'Oh, all right then.' Richie put on his dalek voice again. 'Search – and – recover. Search – and – recover. What are you searching for, sweetiepie?'

'Doubloons, of course, darling. What about you?'

'Um. I hadn't really thought about it. How about my *raison d'être*?'

'Oh.' Ella considered. 'I'm not really sure I want to search for my *raison d' être*. What if it turned out to be non-existent, like in a Beckett play? Oh shit – I'm meant to be heading west now, aren't I? One, two, three, four paces. And – turn.'

'Six paces, Ella. We're doing expanding squares now.'

'Oh hell,' she said. 'Why did I ever let you talk me into doing this, Rich?'

'Because I'm a dangerous, silver-tongued bastard, of course,' he replied, flashing her a smile. 'And you can't resist me.'

'Oh yeah,' said Ella. 'I forgot.'

After the navigation dive came a deep dive. ('It'll be dark. If you get disoriented, just hug yourself to double-check you're still alive,' said PJ reassuringly, 'and make sure your bubbles are still going in an upwards direction.' Thanks, PJ, thought Ella.) Then there was a dry-suit dive, a search and recovery dive, and finally a boat dive. Ella spent an entire weekend clambering in and out of the quarry known as the Blackpits in County Wexford. The weather wasn't great, but she didn't mind that the water temperature was only 10 degrees now that she was in a dry-suit. When she first emerged from the latex-sealed garment she was amazed to find that she was indeed bone dry – just like James Bond when he unzipped his dry-suit to reveal a tux. OK, so she wasn't wearing anything as glam as a tux – just a cosy fleecy thing like a babygro called a 'woolly bear' – but she was snug as a bug in it. That, for her, was the biggest plus of the advanced course. Now that she knew she would never have to peel off a wetsuit again she had a real incentive to investigate diving in the cold Atlantic. She and Richie had signed up for one of the dive weekends away in the West. That's where Ferdia was now, Richie had told her. Supervising trainee open water divers.

The dive Ella had most fun with was the search and recovery dive. You had to locate an object underwater, attach a line to it and send it to the surface by filling an air bag with compressed air. She'd finally mastered the art of underwater navigation, and she couldn't help feeling chuffed with herself when her newly acquired compass skills led her straight to the lead weight that PJ had deposited on the bottom for her to find. It was really just like being in the Boy Scouts, she thought, as she deftly twisted the nylon rope into two half-hitches.

Except Boy Scouts weren't allowed to go drinking after their pow-wows or whatever they were called. Once this group of ten students and five masters had completed their briefs and packed up their gear for the day, they would head straight to the local pub. Most of the students were knack-ered and bruised and stiff-muscled after all the exertion, but once through the pub door, second-wind syndrome invariably set in. Ella found that what the manual had predicted was coming true. She was having fun, she was buoyed up by a sense of adventure, and she was making new friends.

Chapter Eleven

One sunny Monday morning developers moved into the building next door to Nesbit & Noonan. It had recently been sold to a firm of accountants. Uh-oh, thought Ella when she saw a skip parked outside. Patrick made no reference to it when he arrived in, but the expression on his face was more eloquent than words. This was going to cause problems, and possibly major ones.

Halfway into her first session of the day, the hammering began. She was working on a television commercial for a cosmetics company who were launching a new range of body lotions. The visuals were stunning, the backing track was silky, the voice she was recording sexy and persuasive. 'For satin-smooth skin,' read the voice-over artist (Bang! A mighty crash came from next door) 'soft as rain-kissed petals' (Bang! Another – even higher on the Richter scale) 'sweeter-smelling than summer in Provence . . .' (Bang!) The voice-over artist hesitated fractionally and then continued. You could hear the uncertainty in her voice. 'That starts to work from the moment you smooth it on in the morning . . .' (Bang again!)

This was useless. There was no point in continuing. 'OK,' said Ella. 'Sorry to stop you there, Lauren. We'll just have to wait until the banging stops.'

'What on earth's going on next door?' asked the agency copywriter who was sitting in on the recording of the commercial.

'They're renovating the building.'

'Oh.' The copywriter frowned. 'That's going to make life very awkward for you lot, isn't it?'

Ella knew it was a potential headache, but she couldn't have word getting around advertising agencies that future recording sessions in Nesbit & Noonan could be problematic. She tried to sound careless. 'Nah. Shouldn't be a problem. I've known this to happen to other studios. Generally speaking the builders are very understanding, and will stop working when you let them know you're about to record. I'm sure Patrick will talk nicely to them. And if they don't want to play ball, we can always threaten them with legal action.' Ella knew she was bluffing. Legal action was something of an empty threat. It could take a year for the case to be heard, and by that time the building work would have finished and the developers would have scarpered. She paused, and cocked an ear. There was a reassuring silence. 'Good. Seems like they've finished. OK, Lauren? Ready to have another go?'

'Sure.' The actress's warm voice came over the speakers.

'Go ahead, then. In your own time.'

They heard Lauren clear her throat and take a deep breath. 'For satin-smooth skin,' she began again (Bang!) 'that feels soft as rain-kissed petals—' (Bang! Bang! Bang!) 'Oh, for Christ's sake!' The actress gave a rather exasperated laugh. 'There's no point in me going on with this, is there?'

'Take five, Lauren. I'll phone up to Patrick now, ask him to check out the situation next door. He'll have things sorted in no time.'

Ten minutes later the banging was as relentless as ever, and the copywriter was 'tching' irritably. She turned to Ella. 'Honestly – this is bananas!' she said. 'You guys are going to have to get something done about this, Ella, and the sooner the better. I'm not prepared to run into another hour of studio time. I've to be somewhere else at eleven.' She gave her watch a fractious glance.

Uh-oh, thought Ella for the second time that day. Things were not looking good.

*　　*　　*

And they got worse. The entire interior of the building next door was disembowelled with painful slowness, its guts dumped unceremoniously in the skip outside. Many skips were filled over the course of the next few weeks. The builders were so noisy and disruptive and so cavalier in their attitude that eventually legal action had to be threatened. Patrick consulted his solicitor and was told that he could sue for loss of income incurred if regular clients had taken their business elsewhere – as they had done, in their droves. The threat of legal action had the effect of making the developers a little more compliant, but there were still inevitably occasions when a session was disrupted by the sharp whine of an angle grinder or the dull vibrato of a drill. Ella developed a perpetual headache, and took to dropping paracetamol. She felt knackered after work every day, sometimes going straight to bed when she got home. The last straw came when the geezer in the house next door to hers started to do home improvements. The noise of drilling pervaded her entire life. She was incensed enough to write to her local political representative – smiling Jim Moran – to ask what he intended doing about the level of noise pollution in Dublin city, but because there was currently no election to curry votes for, she never received any reply to her letter. Neither, unsurprisingly, did Leonie.

One Thursday she staggered out of the studio and made straight for the refuge of her little artisan house in the Liberties, praying that the DIY merchant wouldn't be wielding his drill this evening. The display on her answering machine indicated that there were four messages. Ella poured herself a huge glass of red wine, grabbed a packet of Kettle chips, curled up on her couch and pressed play. No, she didn't want to talk to her friend Tom the trombonist whose message informed her that he was deliriously in love and was coming out of the closet at last. No, she didn't want to talk to her other friend Iseult, who wanted to know if she was going clubbing over the weekend. No, she didn't want details of a new insurance plan. The fourth message was from Richie. 'Hello, my little dive buddy. How's it going? Give me a buzz when you get this. And never forget – Begin With Review And Friend.'

It was the ridiculous mnemonic that divers use to check that their buddy's safely kitted up. Ella laughed for the first time that week. She thought for a minute, and then reached for her Filofax and accessed Richie's number. 'Begin With Review And Friend yourself,' she said when he picked up.

'Ella! Are you all set?'

'All set for what?'

'For our dive weekend away, of course. Don't tell me you've forgotten. We're meant to be going to Lissamore.'

Ella bit her lip. 'Oh, hell, Richie. I'd completely forgotten.'

'But you *are* still coming?'

Oh God. She really just wanted to take it easy this weekend. The idea of kitting up and plodding around weighed down by pounds and pounds and *pounds* of equipment held no allure whatever for her.

'Oh, Richie. I have had the week from hell. I've been working under the most godawful circumstances. I really don't think I could hack it. I'm sorry.' She heaved a big sigh.

The sigh obviously sounded heartfelt, because:

269

'Look, Ella, it's not important,' he put in with alacrity. 'No problem at all.' But she could tell he was trying hard not to sound disappointed. 'I'll see if there's someone else I can buddy up with. I'll ring Ferdia and ask him who else is going. He's organizing this weekend.'

Ella thought hard. She knew it was highly unlikely that Richie would find another buddy at this late stage in the proceedings. It was Thursday evening – they were scheduled to head west in less than twenty-four hours. And for some reason she was goaded by the idea that Ferdia would more than likely assume that she'd wimped out again if she didn't show.

'No, no, Richie,' she said with decision. 'It's OK. I'll go.'

'Look, Ella – you mustn't do it just on my account. If you're not feeling up to it—'

'I'm not feeling up to it right now, but I'll be fine by tomorrow. I've an easy enough day.' There were very few gigs booked. Business was not booming at Nesbit & Noonan.

'Are you sure?'

'Absolutely.' She injected her voice with as much enthusiasm as she could. 'In fact, I can't think of a better way of recovering from the week in hell than by escaping to twenty-five metres.'

'So! We're sorted!'

He sounded so relieved she was glad she'd changed her mind. 'Where'll we meet up?' she asked.

'Wherever suits you.'

'Um. Let's see. Why don't you come by the studio around five? I should be finished before then. My last session's at four, and it's a dawdle.' As long as the fucking drills don't start up, she thought grimly.

'What constitutes a dawdle in the recording world?'

'A producer who wants out of there ASAP after a stressful week. The lure of the pub on Friday is the biggest incentive I know to get the job done fast.'

'OK. I'll get to you by five at the latest.'

'Excellent. We could be in Lissamore by around nine o'clock if the traffic isn't too hellish.'

There was a slight pause at the other end of the phone. 'Hang on a sec, Ella. I know you're mad about that little Renault, but will it get us all the way down to Lissamore? It's a long journey, and the roads after we hit Galway are shite.'

'Ah. You're right.' She'd ask Patrick to lend her the car if he didn't need it himself. He owed her a favour, what with the hard time she'd been having from advertising executives and copywriters about the construction work over the past few weeks. 'Don't worry, Rich. I'm pretty sure I can get my hands on the Merc.'

'Way to go! We'll do this weekend in style, Ella!'

He sounded so pleased that she found herself smiling in spite of herself when she put down the phone. She swigged back her wine, then got up from the couch and wandered into her bedroom, looking out stuff to pack for the weekend. She located her mask and her snorkel and her dive manual in case she needed to revise anything. She stuffed underwear into an overnight bag, along with tracksuit bottoms, T-shirts, jeans and Timberlands. Her suede jacket. It was a Ralph Lauren jacket that had cost her a bomb four years ago, even at its reduced sale price, but she had ripped one of the pockets and had had to demote it to the scruffier section of her wardrobe. She filled a washbag with basics, then added a tube of tinted moisturizer. A waterproof mascara. Lip gloss. Her Chanel 19. Concealer for the horrible zit on her chin. That was the bloody builders' fault, she thought bitterly, peering into the mirror. She only ever got spots when she was run down, and during the last few weeks she'd been run into the ground. She plucked away one or two stray hairs from her eyebrows with tweezers, and reminded herself to add her eyebrow brush and a tub of Vaseline to the contents of her bag. Then she looked more closely at her reflection. The bags and dark circles under her eyes, the pallor and the blotches on her skin sent her flying straight off to bed. She badly needed her beauty sleep.

*   *   *

Patrick did lend her the car. 'Make the most of it,' he told her. 'It's probably the last time you'll ever drive it.'

'Oh? How come?'

'It's too damn expensive to run. I'm in the market for a new car that will cover a mile on a teardrop of petrol.'

'Shame,' replied Ella. 'But mere budgetary constraints have never stopped you buying groovy cars before, Patrick.'

'I never had *real* budgetary constraints before, toots.'

Ella shot him a questioning look, but he just put a finger to his lips. 'I don't want to talk about it, OK?'

'OK.' She put a lid on her curiosity. She knew better than to ask her uncle questions he wasn't prepared to elaborate on. But somewhere in her subconscious a tiny warning bell started to go off. She knew something was up.

When she finished her final session of the day she went through to reception to find Richie chatting to Julian.

'You never told me you worked with someone who was into diving,' said Richie.

'Oh. Hi.' Ella looked at Julian and then she looked back at Richie. 'You two have met, have you?' she asked without enthusiasm.

'Yeah. We've been dive-talking since I spotted the snorkel sticking out of Richie's bag,' said Julian.

'Julian's doing the deep diver speciality course the same weekend I am, Ella. We thought we might buddy up together.'

Ella tried not to look too aghast at the idea of Julian poaching her dive buddy. She made an attempt to change the subject. 'How can you afford to go on a speciality weekend so soon after forking out for this one?' she asked.

'I've got a part-time job doing telesales. I've discovered I'm kinda good at it,' he added, sounding rather perplexed.

Ella wasn't surprised. Richie had a knack of making friends quickly. He'd done it with her, and now, much to her chagrin, he'd obviously gone and done it with Julian. She wished she'd had the nous to warn him off in advance, and then she copped herself on. What business was it of hers who Richie chose to be friendly with? It wasn't as if she had exclusive rights to him, after all. But part of her couldn't help feeling extremely miffed that Julian had now started hijacking her friends. It was bad enough having to work with him.

'Why didn't you *tell* me you were going diving this weekend, Ella?' he asked now in an aggrieved tone, sitting up on the reception desk and swinging his legs. 'You should have done. We could've all three of us gone down in my car.'

'What do you mean?'

'I'm heading down to Lissamore myself. I haven't done a dive weekend for months, so I rang ActivMarine on an impulse yesterday. I was lucky to get a place. They were fully booked, but someone had dropped out at the last moment.'

Oh no! Her weekend was ruined!

'Why *don't* we travel down together?' suggested Richie. 'It would save on petrol money.'

'No!'

Two pairs of eyes turned to Ella. 'Why not?' asked Richie reasonably. 'It makes sense to me.'

'I er – I'd rather have my own transport. I get antsy if I'm somewhere and I have to rely on other people for lifts.'

'Well, maybe I should travel down with you, then,' said Julian.

'No!'

'Why not?'

'Because I'm taking Patrick's car, not the Renault. The Merc's only a two-seater.'

Julian shrugged. 'Oh well. A missed opportunity. Next time you're going diving, Rich –' Rich! How dare he! '– give me a buzz. I'd be glad to give you a lift and buddy up with you.'

Ella looked at her watch. 'Come on, Richie. We'd better head if we're going to try and avoid the worst of the traffic. What a shame you've another session, Julian.'

'No worries. It's a nice gig. Some ISDN with Gabriel Byrne. That guy's a gent.'

'Gabriel Byrne?' exclaimed Richie. 'Holy shomoly! Maybe we could hang about for a bit, Ella? My sister would love his autograph.'

'I'll get it for you another time,' said Ella, shooshing Richie towards the door.

'I'll get it for you this afternoon, if you like,' offered Julian. 'No problem.'

'Hey! Thanks, Julian. I'll be able to bribe my sister to introduce me to all her foxiest friends for that. Nice one! See you later.'

'Yeah. I'll catch up with you in Sweeney's.'

'Sweeney's?'

'The pub next door to where we'll be staying. It's where all the boys go after a day's diving.'

The boys! 'What about the girls?' asked Ella sweetly.

'Oh, they're welcome too,' said Julian with a laugh. 'But I think you'll find that they're outnumbered. You might find that you're very popular all of a sudden, Ella.' He gave her a big wink. 'Even dogs are popular on dive weekends.' *Jesus!* 'That's not to say you're a dog, Ella, or anything like one,' he added hastily, on seeing the look that crossed her face.

Ella swung her bag up over her shoulder and legged it through the door. Fuck, fuck, fuck, she thought as she zapped the locks on the Merc that was parked just outside. Julian Bollard was becoming the bane of her life.

'He seems like a nice bloke,' remarked Richie, sliding into the passenger seat.

Ella made a noncommittal sound as she slid the car into gear. She would have loved to tell Richie the truth, but she knew it wasn't fair to poison his mind against Julian just because *she* had a problem with him. In fact, she supposed, when she allowed herself to think about it, the only person who *did* seem to have a problem with Julian was her. She had just never allowed herself to overcome the rivalry that had sprung up between them from the very first day they had met.

*   *   *

At half-past nine that evening they pulled up outside Sweeney's pub. It was a typical country pub with no pretensions whatsoever. The furnishings were basic, there was worn lino on the floor, and the place looked as if it hadn't had a facelift since the sixties. A fire was burning even though the evening was mild, and there were posters advertising traditional music sessions on the wall.

The place was Friday night crowded, mostly with locals. Looking around, Ella recognized some faces from her ActivMarine course, and was glad to see Sporty Jan's among them. At least there was *one* other girl on this dive weekend. She sat down beside Jan on the end of the vinyl banquette and made small talk until Richie arrived with her pint. She learned that Jan had done her advanced course immediately after Christmas, and had notched up an impressive number of dives. She also learned that Duffer Dan had gone into orbit, and was now aiming for master diver status. How weirdly misleading first impressions were, she thought. She would never have believed that Duffer Dan would make it through even the preliminary course.

As the evening wore on, more diver types

arrived, and a serious party element started to manifest itself. Ella was standing by the bar trying to attract the barman's attention when she had that peculiar sensation you feel when you know instinctively that someone is looking at you. 'How's it going, Ella?' came a voice from behind. She turned round to find Ferdia MacDiarmada standing there. 'I saw your car outside,' he said. 'Are you down for the weekend?'

She nodded. 'Yeah. I got hooked.' She hadn't seen him for six months. He was taller than she remembered, his dreadlocks were blonder, the jagged silver line of the scar on his cheekbone was more marked in contrast to his tanned skin. He'd obviously been away somewhere in the sun.

'So you certified in Jamaica?' he asked.

'Yes.'

'I knew the Caribbean would suit you.'

There was a hiatus while Ella flailed around for something to say. 'Desirée sends her love, by the way.'

Ferdia smiled. 'She's a class act, isn't she? Did she go down with you?'

'Yes. When I told her I'd trained with you she said she would finish the job for you.'

His smile grew broader. 'I'd better drop her a line to say thank you. You're a privileged girl, Ella Nesbit. Desirée doesn't usually have much truck with trainees. She's too busy running the joint.' There was another slightly awkward pause, and then Ferdia said: 'Is this your first time to dive in Irish waters?'

'No. I did the Blackpits.'

'No shit.' He gave her an interested look, which took her off guard. 'You did the advanced course? When?'

'Um – oh, when was it? About three weeks ago.'

'I'm impressed. How was the visibility?'

'Two metres.'

'Well. Sheep's Head Bay will be a cakewalk for you now. Congratulations.'

'Thanks.' She could feel herself going a bit pink. It was time to lob another shot into the conversational vacuum that was spreading uncomfortably between them. 'How's Perdita?' she was inspired to ask.

'Doing well. She's had her first litter.'

'Oh! How old are the pups?'

'Four weeks. Do you want one?'

She shook her head. 'I couldn't. I've no garden. It's a shame. I haven't had a dog since I was little.'

'What kind had you?'

'A shih-tzu.' Ella actually hadn't much liked the dog. It had been overbred and highly strung. She'd always preferred the mongrel next door who looked like Just William's dog. She was just about to explain how they'd been bequeathed the shih-tzu by a neighbour who'd emigrated to Australia, when she heard her name being called.

'Ella! Hi! I just got here.' Julian was shouldering

his way towards her through the crowd. 'God – that was the drive from hell. I got a flat – can you believe it? – just outside Galway. Boy, am I glad to be here at last! I badly need a drink. Anyway, how are *you*, toots? Sorry, sorry – I know you hate being called toots! Maybe I should call you "buddy" instead.' He leaned over and kissed her on the cheek.

Ella was too totally gobsmacked to say anything.

'Let me get you a drink,' said Julian. Then: 'Hey! Ferdia! I haven't seen you in a while. How's it going, man!' Julian looked as if he was going to give Ferdia a high five, but then obviously thought better of it.

'Fine. And you?'

'Cool. Yeah, yeah. Ella can testify to that, can't you, Ella?'

Ella looked blank. What had happened to Julian? He'd transmogrified suddenly into some kind of wannabe blokey dive type.

'Any good dives lately, Ferdia?'

'Yeah. The Red Sea.' Ella noticed that Ferdia's eyes were starting to scan the crowd, as if looking for an escape route.

'Hey! That *Thistlegorm* wreck! Wow. Something else, yeah?' He made a clicking noise with his tongue against the side of his cheek. 'And did you manage to dive the reef at Gebr El Bint?'

Ferdia gave a vague nod.

'Cool, isn't it? Yeah – I got some of my best dives ever there. I'll never forget—'

'Sorry – excuse me, Julian, but PJ's just come in. I need to go over tomorrow's briefs with him. I'll talk to you later.'

And Ferdia disappeared through the crowd.

'Keep blowing bubbles, man!' Julian nodded at his departing back, and did that thing with his chin that Ella hated so much. 'Sound bloke,' he said. He turned to Ella and winked. 'Hope you're not feeling too outnumbered, Ella. I told you there'd be a lot more men than women on this weekend, didn't I? You must be glad you've got me to look after you. Hey – bartender! A bottle of Coors Light! By the neck!!'

Ella looked over to where Richie was roaring his head off in response to some joke of Duffer Dan's. Jan was having an animated conversation with a very sexy-looking divemaster. Ferdia was nowhere to be seen. And then she spotted him over by the door. A stunning-looking woman had just come in, and was greeting Ferdia like someone long lost to her.

'Let's join the gang, Ella,' said Julian. 'We can just squeeze into that corner by the fire if Dan shifts up. You know Dan? Let me tell you about him. He only started diving last October, and already he's got over forty dives notched up. That man is heading towards master scuba diver, no problem. He's doing the rescue diver course next week, and immediately after that he intends to—'

Julian had taken her by the arm and was steering

281

her towards the corner of the room. She didn't hear any more of what he was saying because she was too busy desperately trying to work out an escape plan.

*   *   *

It didn't work. She spent the rest of the evening miserably sandwiched between Julian and the wall. The wall was marginally more interesting, but even more interesting than the wall was the woman who had hijacked Ferdia. She was at least ten years older than him, and elegant in that very *county* way. Her jumper was of butter-coloured cashmere, she was wearing soft suede jeans that shrieked 'expensive', and her glossy chignon could have been styled by Nicky Clarke. She looked a bit like a younger Sophia Loren, smoked Sobranie cigarettes and touched Ferdia on the arm a lot.

As the pub became crowded, Ella's view of the pair was obscured more and more. Two extremely overweight farmers had positioned themselves directly in front of her and she could no longer indulge her voyeuristic tendencies unless she craned uncoolly to one side. When Julian started to drone on to someone about his dives on the Great Barrier Reef yet *again*, she returned her attention to the wall. Finally she announced that she was heading for bed, using the long drive as an excuse for being a party pooper.

'See you for breakfast at eight-thirty, Ella,' said Julian. 'Be sure to eat a hearty one. It's not a good idea to dive on an empty stomach.'

Oh, shut *up*, Julian, she thought as she headed towards Richie to say good night.

'Ella! How art thou, my beloved buddy!' said Richie when he saw her. He got to his feet a bit unsteadily, and wrapped his arms around her. 'Why are you abandoning me so soon? Stay for another.'

'I won't. I'm knackered, Richie. If I don't get a decent night's sleep I might have to wimp out of the dive tomorrow. Remember what happened that time in Sheep's Head Bay.'

'But that was a hangover, not mere tiredness.'

'That was a *colossal* hangover, and if I stay on here drinking I'll run the risk of yet another one. Good night, Rich.'

'I can't let you walk to the hotel on your own. Allow me to escort you.'

'Richie – I'll be fine! It's just across the road!'

He looked dubious but was distracted by the arrival of Duffer Dan. 'There you go, Richie,' said Dan, setting a pint down in front of him.

'Thanks, Dan.' He turned back to Ella. 'Well. If you're sure, Ella?'

'Of course I'm sure, silly. See you in the morning.'

'Well. Good night, then, gorgeous.' Richie leaned down and gave her a big kiss on the cheek.

She took her leave of Jan and Dan and PJ, and left the pub. She noticed, as she headed towards the door, that the two fat farmers who'd obscured her view earlier were now sitting in the place previously occupied by Ferdia and his friend.

Chapter Twelve

The hotel was an old-fashioned place, comfortable, but not remotely luxurious. Ella's room had two single beds, no bathroom, and a shelf with an assortment of books. She ran her eyes along the spines. There was a volume on fly-fishing, a selection of writing by Myles na Gopaleen, the ubiquitous *Men are from Mars, Women are from Venus*. Some paperback romances. She chose one at random. *Passion's Monument,* she read on the cover. *A Tale of Romance, Desire and Lust.* The picture on the front was of a man stripped to his waist with big bulging muscles on him, clutching to his bare chest a fragile-looking chick with long flowing hair. The book fell open at what was obviously a very thoroughly read page.

'Hah!' he laughed, showing his white teeth. 'You little spitfire! You don't want to make it too easy for me, do you?' He jammed his bronzed thigh between her legs and forced them apart. She felt the powerful muscles rub against her pleasure kernel, and in spite of herself felt a shameful stirring there in her most secret place. 'No,' she murmured, drawing the delicately embroidered strap of her gown back up over

her shoulder. 'Please – no.' He raised a hand, and, before she could prevent him, he had wrenched the flimsy fabric asunder. He pulled aside the satin of her bodice and put his mouth to the creamy skin of her breast. She felt her nipples blossom into miniature rosebuds under his tongue, and then she––

'You bastard.'

It was a woman's voice, raised in anger, and it came from the room next to hers. She heard a man's response, but it was pitched so low it was difficult to make out what he was saying. It went on for quite a long time. Ella could make out the occasional isolated phrase – 'going away', 'can't commit', 'please stop beating yourself up, Philippa –'

The woman's voice came again, tearfully this time. 'This is the last time I'm going to allow you to make love to me. I mean it. I just can't *handle* the deceit any more.' As she spoke her voice got quieter and more reasonable, and it became more and more difficult to hear what she was saying. When Ella realized that she was actually straining to hear, she copped herself on at once.

There was silence for a while, and then came a long sigh of pleasure.

Eavesdropping on a row was one thing, but Ella was damn sure she wasn't going to eavesdrop on her neighbours' lovemaking. She'd escape to the bathroom and leave them to it. Quickly she stripped off her clothes and got into her robe. It was a rather gorgeous creation that her father had brought back for her from a tour in Japan – a kimono in rich pink silk, handpainted with lotus flowers. It was far too special to be wearing on a dive weekend in a not-very-groovy provincial hotel, but she'd spilled the contents of an entire cafetière all over herself that morning, and the towelling robe she usually wore was now soaking in her bath at home. She grabbed her washbag, a couple of hotel towels and an apple, and tucked her dive manual under her arm. Suddenly she had second thoughts.

She chucked the manual back into her overnight bag and tucked the steamy paperback under her arm instead, then headed down the corridor to the bathroom. As she kicked the door shut behind her, the paperback slipped to the floor. She picked it up and was instantly arrested by what she read. *You bastard. This is the last time I'm going to allow you to make love to me. I mean it, Dashiel.* Hey! She'd just heard those very words articulated in the bedroom next to hers! Truth *was* stranger than fiction!

Ella turned on the taps and sat on the edge of the bath, running her eyes over the pages. The words 'pleasure kernel' featured a lot, and when she fast-forwarded to the end of the book, she found that it *wasn't* the last time the heroine allowed Dashiel to make love to her. In fact, he 'took' her on numerous more occasions, and in numerous locations – in a box at the opera, in the conservatory of his mansion, on a massive leather couch in his gentleman's club (she'd disguised herself as a serving boy). God! Were women *really* that much of a walkover when it came to great sex? She couldn't remember.

She turned off the taps and got into the bath. She'd been sensible enough to bring Badedas with her – after the last dive weekend she'd been stiff for days – and she soaked for a long time, scanning the paperback romance for more sex scenes. It was risible stuff, but undeniably steamy – full of thrusting, throbbing and 'damp softness'. 'Damp' was such an unattractive word, she thought, casting around for some alternatives. Moist? Yuck – no! That was just as bad. Squelchy? Oh – *gross*! All the synonyms she could think of for women's sexual arousal were horrible.

She flicked on through the pages. The adjectives used for the men bordered on the aggressive: they were all hard and lean and craggy. The women were all soft and supple and yielding. Out of curiosity, she took a disinterested look down at her own naked body. It was . . . Well. She supposed it *was* soft. And kind of supple. And her breasts were . . . creamy. The novelette was pretty damn accurate after all, she thought, as she reached for the soap and ran it over her breasts, noticing that her nipples actually did look a bit like miniature pink rosebuds . . .

Suddenly the door opened and Ferdia MacDiarmada walked in wearing nothing but a towel around his waist. Ella's mouth fell open with shock, and she slid under the Badedas foam like an electric eel. Water swilled into her mouth and she surfaced again, spluttering like a drowning person. Ferdia instantly turned round, his eyes going automatically to her miniature pink rosebuds before being wrenched upwards. Ella crossed her arms over her breasts, made an inarticulate noise of indignation, and tried to conceal her face with the book.

'Ella. Oh, shit – I'm sorry. I should have knocked.' He spread his hands apologetically and backed out of the room before she could say a word.

Across the room she could see herself reflected in the steamy mirror. Her face was bright purple, her mouth was a big round O, and the title of the book screamed at her from the mirror in swirly neon letters nearly as purple as her cheeks. *Passion's Monument,* she read again. *A Tale of Romance, Desire and Lust . . .* It might as well have read: *Passion's Monument. A Tale Told by an Idiot.* Or: *Passion's Monument. A Tale for Sad Singletons with the IQ of Pond Life . . .* Oh fuck. How completely, how *utterly* humiliating.

Ella hurled the book across the room. If the pages had been contaminated with radioactivity she couldn't have hurled it harder. Then she dragged herself out of the bath, wrapped herself in her robe and tiptoed back to her bedroom. In the room next door the couple were still making love. It wasn't loud, huffing and puffing, moaning and groaning kind of lovemaking, but she could tell they were still

289

at it by a kind of gentle susurration that emanated from the room.

She looked crossly at her travel alarm. Jesus – she'd been in the bath for nearly an hour – you'd think they'd have run out of steam by now. Ella got into bed, set her alarm for eight o'clock, turned off the light and shut her eyes. It was no good. Knackered as she was, she just couldn't sleep. The faint murmurings and sighs and low, low laughs from the next door room sharpened the knife edge of her consciousness, keeping longed-for sleep at bay. The minutes dragged on. What was she to do? She'd be like a dog's dinner in the morning if she didn't get to sleep soon.

Suddenly the activity level next door accelerated. Ella could tell from the urgency of her breathing that the female half of the partnership was approaching orgasm. There was a crescendo of little moans, then one loud shuddering sigh, and then a cry of pure pleasure that seemed to go on for ever, followed by a euphoric: 'Oh *God* that was good!'

Wow. Lucky lady, thought Ella. She turned over in bed and made herself comfortable again, thanking God that the bonking couple had stopped at last. The silence was a blissful relief. She had descended to the very verge of oblivion when something brought her back. There was movement in the room next door, followed by a murmur. Followed by a sigh. Followed by a low, low laugh.

Excuse me? she felt like saying. *You said something*

290

earlier about that being the last time you'd ever allow him to make love to you? This wasn't funny. Either the woman was insatiable, or she had an indefatigable lover, or both. Not only was Ella cross now, she was also very jealous. As the sighs from next door increased in volume, she was seized with rage. She flung back her duvet, knelt on the bed and banged on the wall with a furious fist. The sounds stopped. There was one more low, throaty laugh, and then silence fell at last.

Thank God for that, thought Ella, falling on the mattress and then falling fast asleep.

*   *   *

Next door's alarm went off at the same time as hers. She slid out of bed, slung on her silk kimono and shambled doorwards. As she stepped into the corridor someone emerged from the adjacent room. It was Ferdia. Again he was naked apart from the towel around his waist. It was too late for her to dive back into her room. They looked at each other with rather aghast expressions. Then Ella averted her eyes and Ferdia said: 'Morning, Madam Butterfly. Off to the opera?'

She tried to look scathing while still keeping her eyes averted.

'Sorry, that was a cheap gag. I'll let you get through the bathroom first. See you at breakfast.'

Ella gave a gracious nod in his direction and proceeded down the passageway with what she hoped was elegant insouciance. In fact, her progress was more of a kind of reined-in scamper.

'By the way,' he called after her when she reached the door, 'the latch does work. You just have to make sure you shoot it all the way home.'

* * *

Downstairs in the breakfast room, PJ and Ferdia and the other instructors were sitting around a table working out buddy groups. There was no sign of the nymphomaniac Philippa. Ella slunk past them, sat down beside Sporty Jan and helped herself to corn-flakes. There seemed to be rather a dearth of divers. One by one they skulked in, some looking rather the worse for wear. 'You missed a great session last night, Ella,' said Sporty Jan.

'Oh? What time did it go on until?'

'I dunno. I left while the going was good, at around half-past midnight. Your buddy was still there with a rake of pints in front of him.'

'Richie?'

'Yeah. You might want to give him a wake-up call.'

'I will.' Ella put in an order for scrambled eggs and sausages and rashers, then drained her coffee and ran upstairs to Richie's room. PJ had told her he was in Room 27, which was on the other side of the room she'd seen Ferdia coming out of earlier. She wondered, as she tapped on his bedroom door, if Richie too had been kept awake by all that nocturnal activity.

'Rich? Richie!' She knocked harder. 'Hey, Rich,' she called through the keyhole. 'It's time to get up.'

'Uh.'

'Time to get up, Richie!'

'What? Oh. Oh, fuck.' She heard stumbling noises, and then Richie was at the door. He was still fully dressed in the clothes he'd been wearing yesterday.

Ella looked at him in dismay. His hair was sticking up like a brush, his eyes were Basset-hound bloodshot, and his face was as pale as death. He might as well have had a sign hanging around his neck saying: 'This boy will not be going diving today.'

'Richie.'

'Ella. Hi.'

'Go back to bed.'

'No no. No. What time's it? Are we ready to go diving? Um. Oh God.'

'Go back to bed, Richie.'

'What? No, no. I'm fine. Really I am. I'm just a bit, you know . . .'

'Hungover?'

'Mm. Yeah. A bit.' He was having some trouble focusing his eyes.

'Jesus, Rich. You're not just a bit hungover. You're still pissed. There's no way you can dive today.'

'But, Ella, I can't let you down. Look – just give me five minutes. A bit of breakfast and I'll be—' His hand flew to his mouth and he turned a shade which Ella couldn't identify. It was somewhere between jaundiced yellow and poisonous green. 'Oh fuck,' he said. 'I think I'm going to—' He suddenly shut the door in Ella's face and she could hear him stumbling across the room again.

'Throw up,' she finished for him.

There came the sound of violent retching, and then Ella heard him say in a very small voice: 'It's OK, Ella – I made the wash-hand basin.'

'All right, Rich. Go back to bed and take it easy. I'll find another buddy, no problem.'

She trailed back down the stairs and into the breakfast room, almost walking straight into Ferdia. Oh God, oh God. How could she ever bring herself to look him in the face again? She looked into his face. It was the bravest thing she had ever done. 'Richie's not well,' she said.

'You mean Richie's hungover,' he said.

She nodded. 'What'll I do about a buddy?' she asked.

'It's OK. There were a few casualties last night. Richie wasn't the only one. We can re-jig the buddy teams and make sure nobody's left out. Leave it with me.'

Ella meandered across the room to her place beside Jan. The waitress had just set her breakfast in front of her. 'Sorry – that's not mine,' said Jan. 'I ordered boiled eggs, not poached.'

'Oh. It must be for this gentleman, so.' The waitress turned to the table behind Ella's chair.

'Yes – that's mine all right,' said Julian. 'Morning, Ella. How did you sleep?'

Ferdia was passing the table. Their eyes met, and the air between suddenly crackled with – with what? In her case the moment was charged with the purest embarrassment. *How did she sleep?* He knew very well how she'd slept – or rather, not slept. She could tell that he, too, was clearly thinking back to the peremptory way she'd banged on the wall to interrupt his *coitus* last night. However, she wasn't at all convinced that he was embarrassed by it. She was sure she saw his mouth curve in a barely perceptible smile after they'd broken eye contact.

'Um. I slept OK,' she said, pouring herself more coffee, and bracing herself for a further bombardment of dive savvy from behind. Luckily, Julian had found a novice to bore. 'Residual nitrogen . . .' she heard. 'Narcosis . . . decompression limits . . .' Drone, drone, drone . . .

Ella's breakfast arrived and she ate as much of it as she could, although she didn't have much of an appetite. Julian put away all of his, as did Sporty Jan. Before they got up from the table, Ferdia rose to his feet.

'I just want to run the new buddy teams by you. Some of the group are a bit under the weather this morning—'

'Under the weather? Under the influence, you mean, Ferdia! Ha ha ha!' went Julian.

295

Ferdia gave him a wan smile in return. 'You and Ella will be buddying up, Julian. Dan – you and Frank are a team. Jan, you're diving with . . .'

Ella didn't hear any more. She felt like Roy Scheider that time the camera zooms in on him when he first spots the shark in *Jaws*. Like an automaton, she turned to her new dive buddy, her face a mask of rigidity.

'Well, Ella,' said Julian, jocularly raising his teacup to her. 'Here's to the start of beautiful buddydom.'

* * *

He was the buddy from hell. He was a complete martinet underwater, bossing her around and refusing to let her take any initiative whatsoever. Instead of chilling and taking time out to explore their surroundings in a laid-back, leisurely manner, he insisted on swimming off like a NATO submarine, ploughing through forests of kelp without once stopping to investigate what intriguing creatures might inhabit this seascape. He navigated with ruthless efficiency, heading north, south, east and west like a male version of Lara Croft on speed. Any time Ella tried to slow down the proceedings he would hover directly in her line of vision with his arms folded and an expression of terminal boredom on his face under the mask.

He also kept making denigratory remarks in sign language about her buoyancy control. She still hadn't quite mastered dry-suit buoyancy, and every time he criticized her technique or demonstrated to her exactly how she should be venting air, she would find herself ascending uncontrollably, and in total confusion. *I'm up here, you idiot*, she felt like shouting to him the third time she disappeared, while he searched around for her ineffectually below. When he eventually found her, he actually had the temerity to practically manhandle her back down to the bottom.

When they finally surfaced, Julian was smirking. 'Well, Ella,' he said, as they inflated their jackets, 'you've still got a lot to learn about buoyancy control, haven't you? Maybe you should re-read that module in the manual. You see, what you're doing wrong is—'

Ella didn't want to hear any more. She put her snorkel in her mouth, stuck her face in the water, and started finning back to shore. Once there, she began taking off her gear.

'You should wait for me,' shouted Julian. He was floundering around in the shallows trying to pull off his fins. 'We should be helping each other to doff our equipment according to the buddy system.'

'Oh fuck off back to hell, Julian. Some buddy you were.' Ella dropped her weight-belt on the slipway, and pulled at the releases on her jacket.

'Oh! Excuse *me*, Ms Nesbit. I was only trying to help.' She was glad to see that he was continuing to flounder ineffectually.

'I'll help you out of that.' Ferdia was coming

down the slipway towards her. 'How was your dive?'

'Bloody awful,' she said, anger making her forthright. 'My buoyancy control was non-existent – and there's another thing.' She lowered her voice. 'Please, please, Ferdia – let me have another buddy this afternoon. I can't hack Julian.'

'I thought you'd be well matched.' Ferdia hefted the tank off her back and set it down beside her weight-belt. Relieved of all those excess pounds, she felt as if she was levitating. She looked up at him. Because he was further than her up the slipway, he appeared taller than ever.

'What on earth made you think that?' she asked.

'You're obviously very good friends.'

'What?'

'Well – that's the impression I got in the pub last night.'

'We're colleagues, that's all.' How could he think that she and Julian had *anything* in common? He'd obviously totally misjudged her. 'We work in the same studio.'

'So you're in the élite world of recording as well?'

Something about the amused tone in his voice made her bridle. There's bugger all élite about it, macho man, she wanted to say, but didn't. She needed to keep him on her side. 'Yeah,' she replied. 'You see, that's one of the reasons I don't think it's a good idea for me and Julian to be buddies. We work in such close proximity that we know each other too well. I think it's probably a good

298

idea if we take a break from each other this weekend.'

Ferdia pondered. 'OK. Leave it with me.'

Julian was staggering up the slipway. 'Hey, man!' He tried to give Ferdia a high-five and then changed it into a kind of salute when he realized it wasn't going to be reciprocated. 'Great dive.'

'Speak for yourself,' muttered Ella. Under the tight-fitting neoprene hood Julian's face looked like a squashed bun. Realizing that hers probably did too, she hastily pulled her hood off.

'I understand Ella had some problems with her bouyancy,' remarked Ferdia.

'Yeah. She was all over the place, man!' Julian laughed, and started to do an impersonation of her flailing around underwater. Ella was not remotely amused. She also wished he'd stop saying 'man'. As far as she was concerned, the only people who could get away with high-fiving and saying 'man' were black.

'Look,' said Ferdia. 'I'm going to propose a change to the buddy teams. Ella could obviously do with some more tuition, so I'll go down with her this afternoon. You can buddy up with Alex, Julian.'

'Alex? Hey! When did he arrive?'

'Just this morning. He was too late for the first dive.'

'OK,' said Julian. 'That's cool with me. At least I won't have to keep worrying about where Ella's taken off to every five minutes.' And he started his flailing piss-take again.

'Ha ha, Julian.' Ella stomped off up the slipway in search of her sandwiches.

She spent the interval between dives sitting in the car going over the dry-suit chapter in her manual. Within minutes it had sent her to sleep and she drifted off into a dream that started off innocuously enough but became increasingly erotic. Now she was being clasped against some man's muscular torso, and her hair was streaming out behind her in the wind. She could feel her nipples rubbing against his bare chest, but she didn't have a clue who he was, and she didn't have the nerve to look up at his face. A name suddenly came into her mind. 'Dashiel?' she said tentatively, but when she finally plucked up the courage to look at him she found that it wasn't Dashiel, the hero of *Passion's Monument*, it was—

Someone was tapping on the driver's window.

'Ferdia?' she hazarded, groggily emerging from her dream.

'Yeah. Ready to get wet?'

'What?' The dive manual slithered to the floor.

'We're diving together this afternoon, remember?'

'Oh. Oh, yes. Right.' She stepped out of the Mercedes, feeling a bit ridiculous in her woolly bear. Ferdia had his dry-suit only half on so that he wouldn't overheat, the arms knotted loosely around his hips. He looked like something from a sword and sorcery flick. A thick, heavy-duty zip ran from hip to hip across his pelvis. She'd never seen a suit like it before.

'I've been searching for a suit with a fly opening for ages,' he said, when he saw her looking. 'They're difficult to find and they don't come cheap, but it's a real relief when you're doing repetitive dives not to have to get in and out of a suit every time you need to take a leak.'

'What about us girls?' asked Ella, stepping into the legs of her much less glamorous membrane garment.

'Yet another design fault,' he said, laughing down at her.

*   *   *

This dive was a revelation. She had never dreamed that Irish waters contained such wonderful stuff! Once Ferdia had successfully taught her how to manage her buoyancy, she was able to look around at leisure and see for herself all the exotica she'd missed during the earlier disastrous dive with Julian. The marine life wasn't as abundant as it had been in Jamaica, but what she saw was just as awe-inspiring. She remembered how she'd compared the Jamaican reefs to something by Lainey Keogh. That had been her Spring collection: this was her Autumn one. The terrain looked as if it had been scattered with gold dust. There were tattooed crabs, there were starfish ranging from the size of a dinner plate to the size of her smallest fingernail all tangled up in skeins of silk, there were jellyfish, translucent, and ethereal – and so sensuous to touch! He led her through pink algae like giant swansdown powder puffs, and Ella was reminded of her Caribbean mermaids. If the reefs she explored off that far-away tropical island had been the mer-queen's banqueting hall, then this was her boudoir!

She'd sneered at Julian when he'd used OTT adjectives like 'amazing' and 'astonishing' to describe tubeworms. Now she had to admit that he'd been right. The word 'tubeworm' itself was a totally off-putting misnomer. They should be called sea jewels, she thought, or sea fairies – something that did their dazzling beauty justice. Each individual home was a miniature angel's trumpet, while their colonies were the kind of confections you'd see in the window of a prize-winning florist's. Some of the worms had laid claim to an old rubber tyre, transforming it into a stunningly gorgeous iridescent wreath. Ella laughed out loud when a flick of Ferdia's finger sent the muppet-haired worms diving back into their shells, and laughed even more when she tried it for herself. It was just like seeing the lights on a Christmas tree going on and off she thought, as she swam around flicking her fingers at them like a crazed witch casting spells.

But what made her laugh more than anything were the scallops. When prodded by Ferdia they took off up into the water, snapping their shells open and shut over and over again like furious animated false teeth, until they finally settled down on the seabed once more.

When she was able to stop laughing, she became aware that Ferdia was touching her lightly on the arm. She turned to him, and he pointed across a marine valley. On the other side, about ten metres away from them, she could just make out a dozen or so great, streamlined shapes. She turned back to him with alarm scrawled all over her face. He knew by her expression that she was asking if the creatures were sharks. He shook his head. Then he drew a smile across his face with his left index finger, and moved his right hand in an undulating, rhythmic fashion, the way a dolphin swims through the water.

Dolphins! Oh – heaven! *Dolphins!* Ella wanted to cry with happiness. She had never experienced such euphoria in her life as she did now, watching the school's graceful progress into the blue beyond. To judge by their comparative sizes there were about eight adults and three calves. Come back! Come back! she wailed inwardly. Surely they could sense the yearning that was emanating from her like ectoplasm? But the svelte outlines slowly disappeared into the distance like a receding dream.

She turned back to Ferdia, wonder in her eyes. He smiled and spread his hands in an attitude of regret, then indicated that she should follow him.

As they descended into a valley carpeted with billions upon billions of brittlefish – starfish whose filmy limbs floated around them like fronds – Ella realized that they'd gone quite deep. Her gauge read twenty-seven metres. She also saw that she'd used up rather a lot of air with all that laughing and oohing and aahing. She showed Ferdia the level on her gauge, and gave him a questioning look. He responded by signalling: *It's cool, relax. Everything's OK* with his right hand, and then: *Let's get ready to go up* with his left.

Wait, she told him. The legs of her suit had become filled with excess air, and she needed to perform the trick that would help her dump the stuff, otherwise she would make a thoroughly undignified and hazardous feet-first ascent. She tucked herself into a ball and quickly rolled over on to her back, feeling the air rush to the exhaust valve on her arm. Her legs dropped back on a level with the rest of her body, and she couldn't help feeling chuffed with herself for having executed the manoeuvre with such dexterity.

OK, she signalled, readying herself to fin upwards. Nothing happened. Maybe she was carrying too much weight? She depressed the inflator valve on the front of her suit a couple of times to give her buoyancy a boost, and tried harder, concentrating on using her thigh muscles to get her ascent going. It was no good. Something was holding her back. She descended a little, pushed herself off the bottom and made another effort to ascend – again without success.

Ella was no longer feeling chuffed with herself. Claustrophobia threatened, and she was starting to feel scared now. She signalled to Ferdia that she had a problem. As soon as he saw the expression on her face he signed to her to stop moving. *Take it easy*, he motioned with a hand. *Stay calm, everything's cool. Breathe slowly.* She tried to do as he advised, but she could hear her breath coming and going in a rush, very shakily. Ferdia checked the air level on her gauge again, and she saw his brow furrow a little under his mask. When he next looked at her, however, there was nothing but reassurance in his demeanour, nothing whatsoever to indicate that he was concerned. *Trust me*, said his eyes.

He moved round behind her, and in her peripheral vision she could see him withdraw his knife from the scabbard on his thigh. For a split second she felt a surge of pure blind panic. What the fuck was going on? Oh God oh God – she was in some grotesque nightmare, and she just wanted *out* of there! Ella lunged for her inflator valve with her left hand, and for the release on her weight-belt with her right. In a flash Ferdia had pre-empted her, grabbing both her hands with his free one before she could dump her weights. *No!* he signalled in no uncertain terms. *Trust me!* He hovered there, holding her wrists together, looking directly into her eyes, forcing her to think. She remembered the rule that was iterated on every single page of the dive manual that dealt with potential emergencies. Stay calm. *Stay calm.* What she had been about to do had been an act of lunacy. If she'd dumped her weight-belt she would have gone into a runaway ascent straight to the surface, possibly rupturing her lungs in the process, and running a real risk of contracting the bends.

Ferdia waited until he was sure she was calmer, and then pointed to some fine lines of nylon that were undulating upwards. With an articulate hand he mimed a cutting motion, studying her expression closely to make sure she understood what he was going to do. He pointed to her tank and then showed her the knife again.

Oh God. She was entangled in fishing line. It must have happened when she'd done her backward roll. Jesus. Here they were, down deep, consuming air four times faster than they would on the surface, and Ferdia was going to have to waste precious minutes cutting her free of the nylon that had wound itself insidiously around her life support system. She showed him her gauge again. It was perilously low. In response, he showed her his own, letting her know that if they needed to share air, he had enough to spare. He had at least twice as much remaining as she did. How could that be? And then she remembered that, because he was the more experienced diver, he automatically conserved air by always, always breathing slowly.

OK. She'd do the same. She made a huge effort to control her breathing. Stay calm, she told herself. Breathe easy and stay calm. Ferdia had moved around behind her again and was working methodically at cutting away the fishing line. She fought hard against the impulse to try and help him by attempting to wriggle free of the tenacious stuff. She knew that if she did that she ran the risk of making the entanglement even worse. So she just hung there in the water like a puppet, quite inert, trying to breathe evenly.

Ferdia's hands moved to her shoulders. He angled her around to face him and looked intently into her eyes. Was she OK? Yes, she signalled back. She was OK. He showed her the knife again, formed his thumb and forefinger into an eloquent O, and then stowed the blade back in its scabbard. She was free!

The relief she felt drenched her, and she took a long, shuddery gasp of air, realizing as she did so that breathing was becoming more difficult. Again Ferdia could tell by her face that something was wrong. *What's the problem?* he asked with his eyes. She responded with the 'out of air' signal, and Ferdia reached for her gauge. Then he took hold of his spare regulator and indicated that she was to ditch her own and insert the one he was holding out to her. *Trust me?* he asked, and Ella responded with the OK sign. Oh God. She wasn't sure if she *was* OK. She hadn't performed this exercise in sharing air since her training dives in Jamaica. Her hand was shaking as she took her own regulator out of her mouth, dumped it and then reached for Ferdia's spare. For a split second she felt terrifyingly vulnerable. Here she was, twenty-seven metres under, reaching out to the only person on the face of the planet who could help her. She grabbed the regulator, stuck it in her mouth, registered the taste of salt water, purged it, coughed a little into it, and then started to take great gulping breaths. After a few dodgy seconds, she settled down.

OK? his fingers asked her.

OK, replied Ella's.

Shall we go up? This time he signed with his thumb.

She found herself nodding her head. 'Yes please,' she said into her regulator in a very small voice.

Ferdia extended his forearm to her, and for a second Ella wondered what he was doing, offering her an arm as if he were escorting her into dinner . . . Of course! They would have to ascend in tandem, maintaining physical contact until they hit the surface, using the Roman handclasp.

It seemed to take for ever. She kept her eyes glued to Ferdia's; he only let his drop from hers when it was essential to consult his pressure gauge for their ascent rate. Five metres away from the surface he indicated that they had to perform the requisite safety stop for three minutes. Did she feel confident enough to do it? Was she settled? Would she rather go straight on up? Ella knew how important the safety stop was after deep dives, and she found herself automatically giving the OK signal, before realizing that yes, in fact, she *was* perfectly calm now. Her breathing was no longer ragged: it was slow and measured. She could hear it in her head – the rythmical in and out of it. Ferdia had a firm hold on her and his eyes were eloquent with reassurance. He looked at his watch, and then back at her. Two minutes, he signalled. Oh God. One minute. She started counting her breaths. This had to be the longest sixty seconds of her life.

Then at last came the longed-for signal to surface. They finned in tandem, up through the filtered rays of the tantalizing sunlight that was shimmering on the surface. Once they broke through the water Ferdia immediately inflated his jacket, and then he put his mouth to the valve on her BCD and blew into it, steadily, rhythmically. It took only three breaths to make her positively buoyant. 'OK?' he asked, regarding her closely. His eyes were narrowed against the sun and fringed with spiky lashes, and two drops of water were glistening on his earlobes like diamonds.

'OK,' she mumbled. She wanted to kiss him. This man had saved her life. She took the spare regulator out of her mouth. 'You saved my life,' she said.

'Save your breath,' he returned – a tad ungraciously, she thought. 'We've a fair way to swim. Stick your snorkel in your mouth and we'll fin back to shore.'

By the time they made the shore she was exhausted. Ferdia helped her off with her fins and tank and weight-belt and she flopped down on her back on the slipway.

'Thank you,' she said, when she could breathe again.

'No problem,' he said, shrugging out of his BCD and depositing it tank-side down on the ridged concrete. Then he started pulling off his black neoprene gloves, looking down at her with speculative eyes. 'Well. You learned two new facts of life this afternoon, Ella, my girl.'

'Yeah? What did I learn?'

'You learned to keep calm under pressure. And you learned that there's nothing like a near-death experience to give you an appetite. I am fucking starving after that one, I can tell you. I will demolish my bacon and cabbage this evening.'

Ella gave a shaky laugh. 'I don't know about the keeping calm under pressure bit. I got seriously spooked down there. I bet you were tempted to just stick that knife in me and leg it.'

He smiled. 'And leave you to the sharks? I'm too well-mannered to do that.' He pushed his damp dreadlocks back from his face, and then he stretched. The way he did it was easily as sexy as the way Jack stretched. In fact, she decided, it was sexier. 'It's a real plus that you managed that safety stop, Ella. It's like overcoming a psychological hurdle. You'll find that it'll do wonders for your confidence.'

'Well,' she said, pulling off her hood and shaking out her hair. 'I suppose that manual is pretty accurate when they talk about the adventure of scuba diving. I'm not sure about the fun element, though.'

He raised an eyebrow at her. 'Come on. You had a ball down there. You were like a little girl with a toy shop all to herself.'

She thought about it for a minute. Then: 'Yes,' she admitted. 'I suppose I was.' She sat up suddenly, wreathed in smiles. 'Those dolphins! Oh man! I got such a blast!' She realized that she was talking a bit like Julian did when he went into 'I am a super-cool dive god' mode, and she told herself to shut up. 'Have you ever dived with dolphins, Ferdia?'

'Oh, yeah. And with seals, too. They've an amazing sense of humour. They love to play games.'

'Oh!' She wanted to do that! She wanted to play underwater with dolphins and seals. Dolphins were the best endorphins she'd ever had. 'Maybe we'll see them again tomorrow?'

'With a bit of luck I might see them again tonight.'

'How come?'

'I've a night dive scheduled.'

For some reason she felt absurdly disappointed. 'Does that mean you won't be going to the pub?'

He gave her a scathing look. 'Damn right I'll be going to the pub. I'll just hit it a bit later than you guys, that's all. Do you really think I could stay away after what you put me through this afternoon?'

She realized as he smiled down at her that he was focusing on her mouth, and she automatically found herself parting her lips a little.

But he didn't kiss her. He just put out a finger and lightly indicated the area between her nose and mouth. 'You might want to do something about that,' he said.

'About what?'

'You have diver's face.' And then he turned and strode up the slipway, swinging his tank by the valve.

Chapter Thirteen

When they got back to the hotel, Ella nabbed the bathroom. She had a quick shower, washed her hair and scrubbed her teeth. Back in her bedroom she lashed on body lotion and inspected her face in the mirror. Thank God her skin wasn't as blotchy as it had been, but the spot on her chin was still in evidence. She coloured it in with concealer, and then she stuck on some mascara, telling herself that if she was going to be going diving on a regular basis it might be advisable to invest in an eyelash tint from time to time. She combed Vaseline through her eyebrows, slicked a little gloss over her lips, and sprayed herself with Chanel 19.

On her way to the dining room she passed Ferdia, who was emerging from the bathroom with that ubiquitous towel around his waist. His hair was wet, and Ella found herself wondering how often dreadlocks needed washing. He smelt gloriously clean. Musky, masculine, with top notes of . . . vanilla. Ella was reminded of the soap she'd nicked in Jamaica.

'Oh, hi!' she said, trying to sound dead casual. It wasn't easy.

'Hi,' he said. 'I was just about to knock on your bedroom door.'

'Oh?' Oh God! Why? 'Why?' She hoped she didn't sound too disingenuous.

'I found this in the bathroom.' He held up a book. It was fucking fucking *Passion's Monument.* Oh *no*! 'It *is* yours, isn't it?' he asked. 'I couldn't help noticing that you were reading it in the bath last night.'

'Oh – yes. Well, it's not mine really, actually. It's um – the hotel's. I found it in my room.'

'I noticed that you were dozing under your dive manual this afternoon.' He smiled and started flicking through the pages. 'You certainly wouldn't have dropped off if you'd been reading this. This stuff's steamy enough to rouse the dead.' He ran his eyes down one of the pages and shook his head. 'Page sixty-nine's a real eye-opener. Must try it some time.' He handed her the book, raised an eyebrow at her, smiled and strolled off down the corridor. 'See you at dinner, vixen,' he threw over his shoulder.

Vixen? What was he on about? Ella staggered back into her room to jettison the odious book. Before she returned it to the shelf, however, she decided she had time before dinner to have a quick look at page sixty-nine. Dashiel and Victoria were at it again, this time starkers in a lake.

'Oh,' she gasped as his hands moved to her two firm, well separated breasts. She raised her loins to him, unable to resist the overwhelming desire to rub

314

her pleasure kernel against his muscular thighs.

'Hah!' he spat. 'This time we'll do it my way!'

She gasped. 'Which way is that?' she queried. 'You would not wish to harm me, Dashiel?'

'I harm you, vixen? Nay. My aim is merely to pleasure you.' He flipped her over and before she could gasp again he thrust—

Ella suddenly became aware that someone was tapping on the wall.

'Ella?' It was Ferdia's voice. 'Have you got to the bit where he flips her over yet?'

Ella felt her face flare up. 'D'you know something, Ferdia?' she said. 'I'm not very sure about you.'

'That's OK, vixen. You're not the only one.' She heard him laugh in the next-door room, and then he started humming something. A sudden image of him flashed across her mind's eye, standing naked mere feet away from her on the other side of the wall, towelling dry his dreadlocks. She had tried not to look at his physique too much earlier when he'd accosted her outside the bathroom, but it had been difficult not to. He had a wonderful, toned, muscular body – but he wasn't off-puttingly muscly the way some blokes were. Those kind of blokes kept in shape by working out: her gym was full of narcissistic types who didn't impress her at all with their pathetic posing and the way they ostentatiously clanked the weight-lifting equipment.

She doubted if Ferdia even knew what the inside

of a gym looked like. She reckoned it was sheer physical hard graft that kept him in prime nick, the way construction workers often were. There was something incredibly sexy about a guy who could look so good without working at it the way most other people had to. She knew she'd get flabby if she didn't exercise regularly. Hey! Maybe if she kept on diving she wouldn't need to go to the torture chamber that was her gym. Yet another incentive to carry on with her new hobby!

It wasn't the only incentive. She now knew with gobsmacking clarity that she fancied the arse off Ferdia, and would welcome any chance she could grab to see him again – even if it meant diving in that vile quarry. When had it happened, she wondered? There'd certainly been no *coup de foudre* to announce it. Had it kicked in today, maybe, when he'd saved her life? Or had the first seed been planted last night in bed, when she'd been subjected to the unmistakable evidence of his talent for 'pleasuring' women? Or had it been that time in Sheep's Head Bay when he'd told her that he loved her stockings and then wandered away whistling Beethoven's Seventh? No. Something told her that it went back earlier still. Something told her that she'd actually fancied him from that first night in the classroom when he'd told her that he loved the way she looped her L's, and that her infatuation had kicked in irreversibly when she'd witnessed his handling of the poor stray bitch he'd adopted. Something told her that she and Perdita had become smitten simultaneously. But while Perdita had made no secret of the fact, Ella had been in denial for months.

What was she to *do*? She sat down on the bed and chewed her lip, then got up again and checked out her eyebrows, plucking away a few hairs to make them look slantier. She started to think tactically. In the mirror her eyes went narrow with concentration. In the room next door, Ferdia was still humming.

Absent-mindedly Ella started to plait a hank of hair. She was reasonably certain that the stunning-looking woman who'd accosted the instructor in the pub last night was Philippa, the one who'd been at the receiving end of all the 'pleasuring' that had gone on later. Hah! If that was the case, then she, Ella, wasn't even a contender. That woman had been incredibly sexy. Elegant, too. Way too classy for a country pub. Hell's bells! Life was so bloody *unfair*! First there'd been Jack with his string of sophisticates, and now Ferdia with what was obviously a similar preference. What *was* it about classy women? How did you get to *be* classy?

Hang on. She started to drum her fingers lightly on the edge of the dressing table. This was interesting. After all, didn't she have a few classy trappings? Ferdia couldn't know that Patrick's nifty little Merc didn't belong to her. He imagined – like most people – that the recording business was glamorous. He assumed she had the kind of lifestyle that permitted her to go jet-setting off to Jamaica for dive holidays. He even thought she was the kind of dame that swanned around in silk kimonos in preference to more pedestrian high street shop dressing gowns. And Richie had told her the first time he met her that *he* thought she was a classy chick . . .

Maybe she could do it! Maybe she *could* do class . . . She looked at herself in the mirror and adopted the bored expression favoured by catwalk models. It looked stupid. Then she twisted her plait into a chignon like posh Philippa's. Nah . . . Nice try, but no cigar. She ran her fingers through her hair and shook it out. There was nothing much she could do about the way she looked, she decided, or even about the way she behaved. She was no actress. But she'd been handed some very convenient props on a plate. The posh car, the expensive holiday, the 'groovy' job just might have gone a little way towards establishing her somewhere in his consciousness as a gal with style and taste. She took a last look in the mirror. Her eyebrows looked lovely. Hell – it was a long shot. But it was a shot worth aiming for.

Suddenly she noticed the tacky paperback where it lay open on the dressing table, and a wave of despair washed over her. What gal with style and taste would read books like *Passion's* bloody *Monument*? Hah! What was she *doing*, pretending to be somebody she wasn't? She was crap at bluffing: it had always been her Achilles' heel in poker games. And this game involved a whole new set of rules: this game was dangerous because it involved playing with fire. Ella suspected she could get very badly burned. And then she remembered the way she'd felt when she'd watched Ferdia stretch earlier in the day on the slipway after he'd saved her life, when she'd wanted – really, really wanted – him to kiss her . . .

She took a deep breath, opened the door and walked down the stairs towards the dining room, preparing to light the fuse.

*   *   *

At dinner she sized up the seating arrangements. A long table had been set with a dozen or so places. She wasn't the first one there, but she was early enough to take her pick. One place still had unclaimed chairs on either side, so she sat down there.

She ordered seafood chowder to start, and a glass of wine, and was just about to ask what the catch of the day was when Julian walked into the dining room, followed by Ferdia, the *real* catch of the day. She stiffened, willing Julian to sit at the opposite end of the table, and willing Ferdia to sit down beside her. She sent him a smile that she hoped was inviting. Good. He'd seen her. Oh, wow – amazing! He was heading in her direction.

'The catch of the day is hake,' said the waitress.

'Sounds good,' said Julian, pulling out the chair beside her. He sat down and rubbed his hands together. 'I've one hell of an appetite. Always have

319

after a day spent thirty metres under. How did you get on, Ella? Got a grip on your buoyancy control yet?' And he did that stupid jokey imitation of her for the third time that day.

Across the room she could see Ferdia registering Julian's presence beside her. He paused fractionally, obviously reviewing his seating plan, and then he turned and joined PJ at another table. Ella felt full of murderous rage. She wanted to grab a knife off the table and stick it in Julian's heart.

Instead: 'Hake would be lovely,' she said to the waitress. 'And maybe you could bring a banana for the ape who's just sat down beside me.'

'Hey! Lighten up, Ella,' said Julian, with an irritating laugh. 'Everyone else thinks my take-off of you is brilliant. I had people in stitches over it earlier. Someone even captured it on camera for posterity. It'll go down a bomb at the ActivMarine Christmas party.'

'At which you, no doubt, Julian, will be the life and soul,' returned Ella frostily.

'God – what's got into you? I thought, being a new girl, you'd have been grateful to me for joining you and not leaving you sitting there all by yourself like Ms Norma No Friends.'

Richie wandered into the dining room, looking a little green around the gills, but nowhere near as wretched as he'd looked that morning. 'Hello, ex-buddy,' he said, sliding into the chair on her left. 'How did things go for you today?'

'Good,' she said, ignoring Julian's smirk. 'It's a

shame you missed it. There's some amazing stuff down there.'

'I'll give it a lash tomorrow.'

'How are you feeling now, Rich?'

'Um. Better. Well, better enough to have something to eat, anyway.' He took a look at the menu. 'Chowder. Oh, Jesus, no.'

'I've ordered it, I'm afraid.'

'That's all right, if you don't mind me not looking at you while you eat it. I'll go for the consommé, I think. And the grilled chicken.'

'Fancy sharing some wine with me, Richie?' asked Julian. 'It's not much of a wine list, but there's a vaguely decent Chablis there.'

'Oh, God, no. Thanks, Julian – but no. I'm never touching alcohol again as long as I live.'

'There'll be a session in Sweeney's later,' said Julian. 'You can't miss out on that.'

'I'll go, for sure, but I'll stick to Ballygowan.'

'A session?' asked Ella. 'A musical session?'

'Yep.'

'Who's playing?'

'Nobody special,' said Julian. 'Just a shower of locals. They congregate there every Saturday night with fiddles and tin whistles and uilleann pipes.'

'Oh God. Uilleann pipes. I'm not sure my head could hack all that droning,' remarked Richie.

'Trad wouldn't be the same without the pipes, Richie,' Ella informed him.

'I know, I know. You can call me a philistine again if you like.'

'Did I call you a philistine once?'

'Yeah – that time I told you I was fed up with listening to all that classical shite you play in the car.'

She gave him a pitying look. 'I suppose you listen to nothing but house?'

'Hey! I'm not that sad. No – I like trad, and I don't mind the pipes when they're there as an accompaniment, but *solo* piping! I don't understand how anyone can enjoy that stuff.'

'How can you say that, Rich! You should take a listen to Paddy Moloney or Liam O'Flynn. Or Davy Spillane. They're amazing players!'

'How come you know all this, Ella?' he asked curiously. 'You never really struck me as the kind of gal who'd be into trad.'

'Ella's big into all kinds of music,' said Julian. 'She even plays. Or used to. Didn't you, Ella?'

'Yeah. I'm a musician *manqué*,' said Ella, shooting her colleague a resentful look. She didn't like being reminded of the fact.

'No shit. What instrument?'

'The violin.'

Just then Ella's chowder was set in front of her. Richie took one look, turned green, and clapped his hand over his mouth. 'Oh fuck,' he said, getting rapidly to his feet. 'Excuse me. I need to get out of here . . .' He turned and stumbled out of the dining room.

On the other side of the room, Ferdia looked up as his cousin fled past him. Then he rose from the

322

table and ambled over to where Ella was sitting.

'Do you often have such an emetic effect on people?' he asked.

'Emetic?' This sounded good. Like a cross between 'kinetic' and 'electric'. She dimpled up at him.

Julian sniggered. 'Don't know what it means, do you? Emetic means to make someone get sick.'

'Of course I know what it means,' she lied. 'And for your information, Ferdia, it wasn't me who made Richie want to throw up. It was the unfortunate appearance of the chowder. Which –' she took an experimental taste '– is actually very good indeed.'

Ferdia sat down on the seat vacated by Richie. 'How is he?' he asked.

'In much better shape than he was this morning,' said Ella. 'But obviously still a bit queasy.'

'Will he be able to dive tomorrow, do you think?'

'If he's as good as his word and doesn't touch any alcohol tonight,' said Julian.

'Good. That takes care of all the buddy teams for tomorrow, then. Julian – you'll be diving with Alex again.'

Thank you, Ferdia, thank you! Ella wanted to say. Instead she said: 'And I'll be diving with you again, will I?'

'No. Now that Richie's OK you'll be diving with him.'

'Oh,' she said dully. She hoped he couldn't hear the disappointment in her voice. 'Have you a training group to supervise tomorrow?'

'No. I won't be around. Something's come up, and I need to get back to Dublin.'

No! Oh, no! He couldn't go! Not when she'd just realized she wanted him so desperately! Hell's teeth! What was she going to *do*?

'Are you heading back tonight?' asked Julian.

'No. I've a night dive to do, and I don't want to drive back in the dark. I'll hang around for the session in Sweeney's, and head off at the crack of dawn.'

At least he'd be around later. Nothing in the world could keep her away from that session this evening!

'I don't envy you your early start, after a session,' said Julian. 'Must be something urgent.'

'It is. I got a call to say that Perdita's sick. She's not able to feed her pups and she's very distressed.'

Ella's eyebrows furrowed. 'Oh no! How awful!'

'Yeah. She hates me going away. I don't know how she'll cope when I disappear for good.'

'Where are you off to, man?' She hardly heard Julian's question. She was too busy registering what Ferdia had just said. *Disappear for good* . . .

'I'm heading off around the world. Jamaica first.'

'Hey! Working the dive outfits?'

'If they'll have me.'

'You know they'll have you, Ferdia. With your credentials? You could work anywhere in the world you want.'

The waitress set an open bottle of Chablis in front

of Julian. 'It's customary to open it at the table,' he said.

'Sorry, sir.' The waitress shrugged and ambled off.

Julian heaved a heavy sigh. 'I suppose that's the provinces for you,' he said. 'Full of peasants. Knock back that plonk, Ella, and have some of this.' He poured himself a glassful. 'Ferdia? Will you join us for a glass?'

'No thanks. I've a dive to do.' He stood up from the table. 'Catch you later.'

'Yes,' said Ella automatically. 'See you in Sweeney's.'

He paused. 'You do know there's a session on there this evening?'

'Yes.' Something about his tone puzzled her. 'Why do you ask?'

'I just wouldn't have thought it was your scene, that's all. Enjoy your Chablis.' And he walked back to the table where the waitress was setting a plate piled with bacon and cabbage in front of his empty chair.

'Top bloke,' observed Julian, after a beat.

'Yeah.'

'Fancy him, do you?'

She looked Julian directly in the face. 'No,' she said, with emphasis. 'As if it's any business of yours.'

'I find that surprising, somehow. All the chicks seem to fall for him. Especially the bored married ones with wealthy husbands. Never underestimate the appeal of a bit of rough, Ella.' He stretched ostentatiously in his chair.

Aagh! So that was why Julian was going around talking in cool language and being blokeish! He was trying to impress! But *who* was he trying to impress? She and Jan were the only women diving this weekend. Maybe he had the hots for Jan? She doubted it, somehow. She didn't think she'd seen them exchange more than two words. Oh God. Could it be – was it possible that Julian Bollard had the hots for *her*? No, no – life couldn't be that grotesque . . .

Beside her he was droning on. God – if Richie thought the uilleann pipes were bad, he wanted to get a load of Julian in full flight. 'Yeah – I've seen some very classy broads indeed make idiots of themselves over Ferdia. You saw the one that was in the pub last night? She's married to local landed gentry. She's on the society page of *Individual* magazine every other month. But every time there's a dive weekend scheduled here in Lissamore she turns up and slums it in Sweeney's just so she can join Ferdia in bed later.'

So she was right! Ferdia MacDiarmada had a thing about class ass.

'I suppose it's a bit like being a rock star and being surrounded by groupies all the time.' Julian suddenly couldn't keep the resentment out of his voice. He was so obviously seething with jealousy that Ella intuited that the only reason he tried so hard to be chummy with Ferdia was to enhance his own credibility. Maybe he thought that some of the instructor's sex appeal would rub off on him if he high-fived him often enough.

She looked over to where Ferdia was sitting laughing with PJ, and started to do some more strategic thinking. So. He would be gone in the morning. He had a dive tonight. That gave her very little time to put her campaign into action. She'd just have to make sure she bumped into him in Sweeney's. That would be difficult if there was a session on. She knew from experience that men tended to get so wrapped up in the sexiness of the music and the whole session vibe that lovemaking was – paradoxically – sometimes the last thing on their minds. Hell's bells. If she wanted to end up in Ferdia MacDiarmada's bed tonight she was going to have to be very, very clever. Imagining what could be in store for her if she played her cards right provoked that half-enjoyable, half-unsettling feeling that the anticipation of good sex always gave her – that feeling as if a small animal somewhere in the pit of her stomach was curling itself up into a ball.

'You're looking very pensive, Ella,' remarked Julian. 'What are you thinking about?'

'Nitrogen narcosis,' she said.

*   *   *

Ella kept her fingers crossed that posh Philippa wouldn't be in the pub. She cased the joint as soon as she got through the door, and was glad to see that there was no sign of her. Maybe she was off at a hunt ball somewhere, or at a nobby dinner party. Ella pictured her sipping sherry, chatting to some chinless type, all the time pining for her bit of rough. She looked around to see if there were any other likely fillies who might be in competition with her for the attention of Ferdia, but she couldn't spot any contenders. There was an ostentatiously foxy girl sitting up at the bar wearing a belly top, but she was way too vulgar for his tastes.

Ella tried to take it easy on the Guinness, but it was hard because Richie kept putting pints in front of her. He tried to stick to water, but got bored with it very early on, and started experimenting with soft drinks. He even tried a Pirate's Punch. 'Sweet Jesus Christ!' he said, pushing the glass to the other side of the bar. 'This stuff is undiluted shite! It nearly made me throw up again.'

'I will hear no evil talked about Pirate's Punch,' said Ella. 'They paid for me to have the best holiday of my life.'

There was a palpable sense of anticipation in the crowd, as there always was in pubs on session nights. The place was even more jammed than it had been yesterday, and Ella was far too hot in her Ralph Lauren suede jacket. She slung it over the back of her chair, feeling quite glad that she could now show off the sexy little T-shirt she was wearing underneath.

She caught Richie looking. She wasn't wearing a

bra, and she knew that her miniature pink rosebuds must be pretty prominent. She'd got so used to her easy friendship with Richie that she'd almost forgotten that he was as susceptible as any man to the red-blooded male thing, and she remembered that she'd read somewhere that there was no such thing as a 100 per cent platonic relationship between a man and a woman.

'Will you – um – go back, do you think?' he said. 'To – um – to Jamaica?' Ella got the impression that he was trying too hard to make small talk.

'I hope to. My grandmother's getting married there in the autumn, and her affianced has offered to fly the family over for the wedding.'

The musicians were warming up now, and the atmosphere was tense with reined-in excitement.

'Jamaica's Ferdia's first stop.'

Of course it was! Maybe he *wasn't* about to disappear from her life for ever! Maybe there'd be a chance of running into him there . . . She knew she was clutching at straws, but at least she had *something* to be optimistic about. 'Oh, yeah,' she said, trying to sound casual. 'He mentioned something about travelling round the world. When's he off?'

'End of July.'

The crowd settled and a hush descended as a single tin whistle piped out the first notes of the evening. Ella recognized the tune immediately. It was 'Wallop the Spot', a rousing jig.

'How long's he going for?' Ella lowered her voice. It was considered very unclued-in to indulge in prolonged or loud chat during a session.

'Kinda indefinitely.' Richie had lowered his voice correspondingly.

'And he's guaranteed work in any dive outfit in the world?' The bodhrán joined the whistle, drumming out the heartbeat of the tune.

'Well, work's never guaranteed anywhere. But Ferdia shouldn't have much of a problem. He's one hell of a pro. And he's one of the luckier bastards who can afford to take it easy until the right job comes along.'

'Oh?' Ella was perplexed. 'Why do you say that?'

'He's a man of some means. He's selling his horse.' A fiddle – no, *two* fiddles took up the air. The decibel level of the music soared.

'His house?'

'No. His *horse.*'

'What?'

'He has a *mumble mumble mumble.*'

'A *what*?'

'*Mumble* beautiful thoroughbred. He's *mumble* to sell it. *Mumble* load of money. *Mumble mumble* thousands. *Mumble* surprised you hadn't heard. Everybody in *mumble* talking about the mega *mumble* farewell party he's *mumble* to throw.'

Richie had leaned in to her and was speaking directly into her ear, but it didn't make any difference. The uilleann pipes had blared in. There was no more point in trying to talk.

'*Mumble* clever bloke,' she heard vaguely. 'One

mumble mumble.' Or was it 'won *mumble mumble'*?

'What's the name of the horse?' She made one last-ditch attempt to worm a nugget of information out of him, wondering why she was asking such an irrelevant question when there were millions more important ones she wanted to ask.

He squinted at her, with blank enquiry in his eyes. He obviously hadn't heard her. There was no point in repeating the question. It was a stupid one, anyway. But Richie must have guessed correctly what she'd asked him. His answer coincided with a pause in the music. 'Black Jack,' he enunciated loudly, and then made a cringy face as people around them shot cross looks at him. He turned back to her, drawing an index finger across his mouth to indicate that he'd better zip his lip, then turned his attention to the remaining bars of 'Wallop the Spot'.

She was so flummoxed by what she'd just heard that she could barely concentrate on the session. She smiled vaguely and tapped her foot automatically, but her mind was awhirl, trying to make sense of what Richie had said. Ferdia owned a thoroughbred horse. It was worth thousands of pounds. He was a man of means. Of enough means, apparently, to be able to afford to bugger off around the world without having to bother too much about how he was going to subsidize himself.

Now things started to pan out! So Ferdia really *was* part of a jet set! Now his dalliance with Posh

Philippa made sense! A woman like her wouldn't 'slum it' with a 'bit of rough', as Julian had so charmingly put it.

Hell's bells! This was some revelation! Ella felt a bit like Jane must have done when she'd discovered that Tarzan, King of the Jungle was actually the Earl of Greystoke, or like Cathy in *Wuthering Heights* when Heathcliff reinvented himself as a man of wealth and taste, or like the heroine of *Passion's Monument* when she found that Dashiel (whom she had initially mistaken for a lowly groom) was in fact the heir to a shipping fortune . . .

Ella realized that she was watching the door now, more than she was watching the musicians. Although the playing was top-class, this was the worst session she'd ever had to sit through. She just sat there stewing, waiting for the door to the pub to open and for Ferdia to come through.

The band took their first break of the evening. A respectful path was being cleared through the crowd for the thirsty musicians, and just as a pint of Guinness was being put into the fiddle player's hand by the barman, Ferdia materialized beside him, as if by magic. She noticed that the foxy lady at the bar prinked visibly. Ella gazed at her dive god with parted lips and dewy eyes, unaware that Richie was looking at her sideways.

'Oh Christ,' he said. 'Not you as well.'

'What do you mean?' she asked, colouring slightly.

'It's called Dive God syndrome. And you've got it for my cousin.'

'No I haven't,' she replied, sounding snappier than she meant to, and regretting it immediately. She should just have admitted the truth, and then asked Richie all the questions about his intriguing cousin that she wanted to know the answers to.

Richie gave her a sceptical look, and she looked away. 'Well, if you're not suffering from Dive God syndrome,' he said, sounding resigned, 'you're definitely suffering from dehydration by now. You finished that pint ages ago. Let me get you another.'

Common sense told her that she'd had enough Guinness, and that she should follow Richie's example and remain teetotal for the rest of the evening, but now that Ferdia was finally here, she felt the need for a little more Dutch courage. 'Thanks, Richie,' she said, as he got to his feet and began to struggle his way up to the bar.

As soon as he was gone, she returned her attention to Ferdia. The fiddle player had greeted him with great gusto, slapping him on the back and smiling broadly. Ella supposed that all the ActivMarine instructors were familiar faces in Sweeney's. According to Richie they'd been coming here for years. She sat there rigidly, hands clasped in her lap, preparing herself to send him her best smile when he finally turned round, but he just carried on talking to his fiddler friend, and kept his back squarely to her. Then the pair of them picked up their pints and headed over to the other side of the room where the musicians were reconvening.

Stop it at once, she told herself briskly, as sick disappointment threatened. You are not to go all moony and pathetic with love, Ella Nesbit. You are a fighter. Desirée told you so. You will do your very best to hook Ferdia this evening, and if your very best doesn't work, then you will just have to try a lot harder.

She tried to think rationally. He hadn't seen her, after all. If he'd seen her, he might have come over and joined her, especially since the repellent Julian wasn't hanging around her like a miasma any more. Richie was heading towards her now, a pint of Guinness in one hand and a Coke in the other. He had just set the pint down when an extraordinary thing happened. The fiddler who'd greeted Ferdia handed him a fiddle and a bow with an air of casual camaraderie. Ferdia took the instrument from him, rose to his feet, ran an experimental bow across the strings and began deftly to tune up. Then, with a slow, sexy slur of an introduction, he launched into 'Tom Ward's Downfall'.

Ella sat there with her mouth hanging open. She simply could not believe what she was seeing. Ferdia MacDiarmada was *good*!

The initial long, teasing way he'd stroked the instrument with his bow accelerated almost immediately into more conventional jig time. The fingers of his left hand flew up and down the board of the instrument as fast as the wings of the hummingbirds she'd seen in Salamander Cove. His right hand manipulated the bow with assurance, the short light strokes coaxing a flurry of notes from the belly of the fiddle. The bodhrán joined him now, setting feet tapping involuntarily, then the whistle, another fiddle, the pipes – and they were off!

The crowd was in rollicking form – punctuating the rhythm of the jig with whoops and yells of enthusiasm and encouragement. Bodies swayed in time to the music: hands were clapping, heads nodding, fingers beating time on tabletops. Faces – most of them red with Guinness and heat and excitement – were smiling, foreheads were sweating, camaraderie mixed with the fug in the air. The music gained momentum, racing towards the finale. And now the spoons were in there, frantically stirring the frenzied crescendo that announced the final phrases.

After Ferdia's bow had slid across the string, producing that last, long note, there was a momentary silence. Then the crowd whooped again, and showed their appreciation with claps and cheers and whistles. The applause was well deserved. And hard-earned, thought Ella, noticing the sweat on Ferdia's forehead and the stains that were spreading under his arms.

The audience finally settled down, and Ella turned to Richie to voice her astonishment that this man was a master fiddler as well as a master diver. What a dark horse he was proving to be! But Richie was no longer there. She searched the room with her eyes until she saw him standing in the opposite corner, talking to his cousin. She felt washed with a kind of rapturous agony when Ferdia turned and looked directly at her with interested eyes, then beckoned her over. Ella rose and wove her way between the tables, drawn across the room as if there was a compass in her heart and Ferdia was north.

'Richie told me you play,' he said, when she drew level with him.

'I do.'

'Trad or classical?' enquired Ferdia.

'A bit of both.'

'Play a tune with us, then.' Ferdia indicated a fiddle case on the shabby vinyl banquette next to him. It was obviously a spare kept in reserve for any visiting players.

'What are you going to play next?'

Ferdia consulted with the geezer who'd handed him the fiddle earlier. '"Toss the Feathers,"' he said. 'Do you know it?'

This was perfect!

'Yes,' she said.

'Well,' said Ferdia. 'Let's see you rip this joint, Ella.' His eyes as he handed over the instrument had that incredibly flattering interest in them again, but there was a challenge there too. She felt that small animal in the pit of her stomach curl up again: but this time it curled up even tighter.

Ella took the fiddle. It was an old one – she could tell from the scars on the rosewood – but a little beaut, with a tiny flower wrought in mother-of-pearl on the tailpiece. She ran expert eyes over the board and then raised the body of the violin to her face, pressing the patinated wood against her cheek for an instant, checking it out like a cat before tucking it under her left arm. Then she took a couple of steps backwards, distancing herself a little from the rest of the group. She wanted to hold back for the first couple of bars until she felt comfortable with the other musicians' form.

One. Two. Three. Ferdia's bow swept over the strings, and the music surged out. Whistle and bodhrán were in like Flynn, and then it was the piper's turn to elbow out the melody. *One* two three, *four* five six; *one* two three, *four* five six . . .

Ella started to move. It was impossible not to. She began by swaying almost imperceptibly, but as the tune got livelier and the rhythm became more and more insistent, she found herself swaying with more abandon. Then the fiddle was tucked under her chin, her left hand was supporting the fingerboard and her right hand was poised at an elegant angle, ready to let the bow hit the strings. Still she waited. When the next opportunity to jump in – in between phrases – presented itself, she grabbed it with both hands.

Ferdia turned round. For a split second he appeared a bit fazed at seeing her there, and then a smile spread over his face as he watched her settle into the swing of things. She smiled back. It was a smile of pure delight, but there was complicity in there too. They were smiling the kind of smile that is shared between two strangers who have suddenly discovered that they speak the same language.

Her head was held proudly as she wielded the bow to and fro, back and forth across the strings, and she felt possessed by a wonderful sense of power. This was the power of music: this was the power exerted by the tradition that had been handed down from generation to generation of Irish. Once upon a time, every household in the country would have had a fiddle, house sessions would have been commonplace, and the people would have played and danced – jigs and reels and hornpipes – till dawn. This was the finest, fastest, sexiest music in the world!

Ella shut her eyes and felt the notes she was creating flowing out of her, diving under the carved wooden bridge into the belly of the instrument, bouncing in a wave off the back, and flooding out through the carved arabesques. She smiled to herself as the music took hold of her and transported her effortlessly into the realm of embellishment. This was where you strutted your stuff and displayed your virtuosity! This was where you improvised and cut notes with deft fingers and showed off with triplets! She could tell by the vibe emanating from the other musicians that they were all having a blast; her smile grew broader and behind her closed lids her eyes grew dreamier as she lost herself in the magical maze of the music.

And when she returned, minutes later, Ferdia

was still watching her, with something new in his eyes that she had never seen there before. There was respect there, the respect that one peer feels for another. But there was more. There was also a gleam that was unmistakable, and it was the gleam of very, very strong sexual attraction. Oh God! Yes! She had hooked him! And she had done it without recourse to any wiles, any pretence, any stupid game-playing. She had done it all by herself! She bit her lip to stop her smile becoming any broader, and looked back at Ferdia with challenge in her eyes as she treated him to a sample of ornamentation that sounded effortless, but was actually breathtakingly elaborate. He responded by moving nearer, echoing the notes she'd just played to prove to her that he could match her. She tried something else. A whole sexy galaxy of starry notes fluttered out of the instrument. Again he answered her, with an extra dollop of embellishment to ice the musical cake.

But the next few phrases, the ones that anticipated the climax, were all hers. She outclassed him, playing without thinking. Now it was *she* who was in charge! The laughter and naked admiration in Ferdia's eyes told her that, and he stepped back and surrendered centre stage to her. Ella swayed, every fibre of her being responding to each note she teased out of the instrument she was holding in her arms like a lover, feeling every pulse of the bodhrán's beat, still looking at him, and still smiling. She felt as if the animal inside her – the one that had been wound taut as the G-string on her violin – had uncurled, stretched like a panther, and found its voice at last. The final exultant phrase came. And then the last drawn-out shuddering note as Ella drew her bow down over the singing strings and let her right arm drop to her side.

Again there was that electric moment of silence before the crowd rose to their feet and roared their appreciation. Ella stood there breathing hard, her face slicked with sweat, her hair sticking to her fore-head. There were damp patches on her tight cotton T-shirt, and she was still wearing that blissed-out smile. She looked positively post-coital. As she lifted her jaw off the hard edge of the chin-rest and shook her hair back over her shoulders, she became aware of Ferdia advancing towards her. He stood for a moment, looking down at her, and then he bowed his head until it was on a level with hers. The crowd went even wilder, thinking he was going to kiss her. But his mouth went to her ear, not to her lips. For a second she was bewildered by the warm sound of his voice in her ear. She, too, had been preparing herself yet again for a kiss from him – a kiss that was simply the inevitable finale to what had just gone down on the makeshift stage in the dingy pub. And then she registered what he was saying.

His voice was trickling into her ear like the sweetest honey. Acacia blossom honey. Or drip-ping clover. 'I am going to make you come,' he was saying. 'And come. And come. I am going to make you come like you have never come before in your life, and I am going to do it now. Get your coat.'

Ella thought she was going to swoon. In a daze, she made her way through the crowd, too muzzy with sexual arousal to be able to acknowledge the compliments that came her way. She reached the chair where she'd left her suede jacket and slung it over her shoulders, not bothering with the sleeves.

Just as she and Ferdia reached the door of the pub, it swung open violently. A white-faced garda pushed his way into the room. 'Jesus, Ferdia – thank Christ you and the boys are here. Can you get kitted up ASAP? A car's gone off the road into the Salt Lake. We need divers down there now.'

Chapter Fourteen

Ella went back to the hotel room on her own. She sat wretchedly on her bed for a while, doing nothing, not even twisting her hair. She could think of nothing but Ferdia. It felt as if her mind had been vacuumed clean of everything and everyone else. Hell's bells – how could it be otherwise, after what had happened between them? How to *describe* what had happened between them? It had quite simply been the mother and father of a *coup de foudre.*

She sat and she sat, sneaking frequent looks at her watch and wondering how long it would take to locate the car that had gone into the lake – and the unfortunate individuals who might have gone in with it. She hoped they were OK, and this filled her with self-loathing, because she knew that the principal reason she wanted them to be OK was a supremely selfish one. She figured it was more likely that Ferdia would get away sooner if no-one was injured, and the sooner he got away, the sooner he would come looking for her . . .

Oh God – what a let-down this evening had turned out to be! What a total, utter bummer! If someone had written a recipe for disappointment, it couldn't come much more *haute cuisine* than this. She consulted her watch again. It had been one minute and thirty-five seconds since she'd last looked at it. It reminded her of how she felt in the gym every time she used the treadmill. She would program the machine for a twenty-minute run, and after running for what felt like at least eighteen of those minutes, she would access the timer. It would tell her she'd been running for nine, and that she had eleven more excruciating minutes to run. She *hated* that timer, and now she hated her watch even more.

She heard movement in the corridor outside and tensed, suddenly alert as an Indian scout. But the footsteps went on by, and her shoulders slumped again. Then she became aware of rowdy noises coming from the car park outside. She ran to the window and peered round the curtains. A bunch of divers returning from the pub.

She wondered how many divers had been enlisted for the search, and how long it was likely to take. It was a pointless exercise. She knew nothing about the conditions that would affect the dive and dictate its duration. They might be diving in shallow water, or deep. They might or might not have spare tanks and facilities for refilling them.

The only thing to do to take her mind off Ferdia was sleep, and she knew sleep was impossible because her mind was too full of him. It was Catch 22.

But hey! she thought. If he was to come to her tonight, she needed to be ready! Immediately she sprang into action, taking off all her clothes and spraying herself very, very sparingly with Chanel 19. She didn't want to overwhelm all those sex pheromones that her body had gone to such trouble to manufacture earlier. Then she got into bed, turned the light out, and lay there staring at the shadows on the ceiling.

She focused in on a particularly interesting shadow. It looked a bit like the shape of Ferdia's thigh with his dive-knife strapped on. Dear God, she was a sad bitch! Try and think of something else, Ella, she told herself. Something terminally boring that you know you really have to concentrate on, and it ends up making you fall asleep whether you want to or not. Like her dive manual. Maybe she should turn the light on again and re-read the Search and Recovery chapter? No. She'd been subjected to enough punishment tonight. Something scientific, then. That would be good and boring. Pheromones? What was the scientific theory behind them, for instance? The pheromones in our sweat activate our base animal instinct for . . . No. Pheromones were synonymous with sex, and she'd just end up re-running that outrageously sexy mental video of her and Ferdia playing 'Toss the Feathers' together, and fantasizing about what might have been.

Oh *God* this was awful! What had she done to deserve this torture? *When* would he come? And how should she behave when he did? Should she be brazen? Coy? Cool? Flirtatious?

There was a creaking noise in the corridor outside her room and she stiffened again – but it was just the ancient fabric of the hotel shifting in its sleep. Then she remembered how someone had once told her that if you shut your eyes, it makes your sense of hearing more acute. Maybe she should try it? Then she'd be able to hear him when he finally arrived back.

As soon as Ella shut her eyes, all the physical activity that had taken its toll on her body that day kicked in. Within seconds, she was fast asleep.

* * *

She was woken by the sound of knocking at the door. She sat up in bed instantly, hair cascading over her bare shoulders, trying to ignore the hammering of her heart. Then she drew the sheet up over her breasts, pushed her hair back from her face and quickly smoothed a forefinger over her eyebrows. 'Come in,' she said, breathlessly.

'Ella. Hi.'

Richie came through the door and she felt sick with disappointment. 'Richie! Hi!' she said, trying not to look too let down. 'What time is it?'

'Nine o'clock. I thought it was about time to wake you. We should be ready to rock and roll in half an hour, and I thought you'd want to get some breakfast first.'

'Oh. Oh – sure. I'll be down in ten minutes.'

As soon as the door closed behind him she raced to the bathroom, had the most perfunctory of showers and flung on her clothes. Why hadn't she set the alarm? She was so *stupid*! What had possessed her to think that Ferdia would steal into her room some time before dawn to wake her with a kiss? He would have been too knackered after trailing around doing underwater search and recovery half the night to even think about sex. She gave herself a quick spray with Chanel 19, and then flew down the stairs to the dining room.

She surveyed the room with eyes that hadn't completely woken up yet. There was no sign of Ferdia. Ella made her way over to where Richie was sitting in front of a plate of bacon and eggs. She was glad there was no-one else at the table.

'Well, Ms Nesbit. You are some mean fiddler. That was a splendid display of virtuosity last night.'

'Thanks,' she said briefly. She didn't mean to sound ungrateful, but her fiddle playing of the previous evening was the last thing on her mind. What *was* on her mind was the whereabouts of Richie's cousin. 'Um – what happened about the accident?'

'What accident?'

'You know – the car that went into the lake?'

'Oh – that was a complete disaster.'

'Oh God – was it?' Ella clamped her hand to her mouth, flooded with remorse and guilt. She'd only asked the question as a preamble to the detective

346

work she needed to do. 'Anyone – anyone dead?' I will hate myself for the rest of my life if there is, she thought.

'No. No-one dead, no-one injured.' Thank God for that. 'In fact, the whole exercise was a complete waste of time.'

Ella thought she didn't want to be hearing this. 'What do you mean, a waste of time?'

'The car belonged to a local man. He was exceedingly drunk. So drunk that he was beyond panic – and very lucky indeed that his window was rolled down. When he hit the water he simply opened the car door, made it to the surface and walked the rest of the way home.'

'*What?*' Ella was aghast. 'Well – why didn't someone tell the police that?'

'The person who'd witnessed the car going into the water didn't know the driver had got himself out. They were already on the phone to the police, apparently, when the drunk calmly emerged from the lake without a scratch on him. Some story, eh?'

Ella felt like asking for the drunk's address. She wanted to run off to his house and give him a good kick up the arse. 'So everyone got kitted up and spent a load of time doing search and recovery for nothing?'

'Yeah. Ferdia and PJ were at it for ages. The search and recovery garda divers were halfway down from Dublin before they got the word to turn round and go back home.'

'Would you like a cooked breakfast?' The waitress was at her side, pen poised over pad.

Ella's appetite had vanished into the ether. 'Um, no thanks. I'll just have toast and coffee, please.' She turned back to Richie. 'When did they hear that the driver was OK?'

'When he eventually reeled through the door of his house soaked to the skin. His wife put two and two together, and rang the Guards. She was in agonies of mortification, apparently. It's the second time he's gone into that lake.'

The wife might have been in agonies of mortification, but it could be nothing compared to what she'd been put through. She, Ella Nesbit, had been in agonies of sexual frustration all night because of the drunken bloody driver's deficiency in the IQ department.

'What a fucking fiasco!' she thundered.

Richie gave her a curious look, and she realized that her reaction had been totally out of proportion to the incident. She tried to look as if it had merely offended her civic-mindedness.

'I mean, just imagine dragging out the Dublin search and recovery team! What an irresponsible thing to do!'

'Yeah. It's also messed up the dive schedule, bigtime.'

'What do you mean?'

'Well, neither PJ nor Ferdia can dive today. Too big a build-up of residual nitrogen. I know Ferdia was disappearing anyway, but PJ was to supervise the trainees. He's re-jigging the buddy teams now.'

'Oh.' There was one last question Ella needed to ask before her entire world collapsed around her. 'Is Ferdia still around?' She made her voice as careless as she could.

'No. He needed to get back to Dublin and his pooch. Perdita has him wrapped round her little claw. Had you heard she's not well?'

'Yeah.'

'He'd planned to head off first thing this morning, but he hung around until he got a phone call telling him that the dog had taken another downturn. I think he'd have liked to have stayed here and chilled for a while. That dive last night must have been pretty gruelling.'

'When did he leave?'

'Just before you came down. We had breakfast together.'

She looked across the table at Ferdia's unfinished breakfast. The waitress had arrived with her coffee. She set it down in front of Ella, then started to clear away the used dishes. Ella co-operated by mechanically handing the woman Ferdia's side plate and coffee cup. The cup was still warm! Oh God! She wanted to weep for her witlessness. Why oh *why* hadn't she set the alarm?

'Hi.' PJ sat down in the chair so recently vacated by Ferdia. Ella wondered if the chair was still warm, as well as the cup, and wished she'd sat there instead. 'I expect you've heard that we've had to review the buddy teams, Ella?'

She nodded, and then a warning bell went off in her head. This was a *déjà vu* from yesterday. What had Ferdia said then? *We can re-jig the buddy teams and make sure nobody's left out . . .* And she'd ended up with Julian. 'I'm still diving with Richie, aren't I?' she asked quickly.

'Yes.'

Thank you, God.

'But you'll be diving as a buddy team of three.' He consulted a list. 'Let's see – who have I down here with you? Ah yes, Julian Bollard.'

Julian chose that moment to walk past their table.

'Hey, Julian – you're diving with us today!' announced Richie.

Ella felt like the dame in *The Scream* by Edward Munch. She didn't know what to do, but she would do whatever it took to avoid diving with Julian Bollard. She knew she'd gone white. She knew she looked shellshocked. And then she had a brain-wave. Slowly she got to her feet and stood there swaying a little, holding onto her chair.

'Are you OK, Ella?' asked Richie curiously. 'You look a bit weird.'

'No, I'm not OK,' she said in a whispery voice. 'I feel very strange, I think – I – I think I'm going to—'

And then she fell over.

'Oh, God – she's fainted!'

There was a sound of chairs being pushed back from tables and low excited murmurings in the room.

'OK – just keep back, will you?' It was PJ's voice.

Ella heard footsteps coming toward her, and then someone was uncurling her legs from under her. She felt herself being lifted and repositioned on her back. 'OK' – PJ again, taking control: 'will you all head on down to the dive shop? You may as well start getting kitted up.'

'Is she going to be OK?'

'Sure she is. She'll recover in a minute.'

Ella felt like a total fraud lying there listening to all those concerned people shuffling out of the room. But she had found herself stuck between the biggest rock and the hardest place she had ever been, and there had been no other way out. The prospect of diving with Julian – especially after the agonizing bodyblow she'd just been struck – was simply insupportable.

'Ella? Ella?' PJ's voice was low and in her ear now. 'Wake up. Come on, Ella, wake up.'

She wasn't sure how long to maintain this masquerade. One minute? Two? She'd never fainted before. She tried to think of a film where someone had fainted, so that she could get her timing right, but nothing came to her.

Then she heard Julian's voice. 'Shouldn't we loosen her clothing?'

That was her cue. She opened her eyes and fluttered the lashes briefly, then looked up at PJ. 'What happened?' she said, trying to look confused.

'You fainted,' said PJ.

'Oh. Oh, God – how weird. How did that happen?'

'Beats me,' said PJ. 'The only person who's ever fainted on me before is Ferdia. I have to hold his hand every time he goes to the doctor for his jabs. Did you get some kind of emotional shock, maybe?'

'No,' she lied. She sat up. 'Maybe it's just some kind of physiological girl thing.'

'How do you feel now?' asked Richie.

'A bit woolly.'

'Will you be able for the dive?' he asked dubiously.

'I don't think that's a good idea,' said PJ.

Ella tried to look disappointed.

'I'm sorry, Ella, but it would be irresponsible of me to let you go. I think you should take things easy.' He helped her to her feet.

'Here. Have a glass of water,' said Richie helpfully. He sloshed water into a glass for her and held out a chair. 'Sit down.'

She saw Julian look at his watch, and she knew he was getting antsy about being late for his dive.

'Please don't let me hold you up,' she said with alacrity. She wanted to be shot of him ASAP. She wanted to be shot of all of them. She just wanted to be on her own.

'Are you sure?' Richie looked uncertain. 'I feel awful abandoning you like this.'

'No, no, please don't worry. I'm fine – really and truly I am. I'd just like to get back to Dublin.'

'Will you be OK to drive?' asked PJ.

'Yes, yes, honestly I will.' A thought struck her. 'But what about you, Rich? *I'm* the one who's abandoning *you*! How will you get back?'

352

'I'll take him. No problem.' Some manly-chin acting from Julian. 'We can dive-talk all the way home.'

Oh, poor Richie! Her heart bled for him and she felt horribly guilty, but she just had to save her own skin.

'I'll see you – when, then?' Richie bent down and kissed her on the cheek.

'I'll ring you.'

'And I'll see you in work tomorrow, Ella.' Ugh! Oh, God! Julian was actually making the 'OK' sign with his thumb and forefinger. The pair of them shambled away backwards, and then turned and left the dining room.

'Hey,' she could hear Julian saying as their voices receded. 'Did I ever tell you the story about the time I went diving in Ko Phi Phi? I'd been using a double bladder BCD, you know the . . .' And then thankfully she could hear no more.

'Can I get you anything?' PJ was looking at her with concerned eyes.

'No, thanks.' She gave him a mournful look, which he misinterpreted.

'Don't worry about missing out on your dives, Ella,' he reassured her. 'We can either send you a refund for the ones you missed, or we can offset it against another dive weekend. Which would you prefer?'

'Another dive weekend, please,' she said automatically. She wanted to see Ferdia again.

PJ ran his eyes down the list of ActivMarine

activities on his clipboard. 'OK. Let's see. Where are we now? End of May, June, July . . . The next one's scheduled for the first weekend in August.'

'But that's ages away! I thought they were supposed to be every month!'

'Someone messed up the booking. We had to be flexible, and that's the earliest the hotel can accommodate us. Hey! I've just realized that that's the weekend after Ferdia's farewell party. He'll be on his way to the Caribbean, lucky sod.' PJ scribbled something on an A4 sheet, and Ella felt even more like the dame in the Munch painting. 'You're down in heavy pencil, Ella, and your timing's excellent. You got the last place.'

No, no, no, PJ. Her timing was not excellent. It was totally, devastatingly, derangingly awful.

*   *   *

She arrived at work the next day to find that she had no sessions booked at all. Everyone who'd booked studio time had wanted to use the new facilities out the back. She sat mooning over the tropical fish screensaver on her computer, trying to dream up excuses for phoning ActivMarine. Maybe she could pretend she'd left something behind in her room at Lissamore, and was wondering if it had been handed over to one of the ActivMarine staff? What could she have left behind her? A book. On an impulse she picked up the phone and punched in the number. An answering machine picked up.

Hell, hell, hell*fire*. 'Um. Hi. It's Ella Nesbit here,' she said, after the tone. 'I just wondered if any of you guys might have been given a book that I left in my room in Lissamore.' She was suddenly flooded with the most appalling confusion. 'It's – um – it's not *Passion's Monument*, by the way,' she found herself saying to her own incredulous horror. 'It's – um – it's –' As she cast around desperately, her eyes fell on a CD Rom that Jack liked to play on the computer during idle moments of the day. It was called *Monster Truck Madness*. 'It's called *Monster Truck Madness*. Thanks a bunch talk to you soon bye.'

She put down the phone and banged her forehead against the console. Oh God. What had she just *done*? What were they going to *think* when they got that message? As if she hadn't made enough of an idiot of herself at Lissamore, forgetting to lock doors, banging on walls in the middle of the night, pretending to faint . . . She was damn sure Ferdia'd been filled in on that. 'Ella Nesbit *fainted*? What a wimp . . .'

Oh God, oh God. She wished someone would call 'cut' on this disaster movie that was her life. Could anything else happen to make it worse?

It could, and it did. The door opened and Julian walked in.

'Hey!' he said, throwing a brochure onto the console. It was folded over at a page featuring a blue sky resort in Belize. Happy-looking scuba divers were pictured larking about on a dive boat. 'I'm booking this today. Want to come?' he asked.

Ella lifted her head from the console. She looked down at the glossy images and almost said 'yes'. Instead she tried to look unimpressed. 'Ha, ha, Julian,' she said. Then she looked a bit closer and added: 'It's not one of the ActivMarine packages, is it?'

'No. Kuoni. I'm having to fork out a lot of money for it.'

Kuoni on his Nesbit & Noonan salary? Unlikely. Ella suspected that Julian's daddy was more likely to be financing this little junket.

'So? Are you interested?'

'What? Get real, Julian. Even if I had the money I wouldn't be allowed the time off. I've had my holiday, remember?'

'We've not been busy. And it doesn't look like we're going to be, to judge by the Nesbit & Noonan agenda. I'm sure Patrick could let his favourite niece spend ten days in dive heaven with his favourite sound engineer.'

He *was* joking. What a jolly little japer Julian was! What a killing sense of humour he had!

She looked up at him and raised an unimpressed eyebrow, but there was nothing jokey about the expression on his face. Oh my God, thought Ella. This was for real. Julian Bollard was asking her to go away on holiday with him! In an attempt to disguise the look of gobsmacked incredulity that she was sure was contorting her features, Ella looked back down at the brochure and turned the page.

'I know it's expensive.' Julian's voice drawled on.

She realized abruptly that she was looking at the price list, and in a panic she turned back to the previous page. Oh hell – she was putting out all the wrong signals! She must look as if she were genuinely considering going along. This was so awful it couldn't really be happening to her.

'I'd be prepared to subsidize you, Ella,' he continued. She looked up, aghast. Julian was smiling down at her. He reached out a hand and cocked a finger under her chin. 'I've always fancied you, gorgeous. You know that. I get off on our little bouts of sparring just as much as I know you do. And when I suspected that Ferdia MacDiarmada was trying to muscle in, I decided to pre-empt him.' He picked up the brochure and gazed at the glossy photographs of the luxury resort. 'Just picture it,' he said. 'You and me in Dive Holiday Heaven. What do you say, toots? Sorry,' he gave her a complicitous smile. 'I mean, buddy.'

Ella didn't know whether to laugh or cry. Instead she shook her head dumbly. 'No, Julian,' she said. 'I wouldn't dream of going with you. I can't think for a minute how you thought I would ever say yes.'

He looked perplexed, as if she was speaking a language he couldn't understand. 'But why not?' he said. 'Where's the problem?'

She could see she was going to have to be brutal. 'Because I don't *like* you enough to go away on holiday with you, Julian. That's why not.'

Julian looked perplexed for another moment or

two, and then his eyes went all narrow and his mouth set like a trap. 'Ah. *OK*, Ella,' he said with contrived nonchalance. 'That's your lookout. Ab-so-*lute*-ly. I'm glad we know where we stand now.' He rolled the holiday brochure into a kind of truncheon and slapped the palm of his left hand with it twice. Then he looked down at the console. 'You do realize your gains are set very high there, don't you?' He gave her an ominous look, before turning and striding out of the room.

Ella knew she should have laughed, but she didn't. She felt horrible, and it was all bloody Julian's fault. *He* had made her feel horrible. God! As if their relationship wasn't bad enough without him adding a new dimension of the grotesque to it. And it wasn't *just* horrible he'd made her feel, she realized, as she returned her attention to the exotic fish swimming across her computer screen. He'd made her feel uneasy.

*   *   *

Over the course of the day she had even more cause to feel uneasy. Her uncle was antsy about something, she could tell, and even easygoing Jack looked grim.

'What's wrong with you two?' she asked after work in the pub. 'You've both been really uptight for the past while.'

'Business worries, Ella,' said Patrick, pulling hard

on his Marlboro Light. 'Count yourself lucky you don't have 'em.'

'What's the problem?' asked Julian. 'Or is it confidential?'

'There's no point in keeping it confidential any more,' said Jack, sounding uncharacteristically fatalistic. 'It's staring us all in the face at this stage. We've overstretched ourselves.'

'What do you mean?' Ella leaned forward in her chair.

'The new studio. It's not making money back fast enough. You must have noticed that there's been a falling off in bookings lately. And the building work next door has messed us up bigtime.'

Uh-oh, thought Ella, casting her mind back over the past few weeks. Everyone in the business knew that recording studios often had lean times when bookings weren't coming fast and furious. It was usually written off as a seasonal thing. But this lull had gone on longer than usual. Things should have started to liven up a little at this time of the year. Agencies needed to grab studio time before everyone disappeared on summer holidays.

'But why should there be a fall-off?' she asked. 'That new studio's so *sexy*! Everyone who uses it says how hi-tech and gorgeous it is.'

'It's not hi-tech enough, unfortunately,' said Patrick darkly. 'We just missed the boat. On Line Studios is having a shit-hot digital desk installed. It's the one facility everyone's raring to use. Our regular clients are starting to defect, and I suspect that they may not come back, even when the construction work next door's finally finished.'

'Oh.' Ella's brow furrowed as she tried to think of some solution to the problem. 'Well – couldn't we just install a digital desk of our own? And the building work's due to finish soon. The agencies are bound to come back then.'

Her uncle gave her a pitying look. 'Come on, Ella. We already pushed the boat out with that new Audiofile. We're in no position to crawl to the bank looking for extra money for more equipment. We're going to be crawling to them soon enough anyway. Crawling major league,' he added, gloomily.

She felt a sudden rush of alarm. 'Oh, God, Patrick. Are things really that bad?'

'Fraid so. We need someone to bail us out fast if we're not going to go under. I'm sorry to have to tell you this, sweetheart, but your job's on the line. And yours, too, Julian.' Patrick ground out the stub of his cigarette and immediately lit up another. Things must be really bad, thought Ella. Her uncle usually smoked a maximum of ten cigarettes a day. 'However,' he continued – and Ella knew he was trying to inject his voice with a reassuring note – 'you're both so good at what you do that I can't see you having any problems finding work elsewhere. You two babies will land on your feet.'

Ella felt awful. 'Hell, Patrick,' she said. 'I might be able to get work elsewhere, but what about you? It's your *business*!'

He shrugged. 'I've always wanted to downshift, you know that. And the kids are nearly grown, so I won't have them to worry about soon. It's going to be tougher on Jack.'

'Oh? Why's that?' Ella turned to her other boss and noticed for the first time how exhausted he looked. There were lines she hadn't noticed before etched around his mouth and eyes. She felt even more wretched that she hadn't sussed the situation ages ago. 'Oh, God – I don't mean to sound unsympathetic, Jack, believe me, but at least you've no family depending on you.'

'I will have soon,' he returned, giving her a tired smile. 'Angie's pregnant.'

'What?' Ella was taken aback for a split second before copping herself on. 'I mean – that's wonderful! Congratulations – you clever man!' She threw her arms around him, and as she did so she realized that once upon a time she wouldn't have been able to make the slightest physical contact with him without feeling a sexual *frisson*. Now here she was, clutched in his embrace, feeling – well, *happy* for him. If he'd made this announcement last week she would have been completely gutted by this revelation that he was now lost to her for ever.

'Cleverness didn't have a lot to do with it, sweetheart,' he replied, giving her a wry smile.

'Oh – you know what I mean,' she said, kissing his cheek and then sitting back. 'Tell me – how does Angie feel? Is she doing all right?'

'She's sick as a parrot every morning. But pleased as – well – punch.'

'Parrot. Punch. Parrot's punch,' she said, bemusedly. 'That rings a bell somewhere.'

'It's actually Pirate's Punch,' said Patrick. 'They paid for your junket in the Caribbean, remember?'

'And you'll be amused to learn that Angie's become addicted to it since she got pregnant.' Jack gave another tired smile. 'That punch is what she craves most after marshmallows.'

'Pirate's *Punch*! Oh – gross! She never used to be able to stomach the stuff.'

'It's strange but true. I spend my Saturdays trailing around the supermarket pushing a trolley piled high with crates of Pirate's Punch and giant-sized packets of marshmallows.'

'When do you have to let the bank know?'

It was Julian's Dun Laoghaire drawl, and it was the first time he'd spoken for ages. Everyone turned to look at him. He was sitting back in his chair, outwardly relaxed, but with a strangely intense, watchful glitter in his eyes.

'You mean about our financial problems?' queried Patrick.

'Yes.'

'I've a suspicion they already know that everything in the Nesbit & Noonan garden is far from rosy.' Patrick sighed heavily and reached for his pack of cigarettes. 'Shit. I'm out of them. Be a doll and run up to the bar for change for the machine, Ella. And order another round while you're at it.

I'm out to get slaughtered tonight.' He handed her a crumpled twenty.

Ella got to her feet and started to negotiate her way towards the counter, but before she'd gone two paces something made her stop dead.

'What if the name of the garden changed?' Julian was asking the question. Ella turned around. There was something smugly suggestive about his tone that she didn't like.

'What do you mean?' Patrick was rubbing a bleary eye with a forefinger.

'What if the garden known as Nesbit & Noonan became known as Nesbit, Noonan & Bollard? That might make the bank look on it as a rosier prospect.'

A silence fell. Patrick's finger froze mid-rub. Then he leaned forward and automatically reached for a cigarette, forgetting that he was out of them. 'I'm not quite with you, Julian,' he said. 'You're suggesting, are you, that – er – that we take you on board as a business partner?'

'Well, not me, strictly speaking. I mean my father. He's been looking around for a new business to invest money in. And he knows I'm keen on setting up on my own one day. What better experience for me than to be involved more directly in the day to day running of a recording studio?'

Oh God. Ella was gazing at Julian with an expression of sick dismay. She transferred her gaze to her uncle's face and started to send him urgent messages by thought transmission. No, Patrick. Please say no. Oh, God – say no! Things can't be so bad that you'd consider taking Julian *Bollard* on as a business partner! No, no, no, no, no, no, *no* . . .

Patrick was tapping his empty cigarette packet on the table. He was looking ominously thoughtful. 'Well, Julian. That's a very interesting proposition.' He stopped tapping and looked directly across the table at his prospective new partner. 'When do you think you could sound your father out as to whether he'd be interested?'

'Tonight,' said Julian without hesitation. 'And if you can come up with an attractive package for him tomorrow I'd be prepared to bet that he could give you a definite answer by the end of the week.' He leaned forward and put his elbows on the table. 'I'll help sell you as hard as I can, Patrick. It's in my interest to do so. I'll back you to the hilt.'

Patrick drew in a deep breath. 'Hell,' he said. Then he exhaled loudly, and with evident relief. 'Sure. Fire ahead and run it by him. If he agrees, then we're off the hook.' Patrick was smiling for the first time that evening. 'I really appreciate this, Julian. I owe you.'

Julian's expression was horrifically smug as he nodded acknowledgement that, yes, Patrick owed him. Then he looked up at Ella and did something even more horrific. He actually winked at her and *smirked.*

Ella turned and reeled towards the bar, still howling *Nooooooo!* inwardly. Oh God – how fucking, *fucking* awful. Her life was not going to be worth living if Julian Bollard's name was added to the Nesbit & Noonan sign above the studio door. And to the logo on the letterhead. And to the cards that she slid into those dinky little DAT boxes every day. He would make her life unbearable. He'd call her 'toots' and she wouldn't even be able to tell him to fuck off because, to all intents and purposes, he'd be her boss. She leaned her elbows on the bar and then she leaned her chin in her hands, wanting to cry.

'Evening, Ella,' said the barman amiably. 'Another round for the corner table?' He looked at her a little closer. 'Hey – what's the matter with you? You look white as a sheet.'

'Oh. I just need a drink. Badly.' She caught a glimpse of her reflection in the mirror behind the bar. She looked utterly shell-shocked. 'Um. Let's see. Three pints of Guinness please. And a Coors Light. Oh – and change for the cigarette machine.'

The barman looked puzzled as he handed over the change. 'Didn't know you smoked, Ella,' he remarked.

'I don't,' she answered. 'But I'm thinking of starting.'

*   *   *

When she got home there were two messages on her answering machine. One was just spooky heavy breathing. Could it be Julian? The unwelcome thought skittered through her head, and she erased the 'message' immediately. The second one was delivered in Ferdia's Galway accent. He sounded amused. 'Hello, Ella Nesbit. Sorry to disappoint you, but no book called *Monster Truck Madness* was handed over to anyone here. I suggest you phone the hotel and ask them to post it on to you. You never know – if you ask nicely, they might even throw in *Passion's Monument.* Hope to see you on a dive some time soon.'

Oh God, oh God, oh God. She would never have the nerve to book a dive now, not after making such a prize eejit of herself. She wanted to laugh out loud – very hollowly indeed – when she thought about how she'd planned to pull the wool over Ferdia's eyes and pass herself off as a classy dame. *Passion's Monument* had been bad enough, but *Monster Truck Madness*? *Ow!* Ella cursed herself for not having hit on something by Proust instead. She was just about to erase the message when something made her press 'play' again, just in case she'd missed something.

'Hope to see you on a dive some time soon . . .' No. That was definitely the end of the message. There was no reference to the musical foreplay they'd indulged in on Saturday night, no suggestion that they might take up where they'd left off, no reiteration of his promise to make her come like she'd never come before . . .

She hit the 'off' button and slumped back in the sofa. Hell's bells – what was she going to *do* with her life? She and Ferdia would never get it together before he went off round the world in July. And if

Julian's father came to the rescue and hauled Nesbit & Noonan out of their financial quagmire she might as well resign. She would not be able to bear having Julian Bollard lord it over her.

She went to bed that night thinking that her life sucked.

*　　*　　*

Julian's father did come to the rescue. He did it very quickly and very efficiently. The sign above the studio door was changed to Nesbit, Noonan & Bollard. Alphabetically speaking it should have read Bollard, Nesbit & Noonan, but Julian was careful to defer to his new partners' seniority. He still needed Patrick and Jack enough to brown-nose them. His attitude to Ella, by contrast, became one of total condescension whenever the other two weren't around. He made disparaging comments about her work, and needled her constantly. He poached some of her favourite clients by taking them out to restaurants that she could never afford in a million years, and he made sure he was booked in on any of the recording sessions that involved film stars. He hogged the new studio and made sure that most of Ella's work was confined to the old studio in the basement, which had definitely reached its best-before date compared to the gleaming new joint out the back.

Business picked up again once the heavy work in the building next door had been completed, and

Ella was kept busy. A series of half-hour television documentaries had been booked in to be dubbed, and Ella spent a week in July mixing sound effects, voice-overs and music. By the end of the stint she was seriously knackered. For some reason she hadn't been sleeping well, and her concentration was dodgy. At around nine o'clock on the evening she finished work on the series, her first priority was to get to the pub. She'd arranged to meet some of the staff from a nearby studio there. Their receptionist was getting married, and a serious hen night had been organized, kicking off at eight o'clock in Daly's. Ella had brought her party dress into work – the same little slip dress she'd worn to Jack's fortieth. As she struggled into it in the Nesbit & Noonan loo (Uh-oh. Of course she meant the Nesbit, Noonan & *Bollard* loo, as everyone was very careful to call it these days), she suddenly remembered that, in her hurry to get out of the studio, she'd forgotten to back up the project on the Audiofile. *Shit*, she thought, banging her forehead with a fist. She was going to be seriously late for her hen night. Quickly she tied the thongs on her sandals and ran into reception to retrieve the keys to her studio. Julian was there, scribbling something down in the diary.

'Very nice,' he said, when he got a load of what she was wearing. She hated the way his eyes roamed over her body. 'Off clubbing, are we?'

'Yeah,' she said. 'But I've to back up the project first. I bloody forgot.'

'I'll do it for you,' he offered. Ella almost did a double-take at his uncharacteristic helpfulness. 'I've to hang around here for a while. I arranged to meet someone in the pub at nine-thirty, so I've half an hour to spare.'

'Oh – would you, Julian? I'd really appreciate that. I'm running late.'

'It's no problem.'

'You're a star!' Desperation made her effusive. 'I'll buy you a drink later.' She flashed him the best smile she could muster and swung through the door.

Two hours later she was feeling no pain. Her tiredness was forgotten as she merrily drained another pint of Guinness in the pub. It was to be their last drink before they hit the Kitchen. As she slid her arms into her shrug, she spotted Julian making his way towards the bar. 'Hi!' she called, shimmying over to him. 'Did you back that up for me?'

'Yeah. It's sorted.'

'Brilliant. Thanks, Julian.' She signalled to the barman. 'A Coors Light for this man, please.' She hopped up on a barstool that someone had just vacated and started to rummage in her bag for money. When she finally located her purse and looked up again, Julian's gaze was focused on the expanse of her thigh that had been revealed when she'd climbed onto the barstool. She pulled the hem of her dress back down over her lace-top.

Julian gave her an unpleasant smile and ran his

tongue over his lips. 'I love the stockings,' he said.

Ugh! Ella quickly handed money over to the bartender. She didn't bother waiting for the small amount of change that was due – she just wanted to get out of there.

'See you on Monday, Ella,' Julian threw at her departing back. It sounded like a threat, and the bubble of Ella's buoyancy was punctured, suddenly. Fuck him, she thought, feeling tired again. Yes, she would see him on Monday. And on Tuesday, and on Wednesday, Thursday and Friday. She'd see him every bloody day of her working life until he buggered off and set up somewhere on his own, and they could take the hateful Bollard name off the logo at last. She fought her way through the crowded pub towards where her gaggle of girlfriends were getting ready to leave.

'Ella! Hi!' It was Angie, looking radiant and only just discernibly pregnant. Jack had a protective arm around her shoulder. 'Off clubbing?'

'Yeah,' said Ella.

'You don't sound very keen.' Jack raised an eyebrow at her.

'I was until five minutes ago. I was full of endorphins then.'

'What happened to them?' asked Angie.

'He –' Ella nodded her head in the direction of the bar where Julian was lounging, boring yet another sound engineer – 'hijacked them.'

'Not fair. You shouldn't allow anyone to hijack

370

your endorphins, Ella,' reprimanded Jack. 'That's one of the first rules of having fun.'

'He's always doing it,' returned Ella gloomily.

Angie smiled at her. 'I know a good way of getting them back,' she said.

'Oh? How?'

'Listening to someone showering you with compliments.'

Ella gave her a sceptical look. 'Convince me, then, why don't you?'

'OK. Here goes.' Angie took a deep breath and launched into laudatory mode. 'Wow – Ella! You are looking totally amazing! Look at your hair, all glossy and gorgeous like something out of a shampoo commercial! And where did you get that lipstick? The colour really suits you!' Angie leaned forward and inhaled. 'Let me guess. Chanel 19? How did the copy for that use to go? Witty, confident, *devastatingly* feminine . . . Come on, Jack – join in!'

'Witty, confident, devastatingly feminine?' he echoed. 'You to a T, Ella Nesbit.'

He reached for her hand and kissed it, and Ella found herself smiling.

'See? It's working! More, Jack!' urged Angie.

'Wow! That dress! It's *incredibly* sexy, Ella . . .' Jack let his eyes wander down her body, but this time she didn't feel icky. 'Mm-hm. Those heels – they make your legs look *so* elegant! And hey! Something tells me you're wearing lace-tops. Show me!'

Laughing, Ella pulled up the hem of her dress and gave him a provocative flash of stocking top. She was rewarded with an appreciative leer, and the endorphins started to kick back in. Life was weird, really, she thought. How come a man like Jack could make her feel good by ogling her legs, and a man like Julian just made her feel cheap and nasty?

'Oh, Ella!' Jack was panegyric. 'I *love* the stockings!'

The line Julian had used earlier. But someone else had once come out with that line, she remembered. *I love the stockings* . . . It had been Ferdia.

For some time now she had been mentally counting down the weeks until his departure date. Now she was counting down the days.

* * *

On Monday morning she sat down in front of the computer with a big mug of coffee and a doughnut and logged on. Friday's work would be backed up on exabyte tape number 247, she was told. She accessed the exabyte. It took ten minutes to perform the search. There was nothing on the tape. She bit her lip. OK. This had happened before. The stuff had to be on *one* of the exabytes that had been backed up on Friday. It must be on 246. She accessed 246. Ten minutes later it found a commercial for Esat Digifone. 245. It had to be on 245. She was panicking now. Her coffee had gone cold; her doughnut was only half eaten. She felt sweat break out under her armpits. There was a corporate narrative for a multinational conglomerate on tape 245. Oh fuck. She started to trawl through more of Friday's stuff, and then the phone went.

It was Georgia, the receptionist. 'There's a courier here for the Irish flora and fauna documentaries,' she said cheerfully. 'Can you drop in the DAT?'

Ella cleared her throat, but the voice that came out still sounded croaky. 'I'm afraid there's been a problem. I can't locate the tape that Friday's stuff should be on. Could you ask Patrick to come down here?'

He came down with a face like thunder. 'What the fuck has happened?' he asked.

'There's nothing on the exabyte,' she said piteously. 'Julian must have punched in the wrong number.'

'What do you mean *Julian* punched in the wrong number?'

'I was in a hurry to get out of here on Friday night. Julian volunteered to back up my stuff for me. He obviously screwed up.'

Patrick crossed his arms and stood looking down at her. She felt as small as a flea. 'Julian did not screw up,' he said. '*You* screwed up, Ella. You can't go passing the buck here. It was your responsibility to back up that tape and nobody else's. You have dropped me in the shit. Tell me what you're going to do.'

'Go back through the tapes?'

'Ella, if Julian punched in a wrong number as you suggested, you could have to go back through 247 tapes. At ten minutes minimum per tape, that's going to take – how long? Do some mental arithmetic for me.'

'Two thousand four hundred and seventy minutes,' she said in a very small voice.

'OK. How many hours is that?'

'About forty?' she said, in an even smaller voice.

'Forty, minimum,' said Patrick. She had never seen her uncle look so angry. 'I suggest that it would be quicker starting Friday's job from scratch.' He looked at his watch. 'You can't start now because you've a client due in at ten. You're going to have to work through lunch, and you're going to have to stay on working this evening until you drop. And you're going to have to work lunchtimes and evenings every day this week until the stuff's restored.' Patrick turned and walked away. At the door he turned. 'It goes without saying that you won't be getting overtime.'

Ella put her head in her hands. She wanted to weep. She wanted to scream. If she thought last week was tough, this week was going to be a killer. And it was all fucking Julian's fault. She was filled with blinding rage. She reached for the phone and punched in his extension number with furious fingers. 'Julian?' she said when he picked up. 'Do you know what you are? You are a fucking, fucking bastard.'

'Oh, hello, Ella,' came the smooth rejoinder.

'What a pleasant salutation to start the week with.'

'Tell me what exabyte number you punched my job in on Friday.'

'Mmm. Let's see. 247, wasn't it?'

'No, Julian. It's not on 247. And it's not on 246 or 245 or 244.'

'Oh dearie me,' said Julian.

'You did it deliberately, didn't you?'

'Did what deliberately?' His tone was suavely disingenuous.

'You deliberately punched in the wrong exabyte number, didn't you?'

'Ella, you may recall that you reeled exhausted out of the studio on Friday night, leaving me to finish your work for you. Did you ever stop to think that I might be as knackered as you? It's very easy to make a mistake at the end of a busy working week.'

'You don't fool me, Julian. I know you did it deliberately.'

'El-*la*,' he drawled, elongating the syllables of her name. 'Why would I do such an unprofessional thing?'

'To get your own back.'

'To get my own back for what?'

'For me telling you I didn't like you enough to go away on holiday with you.'

He gave an unpleasant laugh down the line. 'Don't flatter yourself, Ella Nesbit. There are hundreds of girls a lot better looking and more charming than you who would love to come away on holiday with me. I only asked you because I needed a dive buddy.'

'D'you know something, Julian? You are a fucking bastard. You have landed me in the deepest shit I've ever been in.'

'If I'm a fucking bastard, Ella,' he hissed, 'you are a fucking bitch. And I'll tell you something else for nothing. It never pays to speak to the boss like a fishwife.'

She put the phone down, white-faced and shaking with anger. The man was making her life intolerable.

'Ella? Are you all right?'

She turned to see Angie standing in the doorway.

'Oh – Angie! What am I going to do? Everything's going wrong in my life! I *hate* Julian Bollard!'

Angie shut the door and moved swiftly to an adjacent chair. 'What's happened?'

Almost inarticulate with rage, Ella filled her in on what had just gone down.

'Oh, Ella,' said Angie when she'd finished her stream of invective. 'You mustn't allow him to do this to you. You mustn't allow him to best you. You know that at the end of the day you're an infinitely more gifted sound engineer than he is. That's why I always book my sessions with you. You're a *creative*, Ella. Julian's a mere technician.' She invested the word 'technician' with utter contempt.

Ella managed a weak smile. 'Thanks, Angie. You're a total doll. Sorry for letting rip like that. It's just that the bastard really got to me this time.'

'Don't let him.' Angie gave her a catlike smile. 'Shall I tell you the best way to get back at him?'

'Oh yes! Please do!'

'Be happy.'

'Be *happy*?'

'Yes. Pretend he hasn't fazed you in the slightest. Act as if you haven't a care in the world. Smile, laugh, sing. He won't be able to handle that. But if you go around glowering the whole time, Ella, he'll know he's won.'

Ella contemplated this tactic. 'Oh, God, Angie. It'll be tough . . .'

'It'll be worth it. Believe me.'

* * *

It *was* worth it. The more she behaved like some sunny heroine in an old Disney movie, the less Julian liked it, and the blacker his mood became. But, as she had predicted, it *was* tough. Smiling at Julian Bollard was the most difficult thing she'd ever had to do. It made that aborted dive in Sheep's Head Bay seem like a halcyon day.

Chapter Fifteen

Around nine o'clock one evening later in the week, her phone rang. She allowed the answering machine to pick up. She'd been doing this a lot lately, because she'd been getting more and more of those unsettling messages with just breathing on the tape. She was convinced that Julian was behind them.

'Begin With Review And Friend,' she heard, and she picked up immediately.

'Hi, Rich!'

'Ella! How's it going? Have you recovered from your fainting fit?' he asked.

She looked blankly at the receiver. 'What fainting fit?'

'The last time I saw you, you'd fainted clean away on the floor of O'Neill's hotel.'

She'd forgotten about the swoon she'd staged to get out of diving with Julian. 'Oh, yeah. Yeah – I'm fine now.'

'You said you'd ring,' he said, in a mock-accusatory tone.

'Oh, God. I'm sorry, Richie. I've been up to my eyes at work.'

'No problem.' There was a pause, and then he took a deep breath and said – all in a rush – 'I was just wondering if you fancied doing something this weekend?'

'Oh. This weekend's bad, Rich. I'm busy Saturday and Sunday.' Dieter was due, and Leonie had booked special enclosure tickets for the racing at Leopardstown on Saturday, and dinner in the Merrion Hotel on Sunday.

'How about Monday, then? It's Ferdia's farewell bash in the Trident in Howth.'

Farewell! Oh God, how that word hurt! 'I haven't been invited,' she said, resisting the impulse to beg him for news about her dive god. Such as: *Has he sold his horse yet? Is Black Jack a racehorse? And if it is, will it be running at Leopardstown on Saturday?*

'You don't need an invite. Loads of people from ActivMarine are going.'

Hell. What was the point? He'd just look at her as if she was pond life. 'Can I take a raincheck, Rich? Maybe we could do a movie or something the following weekend? I could do with some cheering up by then, probably. And you're the man to do it.'

'Why will you need cheering up?'

She didn't want to say: *Well, because I'm cracked over your cousin and come next week I'll never see him again* . . . Instead she said: 'Oh. I'm just going through a tough time at work.'

'So am I.'

'What's up?'

'One of the people I was selling insurance to over the phone insulted me.'

'I imagine you get a lot of that in telesales. What did he say?'

'He thought I was that eejit radio presenter who makes hoax phone calls.'

'The one on the breakfast show?'

'Yeah. He kept saying things like, "Aaah – ye're a gas ticket. Aren't ye a great man for the crack." In the end I politely got rid of him by telling him I'd play a request for him.'

'What did he ask for?'

'Mr Blobby's song.'

When Ella finally put the phone down to Richie, she was laughing her ass off.

*   *   *

On Saturday she got dolled up in a brand-new tight red leather jacket, an embroidered white petticoat, white lace-trimmed stay-ups and a pair of red leather boots. As well as tickets for the enclosure, Leonie had booked a limo to take them there, and a table for lunch. It had been cloudy all week and drizzling sporadically – dismal weather for July and dismal weather for racing, but Ella was looking forward to it. She was dying to see Dieter and Leonie together again for the first time since Jamaica.

The first race was at two o'clock. At ten minutes to they were sitting at the restaurant bar sipping champagne and consulting the form. Ella leafed through the pages, looking vainly for Ferdia's horse, but there was no Black Jack running in any of the scheduled races.

Dieter had suggested that they hire the services of a tipster, but Leonie insisted that it was more fun to pick horses by their names. Her grandmother was wearing a silk frock that had a discreet – but undeniably provocative – slit on one side. She positively radiated happiness and looked at least a decade younger than her sixty-two years. So that's the effect love had on women! thought Ella. Endorphins were just such extraordinary things!

'Red leather and lace? A bit anomalous, isn't it, darling?' said Leonie, assessing Ella's outfit.

'It's kind of meant to be. I think the leather cuts across the girliness of the petticoat.'

'Oh – I see,' said Leonie with a nod of recognition. 'Is this what they mean by "attitude"?'

Ella smiled at her and shrugged. 'If you like,' she said. 'Although I'm not altogether certain what my attitude to anything is these days.'

'Whatever it is, it suits you, darling. It's actually a very sexy combination. I don't think I've ever seen you with a cleavage before – all that tight buttoned-up leather certainly gives you a boost. Now,' she said, returning her attention to the form, and underlining a name. 'That's an obvious choice for me. There's a filly here called Fleeter.'

Ella looked puzzled. 'Why is that an obvious choice?' she asked.

'Because it rhymes with Dieter of course.' Leonie flashed a smile across the table at her fiancé.

'She's daft as a broom, isn't she?' remarked Dieter to Patrick with a fond smile.

'You mean daft as a brush,' replied Patrick. 'But at least you know what you're letting yourself in for.'

'They're getting along like a house on fire, aren't they?' whispered Leonie in Ella's ear. 'I always knew Patrick would make a good son-in-law. Or is it stepson?' She took a swig of champagne. 'What a pity the odds on this Fleeter are so shockingly bad. Who are you going for, darling?'

'Um,' said Ella, scanning the print. There was a horse called Darling Julian running in the first race. 'Well not that one, anyway. I think I'll go for Big Blue.'

'Why?'

'Reminds me of diving.'

'Oh – of course. Your new passion.' Leonie turned the page. 'Camptown Racer!' she growled triumphantly. 'That's who I'm going for in the second race.'

'Explain?' said Patrick.

'Because Camptown is the capital of Jamaica, of course.'

'No, it's not, Leonie. Kingston is.'

'Oh. Well, then I'll go for Mister Punch, because that stinking punch won us our Caribbean holiday. That's got to be lucky. Who are you going for in race two, darling?'

It was staring her in the face. 'One Love,' said Ella.

One Love came last.

*　　*　　*

Because the weather was so bleak, they spent most of the afternoon in the restaurant, watching the races on television monitors. When the sixth and last race was announced, Dieter got to his feet. 'Come now,' he said. 'It is time to brave the wind and the cold. I cannot go to the races in Ireland and watch every single one on a television screen! We must go out onto the terrace for the final one.'

'Who are you backing in this one, Ella?' Leonie asked her.

'A horse called the Dark Horse,' she said. She'd stuck a fiver on it.

'Why the Dark Horse?'

'Because I met one recently.'

'A real dark horse?'

'A real dark horse.'

'Tell me all about him at once.'

'How did you know it was a he, Leonie?' asked Ella.

'Don't be silly, darling. All dark horses are men. Have you ever heard of a dark mare?'

'Nightmares are dark. I should know. I've been through a living one at work recently.'

'Hush hush.' Leonie narrowed her eyes in warning at Ella, and then she took her arm and drew her away from Patrick. 'Forget about work. I can tell Patrick's not madly happy with the current set-up either. We're here to have fun today. Now. Tell me more about this dark horse.'

Ella didn't need to be persuaded. 'He's this amazing guy I met at scuba, Granny. He's a master dive instructor, but he's also a demon fiddle player, *and* he's loaded. That was the real dark horse bit.'

'Goodness. What an amazing package. He sounds like a terrestrial god!'

'He is,' said Ella glumly.

Leonie registered Ella's tone. 'So where's the catch?'

'I'll never see him again. He's going off round the world.'

'When?'

'Next week. He's throwing a big farewell party soon.'

'So you'll see him then, won't you?'

'No. I haven't been invited.'

'Pshaw.' Leonie was the only person Ella knew who could get away with saying 'pshaw'. 'Gatecrash, darling, for heaven's sake. I did it all the time when I was your age.'

'Oh, Leonie, no. I wouldn't dare.'

Leonie looked surprised. 'What happened to that intrepid streak you were supposed to have inherited from me?'

'Well, it's not that I wouldn't dare to gatecrash a party. It's just that I don't think I could look *him* in the eye again. He thinks I'm a totally sad eejit.'

'Why's that?'

'He thinks I read books with titles like *Passion's Monument* and *Monster Truck Madness*.'

'What's wrong with that? *Monster Truck Madness* sounds very exciting, if you ask me.' Leonie lowered her voice. 'You know, I could really do with some easy reading. Dieter sent me a load of Kafka, and I'm finding wading through all that *Weltschmerz* very tough going. Maybe you'd lend me this *Monster Truck Madness*, darling, for light relief?'

Ella laughed. 'Oh, Leonie! It's difficult to explain, but I actually *don't* read books with daft titles like that.' Announcements were starting to come over the PA system, and people were drifting towards the doors. She checked out her watch. 'Come on – we'd better make tracks. They'll be starting any minute.'

Dieter and Leonie and Patrick and Ella finally joined the crowd of racegoers milling onto the terrace. There was an intense sense of anticipation in the air – not unlike the anticipation that had preceded the session in Sweeney's the night she'd ended up joining in the fiddle playing. The party moved to the far left-hand corner of the terrace, which adjoined the balcony reserved for owners and trainers. These superior beings were filing out of the members' bar, armed with binocular cases all bristling with enclosure tickets, and looking steely.

'I actually saw Menuhin play that piece in the Albert Hall,' came a strident, squirm-makingly posh voice from the adjacent balcony. 'It was an extraordinary experience. I'd go so far as to call it an epiphany, you know.'

'Mm?' A male voice.

'Absolutely. A personal epiphany for me.' The woman indulged in a sigh which she managed to imbue with a kind of nostalgic vibrato. 'Ah! The unabashed rubato of the Maestro! And the exquisite, haunting timbre of that Strad! Sheer heaven! The strains still linger in my mind, all these years later.'

This observation provoked a laconic 'Really?' from the person to whom the remark had been addressed. Ella sensed that the listener was trying to stifle a yawn. She couldn't blame him. This woman was ghastly.

'We met him backstage afterwards. Charming, *charming* individual. You could tell from his aura that he was simply saturated with genius. *Saturated* with it. As incandescent as – as – a *firework*!'

'Sounds like a bit of a damp squib to me,' came the rejoinder in a laid-back Galway accent.

Ella's ears flattened back against her skull in the manner of a cat that has just heard sudden birdsong. Surely that was Ferdia's voice!

'Ferdia!' The woman was playfully indignant. 'You are *so* irreverent!'

Hellfire! It *was* Ferdia! Ella swallowed hard, resisting with mindboggling difficulty the temptation to swing round and confront him. What on earth was *he* doing here? Her mind floundered around like a scuba novice for a second or two before re-establishing neutral buoyancy. His horse – of course. That was it. His horse *must* be running this evening! But she'd scanned the racing form from cover to cover and had seen no Black Jack listed. Maybe she'd got it wrong? Maybe the horse wasn't called Black Jack? It had been so difficult to hear Richie that night of the session when he'd filled her in on Ferdia's turf credentials. Maybe Black Jack was the famous sire or something? Richie could have been making some reference to blood-stock or breeding or whatever that horsy pedigree stuff called itself. The Dark Horse sounded like it could easily be related to a horse called Black Jack . . . Didn't it? Ohmigod, ohmigod – none of these logistics really *mattered* right now. What really *did* matter was – what was she going to do?

'Anyway, the Maestro himself told me that night that that particular Stradivarius—' resumed Mistress Posh in her droney voice, and then suddenly exclaimed: 'Oh! I'll finish the story later, darling. They're about to start. Hello! Isn't this marvellous!' The stalls opened and the horses burst out and started their thunderous procession down the track. 'Come on, come on, the Dark Horse!' exhorted Mistress Posh, in an even more strident tone. 'Well! Not a bad start, Ferdia! Maybe your gamble will pay off after all.'

As inconspicuously as she could, Ella edged nearer the railings that separated the terrace from the owners' and trainers' balcony. The track took the horses from right to left in her field of vision, and as the race progressed, she was able to slide her eyes sideways. She registered first an elegant behatted woman somewhere in her forties, and then Ferdia came into focus. He was decked out in what looked suspiciously like Paul Smith, his dreadlocks were ponytailed, and he was surveying the racecourse through field glasses. He was the most gorgeous sight Ella had ever seen in her life.

A symphony of gasps and groans erupted from the crowd, and Ella tore her eyes away from Ferdia. There'd been a pile-up at the fourth fence. Three of the front runners were down. 'You're OK,' observed Patrick. 'Your horse is still running. But the favourite's down.'

'The Dark Horse!' yelled Ferdia's posh companion, and Ella's attention swung back to the owners' and trainers' balcony. She saw his jaw muscles tense and his lips move in a barely audible, murmured echo. So! It *was* his horse! All around her people were seething with mounting excitement, waving their arms and shouting encouragement as the sweating beasts rounded the curve in the track and came sweeping up the home stretch. Over the PA system the commentator's voice was so frantic it was impossible to distinguish what he was saying. Suddenly a black horse broke away from the main body of the half-dozen front runners that were tearing towards the finishing line. It was as if it had taken wing, suddenly, like a dark Pegasus.

'The Dark Horse! Yes!' shrieked Mistress Posh.

'He's going to do it! How marvellous! He's won, Ferdia! He's won, won, won!' Ella returned her attention to the action on the next-door balcony, where the beaming female was throwing her arms around Ferdia's neck. Somewhere in the distance she could hear Leonie's voice excitedly congratulating her granddaughter for backing the winner, but she wasn't listening. Over Mistress Posh's shoulder she was suddenly looking directly into Ferdia's sea-green eyes. He smiled at her – a perilously sexy smile – and then politely disengaged himself from his companion, who immediately launched herself at the next available male, continuing her air-kissing ritual without missing a beat. Ella's heart missed at least half a dozen as Ferdia strolled over to the rail that divided them.

'Hello, Ella Nesbit,' he said, looking down at her in a way that made her want to faint at his feet. They looked at each other in silence for a long moment. Neither of them could deny the sexual vibe that was practically shimmering between them. Her eyes went to his mouth and the lust crescendoed. She had never wanted to kiss a man's mouth so badly in her life – not even Jack's. And then Ferdia spoke. He said: 'I hope you don't mind if I come straight to the point? I have a question for you. Do you remember what was the last thing I ever said to you?'

'You said that *Monster Truck Madness* hadn't been handed in at the hotel,' she found herself stammering. *Nooooo!* her internal voice yelled at her. *Ella, you klutz! Get it right for once, can't you?*

The amused look in his eyes intensified. 'No,' he corrected her. 'I'm referring to what I last said to you in person. I made a promise, I seem to recall. A promise motivated by extreme, unapologetic horniness. Shall I remind you?'

She nodded. She couldn't trust herself to speak.

He leaned in to her and the sensation of his voice in her ear was warm and liquid. The silken water of the Blue Lagoon came to mind. 'I told you I was going to make you come. In fact, if my memory serves me correctly, I told you that I was going to make you come like you've never come before in your life. I just hope I wasn't jumping the gun,' he added in a tone that smacked of a kind of amused afterthought. 'I hate hubris. Now.' Ferdia straightened up and looked directly into her eyes again. 'Will you leave here with me right now and let me take you somewhere breathtakingly romantic?'

She nodded again.

'Then get your coat,' he said to her for the second time ever. 'And meet me outside the owners' and trainers' bar in five minutes. Do you know where it is?'

She did. She'd passed it on the way in.

'Five minutes long enough for you to make your excuses?'

She nodded yet again. She couldn't manage to force a smile, let alone articulate a sentence. The muscles around her mouth felt atrophied.

Ferdia turned away without another word, smilingly negotiating his way around the ladies in oversized hats who fluttered on the balcony before disappearing through the door that led into the members' bar. Leonie was at her side in a flash. 'Who was *that*?' she demanded.

Ella was wearing a completely dazed expression. 'That,' she said, 'was the Dark Horse I was telling you about.'

'*The* Dark Horse? The diving Dark Horse?'

'Yes.'

'Wow.' Leonie's mouth dropped open. 'What a dude.'

'He's asked me to go off somewhere with him.' She spoke the words without conviction, like a bad actor, still unable to believe what had just happened.

'What? Where?'

'He didn't say. He just said somewhere breathtakingly romantic.'

'Oh, Ella! Go! Go at once!'

Ella turned beseeching eyes on her grandmother, desperate for advice. 'Should I? But what will I do when he finds out I'm an impostor, Leonie?'

'What do you mean, darling?'

'He thinks I'm some kind of groovy socialite.'

'But you said earlier that he thought you were a sad eejit who reads pulp fiction?'

'He thinks I'm that too.'

'Well, there you go. He obviously finds you

intriguing. Like a riddle wrapped in a mystery inside an enigma. Who said that?'

'Winston Churchill.'

'There you are, you see. You're not an eejit. You're an intelligent girl who knows these kind of things, and you're also a hugely accomplished musician and a respected professional sound engineer.'

'Oh.' Ella considered, winding a strand of coppery hair around her index finger. 'I suppose when you put it like that it gives me *some* credibility . . .'

'It's nothing but the truth. Look at you, Ella! You're gorgeous!'

'I get that from you. Thanks, Leonie.'

'Don't discount your mother. Entire orchestras were in love with her. Now run along while you're buoyed up with self-esteem. It's amazing what it can do for a girl.'

It was true. Angie had been right about compliments. They really *did* make you feel better. But still Ella remained unconvinced that she was worthy of the *Überdude* who had promised to transport her to hitherto uncharted realms of sexual delight. What would he expect of her in return? What if she was crap? She was seriously out of practice, for starters. And there was something about Ferdia, something about the way he looked at her, that made her self-confidence evaporate into the ether and turned her into a gibbering idiot.

Dieter was moving towards her, brandishing a bottle of champagne. Ella dithered a little more, and then made a last-ditch attempt at extricating herself from her imminent, nerve-racking tryst with Ferdia. 'Oh – I really can't do this, Leonie. I can't walk out on your celebrations . . .'

'Pshaw and phooey. Run! I'll make your excuses to Dieter. He'll understand. And if things pan out, don't worry about dinner in the Merrion tomorrow night. We'll simply toast your success if you don't turn up!'

Ella didn't say another word. She gave her grandmother a big hug and a kiss on the cheek, and then she turned and skittered back through the restaurant and down the stairs.

Outside, horses were just coming into the parade ring. She wondered which one was Ferdia's. She hadn't had a chance to get a decent look at it while it was running, and anyway, all dark horses looked the same to her. Ella reached the owners' and trainers' bar and peeked through the window. At the opposite end of the room she could see him. He was leaning with one hand against the wall, talking on a mobile. Half his face was in shadow, half was illuminated by the watery sunlight that filtered in through the plate glass. There was something businesslike about him, which was at odds with his relaxed physical stance – something *authoritative.* She'd seen the film *Tango* on video recently, and had found the dominant male stuff gobsmackingly sexy. Her politically correct persona had opened its mouth in a little momentary Oh! of indignation, and then, to her secret relief, it had turned its face to the wall and thoroughly connived at the thrill engendered by illicit concupiscence.

Across the room Ferdia shifted his stance, angling his body so that his broad shoulders were supported by the wall and stretching out one long, lazy leg to rest it on the rung of a barstool opposite. He was in three-quarters profile to her. The contours of his face were more than usually accessible, unobscured by his trademark dreadlocks and undisguised by his dive mask. In fact, his face looked so indecently exposed that Ella felt obliged to examine it in lingering detail. It wasn't a classical profile, or a handsome one. There was really very little that was symmetrical about it . . . but . . . But *that's* what made it sexy! OK – so his nose was broken – in fact, it had probably been broken more than once, by the look of it – but the other bones in his face looked as indestructible as Achilles'. His eyes were downcast and heavily hooded, his mouth was curved and gutwrenchingly sensual, and his skin was the dark gold-bronze of a weathered Adonis. Well, of course it was, Ella Nesbit you eejit! He hadn't been tagged with the moniker 'Dive God' for no good reason!

She watched as his right hand snaked into his trouser pocket, delved there for a tantalizing moment, and then emerged hefting a handful of small change. With his thumb he flicked over the coins, obviously checking their denomination. Then he turned and, still holding the phone to his left ear, disappeared in the direction of the Gents.

Ella visualized him sliding the coins into the slot of the vending machine (which would he opt for? she wondered. Ribbed for extra pleasure, satin finished for sensitivity, or heavy-duty for added protection?), and then pulling open the little drawer and extracting the packet. Or packets.

Suddenly he was in the bar again, moving towards her, looking directly at her through the window, still talking on the mobile. Ella turned away immediately, hoping to God that her face was well concealed by the curtain of her hair. She knew the expression of naked desire scrawled all over it made her look way too vulnerable, and she suspected she was going to need all her defensive wits about her. Be cool, she warned herself. Be grown-up. Be worldly.

When she next dared to look up, she saw that he had finished his phone call. Mistress Posh had joined him. He talked to her for a minute or two, then handed her the phone. As she tucked it away in the dinky little Vuitton purse that dangled from her wrist, he leaned towards her, disappearing momentarily under the giant, ostrich-feather-trimmed pagoda of her hat. Mistress Posh laughingly threw back her head, and laid what looked like a restraining hand on his arm. Ferdia shrugged, removed her hand with a smile, kissed her lightly on both cheeks, and turned away from her. Then he was moving towards Ella once more. He swung through the door, reached her, scooped her right hand into his left and started to pull her through the crowd. For Ella it was like being in a slow-motion action replay of the night in Sweeney's. She felt weak as water.

'Where's your car?' he asked.

'I don't have it.'

'In that case we'll have to get a cab. I'm not driving today either.'

'How did you get here?' She didn't care how he'd got there. He'd probably just swooped down from heaven. But she craved the convention of small talk the way an addict craves a fix.

'Helicopter.' Of course he did! 'You?'

'Limo.'

'Of course you did.' He threw her an amused look.

'Where are we going?' She was practically having to trot to keep up with him.

'I've booked a hotel room.'

She felt a rush of pure lust. It started in her groin, surged upwards through her stomach, and then gushed into her brain and erupted with the force of a geyser. She was drenched with it.

'Oh? Where?'

What? Who had said that? Oh, God – it had been her. She was speaking on automatic pilot, now.

'The Clarence Hotel.'

Holy fucking shomoly! 'Ah. Was the penthouse available?' A little joke. Oh, *God*! Her automatic pilot was obviously totally challenged in the humour department.

'Sorry. We're out of luck. There must be rock

stars in town tonight. But I've been assured that the room they've booked us into is the next best thing.'

Wow! she thought. Hip hip hooray! Shazam and pow! Yes yes yes!

'Cool,' said her automatic pilot.

'Ella! Hi!' said somebody else. They had reached the private Pavilion, and were obliged to stand back as a flurry of racegoers emerged. Oh no, thought Ella, stapling a reluctant smile onto her face before turning in slow motion, and thinking these thoughts as she did so: I don't want to run into anyone right now. I just want to be spirited straight into a bedroom in the Clarence Hotel. I just want to shag Ferdia MacDiarmada senseless. I just want to be shagged senseless by Ferdia MacDiarmada. This is hell. And, as she braced herself to face her inter-locuter, the last thought that went through her head was: Well, at least it was a woman's voice that greeted me, so it's not Julian. At least I've been spared the worst nightmare scenario ever projected onto the life of Ella Nesbit. If it had been Julian I'd have ended up in Mountjoy prison on a murder charge (no, make that manslaughter. No judge in his right mind wouldn't sympathize with me) and I'd never have got near to shagging Ferdia senseless in the hippest hotel in the world.

'Well. Hi . . .' said Ella's automatic pilot voice. It was even more lacking in conviction than her bad actor voice. 'It's nice to see you again – Sophie.'

Sophie Burke was standing there, looking just like she did in the shampoo commercial she was currently starring in. Her chignoned blond hair was a skein of silver silk, her complexion was flawless, her smile was pearly, her lips were prettily plump with collagen. She was wearing a skirt that was too tight for her and a tart's blouse that exposed practically all of her bosom, noticed Ella. (Actually, Sophie was wearing a beautifully cut, discreetly sexy skirt and an expensive little tailored shirt that showed an inviting inch of cleavage.)

'Nice to see you, likewise,' fluted Sophie, air-kissing expertly. Behind the dark glasses Ella saw the actress slide a look of assessment at Ferdia. He must have passed the test, because: 'Come and join us for Pimm's, why don't you?' she trilled, indicating the group of unsmiling cool Calvin Klein clad sunglasses-wearing individuals who flanked her like bodyguards. Ella couldn't see Ben among them. 'It's my last day in Ireland – I've spent a whole week visiting family – and we're celebrating.'

Ella didn't ask. Sophie could have been celebrating a birthday or a film deal or an Oscar nomination or the successful housetraining of a pet poodle for all she cared. In fact, Sophie really *was* celebrating her last day in Ireland. She couldn't wait to get back to her *pied-à-terre* in South Ken and leave behind the more embarrassing of her Irish connections. The north Mayo contingent had descended on Dublin when they'd heard that their movie star relation was granting Mummy and Daddy Burke a flying visitation, and Sophie had spent a lot of time in her childhood bedroom clutching her childhood soft toys and bravely battling a migraine.

'Oh. Thanks for the offer, Sophie, but I'm afraid we can't. We're just on our way out.'

'Shame!' Sophie slid off her sunglasses and looked up at Ferdia with startlingly blue eyes. Hang on, thought Ella. *Blue* eyes? They'd been green the last time she'd seen her . . . Coloured contacts. Of course. 'Hi,' Sophie said to Ferdia in her best husky little-girl voice. 'I'm Sophie Burke,' she added with a coy little bite down on the lower collagen-packed lip, as if she knew the introduction was just a formality to be got through. After all, of course he knew – of course *everyone* knew – who she was.

'Loved you on the cover of *GQ*.'

'Thanks,' simpered Sophie.

'Very taste . . . ful.' Ella shot Ferdia a look. For a split second she had wondered if he'd been going to say 'tasty', but there was nothing salacious about the urbane smile he was bestowing on the film star.

'I thought so too. They eventually convinced me that the nude shots were a good idea, and I must say I was pretty pleased with them. I wasn't sure about the interview, though. I'd just split up from Ben – my husband – and I was feeling very vulnerable. You don't think I came across as someone who'd been too irreparably wounded, did you?'

'I didn't read the interview,' said Ferdia. 'I only looked at the photographs.'

'Oh.' Sophie tried hard not to look put out, but didn't succeed very well.

'I'm sorry to hear you've split up from Ben,' Ella interjected quickly. 'When did that happen?'

'Not long after I got back from Jamaica. Actually, I'm surprised our relationship lasted as long as it did.' So was Ella. 'I'd tried for years and years to make a go of it, but I should have listened to my father when I first told him we were getting married.'

This was so patently a cue for Ella to say: Oh? What did your father say to you? that she found herself saying it.

'He said that Ben wasn't good enough for me.'

'He wasn't, Soph,' said one of the Calvin Klein clones stalwartly.

'Thanks, Tarquin.' Sophie smiled at the clone, but there was a becoming tinge of sorrow in her beautiful blue eyes. She turned back to Ferdia, reassessed briefly and expertly, and obviously thought he was worth another try. 'Are you sure we can't persuade you to join us for Pimm's?' What man in his right mind could turn down the invitation implicit in those twelve words? Sophie wasn't asking Ferdia if he wanted to join her in a sickly beverage of lemonade laced with alcohol. She was asking him if he'd like to fuck a hot-shit movie star until she begged for mercy.

Ella was in like Flynn. 'We're sure, thank you, Sophie,' she said firmly. What she was actually saying was: *Back off, bitch. He's fucking* me *this evening, OK?*

'Shame,' said Sophie again. 'We could have

400

shared memories of Jamaica. Remember the day we went to Navy Island with that Rasta? It was quite extraordinary – I'm sorry – I don't know your name?'

'Ferdia.'

'Ferdia. Anyway, this Rastafarian took Ella and my friend Eva – you know Eva Lavery, the film star? – to a place called Navy Island, off the north-east coast of Jamaica. It was a deeply spiritual experience just to walk through the rain forest and be at one with nature. Not to have to fend off fans – well, for me and Eva, of course. It's not as if Ella has her own web site!' And Sophie went off into an enchanting little peal of laughter.

If Ella didn't get out of there *now* she ran yet another serious risk of being hauled up for manslaughter. But what to do? If she suggested they make tracks it would only make her look as if she was dead keen to get Ferdia into bed. Which she was, of course. But she didn't want *him* to know that . . .

'Oh, look,' said Ferdia. 'Serious VIPs having their photographs taken.'

'What? Where?' Sophie spun through 360 degrees to locate the VIPs, and, more importantly, the photographer.

Ferdia indicated with a casual hand the parade ring, where a triumphant owner – a prominent ex-government minister – was posing with his wife. 'Why do most of the women here go out of their way to disguise themselves as giant mushrooms?'

he asked no-one in particular. 'Those hats are insane.'

'Oh – it must be for the Society page of *Individual*,' Sophie declared. 'There's Oliver – he always does their photos. Olly! Hi! Long time no see!' And for the second time in Ella Nesbit's life, Sophie Burke turned away and shimmied towards the main event, abandoning her without a backward glance.

Ferdia watched her go, sycophants stumbling in her wake in their attempts to keep up with her.

'It girls rule,' he said.

'Do they?' countered Ella.

'Well, darling. You should know.' He reclaimed her hand, raised it to his lips and kissed the palm, rendering her speechless. Then he strolled through the gate and down the long curving driveway towards a taxi that was disgorging more dames in hats. 'I hope he had the nous to charge them double,' he said. 'One of those hats takes up as much room as a paying passenger. Come on – let's grab it.' He quickened his pace, striding towards the taxi with Ella's heart accelerating at the same rate as her feet. He held the rear door open for her, and slid in beside her.

'Where to, guv?' said the driver, and Ella's heart decelerated instantly. She could tell at once that this driver was in chatty mode, by the self-referential irony with which he'd invested the word 'guv'.

'We're going to the Clarence,' said Ferdia.

'Bono's gaff! Ha ha ha! No better man. No – I

mean it. Gave him a ride once. He was late for an interview on RTE. I think it was around the time they were doing the Zoo tour. There's a funny story about that, too. My sister had tickets for one of their gigs – Lansdowne Stadium, I think it was. Anyway, for some reason she was really on edge on the day of the concert – "on edge" hahaha, d'you get it? And the friend she was going with didn't turn up so my sister rang me and said . . .'

Oh sweet Jesus, thought Ella.

'Ah – ye're a right bastard!' The taxi driver blared his horn at a BMW that had shot in front of him without indicating. 'Bastard Beamer drivers think they own the road.' He swerved angrily around the Bastard Beamer, and Ella was slammed against Ferdia. He looked down at her and smiled, and Ella couldn't stop herself from focusing on his mouth and wondering just when he was going to kiss her and just what it was going to be like when he did. His eyes slid away from hers, downwards. They travelled to her mouth and lingered there, and then they travelled to her breasts and lingered even longer. Finally, they moved down to her thighs. If he'd touched her there she couldn't have felt sexier.

And then he did touch her there and actually Jesus Christ it *did* feel sexier. The touch was so light it was barely perceptible. An index finger grazed her knee, and then he was lifting her skirt slowly – *agonizingly* slowly. Millimetre by millimetre, until the tops of her stockings came into view. She was aware that her thighs had parted automatically, and some circumspect voice miles away down some corridor in her head was telling her to put her legs back together at once because nice girls don't do things like that, but she just told the voice to shut up. Then she steeled herself to look up at him, this man who made her want to be the most wanton, abandoned creature on the planet. He traced the lace top of her stocking with his thumb and his full lips curved, and his eyelids looked heavier than ever. Then his eyes travelled back up her body until they met hers. 'What a very clever girl you are,' he said in a very low voice. 'To have worn stockings.'

'Anyway,' resumed the cab driver, back on form after having taken out the Bastard Beamer. 'My sister rings me at about seven o'clock in a tizzy and says to me "Kevin," she says, "I can't find the tickets! And Dolores has gone AWOL" – Dolores was the friend. And I said to her . . . Jesus! Aren't Beamer drivers the pits! Did you ever see driving the cut of that? Well, did you? You can't deny that that's the worst piece of driving you've seen in a year. In a decade! Now can you?'

'If you ask me,' said Ferdia, tearing his eyes away from Ella's stocking tops and pulling the hem of her skirt over them. 'It's the worst piece of driving I've ever seen in my life. It's a tough job you have, mate.'

'Tell me about it!'

Oh, no! thought Ella. Why did you have to go and call him 'mate', Ferdia! She could tell that the word had established camaraderie beyond the shadow of a doubt in the mind of the driver. 'You wouldn't believe some of the stuff I've seen, mate! Let me tell you about the time . . .'

There was nothing else for it. Ferdia and Ella sat back and let him tell them about 'the time'. In mind-numbing, freeze-frame detail.

Chapter Sixteen

In the Clarence, Ella sat in the study just off the main lobby while Ferdia did all the bureaucratic stuff at the reception desk. She sat with her legs crossed, one 'relaxed' arm draped over the leather back of a chaise-longue, pretending to read the *Irish Times* and feeling like someone in a Terence Rattigan play. Beneath the carapace of insouciance she was limp, soft as kapok, and thrumming with lust. Ferdia had not made physical contact with her since he'd pulled her skirt back down over her stocking tops in the taxi, and she ached for his touch so badly that she wanted to scream. Hell! Everything seemed to be taking so *long*! The taxi driver hadn't had change for the £50 note that was the smallest denomination that Ferdia had on him, and then Ferdia had finally lost patience with his matey dithering and told him to keep the change. And now there were computers to be accessed and forms to be filled out and plastic to be swiped.

Ella snuck a look at her dive god over the top of the paper as he filled in the registration card and signed 'just there, please, sir', and flirted with the girl behind the desk. God, was he cool! He looked so in *control,* as if he booked into smart hotel rooms every day of the week! And then a nasty little niggle of a thought struck her. He'd done this before. Loads of times. He was a smooth operator, and she was handing herself to him on a plate . . . She found herself thinking about all the opportunities Ferdia must have had to screw the kind of women for whom the price of a dive holiday would be small change. He probably had a serious track record in seduction. Hell – he probably had a logbook for recreational sex as well as one for recreational diving. Did Ella really want to add her name to the logbook? How would he log her if she did? *Ella Nesbit. A complete walkover, but not a bad shag.*

She felt utterly miffed suddenly, like a spoilt child who'd just found out that everyone else in the class had got the latest, most desirable Barbie for Christmas, too. Oh, God. Had he done this with Philippa, the woman at the hotel in Lissamore? Or with the dame in the pagoda-sized hat who'd been so reluctant to let him go at the races earlier?

She didn't care. It was none of her business and as she looked at him she realized it never would be. He'd be gone in a week, and she might never, ever see him again.

So what was she doing here? Was this really what she wanted? Was she destined to spend the rest of her life meeting the wrong guy? She should stop this now. She was getting in too deep, and if she went to bed with this man she might never extricate herself from the morass of emotions that were swilling around inside her. And then Ferdia turned to her and smiled (oh, God! That smile!) and held out his hand . . . and she found herself getting up and trotting over to him like a puppy to its master.

They were shown up to the room by the manageress, who was professionally friendly (a huge relief after the relentless mateyness of the taxi driver), and who was totally unfazed by their deficiency in the baggage department. She showed them round – the balcony, the sound system, the champagne ready in an ice-bucket – and then she slid back out through the door and shut it softly behind her.

Ferdia and Ella stood on either side of the conker-brown leather chaise, looking at each other. It seemed to her that his look was one of unsmiling assessment. He narrowed his eyes and then indicated her jacket with a brief nod of his head. 'Take it off,' he said.

She hesitated, then she raised a hand and started to undo the buttons with shaky fingers. Because the leather was so new, unbuttoning was no easy task. It seemed to take for ever. Ferdia watched as she fumbled, but he made no move to help her. He just stood there with his right hand on his hip, his thumb hooked through the strap of his belt. Ella's fumbling became even more ineffectual, and she knew she was blushing. God, how uncool she was! Did his other women do this for him? Did his other women perform expert stripteases like Demi Moore in that awful film? Did they do all that stuff men were

408

meant to find such a turn-on – shaking back manes of lustrous hair, slipping lacy straps off perfect shoulders, sliding tongue tips suggestively along parted lips? She felt like a rank amateur.

She'd reached the last button. Her red leather jacket hung open, exposing her small breasts in their broderie anglaise bra. Ella resisted the impulse to cover herself with her arms. She had never felt so vulnerable. With an eloquent gesture of his hand, Ferdia indicated to her that she should lose the jacket. She shrugged it from her shoulders and let it crumple to the floor.

'Your skirt.'

This was easier. Two buttons and a zip. For one blindingly awful instant she thought the zip was going to get caught in a bit of loose embroidery, but it came away with a not-too-indiscreet tug. Ella bit her lip as the white cotton of her petticoat joined her jacket on the indigo-blue rug, and then she stepped out of the lacy circle it had formed around her boots with the delicate precision of a circus pony.

Still Ferdia stood looking at her without moving. She wasn't sure what to do next. If he instructed her to lose more of her clothing at this stage she'd feel – well, naked. Uncomfortably so. But he said nothing. Finally he took in a deep breath and let it out again in a long sigh. 'Jesus,' he said. And then he started to move towards her.

She knew her chest was rising and falling visibly, she knew he could hear her breathing, she knew before she dropped her eyes that he had seen the glimmer of arousal in them. When he reached her he lifted his left hand, and she stood immobile as he cupped his palm hard against the back of her head and let his fingers explore the contours of her skull. Then he entangled his fingers in her hair and dragged his hand down through it, down across the side of her neck, down over her collarbone, until he made contact with the lace trim of her bra. He rubbed the broderie anglaise between thumb and forefinger, and she felt his knuckle dig into the soft flesh directly above her nipple. She could not lift her eyes. His other hand was on her buttocks now, and he exerted a little pressure, moving her closer into him, so that his thigh was between hers.

An image flashed across her mind's eye of that time in the pool, when she had felt the over-whelming impulse to grind herself against him, and now this impulse was driving her again, only a thousand times more urgently. She shut her eyes, and when she opened them again a minute later, his head was bent over her breast. She felt his warm breath on her skin, and then she felt his tongue – and his hand. Oh! His hand was between her thighs now, and he was doing something so persuasive with his fingers that Ella felt compelled to strain against his palm. She snaked an arm around his neck and pulled herself into him, letting out a long, shuddering sigh . . . And suddenly she was coming. Oh, God! She was coming so hard she thought she would never stop . . . She could feel his fingers moving inside her, his rhythm matching her urgency, and then she tensed, eyes closed, breath bated, frozen for an infinite, ecstatic moment before winding both her arms round his neck and clinging to him desperately as her legs gave way beneath her and they dropped together to the floor.

She lay motionless, eyes still closed, lips parted, chest lifting and falling with exertion. She could feel him move beside her as he extricated his limbs from hers. She couldn't look at him. She knew her chest, her neck, her face would be slippery with sweat and scarlet from her orgasm. She felt his hand slide away, and then his mouth was on her there. Ella sucked in her breath and flinched. She was so tender she almost couldn't bear it. But his tongue was so gentle! It was so soft it soothed, and so languorous in its unhurried exploration of all the folds and whorls and intricate, velvety furls of her flesh and – oh *God* don't do that! she thought as she reached out and clutched his head . . . Oh! Jesus Christ, that's too much! (as she pulled him harder against her) . . . Oh, God, stop! And then she was coming again. And again. And again. Ella Nesbit was coming like she'd never come before in her life.

When Ferdia finally raised his head from her she found she could not move. She half opened her eyes, but when she saw him looking down at her she couldn't meet his gaze and so she shut them again. She tried to say something (What? 'Thank you, Ferdia?' How cringemakingly inadequate!) but she could manage nothing more articulate than a kind of croak. Then she cleared her throat and tried again. 'Well,' she said, in the kind of voice an alien might use. 'You certainly keep your promises.'

'Meaning?'

'You made me come. And come. You made me come like I have never come before in my life.'

'My pleasure, ma'am.'

Ella finally opened her eyes and looked at him. 'D'you think I should have a go at returning the favour?'

'I think that's a stunningly good idea, Ella Nesbit.'

Ella blinked and cleared her throat again. Then she started trying to rearrange her arms and legs into a sitting-up position before discovering that her limbs weren't being particularly co-operative.

'Um. I don't think my muscles are functioning properly. I don't seem to be able to—'

'Allow me,' Ferdia leaned over her and suddenly she was being airlifted onto the bed, and her bra and pants were dematerializing.

'You've still got all your clothes on,' she observed unnecessarily.

'Not for long,' he said, losing shoes and socks, jacket and shirt.

'Paul Smith?' she asked.

'All that coming has obviously affected your brain, Ella Nesbit. I'm Ferdia MacDiarmada, remember?'

'No. I meant your threads. Are they Paul Smith?'

'I haven't a clue. Who's he?'

'A designer.'

'Well, if he did design these trousers he obviously never bothered to find out how they'd feel if the wearer got a load of a broad sprawled on the floor wearing nothing but red leather boots and scanty lace underwear. Jesus! Relief at last!' He unzipped his fly – extracting the condom packet from his hip pocket before kicking his trousers onto the floor – and then he shucked off his underpants.

Ella's mouth fell open. 'Oh,' she said, in a kind of whisper. She raised her eyes to his. 'How may I accommodate you?' she asked, sending him a disingenuous smile.

'I'm sure you'll come up with something,' he said, expertly rolling on a condom.

Ella lay back against the bank of pillows and parted her legs.

'That looks good,' he approved. 'For starters.'

And then Ferdia MacDiarmada spread her legs further still, took his cock in his hand, and sank very, very slowly into her.

*　　*　　*

They left the bed twice that evening. Once to admit room service because all that sex had rendered them ravenous, and once to have a shower together.

'Why have you got "The Birdie Song" tattooed on your shoulder blade?' asked Ferdia, as he massaged shower gel over her back.

'It's not meant to be "The Birdie Song",' said Ella,

413

feeling foolish. 'It was supposed to be the first bar of the slow movement of Beethoven's Seventh. The tattooist got it wrong.'

'What an intolerable cross to bear – going through life with the naffest song ever composed branded indelibly on your flesh.'

'You're the first person who's looked at it closely enough to find out. I tend to keep it under wraps when I'm around people who know the score.' She leaned back and rubbed her cheekbone against his chest. 'Why have you no tattoos, Ferdia? I thought they were *de rigueur* for all you diver types.'

'I think I told you once – I hate needles. They make me faint. I anaesthetize myself with Jack Daniel's before getting injections. If I didn't suffer from such overwhelming wanderlust I'd never travel anywhere where vaccinations are necessary.'

'That kind of makes nonsense of that Dive Deep, Dive Hard, Fear Nothing ethic, doesn't it?'

'Yup,' he said, squeezing more shower gel between her shoulder blades and letting it drizzle down her spine. 'But it all pans out when you get hit by the rapture of the deep, don't you reckon?'

'The rapture of the deep?' she repeated. 'You mean nitrogen narcosis? I've never had it. How deep do you have to go to get narked?'

'You obviously haven't studied your manual for a while.'

'Remind me.'

'Well. In order for me to experience narcosis, it really depends on how deep you want me to

414

go.' He sucked her earlobe, and she smiled.

'You can forget your decompression limits, for starters.'

'But remember – the deeper I dive, the more pronounced the narcotic effect.'

'On you? Or on me?'

'On both of us.' His tongue slid from her earlobe to her collarbone, and his hands trailed across her belly. Ella let out a long shuddery sigh. 'All right, Ms Nesbit,' said Ferdia with decision. 'You're obviously in no mood to concentrate on the academic side of things, so let's get down to the practical stuff. D'you know something? You have the most intriguing belly button I have ever seen. Or felt.' He inserted a finger and she spooned herself against him, revelling in the sensation of his erection nudging against her spine.

'Ow! That tickles!' she said, not wanting him to stop. He probed a little deeper, and she returned the pressure, straining her hips against him, feeling him harden correspondingly. *Dive deep, dive hard . . .* It was like a refrain in her head now. *Fear nothing . . .* 'Oh! What else are you afraid of, Ferdia? Apart from needles? Sharks?'

'No. I've done a lot of shark dives. I'm seriously freaked by bristleworms, though.'

'Bristleworms? They sound benign enough.'

'Not when they sting your balls, they're not. One crawled out of a conch shell that I'd stuffed down my swimming trunks when I was snorkelling in St Lucia once. I was just twelve, and I've lived in fear of those little bastards ever since. I suspect that experience was what triggered my antipathy for needles. Arms up, sweetheart.' He started to rub gel around her armpits.

'No-one's said that to me since my mother bathed me when I was a little girl,' said Ella. The feel of his fingertips as they circled the contour of her armpit was incredibly erotic. She eased her arms into a luxurious stretch, allowing him even more access.

'You still are a little girl,' he said, letting his hands travel to her breasts. 'You have the most delectably small breasts it's ever been my privilege to fondle.'

'*Delectably* small? I thought most men liked big boobs? I've often wondered whether I should investigate having implants.'

'Don't you dare! I've fondled a lot of implanted breasts in my time. It's like fondling a life-sized Barbie doll. Anyway, I have this theory that small breasts are more sensitive.' He circled the nipple of her left breast with his ring finger, so lightly his touch was barely perceptible. Her nipple sprang to attention instantly. 'See what I mean?' he said, with a lazy laugh.

She leaned back into him, aware that his cock was stiffer than ever where it rubbed against the small of her back. He cupped her left breast in his hand and trailed his other hand back over her shoulder, returning his attention to her tattoo. She felt him trace a finger along the treble clef and then run it down the stave, as he followed the notes. 'He certainly did get it wrong. It bears no resemblance to the Beethoven piece,' Ferdia said.

'It was my fault. I was pissed when I had it done, and I obviously didn't give explicit enough directions.'

Ferdia whistled the first couple of bars of the allegretto very softly between his teeth.

'You know it?' She knew he knew it. She'd heard him whistle it once before.

'I played it with the college orchestra.'

'Oh? Where did you study?'

'Trinity. You?'

'College of Music.'

'Did you want to play professionally?' He pushed the damp mass of her hair to one side and kissed the nape of her neck.

'Yes. More than anything. But I couldn't get work. I still fantasize about it.' She ground her buttocks harder against him, inviting him to enter her again. The pressure of his hand on her breast increased. Oh God! Playing professional violin wouldn't be the only thing she'd be fantasizing about in future. 'What about you?' she resumed, trying hard to sound normal.

'I never took my degree. I got bitten by the diving bug and dropped out of college halfway through my first year. Anyway, I could never have hacked it as a professional. I lacked application, according to my tutors.'

'But you still play, obviously.'

'Only the occasional session. I was always more into trad than classical. What about you?'

'A bit of both. They're both in my genes.' She felt sticky as honey and sweeter than syrup. This shower was doing nothing to freshen her up.

'And what beautiful, beautiful genes they are,' he murmured in her ear, sliding his hands down over her belly. The honey inside her started to drip. 'Your parents are musicians?'

'My mother was first violinist in the – um – National Symphony Orchestra for a few years. And my father's in a – in a – band . . .' She was having difficulty getting her words out. And when they eventually did come out they were so breathy she could hardly hear herself.

'Which one?'

'Celtic – oh! – Celtic Note.'

Ferdia gave a low whistle, and turned her to face him. 'Your old man is Declan Nesbit?'

She nodded.

'Well. I am impressed. No wonder you strutted your stuff with such chutzpah that night in Sweeney's, Ms Nesbit.' He pulled her closer to him. 'Come here. I've always wanted to fuck a real live princess.'

'What do you mean?' It was the smallest voice in the world, and it was coming from somewhere very far away.

'You're directly descended from the king of Irish fiddle players, aren't you?' His hand was between her legs now.

'But I'm a classicist at heart,' she managed, valiantly.

'That's cool, too,' he said. 'You might help me brush up on my vibrato. I'm sure I've lost the knack since I dropped out of college.' He was rubbing her clitoris with gentle, insistent fingers.

'Oh no you haven't,' said Ella, taking his face in her hands and smiling up at him. 'You are quite simply a *maestro*, Ferdia MacDiarmada. Your fingering is perfect.'

Those were her last articulate words for a very long time.

*   *   *

Much later, back in bed, Ella lay on her tummy, scoffing the last of the smoked salmon sandwiches they'd had sent up.

'Mm. Excellent, excellent grub,' she remarked. Ferdia was refilling her glass with champagne. 'This has to be the most welcome supper I've ever eaten.'

'It's more like breakfast,' said Ferdia.

'Oh? What time is it?' she asked, cursing herself the moment the words were out of her mouth. She didn't want to know what time it was. She wanted this rapturous idyll to go on for ever.

'I dunno,' he said, handing her the champagne flute and then wandering out through the glass doors that opened onto the balcony. 'But the sun's about to come up. Look over there.'

She joined him by the railing of the massive private balcony. The horizon of the untidy cityscape that lay stretched all around them was smudged with the rosy glow of imminent dawn. To their right were the roofs of Temple Bar, to their left, five storeys below, the River Liffey slid through the city on its way to the Irish Sea. Ferdia slung his arm around Ella's shoulders and she leaned into him. It felt wonderfully liberating to be standing stark naked on the balcony of this quintessentially charismatic hotel, watching the slow ascent of the sun over Dublin. How right he had been earlier when he'd told her he was going to take her somewhere breathtakingly romantic! She couldn't imagine that a more blissfully romantic scenario existed right now anywhere on the face of the planet. It was as if they were the only two lovers awake in the world. She took a sip of champagne, and then held her face up to be kissed. They transferred the wine between their mouths, letting some spill as the kiss became more passionate. Finally, Ferdia broke away from her mouth and lapped up the little pool that had accumulated in the hollow of her collarbone.

'I don't want to waste it,' he said, as he licked her clean. 'That's the last drop of vintage stuff I'll be indulging in for some time.'

'There's a half-bottle of Veuve Cliquot in the minibar,' said Ella. 'We could crack that.'

'No, no, my sexy little princess. I'm diving today. I'll need my wits about me.'

'You're diving today?' repeated Ella stupidly.

'It's Sunday now. I've to be in Portdelvin at half-past eight to get kitted up.'

'Oh.' Ella didn't want to be hearing this. She thought she might burst into tears. *Go away, real life! You suck!*

'But I think I'd like to see you come again before I go.' Suddenly Ferdia was swinging her up in his arms again. Dear God, he was strong! He made her feel as eensy and petite as the woman on the cover of *Passion's Monument* . . . He carried her back into the bedroom, deposited her on the bed, and looked down at her with a wicked smile. 'Before dawn he took her again,' he said, in an actor-ish sort of voice.

'What?'

'*Dashiel flung her roughly on the bed. "I see I am unable to tame your fiery temper by force, vixen", he said, "Let's see if this will help you to submit to me of your own free will." He licked a finger –*' Ferdia did just that – '*and before she realized what he was doing, he was touching her pleasure kernel.*'

He slid his hand between her legs. Ella burst out laughing.

'"*You dare to laugh, vixen?*" said Ferdia. '"*Damn your impertinence to hell! I will soon have you sobbing with desire and begging me for more!" Dashiel roughly parted her thighs with his other hand*'

'Yes!' thought Ella. She laughed again, and then she gave a little, theatrical gasp. '*Victoria gasped,*' she said. '"*Stop!" she pleaded, as she felt his finger explore her moist, most secret place. Despite herself, she could feel her pleasure kernel swell with shameful lust.*'

'"*Hah! You want me to stop?*"' barked Ferdia.

'"*Yes, yes" she panted. "Please stop!"*'

421

Ferdia took his hand away. '*He took his hand away. "Very well. I will desist if you insist."*'

Ella almost couldn't speak, she was laughing so much. '"*Yes! No! I mean—*"'

'"*What do you mean, you inarticulate bimbo? You mean you want me to touch you, do you not?*"'

'"*Yes," she said, lowering her eyes with shame.*' Ella lowered her eyes and was delighted to see that Ferdia was clearly aroused again.

'"*Where do you want me to touch you? Tell me," he demanded roughly, flipping her over.*'

'"*On my – my p-pleasure kernel," she faltered.*' It was too much. Ella doubled up with laughter as Ferdia, laughing, too, turned her over and entered her from behind.

'Roughly?' he asked.

'Yes, please,' said Ella. Then: 'Ow!' she said. And then she said: 'Oh, God . . .' And finally: 'Thank you . . .'

*　　　*　　　*

Some time later she awoke from a dozy half-sleep to see him standing by the side of the bed, looking down at her. She blinked, and smiled up at him.

'Look at you,' he said. 'All beautiful and aslumber.'

Oh, God, she thought. He even uses words like 'aslumber'! How divine! I couldn't have dreamt this man, could I? Ella stretched luxuriously, and then winced. 'Ow,' she said.

'What's wrong?'

'I'm stiff. I used muscles last night that haven't been used for a while.'

'And most captivating muscles they are, too,' he said, leaning over her and kissing her bare shoulder.

'Look who's talking.' Ferdia had the muscles of a sleek beast. She reached out and ran a hand down his chest and over the tanned skin of his stomach. 'Do you work out?'

'I wouldn't dream of it,' he said. 'That stuff's for blokes who sit on their backsides all day. I get enough exercise in my line of work.'

With her index finger she traced the line of a scar on his chest. 'How did that happen?' she asked.

'I had a close encounter with a Moray eel.'

'Ow!'

'Those bastards don't let go in a hurry,' he said. 'I had some difficulty tearing myself away. Literally.' He flashed her a pained smile, and then reached for his underpants.

'Where are you going?' she asked, sitting up in a sudden panic.

'I'm going to work,' he said.

'Oh, God. Is it that time already? It can't be.' She looked at her discarded watch. 'No, Ferdia – it's far too early. Look – it's only half-past seven. We needn't order a cab for at least another half-hour.' She felt like Juliet when Romeo gets up to leave after their first night together. 'And you'll need some breakfast. You can't dive on an empty stomach.'

'Don't teach your grandmother to suck eggs, new girl. I've dived on far less sustenance than smoked salmon and vintage champagne. Anyway, I can pick up a sandwich on the way to the DART.'

'The DART? Aren't you getting a taxi?'

'What? After forking out fifty quid for that cab yesterday? Are you out of your mind?'

She'd thought that money would have been no object. He was buttoning his shirt now. Ella jumped out of bed.

'Don't get up, princess,' he said. 'Stay on in bed. Phone down for breakfast and the papers and have a bath. Treat yourself. And don't forget to grab the freebies from the bathroom. I'll settle up on the way out.'

'No.' Ella stood naked and uncertain in the middle of the room. The balloon of her idyll had been pricked suddenly, and a slow puncture was setting in. She didn't want to stay on here without Ferdia. She didn't care that the joint was the height of sybaritism – she wouldn't be able to enjoy it. It would be like trying to play an out-of-tune instrument. She started to wander around the room, picking up items of her clothing as she went.

A horrible silence had descended and an atmosphere of grim inevitability prevailed.

'When are you leaving?' Ella had sat down on the chaise longue with her clothes piled in her arms. Her voice was croaky again.

'For Jamaica?'

She nodded.

'Next week.' Another silence fell, and all the colour drained from her world. She felt as if she was sitting in a picture in some small child's colouring book, but no-one had provided said child with crayons. Ferdia made an effort to sound conversational. 'Did I tell you I'd been offered a job in Salamander Cove? That Desirée's a persistent broad.'

He hadn't told her, and she didn't care. 'So this is your last week with ActivMarine?'

'Yeah.'

Oh God. 'Will I see you again! Before you go?' She couldn't help herself. She was pathetic with love. In a vain attempt to cover up her sudden painful deficiency in self-esteem, she started slowly pulling on her stay-ups. After some moments, when Ferdia still hadn't answered, she looked up. There was something curious about the way he was looking back at her.

'Do you mean . . . will we make love again before I go?' he asked.

'Yes,' she said. There was no point in being coy. They simply hadn't enough time to indulge in game-playing.

There was another long pause before he answered. 'That might be difficult.'

She'd known he was going to say that! Why had she been so stupid as to ask? But it didn't prevent her from carrying on. 'Why?' she said, wanting to slap herself across the face. As she rolled satiny white lycra up her calf she felt a hangnail snag it, and didn't care.

425

'The lease is up on my apartment. I've had to move out. I'm staying with Richie until I leave. Him and two others. I'm on the couch.'

She opened her mouth to say 'You could stay with me', and then shut it again. Ferdia would take one look at her *pied-à-terre* and hightail it out of there. She loved the dinky little artisan dwelling she rented, but it wasn't exactly what you could describe as *des res*, and because she'd been working till all hours last week, the place was in a total mess. An entire week's worth of dishes were stacked unwashed in the sink, no laundry had been done, and her bed looked a bit like the one that had been nominated for the Turner prize.

Oh, God – so *what*? So what if she was exposed as an impostor? Maybe she should just throw caution to the winds and tell him who she really was. An ordinary girl with an ordinary job and an ordinary lifestyle. If he couldn't live with that, then – well, then he wasn't worth wasting her tears on, was he? She knew it made sense. But then another thought infiltrated her brain. He'd be gone in a week. She would never see him again. Wasn't it better – if he ever did think of her again – for her to occupy a place in his mind where she'd be remembered as a contender, an equal? Someone with a touch of class . . .

'Will you come to my farewell party?'

She shook her mind clear of the thoughts that had been preoccupying her. 'Tomorrow evening?'

'Yes. It's in the Trident hotel. Do you know it?'

'Yes.' The Trident hotel was a vaguely seedy joint not far from ActivMarine in Portdelvin. Bit of a comedown from the Clarence, she thought. And then she thought: I can't go to Ferdia's party. I'd just get drunk and cry and make a total idiot of myself, and that would be his abiding memory of me. No. Let him remember me as the girl with the Merc, the girl who gets chauffeured to the races, the girl who fraternizes with film stars, the girl with designer labels, the girl who wears antique silk kimonos. Let him remember me as a princess – not some pathetic lovesick klutz. She looked up at him and shook her head. 'I can't come,' she said.

He moved to the window and stood motionless for a while, looking down at the river. 'I'll never forget you the way you were that morning when I ran into you in the corridor of O'Neill's hotel in Lissamore,' he said out of the blue. 'You were all sleepy and tousled and pouting and you were wearing something beautiful in silk. You were the sexiest thing I ever saw.'

That settled it. That was how he'd remember her for ever!

'Until now.' Ferdia turned and looked at her where she sat on the leather chaise in nothing but her lace-trimmed stay-ups. They gazed at each other for a while, Ella superhumanly resisting the impulse to reach out and draw him down to her. Somewhere a church bell chimed the hour. Ferdia shook his head and finished buttoning up his shirt. 'Gotta go,' he said.

Chapter Seventeen

After she and Ferdia parted company outside the Clarence she stumbled back to her little house feeling like the toad who'd kissed the handsome prince and lived the life of a princess for a day. She spent most of the rest of the day in bed listening to Portishead over and over, crying a lot, knocking back a bottle of rather nasty wine and repeating *Life sucks!* to herself like a mantra. They had actually been the last words she'd uttered before she fell into a sleep flooded with dreams of Ferdia. Ferdia floating over a reef, Ferdia on horseback (where did *that* come from?), Ferdia on the balcony of their hotel room, stark naked . . .

On Monday morning she woke to the sound of the phone ringing. She picked up to hear Julian Bollard's awful Dun Laoghaire accent at its most righteously indignant.

'Ella? You get your fucking ass in here right now. Do you realize what time it is? It's ten o-fucking-clock, and you had a session booked with AL&D at nine-fucking-thirty.'

Ella suddenly felt so weary she wanted to die. 'Oh, go *away*, Julian,' she said.

'What?'

Ella thought for a second before answering. 'Actually – make that "don't go away",' she said. 'Stay right there, Julian. Stay there and do the fucking session yourself.'

'*What?*' He sounded apoplectic. She would have laughed if she'd had the energy. 'What did you say?'

'You heard me.'

There was an outraged intake of breath, and then he said: 'Do you realize I could have you fired for this, bitch?'

'You can't fire me, Julian.'

'Why? Just because your uncle wouldn't let me?'

'My uncle's got nothing to do with this, Julian. You can't fire me because I'm a loose cannon and I'm firing myself.' She'd heard someone say it before in a film, and she'd thought *Yes!* when the actress who'd delivered the line had turned on her heel and walked out the door with her head held high. But she didn't feel any buzz now as she put the phone down. There was no sweet taste of revenge on her tongue, no little voice hissing *Hah! Take that, you gobshite!* in her head. No endorphins.

The phone rang again almost immediately. 'I thought I just told you to go away, Julian?' she said.

But it wasn't Julian's voice that answered her. It was Patrick's.

'What's the problem, Ella?'

'I hate him, Patrick. I can't take him any more. I'm sorry. Will you cope?'

'We'll cope. Just about.' She could hear his heavy

sigh over the phone. 'Look. Meet me after work, OK? Daly's, at seven. We need to talk about this.'

'OK. I really am sorry, Patrick. But if I went in there today I'd stick something sharp in him, I know I would.'

'I know, I know. I saw it coming. But you need to do some serious thinking, Ella. Daly's. Seven o'clock.'

'Julian won't be there, will he?'

'Not a chance. I'll have him working overtime on a hot Audiofile.'

'I'll be there.'

She put the phone down, slung on her old towelling robe, and shambled into the kitchen, opening the window to let in some fresh air. Then she sat down at the kitchen table with her head in her hands and did as Patrick had advised her. She thought. And she thought. She thought about her past and she thought about her future. She thought as rationally as she could, weighing pros against cons. She had no job and no income: but she did have prospects. Picking up a job wouldn't be a problem, she knew that. She was too good a sound engineer, and head-hunting went on all the time in her line of work. She could lift the phone to virtually any studio in town right now and be offered work.

But another voice inside her head kept challenging the rational one. Come *on*, Ella! it said. Think harder. Is that what you *really* want? So she thought harder. She cast her mind back to what the grim-faced careers guidance person had said to her in her final year at school. *Being a professional musician will be tough. You should get some training behind you to fall back on.* It had been good advice, and she'd taken it in the end. But then she remembered what her violin teacher had said to her one evening when they'd been to see Anne-Sophie Mutter perform in the National Concert Hall. *What a way to earn a living, Ella – doing the thing you love most in the world! Wouldn't you kill to be able to do that!* Ella knew a handful of people who were lucky enough to do just that – to earn a decent income doing something they were passionate about. Her father was one of them. Ferdia was another. And so was—

Something made her look up. A breeze from the open window had blown something off her notice-board. She bent down and picked it up from where it had fluttered to the floor. It was the photograph of Raphael that Eva Lavery had taken the day they'd visited Navy Island. She'd stuck it onto her noticeboard along with a handful of her other favourite photographs – including one of Ferdia that she'd taken on the Lissamore dive weekend.

As she looked at it, she remembered the story Eva had told her – of how Raphael had had to turn his life around after he'd been struck down by the bends. *When you have a gift you are grateful and full of praise. Jah gave me my gift. But Jah has the right to take away that gift also. Be grateful for what you have, Ella. Be grateful, and full of praise . . .* And then she thought of what Desirée had written on her underwater slate

431

the day she'd got through her training dive. *I can tell you are a fighter . . .* And then she thought of what Patrick had said to her at Christmas. *Dreams can come true, Ella, if you pursue them hard enough and want them badly enough.*

She knew what she wanted right now. She wanted Ferdia MacDiarmada. She wanted him more than she'd ever wanted anyone – more than she'd ever wanted Jack Noonan. She wanted him so badly it was like a physical ache, deep inside her. And if she didn't do something about it today she'd spend the rest of her life regretting a missed opportunity.

She got to her feet and pinned the photograph of Raphael firmly back on the noticeboard beside the one of Ferdia. He was looking at her with challenging eyes. Ella narrowed her eyes back at him, and then she scooted into the bathroom and rooted out the Chanel 19 soap and body lotion that she kept for very special occasions. She'd done enough thinking. She'd thought hard enough to make a really difficult decision, and now it was time for action.

She would go to his party tonight. She would confess that she was an impostor and a fraud, and that she wasn't the groovy socialite type she'd led him into believing she was. She would tell him that she felt she had to get things straight between them before he left for Jamaica, and she would be completely candid about the fact that she fancied him rotten; after all, she reasoned, if you put all your cards on the table there was very little point in being coy about it.

Oh God – what if he laughed at her! What if he *sneered*? Ella turned on the shower and dived under the spray, shampooing her hair vigorously, as if trying to scrub the scary thoughts out of her head. She wouldn't think about the outcome: she couldn't let herself be spooked at this stage of the campaign. It might all go pear-shaped – of course it might – but Ferdia was worth fighting for, and fighting was something she was very good at. Positive thoughts – that's what she needed. *Feel the fear* and all that shit. She fought hard to conjure a positive vibe. Hey! Maybe they could meet up again in a couple of months' time! She'd be flying over in the autumn for Leonie's wedding – and – and – Well. They could take it from there. That's as far into her future as she dared to project.

*   *   *

At around six o'clock she left the house. She wanted to walk in Stephen's Green before meeting her uncle. A walk would help to clear her head, maybe help her to work out some temporary *modus operandi* for Patrick. She felt like a total shit for letting him down. Maybe he could let her and Julian work separate shifts or something, until he got himself a new engineer? Maybe they could have strict demarcation lines between the studios, so that she and Julian never had to cross paths? One thing was certain – she had done the right thing. She had meant it earlier when she'd said that she'd stick something sharp in Julian slimeball Bollard if she ever had to set eyes on him again.

She was standing at the pedestrian crossing on the corner of the Green when she felt someone touch her elbow.

'Ella?' It was Richie. He kissed her on the cheek. 'Hi!' he said. 'You look great.'

'Thanks!' Ella had toyed with the idea of wearing a party frock to the do in the Trident, and then decided against it and stuck on a pair of jeans and a plain white shirt. She didn't really think she looked great, but – hell. What you see is what you get. Her new philosophy. There would be no more game-playing, no more cases of mistaken identity.

'Have you time for a coffee?' asked Richie.

She looked at her watch. 'Sure.' It would mean she'd have to forgo her walk, but suddenly that wasn't important any more. If she went for a coffee with Richie she could pick his brains about Ferdia. Find out what her chances with him were, now that she was about to come clean about who she really was. The thought of her pathetic masquerade as an 'It' girl still had the power to make her cringe. It had been so *stupid* of her to pretend to be someone she wasn't! She ought to have known that it could only end in tears. And there had been plenty of those last night, she thought, casting her mind back to the mad bitch who'd wept and wailed under the duvet accompanied by Portishead. It was about time she started laughing again. 'You always managed to make me laugh, Richie,' she said, linking his arm. 'Let's see if you can do it today.'

'Make you laugh?'

'Mm-hm.'

'Oo-er. Are things really that bad?'

She laughed. 'Nobody ever says oo-er except in comics.'

He shrugged his shoulders at her and gave her his lop-sided grin. 'Well, at least it raised a smile. Come on. Let's go in here.'

He indicated a nondescript café. They sat down on plastic chairs at a plastic table and exchanged glances as a pretty, overly made-up waitress radiating indifference shambled towards them. 'Not much chance of a grande skinny decaff almond latte here, methinks,' observed Richie. 'Cappuccino do you, Ella?'

'Cappuccino's fine, thanks.'

'Bella Donna!' pronounced Richie in theatrical tones. 'I would feast my eyes a little longer on your pulchritude, but – alas! – it is not to be, for we have come a long and weary way and require refreshment most grievously. What beverages have you to offer for our delectation today?'

The girl looked at him suspiciously. 'Wha'?' she said.

'Might you have some arabica of which we might partake, for instance? Or are the beans which I am certain you grind with your own fair hands of a less exotic provenance?'

'A joker, righ'?' said the girl brusquely, and with great contempt. 'Tell us what yiz want in plain English.'

'Two cappuccinos, please.'

'The cappuccino machine's broken.'

'In that case, make that two ordinary coffees, please.'

The girl slouched away with a venomous backward look, and Richie turned to Ella. 'You just can't get the staff these days,' he remarked equably.

Oh yes, you can, thought Ella, her mind conjuring up recent images of starched linen napkins, and champagne flutes, and plates of smoked salmon sandwiches on a tray set down by a discreet porter. If you can afford them.

'So. What's new?'

'Loads.' She flashed him a big smile. 'I quit my job.'

'Well, knock me sideways with a cocked hat. When?'

'Today.'

'What? Why?'

'Because of Julian Scumbag Bollard.'

'Well, now. I can't say I blame you. He's a bit of a Tartar that Julian bloke, isn't he?'

'How do you know?'

He looked sideways at her. 'I had the pleasure of diving with him, remember?'

'Oh, God – yeah! That time in Lissamore! How did that go?'

'It was bloody awful. He whizzed around under

436

water like someone in a James Bond film. And I wished I hadn't taken him up on his offer of a lift. He talked about himself non-stop. By the time we got back to Dublin I wanted to jump out at the first traffic light we hit.'

'Oh, Jesus, Richie – I'm so glad you found that out for yourself. He's a total fuckwit, and I hate his guts.' A wave of pure relief flooded through her suddenly. 'Hallelujah and Praise the Lord! I will never have to work with Julian Bollard ever again. Oh. Thanks.' This to the waitress, who had set two cups of watery-looking coffee-coloured liquid in front of them.

'Here's to you, then, brave girl. Life's too short to work for an asshole like that.' Richie raised his cup at her. 'But what are you going to do when *real* life comes calling? Will it be easy enough for you to find another job?'

'I haven't a clue. I don't want to think about real life just yet.' She stirred her coffee pensively and then laughed. 'Oh, God! I wish I could have seen his face! I should have done it in person instead of over the phone.'

'Well,' said Richie. 'At least you're laughing.' He took a sip of his coffee and then made a face. 'Jesus. This coffee is shite. Let's go and grab a pint some- where instead. I'll get this.' He put a hand over hers to discourage her from paying, and hailed the surly waitress, who pretended not to see.

'I can't go for a pint with you, Rich,' said Ella, looking at her watch. 'I have to go and do some confrontational stuff with my uncle. He's not going to be crazy about the fact that I've dumped him in it. But I'll see you later.'

'Later? Where?'

'Ferdia's farewell party.'

'I thought you weren't going.'

She gave him an enigmatic smile. 'I changed my mind.'

'Cool! Although it's not going to be much of a party if fucking Ferdia carries on being such a prize jerk.'

Ella's ears pricked up instantly. 'What do you mean?'

'He won a shitload of money at the races recently, but it hasn't made him a happy man. He's been mooning around getting drunk and maudlin and droning on about some dame he met.'

'What dame?' Ella was in like Flynn. Richie glanced at her, registering her sudden interest. She gave a little cough and swiftly changed her approach. 'I mean, it's kind of out of character for him, isn't it? He's such a cool dude, normally.'

'Well, I've certainly never seen him behave like this before. You'd think he was in some sick romantic movie starring Meg Ryan. He's effing and blinding and saying things like: "Why didn't I realize it sooner? Why did I leave it so late? I should have known that weekend in Lissamore . . ."' Richie put on a lugubrious Galway accent. Then: 'Why is that serving wench ignoring me?' he said in his normal voice, looking across at the counter.

Ella didn't answer. She hoped the serving wench would continue to ignore Richie for as long as it took for her to siphon off the information she wanted.

'So, who's the dame?' she asked, as casually as she could.

'Haven't a clue,' he said. 'All I know is he came home drunk late yesterday afternoon and was a pain in the arse all evening. It's no fun living in a flat with three other men and have one of them in a black humour over some tart. Oops. Sorry for the politically incorrect speak.'

'That's OK,' said Ella. She was slowly filling up with endorphins, like an inflating balloon. 'So Ferdia's staying with you, is he?' she asked disingenuously. She already knew the answer, but she was desperate to prolong this conversation, even if it meant that Patrick was kept waiting for her in Daly's.

'Yeah. The lease was up on his flat.'

'It must be a bit crowded. Four blokes in a flat. Yeuch!'

'We're not all smelly Neanderthal apes, you know. Ferdia even showers occasionally.'

She remembered the smell of his soap. Longing washed over her.

'I don't,' remarked Richie.

'You don't *shower*?' She shook herself free of the memory of the scent of his cousin's skin against hers. 'I never took you for a pig, Rich.'

'I prefer baths. That is, when I can get into the

bloody bathroom. There always seems to be someone taking a dump when I want to take a bath.'

'Thank you for sharing the lavatorial habits of your room mates with me, Richie.' Then something struck her. 'Why didn't Ferdia just move into a hotel?' she asked.

'A hotel?'

'Yeah.'

'He couldn't afford to stay in a hotel.'

'But – but you said he won a shitload of money?'

'Yeah. He's a mad bastard. He took all that money that he made from selling his share of that racehorse and stuck it right on its nose. And whaddyaknow, the horse performed, and Ferdia won a fortune.'

'The Dark Horse?'

'Yeah. How did you know that?'

She wasn't going to elaborate. Instead she said: 'I thought you said his horse was called Black Jack?'

'What? No. He *won* it in a game of blackjack.'

Things were moving too fast for her now. She needed time to digest this information. 'Hang about, Richie,' she said, after a long pause. 'You told me that Ferdia had sold a horse—'

Richie laughed. 'Ferdia deal in bloodstock! Jesus, Ella. Cop yourself on. I told you he won a *share* in a horse in a poker game from someone with more money than sense, and then he sold it. He got around ten grand for it – can you believe that?'

'Jesus! What kind of stakes were they playing for?'

'The stakes weren't a consideration. It makes sense to call some booby's bluff when you're holding a royal flush. What was *really* insane was to stick that kind of money on the nose of a dodgy runner.'

'I didn't think bookies accepted bets that big?'

'They don't. He spread the money around a bit. *He's a rambler, he's a gambler . . .*' Richie swigged back some coffee, and then sent the cup skeetering across the table. '*Shit!*' he spat.

Ella did some quick calculations. 'He must have collected around ninety thousand,' she said.

'Yeah, 90 K's about right. He's being understandably coy about the exact amount – he doesn't want ten zillion people hitting him for a loan – but he says it's enough for him to buy into his own dive outfit.'

Her heart did a somersault. 'He's decided to stay on in Dublin?'

'No, no. He agreed to work the outfit in Jamaica for a minimum of six months, and he's a man of his word. He wouldn't let them down. But once he's through there he wants to try and invest in a joint of his own.'

'In Jamaica?'

'He's not sure. He'd be keen on Australia, but the visa thing might be a problem. In the Caribbean they apparently have ways of cutting through red tape if you have enough influence. And money is influence.' He raised a hand at the waitress and was studiously ignored. 'If that bitch doesn't bring me the bill soon I'm going to do a runner. You're looking very pensive all of a sudden.'

'Am I?' She took a sip of disgusting coffee. And another one. And another. And finally she said: 'So. Ferdia's not rich.'

Richie scoffed. 'Damn right he is.'

'No, no, what I mean is—' she took another sip of coffee – 'he wasn't rich till now.'

'No. Jesus, Ella! How can you touch that stuff! In fact, he was even poorer than me.'

'But you're *really* poor, Richie.' She hoped she didn't sound rude. She was just having considerable difficulty in processing all this new information.

'You forget that I have morphed into a whiz-kid telesalesperson.'

'Oh, yeah.' She *had* forgotten.

A silence fell. There was something funny about the way Richie was looking at her. 'Maybe you'd consider me as a serious suitor now that my dive god cousin is no longer going to be hanging around as a contender for your affections?' he blurted.

Ella turned crimson. 'What? How did you find out about us? Did he tell you?' she blurted back.

'What?'

Oh God. What had she said? Backtrack, Ella, backtrack.

'Did he tell me *what*?' insisted Richie.

'Um.' Ella was trying like mad to work out how she could backtrack, but it was no use.

She went redder and redder, and then realization dawned on Richie's face. 'Oh. Shit! It was *you*! It's *you* that's got him all messed up and emotional!'

She didn't say anything.

Richie shook his head in amazement. 'Jesus, Ella, I knew you fancied him, and I suspected it was reciprocated, but I didn't know it had got real. How did it happen? *When* did it happen?'

She relented. 'I met him at the races on Saturday.'

'And took him back to your place?'

Ella demurred.

'Oh, come on, girl! Don't go all coy on me now! Not now I've discovered you're Ferdia's nemesis. Shit. Trust my dive god cousin to rob me of my one and only true love.' He'd said it in a jokey voice, but Ella sensed that there was real regret somewhere under the clown face. She felt a little flash of guilt, and then she shook it off and answered him.

'No. We didn't go back to my place. He took me to a hotel –'

'Jesus Christ! Not the Trident!'

'No.' She permitted herself a small smile. 'Not the Trident. And not my gaff . . .'

She remembered how she hadn't invited him to stay at her gaff because she didn't want him to see how she really lived. What a joke! What a total, total klutz she'd been! How could she ever have thought that it would have made any difference to a man like him? Ferdia MacDiarmada wouldn't ever be taken in by stupid superficial trappings like posh cars and designer clothes and an 'It' girl lifestyle and all that – all that *materialistic* shit. He didn't belong to some horsy set who sat around on exclusive balconies at the races talking about Yehudi bloody Menuhin. She could see that now, and it absolutely made sense. He was suddenly revealed to her in a brand new light, and she liked what she saw. She really, *really* liked it. He hadn't taken her to the Clarence in some smooth display of his wealth and taste – he'd taken her there because he was celebrating the fact that his spectacular gamble earlier that day had paid off! Who *wouldn't* be tempted to cut some swank in a posh hotel if they'd just won a fortune?

This new knowledge was having a strange effect on her. Now that she knew Ferdia *wasn't* rich he was even *more* desirable. She was actually *relieved* he wasn't rich. She wanted to curse herself over and over. Why oh why had she been so foolish as to go around posing as something she wasn't? Why hadn't she picked up the phone to him weeks ago? Why hadn't he picked up the phone to *her*? But there was a reason for that, she figured. Relationships between instructors and trainees wouldn't exactly be encouraged by ActivMarine.

'Well, Ella?' Richie was still waiting for her to answer his question. 'Spill the beans. I want to know how to impress the next girl I fall for. By the sickeningly moony look on your face he obviously took you somewhere pretty special.'

'He took me to the Clarence.'

'The *Clarence!* No shit. You stayed overnight?'

She bit her lip and nodded. She knew she was still

444

a bit pink. 'In Room 508. It's the next best thing to the penthouse.'

'Wow! My cousin is *such* a smooth operator! Did he do the champagne thing?'

'Yeah.' She gave that dreamy smile again. She just couldn't help it. Then she jumped out of her reverie. 'Why? Does he do that with all the girls?'

Richie shook his head. 'Not that I know of. But it's kind of mandatory behaviour when you're staying in a joint as classy as the Clarence, isn't it?' He slumped back in his chair with a bewildered smile on his face. 'Well. Ferdia MacDiarmada really is a dark horse isn't he?'

Ella smiled back. 'You took the words right out of my mouth,' she said.

*　　*　　*

Patrick was looking pretty pissed off when Ella finally showed up in Daly's.

'Please don't be cross with me, Patrick!' she begged, as she threw her arms round his neck. 'I'm sorry I'm so late.'

Her uncle held her at arm's length and gave her a curious look. 'How could I be cross with someone who looks so radiant?' he said. 'What has happened in your life that suddenly makes it worth living again? I thought you'd trail in here looking like the Little Match Girl.'

'Who?'

'Didn't your mother ever read you fairy stories when you were a kid?'

'Um. No, actually.'

'Ask a stupid question . . .'

She sat down beside him and sent sign language to the barman to bring over two pints. Then she turned to her uncle. 'Now,' she said in a businesslike voice. 'Listen to me, Patrick. I did what you told me. I did a lot of thinking today, and I made a lot of decisions about my life. But the first thing I want to say is that I'm really, really sorry about the resigning thing. I'd just reached the end of my tether with Julian and there's no way I could—'

Patrick raised a hand to stop her in her tracks. 'It's cool, Ella. It's all sorted. I've done a bit of underhand stuff.'

'What do you mean?'

'I've poached Dave Leary from On Line,' he said.

'*Dave?* Wow.' Ella was impressed. Dave Leary was a top-notch sound engineer. 'How on earth did you manage that?'

'I'd approached him ages ago, before Julian came on board. He said he'd think about it, and then he said no, but that I wasn't to be put off asking again in a year's time. So that's exactly what I did. And hey presto – the timing was perfect. He's ready to move on.'

'Right now?'

'No. He'll give them a month's notice and in the meantime we'll take a freelance on board.'

Ella made a rueful face. 'Shit, Patrick. This is going to cost you money, and it's all my fault.'

'It certainly is. Freelancers, pay increases – yes –' this in response to her slightly indignant look – 'Dave's looking for more than you ever got, but he'll be worth it.' He lit up a cigarette and leaned back in his seat. 'So *I'm* sorted. How about you? What are you going to do with your windfall?'

'Windfall?'

'Didn't you get the e-mail I sent you on Saturday?'

Accessing e-mail had been the last thing on her mind yesterday as she'd swigged back wine and droned along to Portishead. 'No.'

'Well, then, you're in for some surprise, toots. To the tune of £900.'

'*What?*'

'That horse you backed was a nice little earner for you.'

Ella was perplexed. 'But I only stuck a fiver on it.'

'I know you did. Dieter stuck ninety-five more on, though.'

'What do you mean?'

'He was doing it all afternoon, apparently. Upping the ante behind everyone's back. He must have lost a fortune, but at least you won one.'

Ella prinked. 'Hey! Cool! That'll take the sting out of being unemployed for a while! Good old Dieter.' She gave Patrick a radiant smile, which she turned on the barman as their pints arrived.

'Hello, Ella,' said the barman. 'You're looking very pleased with yourself this evening. What has you in such good form?'

'I'm in love,' she said with a candour so disarming that the barman said: 'Well. That's something to celebrate. These are on the house, so.' He ignored her proffered tenner, and returned to his zone behind the counter.

'In love?' queried Patrick. 'Has this anything to do with your hasty exit from the racecourse on Saturday evening?'

'Yes.'

'I thought as much. Leonie hinted to me that there was some man involved. Is it reciprocated?'

She gave him that radiant look again. 'Absolutely.'

'So tell me about it.'

And Ella proceeded to fill her uncle in on the events of the past couple of days. 'But the most brilliant thing of all, Patrick,' she said breathlessly as she came to the end of her story, 'is that he's not who I thought he was!'

'Translate.'

'He's not rich.'

'And this is a *good* thing?'

'Yes, yes! Oh – it's too complicated to explain –' she shot a quick look at her watch – 'and I'm in one hell of a hurry. He's throwing a farewell party out in Portdelvin tonight, and I need to get out there. He needs to know that I'm not rich either.'

'You're *not* rich.'

'I know, I know! I *told* you it was complicated. But it all has a lot to do with something Dad said to me at Christmas. He said that dreams can come true if you pursue them hard enough.'

Patrick was looking sceptical. 'Darling – it's your dad you're talking about, not the Dalai Lama.'

'Don't be cynical, Patrick – please? I have to try – can't you see that?'

There was a long pause. Then Patrick said: 'So. What's going to happen when this dive god goes away?'

'I've been thinking about that too.' Ella gave a little frown of concentration. 'I could go and visit him in Jamaica. I'll be going there in November, anyway, for Leonie's wedding. And then when he sets up his dive outfit in the Caribbean I could work for him. Help out in his shop or something.'

'He's setting up his own dive outfit?'

'Yes, and—'

'I thought you said he was poor. How can he afford it?'

'Well, he's really loaded, but that's far too complicated to go into right now—'

'Ella, Ella.' Her uncle was looking at her with concern. 'I know your dad encouraged you to chase a dream, but is this it? You're a talented musician. You're a highly respected sound engineer. You're seriously considering giving everything up to go and work in some dive outfit in the Caribbean?'

'Well – it might be Australia. It depends on the visa situation.' She reached for his hand and leaned towards him. 'Look. I've felt *pinioned* for so long, Patrick. D'you know what I mean? I've got to do some flying. I've *got* to take some risks in my life.' She thought of the extraordinary risk that Ferdia had taken. That uncompromising bet he'd put on the Dark Horse. If it hadn't come in first, he'd have lost everything. 'I can't walk on the woolly side for ever.'

'The woolly side?'

'You know. Cotton-woolly. As opposed to the wild side. I've played it safe for too long.'

Patrick still looked dubious. 'Jesus, Ella. First you pack in your job, and now you're running off to the Caribbean with some geezer you hardly know. Don't you think you should take things a bit slower?'

'No.'

Patrick looked at her with thoughtful eyes. Then he laughed and gave a resigned shrug. 'There's no arguing with that "no". I know by the mutinous way you set your chin.'

Ella laughed. 'Thank you. I love you, Patrick,' she said. Then, just as she leaned over to kiss her uncle, the door of the pub opened and Julian Bollard slid through like slime. 'Aagh – look – I'm out of here! There's Julian coming in. I thought you said he'd be toiling over a hot Audiofile?'

'He's obviously finished. Have you any idea what time it is?' Patrick stretched out his arm and showed her his wristwatch.

Ella's hand flew to her mouth. 'Oh, no! My watch

450

is running slow! Hell's teeth – that party will be kicking by now! I gotta run, Patrick.' She dropped another kiss on her uncle's cheek, then jumped up and slung her backpack over her shoulder.

'Ella?'

She turned round. Her face was flushed with excitement, her eyes were bright with love.

'Take care. I don't want to have to start scraping you off the ceiling if things don't work out.'

'They *will* work out, Patrick. All I have to do is hold onto what Dad said. Remember? Dreams can come true if you pursue them hard enough! I'll talk to you tomorrow!'

And then she was weaving her way through the crowded pub, running late for her date with destiny.

Chapter Eighteen

The DART took her to Portdelvin. It was much later than she'd have liked by the time she arrived at the Trident hotel. The receptionist in the lobby told her that the function rooms were on the first floor. Ella ran up the steps with a hammering heart and a mouth drier than 007's martini, abstractedly registering a horrible oil painting of Neptune on the landing. The sea god was standing on a chariot waving his trident, wearing such a ferocious expression that he looked more like a devil than a deity.

The music spilling out through the open door of one of the rooms told her where the party was. The place was jammed. Ferdia was obviously a popular bloke. Ella paused on the threshold and scanned the crowd, looking for him. What would she say when she saw him? As far as he was concerned, she'd said her final farewell to him yesterday morning. She'd told him quite categorically that she wouldn't be able to make his party – how to explain the sudden change of heart? But they'd been lovers, after all! Lovers didn't need words to communicate with each other. Maybe they'd just look at each other and *know*.

'Hey! There you are!' Richie was swinging his way towards her through the crowd.

'Hello again,' said Ella, glad to see her unlikely Cupid. He'd remarked – as he'd finally managed to settle the bill for the disgusting coffee earlier – on the irony of the situation. How bloody, bloody unfair it was that he should be acting as a go-between for his cousin and the object of his own desire!

He dropped a kiss on her cheek. 'I saw you come in. You looked like a frightened doe.'

'Oh, God, did I? I was trying hard to look cool.' She snuck a surreptitious look over his shoulder, but it wasn't surreptitious enough, because Richie copped on at once.

'Don't worry – he's here,' he said. 'Last time I looked he was out on the balcony swigging back Jack Daniel's and gazing at the moon in a sickeningly soulful way. How's that for reassurance?'

She felt a rush of something. Whether it was adrenalin or endorphins she wasn't sure. 'Did you tell him you'd run into me?'

'No. I want to see the expression on his face when he gets a load of you. You look great.'

'You're sweet. That's the second time you've said that to me today.'

'I'll say it again if you like. Hell, Ella – you'd look great to me even if you were wearing Fergie's cast-offs. My cousin is a lucky dog, and I hate his guts.' He took her by the hand and started threading his way through the crowd. 'I should be charging him

453

a fee for this. Maybe I should set up a dating agency. I could call it Richie's Rides.'

She gave him a dig with her elbow. 'Jesus, Richie. You are incorrigible.'

He smiled down at her. 'Although, having said that, I wouldn't have thought you were an obvious match for Ferdia.'

'Thanks.'

'No offence meant. It's just that he has a thing for older women, usually.'

For some reason this produced an unpleasant flutter in the pit of her stomach.

'So I suppose you're the exception that proves the rule,' he added.

The French windows that led onto the balcony were open. Ella was dying for some air. It was hot and muggy in the function room, and her face had flared up and the palms of her hands were slithery with nervous sweat.

'I'll let you go first,' Richie whispered in her ear. She could tell by his voice he was smiling. 'Hell, is he in for a surprise!'

Ella took a deep breath, and then she stepped out onto the balcony.

Ferdia was leaning against the wall to her right. Except he wasn't on his own. He had a woman in his arms and they were indulging in a seriously sexy kiss. Ella froze for a fraction of a second, then spun round and barged straight into Richie, who let out a yelp as she stood on his toe. In her peripheral vision she saw Ferdia glance up, and the woman in his arms turn around. She was svelte, Italianate, forty-ish. It was the woman he'd bonked all night that weekend at Lissamore. It was posh Philippa.

Ella made an inarticulate noise and shouldered her way back into the party, aware that Richie was hot on her heels. Gyrating bodies and unfamiliar faces swam into focus and then receded. She had to get away from this *danse macabre*; she needed air. She wove her way across the floor as slowly as if she was wading through water. She was a drowning woman, a diver who'd gone too deep and whose gauge had hit empty. At last she reached the door. She bolted through it and clattered down the stairs, practically hyperventilating, with Richie still behind her. Satan waved his trident at her from the wall, banishing her to hell.

Richie caught up with her on the front steps. 'Stop, Ella! Stop!' He stretched out a hand and grabbed her sleeve, but she shrugged him off. 'Please stop.' This time he reached for her arm with both his hands and succeeded in physically restraining her. 'Stop.' They were both breathless. Ella's face was crimson, and she was weeping tears of humiliation so hot they scalded her cheeks. 'Oh God, Ella. I'm sorry. I am so, so sorry. I had no idea.' Richie's voice was hoarse with pain for her. She tried to break free again, but he took her in his arms and clasped her against his chest until she slumped like a rag doll, and let herself be held. She sobbed and sobbed, inhaling raggedly. Oh

God! He smelt like Ferdia! That same clean, soapy smell . . . Ella sobbed even more shamelessly. 'There, now. There,' murmured Richie. 'Get it all out. It's OK. Shh, shh.'

He led her to the steps of the hotel, and they sat down, Ella leaning her head against Richie's shoulder. She wept like a child while he rocked and soothed her. 'There, there,' he crooned, over and over into her ear. 'Shh. There now. Good girl. It's OK. Everything's going to be all right.'

It was amazing the effect the clichéd words of comfort produced in her. Gradually, gradually she calmed, until her flood of tears had dried up into a trickle of gulps and hiccups. She felt as she had done once when she was a little girl, when her uncle had comforted her after a bad fall.

When he could see that she had cried herself out, Richie produced a rather grubby tissue from his pocket and wiped her cheeks, and then he held it up to her nose and instructed her to blow. 'Whoa,' he said. 'How could such a pretty little nose produce so much snot?'

Ella managed the wannest smile of her life, and then she stood up.

'Thanks, Rich,' she said. 'You are a chum. I mean that.' There was nothing more to be said. 'I'll see you.' She turned away and started walking down the footpath.

Richie stood and watched her. 'Are you going home?' he asked.

'No,' she said, turning back to him. He looked

quite bereft. 'I'm going to do what stupid girls always do when they make fools of themselves.'

'What's that?' he asked.

'I'm going for a long walk. And I'm going to lick my wounds.'

She started walking towards the pier.

'Ella?' He sounded uncertain. 'Ella – you're not going to do anything – well – *daft*, are you?'

She gave a hollow laugh. '"Men have died from time to time," Rich,' she lobbed back over her shoulder. '"And worms have eaten them, but not for love." Shakespeare.' She walked on.

The people she passed on the promenade were all bad-tempered and ratty looking, and suddenly Ella felt flooded with misanthropy, riddled with nihilism, and swamped with self-loathing. She remembered something her mother had used to chant, in the days before she'd fled to the arms of her lover in Tuscany: *Oh how I hate the human race. Oh how I hate its ugly face . . .*

She heard running feet behind her. In a movie, this would be Ferdia, come to rescue her from hideous reality. But her life wasn't a movie, and of course it wasn't Ferdia. It was Richie. 'Look. Do you want me to come with you?' he said.

'No, no, Richie. Thanks for the offer. I just need to be on my own for a while. Try and shake off these black dogs.'

'OK. I understand.' He hung back, and she advanced a couple more paces. Then: 'Can I follow you down after a decent interval?' he asked. 'I owe you a drink after what happened back there. And you probably need one.'

She stopped again. He was silhouetted against the marine blue spotlight that illuminated the front of the hotel, looking very tall and very authoritative and very reassuring. She smiled at him. 'You are such a nice man, Rich,' she said. 'You are the nicest man I know, and – yeah. I really would like a drink.' She took in a great, shuddering sigh. 'You'll give me about half an hour to exorcize my demons though, won't you?'

'Sure.' He stood and watched her go, and then he turned and went back up the steps of the Trident hotel.

Ella walked fast to the end of the long pier, with her head down and her hands in her jeans pockets. It had been a hot day, but now it was muggy, and the darkening sky was even darker where storm clouds were gathering on the horizon.

Her internal voice was vociferous as it berated her. 'You stupid, stupid bitch,' it said. 'You first-class klutz. What were you *thinking* of? What pooka got into your brain and persuaded you that Ferdia MacDiarmada would be interested in a girl like you? You'd witnessed at first *hand* the kind of women he's into. Why couldn't you have taken on board the evidence of what you'd seen with your own two short-sighted eyes?' Even Julian had pointed it out to her! *I've seen some very classy broads indeed make idiots of themselves over Ferdia* . . . 'Why couldn't you have *recognized* that the only thing the two of you had in common was sex? Common being the operative word. After all, it's pretty *common* behaviour to let yourself be smooth-talked into a one-night stand, isn't it? *Isn't it?* No girl with an ounce of self-esteem, an ounce of self-respect would have been the walkover you were.' What contempt Ferdia MacDiarmada must have felt for her as he got on the DART on Sunday morning: trading an acquiescent bitch on heat for a class piece of ass like posh Philippa – a dame so besotted with him that she'd travelled all the way across Ireland for his farewell party!

Oh God. She was inflicting such pain upon herself that she started to weep again, awash with self-hatred and despair. She slumped against the pier wall, and stopped her ears with her fists, but the voice was merciless.

'"I could go and visit him in Jamaica!"' it mocked her. '"And then when he sets up his dive outfit in the Caribbean I could work for him! Help out in his shop or something!"' Oh, *Jesus.* How could she have been so *naïve*? '"I can tell you are a fighter!"' continued the voice in its relentless mimicry. It sounded like the voice of a ventriloquist's dummy. '"You can make a dream come true if you pursue it long enough!"'

Oh God! Where had she been *living* for the past few hours? She'd taken a first-class ticket to Cloud Cuckoo Land, on a flying visit. But at least it had been a return ticket. She, Ella Nesbit, had been shuttled unceremoniously back to Real Life, for a crash landing with no survivors.

And now the image of Ferdia on the balcony shimmered before her mind's eye, devastating in its lucidity. In his arms, posh Philippa. Everything that she could never be. It was *she* who had lured Ferdia into the emotional rough patch that Richie had told her about. It was staring her in the face now. Ferdia hadn't been referring to *Ella* when he'd mentioned the Lissamore dive weekend to his cousin. He'd been referring to Philippa. Ferdia MacDiarmada was obviously just a bastard who thought with his cock.

She sat there, staring out to sea with unseeing eyes. Were all men like that? No. Of course they weren't. She remembered – she remembered – Raphael. Was he staring out to sea, too, right now, on that green island on the other side of the world? Her gorgeous, gorgeous, gentle Rastafarian. The most soulful, beautiful man she'd ever met. She remembered the altruism that had radiated from his eyes with a lustre that she had never seen in any man's eyes before or since. Until . . . until . . . Tonight. That look had been in Richie's eyes tonight. How concerned he had been for her when he'd registered the enormity of her anguish! How good he'd smelt when he'd held her close, letting her tears soak into the fabric of his shirt! He'd even had a tissue! How reassuring he'd been, how *there* for her, how *caring* . . .

She heard her own shaky intake of breath. Had

her Mr Right been under her nose all along? She'd always thought of Richie as a pal, a mate, someone to lark around with. She'd never thought of him in a sexual way at all. He was just a boy friend. But he wasn't a boy. He was an attractive man . . .

She glanced over her shoulder, and saw him now, a dark shape lounging against the wall at the other end of the pier, watching her. She looked out to sea again, and when she looked back she saw that he had started to make his way along the pier towards her, not hurrying, taking his time, obviously wanting to allow her all the headspace she needed. Ella turned and focused on the horizon. A breeze ruffled the water and the salty, tangy smell of sea came to her, drying the salt tears on her face. And then she became aware of another scent mingling with the sea smells. Clean, musky, masculine – with a top note of vanilla . . .

'Hi, Rich,' she said, in a very small, subdued voice. 'Thanks for looking out for me.' She got to her feet and turned to him. But it wasn't Richie who was standing there. It was Ferdia.

For the second time that evening she froze. He stood quite still, too, looking down at her. Oh, God! Had he taken pity on her? Had Richie told him that she deserved, at the very least, an *explanation* after what he'd put her through? Had Richie ignited the spark of guilt that had prompted him to come down onto the pier and explain, gently, exactly why he wasn't interested in more than just a casual fling? Men had done that to her before in the past, and she'd always had a sneaking suspicion that there was an element of *schadenfreude* in their admissions. They'd dipped their barbs in treacle before they'd shot her down, watching her plummet back to earth with a mildly sadistic pleasure. Was that how Ferdia would do it? Smile as he twisted the knife?

'What do you want?' she asked, dreading the answer.

'You,' he said. And he took her face between his hands and kissed her and kissed her and kissed her.

* * *

They went back to the Trident hotel, but they didn't go back to the party.

It was like a re-enactment of the evening in the Clarence, with Ella loitering in reception while Ferdia booked a room for them. And even though the Trident was vastly inferior to U2's joint, for Ella it was the most beautiful place on earth. She bestowed beaming smiles on the indifferent receptionist, she thought the fabric flowers in the lobby were lovelier than the real thing, and their room – when the key was finally located – was like something out of a fairy tale, with a Gauguin painting on the wall, a charming old-fashioned blue candlewick bedspread on the bed, and a view over the sea. She was in heaven, and there was a god. Her very own beautiful Dive God.

They went straight to bed. And after their first fuck they said, simultaneously: 'We need to talk.'

And then they fell upon each other and fucked each other silly all over again.

Finally, around midnight, they lay exhausted on the bed, not touching, just looking into each other's eyes. From the street below came the usual drunken post-party sounds.

'You missed your farewell party,' said Ella.

'I didn't miss it at all. I was having a horrible time at that party. I had a much better time here with you. Thank you very much.'

She gave him a sceptical look. 'You didn't look as if you were having a horrible time when I walked in on you.'

'I had a *seriously* horrible time trying to extricate myself from Philippa's tender embrace, I can tell you. That took some diplomacy.'

Ella remembered the tearful row that had gone on in the bedroom next door to hers in Lissamore. 'Was she very upset?'

'You could say that. The minute I got away I cornered Richie at the bar and asked him where you'd gone. I needed to clear things up with you before heading off to Jamaica.' She wished he hadn't brought up the subject of Jamaica. She couldn't ask the question that begged to be asked. *Will you miss me?* It hung unspoken on her lips for a long moment before Ferdia said, 'I'll miss you, you know.'

Oh God. 'Really?' She gave a too-casual shrug. A little dismissive laugh that sounded unconvincing even to her own ears. 'But you hardly know me.'

He smiled. 'I've a hunch I know you better than you think.'

'What do you mean?'

'I enjoyed observing you. You were pretending for ages, weren't you? To be somebody you weren't.'

She coloured. 'What do you mean?' she asked again. She knew she was stalling. The expression in his eyes told her he'd seen through her so easily she might have been plate glass.

'You seemed to put on an act. Not all the time; but sometimes I got the impression that you were trying very hard to be – what's the word I'm looking for?'

There was no point in dissembling. He'd got her spot on. 'Sophisticated?'

'That's almost right, but there's a better word. *Urbane*. That's it. It seemed to me that you'd constructed some kind of elaborate defence mechanism. It kept me off your case for ages.' Oh, *God*! What a bad joke her life was! 'I used to find it funny,' he added.

'Funny? Funny as in intriguing?' She remembered what Leonie had said about her being like a riddle wrapped in a mystery inside an enigma.

'No. Funny as in amusing. Especially when the urbane veneer kept slipping, and I'd catch you doing a pratfall. Like that time you turned up hungover for your first dive and flashed your stocking tops at me. That wasn't a terribly urbane thing to do, but it was fantastically sexy.'

OK. So her attempts at being urbane had been

pathetic. But she was starting to like what she was hearing. 'You fancied me then?'

'God, yes.' He leaned on his elbow and looked down at her gravely. 'You'd started stealing into my thoughts like a little cat burglar, Ella Nesbit. At first I tried to ignore you, but then you started visiting me more and more often. Especially at night. You were responsible for some of the sweetest dreams I've ever had.' His head dropped back onto the pillow. She reached for one of the dreadlocks that spilled over the pillowcase and started to twist it round her finger. 'Hell – remember that time you performed your safety stop in Lissamore? I almost couldn't maintain eye contact with you my erection was bothering me so much.'

'Oh!' The endorphin rush she experienced on hearing this was so intense she tingled.

'And then, that time you wandered out of the bedroom next to mine—'

'I heard you bonking in there all night. I hardly got any sleep that time!'

'Sorry about that. When I realized you'd been listening I got seriously turned on.'

'Pervert.'

'Absolutely.' He gave her a smile that made her want to melt. 'But the most apocalyptic moment had to be when you played your fiddle at me. That was the best foreplay I ever had.' She leaned over and kissed him. 'However, some small, smart-arsed voice of reason was warning me off at the same time.'

'Oh? Why?'

'I didn't think my life needed any more complications before I left for Jamaica. And now look what you've gone and done.'

'Complicated things?'

'You, my funny, sexy little violin-playing princess, have complicated things more effectively than a kitten with a ball of twine.'

They exchanged rueful smiles. Then, simultaneously, their smiles faded as lust flared up again. But this time her orgasm, ecstatic as it was, was marred for Ella by one tiny little niggling thought that gnawed at the back of her mind like a miniature terrier. We *really* need to talk, she thought.

And eventually, some time in the early hours of the morning, they did talk. They talked for a long, long time. He told her about his plans for setting up his own dive outfit, and Ella told him about having quit her job. He told her about how his co-shareholders in the Dark Horse had been responsible for the private suite and the helicopter that had transported him to Leopardstown, and she told him how Dieter had been responsible for the champagne and the limo that had transported her there. They talked about loads of things. They filled each other in on their childhoods, and Ella told him how she had spent most of hers rigid with mortification at the antics of her family. She even told him about how she had used to try and disguise her violin case by wrapping it in her coat and carrying it vertically against her chest, because she was sick of being teased about it at school.

'The violin wasn't sexy in those days,' she explained. 'I really resented having to study it. I always wanted to be the girl drummer in some cool band. How did you cope?'

'It never bothered me. People used to make remarks about it being namby-pamby, but I didn't care. I was doing it because I wanted to.' He turned his face to hers on the pillow and smiled. 'Being physically big helped. People didn't make remarks more than once. Your ex-colleague Julian tried to be withering about it on a couple of occasions, but when I warned him to back off he just reverted to bullying the juniors.'

'He mentioned that he'd been to school with you.'

'He was a gobshite even then.' He laughed. 'You should have seen the horrified expression on his face the first time he turned up at ActivMarine and realized that not only was his namby-pamby violin-playing old classmate a master instructor, but that he also had the bad luck to be allocated to my training group. He hasn't stopped bum-sucking me since.'

'And you thought he was my *friend*? How *could* you, Ferdia?'

'Well, he acted very pally with you. It was an easy enough mistake to make. I have to say you went down a bit in my estimation when I thought you were mates.'

'Jesus! He's the reason I am now unemployed.'

'Poor Ella.' He spoke the words lightly, but she read concern in his eyes. 'Any idea as to what you might do?'

'Maybe I could work for you when you have your own joint in the Caribbean,' she said in a jokey voice, hoping he'd say, Hey! What a great idea!

But of course he didn't. He just laughed. 'I'd love to get a load of you lugging tanks about all day, princess.' Then he looked thoughtful. 'Are you going to look for work in another studio, or are you still dreaming about playing professionally?'

'Still dreaming,' she said. 'But reality bites, I suppose. I'll have to start phoning around. See if anyone's looking for a sound engineer.'

'But if someone offered you work as a professional violinist, you'd take it?'

'Like a shot.'

'Anywhere in the world?'

'Except Jury's cabaret,' she said.

'OK.' He was looking at her very strangely. 'I have an idea coming on. Have a look at this.' He reached for his jacket where it lay on the floor, and pulled a sheet of fax paper from the pocket.

'What is it?'

'Read it.'

She scanned the page and found her mouth curving into a slow smile. 'Is she serious?' she asked.

'It's worth a try. Give her a ring.'

'At this hour of the night?'

He looked at his watch. 'It's only ten o'clock in the evening over there.'

Ella picked up the phone and dialled 9 for an outside line. Then she consulted the fax sheet and punched in a lot of numbers. 'Is this completely bonkers?' she asked, as she waited for the connection to be made.

'She liked you, didn't she?'

'Yes. I think so.'

He narrowed his eyes at her, assessing her. 'Did you get a cocktail named after you?'

'Yes.'

'Then she liked you. What did she call it?'

'The cocktail?' She gave him a smug smile, feeling very pleased with herself indeed for having earned such a groovy moniker. 'She called it a Siamese Fighter.'

'Really?' he said, lounging back against the pillows. 'I would have thought Sea Horse would have been more appropriate, myself.'

She looked puzzled. 'Why?'

'Because you're such an astonishingly good ride, of course.' Ferdia grinned at her, but before she could aim a kick at him, she heard the phone on the other end ringing.

In Jamaica, Desirée picked up.

Ella braced herself. She could hardly believe she was doing this. 'Desirée?' she said in as bright a tone as she could muster. 'You probably don't remember me. It's Ella Nesbit here, calling from Ireland. I certified with you last—'

'Ella! My Siamese Fighter! Of course I remember you! Hey! What's this about! Why are you calling me from halfway across the world?'

'You sent a fax today, Desirée – to Ferdia MacDiarmada?'

'That's right, honey! How is that bad boy?'

Ella glanced over to where Ferdia was reclining like a naked pasha against a bank of pillows, yawning expansively and looking sexier than any man had a right to look. The rush of lust she felt made her smile. 'He's bad, all right. And as a matter of fact, he's here with me now. We're in a hotel in a place called Portdelvin.'

Desirée laughed down the phone. 'Raphael done got it right again, as usual! He said you two should get it together! You give that Ferdia a big kiss from me, girl!'

Ella felt shy, suddenly. She was almost too embarrassed to ask what she wanted to ask. It was such a long shot . . . She took a deep breath. 'The thing is, Desirée – you put a kind of jokey PS on that fax. Suggesting that Ferdia bring his violin with him?'

Another laugh from Desirée. 'I was only half joking, honey chile. That Diandra done run off with a wealthy Mexican gentleman, and there's no-one around Salamander Cove to serenade those diners at night.'

'Desirée?' Another deep breath. 'Would I do?'

There was a beat, and then another, during which

Ella's heart plummeted. What a wuss she was to have made this phone call!

'Would you *do*!' Desirée's voice was on the line again, sounding nearly an octave higher. 'As a serenader? Honey – are you serious?'

'Yes. I know it's not your brief, but you're the only person there who will remember me. I'm good—'

'I *know* that, honey. I remember. You had some gentleman from New York offer you a job. And not only are you good, but you're damn easy on the eye. Dem tourists like to look at a pretty girl while they eat.' Desirée's voice slid into a more confidential tone. 'You and Ferdia have hooked up good and proper, yeah?'

'Well – yes. We're – um.' She didn't want to be too expansive while he was lounging there listening. 'We're . . .'

'You happy, honey?' crooned Desirée.

'Oh, *God* – yes I am!'

'Then I cannot have my Leopard Shark unhappy without you, can I? I cannot have him work my outfit, pining all the time for his woman back in Ireland. I know how bad my man Raphael would feel without his Desirée to keep him warm at night.'

'So?' Oh, God. Ella was beginning to allow herself to hope. 'Do you think you could run it by management for me?'

'Well, honey, this strikes me as being something so fortuitous that we will have to *make* it happen! Put me on to that bad boy.'

'OK.' She felt weak with anticipation. 'Desirée – if this pans out, I owe you. Bigtime.'

'If you want something badly enough in this life honey, you can get it. That's what I always say.'

'That's funny.' Ella smiled down the phone. 'That's what my dad says, too. Here's your Leopard Shark.' She handed the phone to Ferdia and sat down on the bed.

'Desirée! Darlin'! How's it going?'

Ella heard an indistinct burble coming over the receiver.

'Yeah, yeah,' said Ferdia, with a broad smile. 'Yeah. I'm looking forward to it, too.'

More burble.

Then: 'She plays a real mean fiddle, Desirée. *Much* meaner than me. It would be kind of nice if we could wangle it so we worked the same joint. I am kind of fond of her, yeah.'

Ella was staring at him, her mouth a little O of anticipation. He smiled down at her, and slid his thumb into it.

'Yeah. Will you do that for me? You are a star. Her? She is a princess. But you know that already. I will hear from you later? Excellent. If this works out, then she's going to have to start packing her bags fast. Oh, you know me. I always travel light. Yeah. Just my dive bag and my backpack. And a bottle of duty-free Jack Daniel's for my favourite dive mistress. You, of course.'

A laugh over the receiver, and then a laconic burble.

'Take care yourself, honey chile. See you next week.' And Ferdia put the phone down.

'It looks like you might have a job,' he said, sliding his thumb out of Ella's mouth.

Her hands flew to her face. 'Oh, God! What did she say?'

'She said yes. She said she would have no problem persuading them. Apparently the staff still talk about the night you played in the Pagoda restaurant.'

'Oh God!' Endorphins surged and bubbled out of her and exploded all around them like glittering angel dust. 'Oh, my God! Are you serious? Are you really, really serious, Ferdia?' She knelt up on the bed and flung her arms around him. 'I cannot believe this! This is like a dream come true!' She sat back on her hunkers suddenly, eyes wide, hands clamped over her mouth. '*Am* I dreaming?' she asked.

Ferdia reached over and pinched her nipple. 'Did you feel that?' he asked.

'Yes.' She gazed up at him, moony with love. 'It felt lovely.'

'Then you're not dreaming,' he said.

* * *

She packed all her belongings into boxes and Ferdia delivered them in the dive van to her uncle's garage. All she needed was her violin case and a backpack and a plane ticket – which was more than adequately covered by the £900 the Dark Horse had won for her. She didn't even need her jabs. She'd had them the last time she'd been to Salamander Cove. Ferdia went white when she told him how the needle had slipped, and she filed that little observation away under: 'Things I Know About Ferdia', resolving to take it out and torture him with it the next time he annoyed her. She e-mailed the manager of the resort, and made another phone call to Desirée to sing her praises for fixing things for her.

Leonie phoned Ella on the evening of her arrival at Salamander Cove, to wish her happy birthday. Arriving in the resort on the day of her birthday was the best present she could have had. Apart from what Ferdia had given her, of course.

'How are things?' asked Leonie. 'Is it as gorgeous as ever?'

'Oh – it's even better!' replied Ella happily, curling up on the bed. She was wearing her favourite sarong and a hibiscus blossom in her hair and absolutely nothing else. 'You know the way there always seemed to be a kind of pink glow in the air?'

'Yes?'

'Well, it was even pinker today.'

'That's what love does to a place,' observed Leonie sagely. 'Unless your sunglasses are rose-tinted. What's your room like?'

'Smaller than ours was, but with the same amazing view.' It was getting dark outside. The sky was like inky blue velvet. On the headland that jutted into the bay, she could just make out the shape of a man sitting, contemplating the ocean. A tiny pinprick of red flared, and she knew it was a joint. Raphael? The figure rose suddenly, and raised a hand high in the air, as in a gesture of benediction. Her guardian angel! She blinked, and he was gone.

Leonie sighed. 'I can't wait to see it again. The sooner Dieter finishes all his wheeling and dealing and wraps up the business the better.'

'Have you finally fixed a date?'

'The last week in November. Around the same time as we went out there last year. Heavens above and eat my socks! A whole year will have gone by!'

'Yup. Just like in *A Tale of Two Cities*.'

'What on earth are you rambling on about, Ella? I suppose you've been doing nothing but smoke ganja since you got there.'

'*A Tale of Two Cities*. "It was the best of times. It was the worst of times." Remember? Famous opening lines. Anyway, that's what last year was like.'

'Ronan!' Leonie spoke crossly to her cat. 'Yeuch! He's just spat a furball out onto my Turkish runner. Bastard. Now – what was I going to ask you? Oh, yes – will you serenade Dieter and me every time we dine in that restaurant? What was it called? The Pavilion?'

'Nice try, Leonie. It was the Pagoda.'

'Oh. Right. When are you starting work?'

'Day after tomorrow. They've allowed us some time to get over our jet lag.'

'How will you spend it?'

Ella looked at the balcony where Ferdia, naked but for a white towel slung round his hips, was looking out over the deep blue Caribbean sea. He turned round to her and smiled. He was wreathed in blue smoke, and his blond dreadlocks were haloed around his head, and she thought she might swoon with love for him. Her dive god!

'Oh. How do you think, Leonie?'

'Aqua diving?'

'Except we divers don't call it aqua diving.'

'Oh? What do you call it?'

'We call it "Going Down,"' said Ella, as Ferdia MacDiarmada took a last toke, tossed away the roach, and walked towards the bed. 'I have to go now, Leonie,' she said. 'I'll e-mail you soon, all right? Goodbye.'

'You don't mean "goodbye", Ella. You mean "one love".'

'Yes,' said Ella. 'Yes. I do. One love.'

THE END